W9-AHN-538

FLESH AND THE WORD 2 IS A DARING, VITAL contribution to the world of gay men's erotica. Stories by established writers such as Anne Rice and Aaron Travis appear alongside twelve original stories by some of the rawest, freshest talents in the field. From bondage to tender romance, from forgotten kingdoms to today's headlines, the stories celebrate the frank excitement of sex between men.

John Preston's infamous *Mr. Benson* and the *Master* series gained him an enormous following in gay men's erotica. In *Flesh and the Word 2*, Preston masterfully shapes today's gay erotic writing into a vibrant carnival of desire, attraction, and passion, each story a small masterpiece.

FLESH AND THE WORD 2

JOHN PRESTON has published over forty books in the past ten years, including the acclaimed anthologies *A Member Of The Family*: *Gay Men Write About Their Families* (Dutton); *Hometowns*: *Gay Men Write About Where They Belong* (Dutton/Plume); and the first *Flesh And The Word* collection (Plume). He is active in The Author's Guild, PEN, the Maine Writers and Publishers Alliance, and the National Writer's Union. He makes his home in Portland, Maine.

OTHER BOOKS BY JOHN PRESTON

FICTION

Franny, the Queen of Provincetown, 1983
Mr. Benson, 1983, 1992
I Once Had a Master and Other Tales of
    Erotic Love, 1984

"The Mission of Alex Kane"
Volume I: Sweet Dreams, 1984, 1992
Volume II: Golden Years, 1984, 1992
Volume III: Deadly Lies, 1985, 1992
Volume IV: Stolen Moments, 1986, 1993
Volume V: Secret Dangers, 1986, 1993
Volume VI: Lethal Secrets, 1987, 1993

Entertainment for a Master, 1986
Love of a Master, 1987
The Heir, 1988, 1992
In Search of a Master, 1989
The King, 1992
Tales from the Dark Lord, 1992 (short stories)
The Arena, 1993

Edited:
Hot Living: Erotic Stories About Safer Sex,
    1985
Flesh and the Word: An Erotic Anthology,
    1992

NONFICTION

The Big Gay Book: A Man's Survival Guide
    for the Nineties, 1991
The Art of Being a Hustler, 1993

With Frederick Brandt:
Classified Affairs: The Gay Men's Guide to
    the Personals, 1984

With Glenn Swann:
Safe Sex: The Ultimate Erotic Guide, 1987

Edited:
Personal   Dispatches: Writers   Confront
    AIDS, 1989
Hometowns: Gay Men Write About Where
    They Belong, 1991
A Member of the Family: Gay Men Write
    About Their Families, 1992

EDITED AND WITH AN
INTRODUCTION BY
JOHN PRESTON

FLESH

AND THE

WORD 2

AN ANTHOLOGY OF
EROTIC WRITING

WITHDRAWN

Ⓟ
A PLUME BOOK

FLIP

PLUME

Published by the Penguin Group
Penguin Books USA Inc., 375 Hudson Street, New York, New York 10014, U.S.A.
Penguin Books Ltd, 27 Wrights Lane, London W8 5TZ, England
Penguin Books Australia Ltd, Ringwood, Victoria, Australia
Penguin Books Canada Ltd, 10 Alcorn Avenue, Toronto, Ontario, Canada M4V 3B2
Penguin Books (N.Z.) Ltd, 182–190 Wairau Road, Auckland 10, New Zealand

Penguin Books Ltd, Registered Offices:
Harmondsworth, Middlesex, England

First published by Plume, an imprint of Dutton Signet,
a division of Penguin Books USA Inc.

First Printing, October, 1993
5 7 9 10 8 6

Copyright © John Preston, 1993
All rights reserved

Pages 413–415 constitute an extension of this copyright page.

Ⓟ *REGISTERED TRADEMARK—MARCA REGISTRADA*

LIBRARY OF CONGRESS CATALOGING IN PUBLICATION DATA:

Flesh and the word 2: an anthology of erotic writing/ edited and
with an introduction by John Preston.
    p.   cm.
ISBN 0-452-27087-1
    1. Gay men—Literary collections.   2. Erotic literature, American.
3. Gays' writings, American.   I. Preston, John.   II. Title: Flesh
and the word two.
PS509.H57F57   1993
810.8'03538—dc20   93–5575
                                                                CIP

Printed in the United States of America
Set in Garamond No. 3 and Futura

DESIGNED BY STEVEN N. STATHAKIS

Without limiting the rights under copyright reserved above, no part of this publication may be reproduced, stored in or introduced into a retrieval system, or transmitted, in any form, or by any means (electronic, mechanical, photocopying, recording, or otherwise), without the prior written permission of both the copyright owner and the above publisher of this book.

PUBLISHER'S NOTE: *Some of these stories are works of fiction. Names, characters, places, and incidents either are the product of the author's imagination or are used fictitiously, and any resemblance to actual persons, living or dead, events, or locales is entirely coincidental.*

BOOKS ARE AVAILABLE AT QUANTITY DISCOUNTS WHEN USED TO PROMOTE PRODUCTS OR SERVICES. FOR INFORMATION PLEASE WRITE TO PREMIUM MARKETING DIVISION, PENGUIN BOOKS USA INC., 375 HUDSON STREET, NEW YORK, NEW YORK 10014.

To:
Mike and Owen
Greg and Ernie
Michael
and
Joe.

Because they liked it so
much the first time.

ACKNOWLEDGMENTS

PUTTING TOGETHER ANY ANTHOLOGY OF WRIT-
ing means assembling a community of writers. The authors in this
book have been as forthcoming and helpful as those in the other
anthologies I've edited, and I thank them.

My agent, Peter Ginsberg, has always been ready to support
me in the many different directions of my career. His willingness
to enthusiastically endorse and promote my forays into the world
of pornography are especially welcome.

I'm grateful to Matt Sartwell, the original editor of *Flesh and
the Word,* and now a freelance editor, for a repeat of his expert
handling of the assembled material. Matt has a way with dirty
words.

Tom Hagerty once again performed miracles as assistant, editor, and constant source of inspiration.

Our artists and writers on all levels should be able to be mad men and mad women. That's the function of Art. We want our mad men and our mad women to be offensive; we need them to be obscene. That's the way culture works. It's only when you have a free artistic marketplace that people have the freedom to create the classics of tomorrow.

—ANNE RICE

Erotic literature and art after all is such an elemental force. Fucking is more than sex. It's just as magical and mysterious as talking about God or the nature of the Universe.

—HENRY MILLER

C O N T E N T S

xi

INTRODUCTION

OUR LIVES

WITH

PORNOGRAPHY

The accepted meaning of *erotica* is literature or pictures with sexual themes; it may or may not serve the essentially utilitarian function of pornography. Because it is less specific, less suggestive of actual sexual activity, *erotica* is regularly used as a euphemism for *classy porn*. Pornography expressed in literary language or expensive photography is *erotica;* the cheap stuff, which can't pretend to any purpose but getting people off, is smut.

From "Feminism, Moralism, and Pornography" in Beginning to See the Light *by Ellen Willis (Hanover, N.H.: University Press of New England, 1991)*

Erotica was never written about gay men. It couldn't have been. We were, by definition, obscene; therefore, anything written about us had to be declared pornography.

1

There were some texts from classic Greece or Rome—Catullus comes to mind—that had an air of literature because of their age, but nearly every literary mention of homosexuality before 1970 had to be sanitized by medical language, or else it was relegated to the status of pornography and denied access to mainstream bookstores or polite discussion.

As a sort of gay life evolved after the Second World War, a few writers began to explore the possibilities of an emotional and sexual life that transcended the boundaries of heterosexuality. James Baldwin, Truman Capote, and Gore Vidal were three who attempted to write erotic (though not very explicit) novels of gay life in the fifties. Their first novels brought down an astonishing critical avalanche. While all three went on to create impressive careers, never again was any of them as unreserved as he had been with his first book. The lesson was learned. The lesson was also learned by Tennessee Williams and other playwrights who might have been interested in a more upfront confrontation with their material. These authors were seldom willing to admit that they were writing about gay men and their experience, although everyone knew it. When critics or commentators did bring up the fact that a homosexual point of view or, perhaps, even a homosexual aesthetic was involved, they did so to attack the work.

These pressures left a great void in writing about modern life.

There was a subtle revolution going on—the social and sexual changes that would eventually lead to Stonewall and the gay liberation movement were already beginning to take form.

Various legal decisions in the 1960s opened the door for an underground publishing movement. Essentially, the Supreme Court decided that, contrary to previous opinion, the *fact* of the existence of homosexuality was not obscene and, therefore, material that reflected homosexual life wasn't necessarily so pornographic that it had to be banned from sale or distribution. Small magazines and publishing houses began to develop to take advantage of the new rulings. In fact, it was *One* magazine, a publication that came out of the old Mattachine movement, that won one of the most important of these decisions; it was allowed to sell mail subscriptions, something the post office had tried to ban.

But legal access didn't necessarily translate into social acceptability. The works could still only be distributed through the channels of the "adult" bookstore or hand-to-hand by the cognoscenti. No matter how good the writing, the material was still perceived as obscene.

The distribution didn't matter to many of us who were growing up and coming out in the sixties and seventies. We found the stories and books by Samuel Steward and Clay Caldwell (aka Gary Collins) and others, and used them as guides to our new and evolving lives. We were a remarkably innovative group, and our innovation was matched by the producers of the material. We understood the buzzwords they used to signal homoerotic content. To me, that meant looking for material whose front cover labeled it as "sociologically important." That was a signal to us in those days. A sociological study of what they were doing in tolerant Denmark was always sure to have a lot of great juicy parts to it.

While the general society was determined to make sure that gay erotic writing was never accepted as "classy porn," in Ellen Willis's words, that didn't mean we had to accept their definition. An evolving gay literature advanced along with the gay political movement that burst out in the seventies. The new writing was blunt and straightforward; that was the way we wanted it to be, just the same way we wanted to be ourselves. Gay erotic writing that developed from the sixties created heroes and myths that were signposts for us as we were getting our lives together; the gay writing of the seventies was about the way we really were.

There were still many attempts to limit what gay writing was about. There were many writers who wanted to avoid the new gay movement as much as possible, hoping that they would be accepted into the canon of mainstream literature in spite of their homosexuality, not through it. Those writers avoided the core of gay life and tried to avoid explicit sexual detail as much as possible. The literary movement paralleled a political effort to convince the American public that gay life was just like everyone else's, surrounded by white picket fences and nicely colored in pastel. While politicians might have wanted us to model ourselves as though we were polite versions of heterosexuality—including being just as sexless as television represented heterosexuals to be—there was an undercurrent of revolt in our writing. Samuel Steward's Phil Andros was sometimes a hustler, always a drifter, forever an adventurer; someone who you could never imagine settling down. The world that Clay Caldwell developed was one that was overlooked by the general population, but that seethed with lustful sexuality between men, even as it was ignored. No matter how much some writers and critics might have wanted to avoid this heritage, others embraced it.

Nowadays, as gay writing has become something of a genre itself, one that has a niche in the mainstream, gay sexual writing is continually shunted aside, left on the back burner, boiling away. Certainly there have been many highly commercial pornographic publications in the past twenty-five years, some of which are quite slick, though few are sold at the neighborhood store. Technology has also changed the landscape of gay sexual images. Video and computer sciences have opened new avenues to distribution, just as they've altered how we look at the material.

Yet, for all the science and the political advances, we still seem to consider gay erotica something that should stay in its own peculiar closet. That constraint has nothing to do with literary merit. We have allowed the world to judge our writing about gay sex on the basis of its content—once again allowing anything that involves gay sex to be deemed obscene just because it is about gay men.

There have been many people interested in gay erotica. The tenacity of the fans of Samuel Steward and Clay Caldwell is just a simple example of that. It has often seemed that the main barrier was the way the material was presented. The package often underlined the message that the explicit writing was deviant in a way that only equally deviant readers would find acceptable. Distribution was still a problem, since most erotic writing, no matter what its merit, could only be found in adult stores. Anything found in these locations still had to be pornography; it couldn't have been erotica.

When I edited the first volume of *Flesh and the Word*, one of my goals was to go into the world of gay sexual writing, find material that had been considered "smut," and bring it out and recast it, to show it as "erotica." My desire wasn't to make it nicer, but to put it in a context and a package where it could be more carefully judged and enjoyed. One of my main reasons was that I was convinced that the writing was *good*. It shouldn't be ignored. It touches some of the deepest and most tender parts of our lives, not because it is pornographic, but because it is the writing of very fine authors. I wanted to take some of the best gay writing and present it to an audience that would be able to see it as that.

The first volume was a great success, in every way. Many copies were sold; many reviews were written; many writers were introduced; many readers were made very happy.

There had actually been a number of pieces that I had been aware of that couldn't fit into that first volume, and there had been some topics—video and its influence on pornography is one example—that I hadn't been able to cover. With this second volume, I hope the record is more complete. *Flesh and the Word* and *Flesh and the Word 2* should be read together, as a set. The quality of some writers' work—Steven Saylor, for instance—becomes even more recognizable for their skill when there's more than one piece to read. While some writers are represented in both volumes, I've also striven to find new voices here in *Flesh and the Word 2,* to balance the more established voices in the first volume. I also wanted to make more of an acknowledgment of how pornography documents our lives. There are more pieces of non-fiction in this book, precisely because writers like Michael Bronski, Andrew Holleran, and Christopher Wittke have used their skills to chronicle and report on the way we live. This is a vital role of our writing, especially under the extraordinary circumstances of the AIDS epidemic.

These two volumes stand as my introduction to you, the reader, to some of the finest writers in the gay world, writers who are not willing to be involved in silencing the gay experience, but who insist on celebrating it.

JOHN PRESTON
Portland, Maine

PART ONE

THE

TRADITIONALS

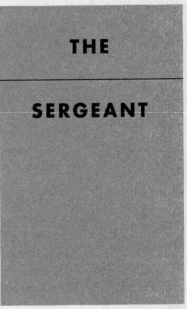

GARY COLLINS

THE

SERGEANT

THE CADRE ROOM AT THE END OF THE BARRACKS
was small and moist-warm. A layer of cigarette smoke lay motionless in the air. The young sergeant slouched back on his foot-
locker and took a final swallow of whiskey from the paper cup in
his hand. Overhead, the bare light bulb glared on his short, golden-
red hair and shadowed his hard-cut, tanned features. Almost lazily,
he drew one hand down along the fly of his fatigue trousers, strong
fingers cupping the bulging mound beneath.

"Fill 'em up again, kid," he said to the dark-haired youth
seated on the iron cot opposite him.

The younger soldier picked up the bottle from the floor and
leaned forward. A thick lock of black hair fell down over his forehead and he did not look at the man as he filled the cup.

The sergeant grinned. "How about it, Mike?"

"How about what, Sarge?"

"We're going to take care of each other, buddy. Stand up."

"Please don't, Burt," the youth murmured hoarsely.

"On your feet."

The youth sucked in a deep breath and then he got up, his eyes closed as if not looking would keep it from happening. His arms hung at his sides, and his youthfully handsome features were tense. He heard the man's slow, heavy breathing close in front of him, and then the fingers were tugging at his jacket buttons, starting at the top and working down. His muscles tightened, and he locked his jaw as his jacket was spread open. Then the man was touching his bared flesh.

"Damned nice, Mike. You've got a real good build for nineteen."

Mike swallowed hard, trembling. "Remember when you were nineteen, Burt? Lemme go, huh?"

"That was only three years ago, kid."

"Burt . . ."

Mike felt the open palms move over his high-curved chest, smoothing the wisps of flat-lying hair. His heart was throbbing almost painfully. The fingertips inspected the wide, flat nipples at either side and rose to push the jacket down from his broad, muscle-ridged shoulders.

"You're okay, buddy." Burt's hands caressed Mike's sides and made slow, circular patterns over his taut-plated stomach, working lower and lower. "Real fine."

The fingers gripped Mike's belt and eased it loose; then his fly was being opened. The hot, uncontrollable pressure surged into his loins, and then his trousers were falling down over his muscle-tensed legs.

"Burt . . ."

Burt was unfastening his skivvies, fingertips slipping inside to stroke the flat curve of Mike's belly and follow the widening trail of silk to the thicket at his groin. The hands moved out to Mike's hips and pressed downward. He shivered as his shorts dropped over

his thighs. He felt the sudden, hard-surging release of his flesh.
The fingers were between his legs, caressing the insides of his thighs
and moving up. An involuntary whimper broke from his throat as
one palm cupped beneath his heavy-hanging power. Then he felt
the warm, sure grip on his swelling body.

"Please don't, Burt."

The sergeant stroked slowly, tantalizing the boy, making him
gasp and whimper with all sorts of the most exciting emotions.
Mike's naked body jerked with tension, and he groaned slowly.

"Damn nice," Burt repeated huskily. "Hold still and I'll show
you how."

Burt dropped to his knees and Mike felt his clothing being
stripped from his ankles. Then the hand gripped his body again,
supporting it in the arc between thumb and forefinger. An instant
later the harsh warmth licked over the sensitive boy and the strong,
damp lips closed about the flange.

A gentle spatter of rain broke against the window and the
dripping from the eaves drummed on the sill.

Burt pressed closer, drawing the massive boy deeper and deeper
into his mouth. His hands pressed up between the young soldier's
quivering thighs, caressing the sensitive flesh, fingering the slippery
flesh, reaching back to rub over the sleek, pinched-in bottom.

Mike's head rolled forward and he half-opened his eyes, staring
down at the man crouched before him. Burt's shoulders were hard-
marked with rigid muscles and his face was buried in the darkness
between Mike's wide-spread thighs. With torturing slowness the
sergeant drew back and the youth saw as he was about to slip free.
Then Burt was rising to his feet, his hands drawing up over the
naked body once more.

"That wasn't the first time for you, Mike."

"No."

"Okay, it's your turn."

Mike stood motionless, staring at the sergeant's powerful torso
before him.

"Go ahead, Mike."

Mike watched the sharp rise and fall of the broad chest, the sleek golden hair gleaming in the dim light, the sharp pointed nipples standing out at either side of the solid curves.

"Go ahead, kid."

Mike's hands rose like dead weights at the ends of his arms, and his fingers touched the front of the man's trousers, finding the metal buttons and unfastening them, one after the other. He brushed against bare flesh and wiry hair, and he knew the sergeant hadn't put on shorts beneath his pants. Without shifting his gaze from the heaving chest, he pressed the clothing down. His heart hammered and he could hear the tight-throated rasp of his own breathing.

"Grab a hold, buddy," Burt ordered quietly. It seemed strange that he should be so calm.

Mike's eyes burned and began to water. He brought both hands up. Numb, he felt the tantalizing fullness of the man's body. Then Burt's palms were cupped on his shoulders.

"Like I showed you, Mike."

The hands pressed down firmly and Mike sank to his knees. The wooden floor was rough and hard-grained, and before him, the man's body stood straight and erect; every part of him was alive and throbbing with raw and naked lust. There was no turning back.

"Go on, Mike. Take it."

Mike watched the sergeant's fingers lock about the base of the potent power and raise it toward his face. He closed his eyes and felt the glass-smooth boy touch his lips. He swallowed hard. The wetness was drawn along his lips and he felt the body warmth and smelled the closeness of masculine scent. Then he opened his mouth.

"That's the way, Mike." Burt reached down and stroked the back of the youth's head. "Take your time, little buddy."

Mike felt the tears brim over and trickle down his cheeks. Then the hands were sliding from his head to the back of his neck, urging his face forward into the mysterious darkness between the man's legs.

"Go ahead, kid, take it."

■   ●   ■

Mike lay back on the cot, staring up at the dimly lit ceiling, his arms folded beneath his head. He could feel the numbed pressure of the naked man resting against his side, and he saw the flare of a cigarette ember. The redness glowed on the crossbeams above for a moment; then the cool breath of smoke blew across his bare belly.

"Want a drag, Mike?"

"Thanks."

Burt held the cigarette to Mike's lips and waited while he inhaled hungrily. Then he dropped his hand to the youth's slow-rising chest. "Okay, buddy?"

"Yeah. Sure."

The sergeant drew back to finish the cigarette and drop it in the butt can. Then his hand was on Mike's chest again, stroking the lightly haired curves.

"Want a drink, kid?"

"No." Mike felt the surprisingly gentle pressure of the fingers. He lay still as they moved over his bare torso. "How come you picked on me, Burt? Why not one of the other guys?"

"You're not the first. It just took you longer to get the idea."

"But why me?"

"I dunno. There's something about a kid that says he's going to try it, sooner or later. That's how I found out." He watched his hand move over Mike's taut stomach. "You're a real rugged young stud, and I figured you were ready."

"I never thought I'd do something like that."

"Some guys don't mind. Some of them like it."

Mike swallowed hard, the unfamiliar taste still lingering in his throat. "It wasn't so bad, I guess. I sure needed to get my rocks off afterwards."

"You've had guys work on you before, huh?"

"A couple of times. Hitchhiking. And there was a kid in high school." Mike drew one arm from beneath his head and fingered the soft hair on his chest, still staring at the dark ceiling. "I never did anything for them."

Burt eased his palm down the flat curve of the youth's lower belly, caressing to the border of the shadows. "You need plenty of action, buddy. Anytime you want to make it, I don't mind taking care of you."

"You want me to take care of you again, too?"

"That's up to you."

Mike reached up and drew a meaningless pattern with his finger on the sweat-glazed window. "Can I have a pass this weekend?"

"Sure, buddy."

"And that leave."

Burt worked his hand down to Mike's heavy-muscled thigh. "You're learning fast, kid. Don't lose your head."

"What do you mean?"

"You liked it, right?"

Mike moistened his lips, watching the water drops run through the lines he had traced on the window. "You said I need plenty of action. I don't care if a guy wants to swing with me."

"That isn't the part I meant."

"Look, Sarge," Mike exploded, his voice suddenly cold. "I did it—just like you wanted me to—so I could get a pass this weekend and a leave. And that's the only reason."

"Sure, kid."

Mike felt a slow, taunting movement of Burt's fingers against the smooth skin lining his thighs and the first hint of sexual excitement warmed his midsection. He squirmed to get comfortable and spread his legs slightly.

"I'm not going to do it to you again, Sarge."

"Okay."

Suddenly Mike reached down and gripped the man's hand, shoving it up to the rapidly heating column at his crotch. "How about you, Sarge? You like that, huh?"

"I take care of my boys, Mike."

"You really like swinging on it, huh?"

"You've got a lot to learn, kid." Burt sat up, gazing at the swelling flesh filling his fist. "Yeah, I like it, little buddy."

He swung over on his knees between Mike's legs and dropped forward. Mike tensed, feeling the warm dampness encircle the swol-

len head of his body. He raised up on his elbows and stared down
at the sergeant slowly taking him.

"You're a real queer, Burt," he muttered, and then he lay back,
closing his eyes as the release-promising pressure began. "Okay,
Sarge, swing!" He reached down to grasp the heaving shoulders,
outlining the powerful muscle ridges beneath the taut flesh. Then
his hands moved to the bobbing head, fingers stroking the short-
clipped hair and then pressing down firmly. "Go ahead. Take it!"

JOHN DIBELKA
WRITING AS JAY SHAFFER

SHOOTERS

"WHY IS IT NONE OF THESE STORIES IS ABOUT jacking off?"

Steve's cue hits the cue ball. The cue ball hits the seven and the seven falls into the pocket, *clunk,* just as smooth as you please.

Steve asks me these questions like I'm supposed to know the answers. Most of the time I don't even know what he means, but I hold my tongue and let him shoot. They always come up when he is just about to sink a killer shot.

Sometimes I hate playing pool with this man.

"I don't know what you're talking about," I tell him. As usual, I really don't.

Steve looks up at me from under his eyebrows. His face is a

17

little green from the light bouncing up off the felt. He looks like an ogre this way, and he knows it. He uses it. On everyone except me. Now he scowls for a second, but stands up to chalk up his tip and fill me in on what he means.

"Gay men's porn," he says patiently, setting the chalk block down. "It's never about jerking off." He sets the thought in my brain with his eyes; then he leans down to set up his shot. "It's all about all kinds of sex," he adds, aiming. "Everything else but the solo stuff."

Smack. Click. Clunk. The three ball has disappeared, and all Steve did was flick his wrist. The man's hand action makes all his shots something special to see.

Now he is standing again and staring at me and waiting for my answer. We both know his next shot will end the game. I have balls all over the table.

"I don't know," I tell him. "I've never thought about it much." I don't, and I haven't.

Steve purses his lips and scowls again; looks at the table and leans back down; sets up his shot and, with a flick of his wrist, turns the eight ball into history. *Everything is a matter of self-confidence,* he has told me more than once. *You can do anything you set your mind to do.*

Maybe so, but I can't shoot pool for shit.

Steve racks the cue and wipes chalk dust from his hands to his butt and the lump of his basket. He walks around the table to reach out and shake my hand.

"Thanks," he says.

"You're welcome," I answer. "All I did was hold still."

"I'm serious," he tells me.

"Okay," I tell him back, not sure just what he means, "so'm I."

"About the porn," he explains. Oh. That. I nod.

"Come on," offers Steve, "I'll buy the beer."

That is an offer I never refuse. I follow him to the bar, where he pays and grabs the pitcher and two mugs and points toward a corner where the jukebox won't be too painful. We walk. We sit. He pours. I thank him.

"To jerking off," he toasts. I laugh. "To pounding puds and yanking cranks and flogging dogs and . . ."

"I get the idea," I tell him. "I'm thirsty." I drink. And I think, and his answer comes to me. I set my mug down. "Maybe I do know," I say.

"Let's hear it." Steve watches my eyes as he places his own mug on the table squarely, exactly where, for some reason, he has decided it should be.

"Well, hold on a second. It makes sense to me, but I'm not real sure I'll get the words right."

"Just say it," Steve prods.

"All right. Shit. I'm working on it." I take a sip.

"Men read porn," I tell him like it's news, "because they want to jack off. They want fantasies. Scenes they can't imagine for themselves, or scenes they can't make happen." Steve's expression doesn't change. "They know what it's like to jack off," I continue. "They don't want reality. Give 'em a story about what they do already and nobody's going to be interested. It'd never sell. So it'd never get printed. It's economics." I'm pleased with myself. I feel like a fucking sociologist.

"I'd buy it," Steve answers. He lifts his mug thoughtfully. I know he doesn't mean my explanation.

"Yeah?" I ask. With Steve, I never know anything for sure. "You'd buy the stories?"

"Yeah," he says. "And I'll tell you why." He sets down the mug on exactly the spot where it rested before. "What you are saying here is that masturbation somehow isn't really sex. The men who buy this stuff want fantasies about reality, or something that could be real sex. That is what it all comes down to, isn't it? You still with me?" I nod. Steve continues, his tone homing in for a kill. "You are telling me guys beat their meat when they can't get the real thing. By which you mean they can't get someone else to get them off. Is that correct?"

"Well yeah," I stammer. "This seems obvious."

"This," says Steve, "is bullshit."

My jaw drops. Steve frowns, but he continues.

"Look at it this way. Who do you play with, of everyone you
play with, who *always* gets you off? We are talking, one hundred
percent of the time." I shrug. "You do. It all takes place in your
mind anyway. All I am saying is, that's just fine. You don't have
to shoot for anybody but yourself. Sometimes it's better to come
just to come. You don't have to worry about anyone's pleasure but
yours. It's some of the best damned sex *I've* ever had."

He leans back, now, and pours us both more beer. I sip mine
and think about his words.

"You mean," I say, "sort of like 'Don't fuck 'em if they can't
take a joke.' " Steve looks astonished for a second before he busts
up laughing.

"Yeah. I think you've got it."

"I'll have to think about this. What about you, then?" I ask
him. "You want to see the story, give me an example." Steve's head
cocks, and his eyes blank out, while he thinks.

"Okay," he says at last. "Picture this. I am driving down to
Denver. In a pull-out on the northbound side of the highway sits
a trailer. No cab attached. You know how it is when some trucker
gets careless and forgets to get his Wyoming permits: he has to
leave his load until he can get the papers to move it. But it's Friday
night, so his trailer is going to sit there all weekend unless the
poor slob can get someone to take out a blow job in trade. And
what do you think is sitting on top of it?"

Steve is watching me closely now, setting me up for something. I love it when he tells me stories. Makes me feel like I'm
the only one around for miles. I hold up my hands and I shrug.
Shit if I know.

"A tank," Steve says. "A camouflage-painted Army vehicle
with treads and a very large-bore weapon." Steve wets his whistle
and waits for his words to sink in.

"I don't believe it," I tell him. "A tank? Unguarded? Army
property?"

"Unguarded," he answers, searching my eyes again. "Think
about it. Who is going to fuck with a tank? In the heart of the
Midwest—or close."

"Oh," I say. "Well; I guess you're right." I nod. "So what did you do?"

"I drove to Denver."

I should have known. I don't even know why I asked. Once Steve sets his mind to something, that something gets done come hell or high water.

"But I had a hard cock all the way down and you better believe I stopped at that tank on my way back home."

I think this story is about to get interesting.

"It is Sunday night," Steve continues. "It is dark. It is cold, and it is lonely. The tank is still there; still unguarded and still pointing its weapon out over the road."

I think I may know where he's going. My dick is getting hard. I squirm to give it room to grow and almost fall off my stool. Steve pretends not to notice. Such a gentleman. The man makes me crazy.

"I pull up," he says, "and park my truck off to the side, out of sight from the road. Then I assess the situation."

Steve is forever assessing situations. No matter where he goes, within fifteen minutes he knows everything there is to know about what is around him and who is there and what is going on. Or is likely to go on. Before he moved west he was either a cop or a spy or a hit man for the mob. He won't tell me which.

"It is around midnight. There is no traffic for miles. No observers. So I climb up onto the vehicle." The mental image is one of Steve in boots and jeans and a hunting jacket, using gloved hands to hoist himself onto the flatbed and from there to any horizontal surface on the tank that does not read, NO STEP. Steve would notice that sort of thing. Even in the dead of night.

My mouth is dry. My cock is throbbing. I can't recall ever having been turned on by a tank. I rub myself through my jeans, as casually as I can.

"I have never been this close to a tank before this," Steve tells me.

This I find hard to believe. Steve seems to me to be the kind of man who would be perfectly at home commanding an entire division of tanks. Then again, Steve never lies. So this was his first time on top of a tank. That fact just makes his story hotter.

"I am thinking about all the soldiers who have used this equipment, or will use it." As he says it, so am I. "Three, maybe four at a time. Shoehorned into tight quarters like these; nervous and sweating like pigs." I've never thought of tanks like this. Steve sees everything this way. To him the world's nothing but sexual objects.

His hands wander now, as he talks. He's getting as worked up as I am. His fingertips draw little designs in the puddles on the table. His palms wrap around the edge, thumbs on top. His biceps bulge, grow harder, as he uses his grip to readjust his seat on the bar stool. I keep one fist wrapped around my beer, but I catch myself sliding it up and down the mug. My other hand drifts to my lap where it ends up, thumb through a belt loop, stroking, palming, fingering my meat to beat the band.

"I climb all the way up to the top of the turret," Steve goes on. His voice is hypnotic like this. "I take a look around. Visibility is unlimited. There is no moon, but the stars are very bright. Very clear and cold. No traffic. I can see a great distance down the highway." I am mesmerized by Steve's eyes. "The whole scene is peaceful and quiet and beautiful."

I can't help myself. I unbutton my pants, slowly and carefully, in the middle of the bar.

"And in the middle of all this," Steve says, "is a war machine. And I am on top of that machine." Steve takes a slow sip and places the beer back down. No way can I look away from his face, even though my eyes are clouding over with the scene he is showing me.

I pop the last button. My dick unreels into the cigarette-stale gray air like an animal on the attack. I get all the way hard right away.

"By this time it is all I can do," Steve is telling me, "to pull off my gloves and open up my britches zipper, because I have thrown a bone like nothing else." I can't look away from Steve's eye. I don't dare look down in my lap.

I reach in and dig out my nuts.

"My meat feels real good in my hand, in the open. Hard and hot," Steve breathes, "and when I look down it gets harder and hotter. I pull my nuts out along, too, and I turn a few degrees until it is perfectly parallel with the barrel of the gun." I can see this scene. I can't see much more of the Steve in the bar, but I sure see the Steve who has claimed a tank and is just about to mark it as his property.

Too hot. I'm settling into a good jacking rhythm, but my palm is dry. What the hell will I use for lube? I can't very well spit into my hand—not here. Besides: my mouth is dry, too. I sip my beer. The mug is sweating. I set it back down and go to wipe my hand off on my pants before I figure out what to do instead. I scoop up more mug sweat and slap it on down on my dick. The stuff is slippery, all right, but it's *cold*. The excitement keeps me hard anyway.

"It is cold, like I told you," Steve says, "but the scene is so hot my cock doesn't even think of shriveling up." Not that Steve's cock would ever do anything without his permission. We both know that. He's just talking for effect now. He knows what his story is doing to me. He knows what I'm doing with his story—and myself. The man misses nothing. He makes me nuts.

The bar has gotten crowded. With half my mind I wonder if anyone around us knows as well. *Hey there, people. Wonder what's going on under this table?* I'm not sure if I want them to or not. I don't need to get busted for waving my whanger in public, but the thought that I might sure as hell turns me on.

I try to take stock, look around; assess the situation. Not possible. All I can see is a midnight sky full of stars and a cock pointing out like the gun of a tank.

"All I can see is the sky and the stars," Steve tells me, "and this tank and the men who will use it and the spots they will find the next time they climb aboard." I moan. "I can see their faces . . ."

My butt cheeks are starting to clamp on my stool.

". . . when they walk up and see those dried-up tracks . . ."

My thighs are so tight that they vibrate.

". . . on their hatch and all over their little windshield . . ."

My chest is constricting; my face is getting flushed.

". . . and they figure out first that it shouldn't be there . . ."

My heart is racing. My nuts are drawn up.

". . . and they start to wipe it . . ."

My come is churning up.

". . . until one of these men stops, and starts to laugh . . ."

My breath is ragged. My dick is drooling. My toes are curling up, down in my boots.

". . . and he tells his buddies what it is . . ."

What it is, is jizz, and it's starting to move into position.

". . . and they all get hard thinking about it . . ."

Loaded. And ready to *fire*.

". . . and they all start to rub their crotches, hoping nobody else—none of their buddies in that cramped, sweaty, stuffy tank—notices what's going on . . ."

Christ. Sweat is pouring down into my eyes. My hand must be a blur. So close. I am . . . *so close* . . .

". . . but they all hold off until next time they are out on the practice range . . ."

Hold off? He has *got* to be kidding . . .

". . . and the first time that big gun goes off . . ."

Yeah . . . ?

". . . they shoot all over the inside of that tank. Hose it down good. Just like I shot on the outside."

Just like I'm shooting this table. I howl. I yell. I don't care who hears me now. This is just the fucking *best*. Nonfucking best. Shit—what*ever*. Shot after fucking hot, crotch-slicing shot builds up in my pelvis and loads and fires and flies out into the bar air, cutting the cigarette smoke like a knife with the smell of loads of fresh, hot come. I get goosebumps. I get cramps. I sweat like a pig.

I get something wet on my hand. Wet—and hot.

Something wet and hot and not mine: I'm shooting out. And this is not dripping down from the table.

I will be damned.

Steve's coming, too. Right into my open fly. Another perfect shot. Even in pocket pool the man's a winner. It's all I can do to keep from falling off this stool, but Steve is cool and still aiming his shots like a champ. Christ almighty.

I grit my teeth. This hurts so *good.*

"And I shoot my load all over hell and back," Steve says (rather redundantly, I think) when he can catch his breath.

"Oh my holy shit," I grunt, shaking my head to clear sweat from my eyes and cobwebs from my brain. *"Yo,"* I say, and bust up laughing.

"Yo," Steve answers, exactly as his last shot lands exactly on my hand. "See what I mean?"

No, I don't. All I see is Steve—the Steve in front of me now, not the one on the tank—looking cool and unruffled, every hair in place and grinning, just a little. Except for the fact that his face is red, no one could tell that he's just shot his wad out all over my crotch.

"What you mean about what?" I ask him. Panting.

"Jerking off. Solo sex. At the risk of being trite, it was good for you, too, wasn't it." This is not really a question. I smile. I laugh. I just about fall off the stool one more time.

"Well, sure," I say. "But it wasn't really solo. You were here. We just had sex." And god knows I've got the stains to show for it. What will I look like when I stand up again?

"Yeah," he leers, "but it works alone, too. Just set your mind to it. And write all about it."

Steve sips his beer and wipes one finger off on his mustache. One huge drop of my come glitters in the barlight glow before he scoops it off again and reaches across the table to deposit it on my tongue. I taste just great.

"Write about it?"

"Sure. You can do it. You know you can." The idea turns me on.

"You know," I say, "I think you're right." It turns me on a lot. "But can I write about this first?" I ask.

Instantly I kick myself for asking Steve's permission. I can do anything I set my mind to.

"Don't ask me," Steve says, drinking his beer with one hand while he closes his fly with the other. "Just do it."

WILLIAM COZAD

THE

PAWNBROKER

AFTER I WAS LAID OFF WORK I RAN LOW ON CASH.
Unemployment insurance, or "cool aid" as they called it, wasn't
nearly enough to hold body and soul together.

About the only thing of value I had was a diamond-cluster
gold ring which my ex-lover gave me. He took everything else
when he split, probably because he couldn't get the ring off my
finger while I was asleep. I thought about giving him back the ring
and keeping the stone, but I didn't.

I made a visit to the pawnshop down in the sleazy part of
town. The store had the three dangling balls in the window. I'd
heard that there were twice as many hock shops as banks where
people went for loans.

Entering the store, I noticed all the business equipment, like
small copying machines. Bad sign, like the economy was in a reces-

sion. I sure was. I'd heard that most working people were three paychecks away from being in the streets. Losing my job made a believer out of me.

But I stopped thinking about dollars and cents when I saw the clerk. The guy almost blew me away. Dynamite-looking. Short and slender, around twenty-four. Curly black hair and big brown eyes. Just my type.

"I'd like to hock this ring," I said.

"How much?"

"A hundred. It cost nearly a grand."

"Let me check it out."

He called to the office in the back. Out came a wizened old man with a jeweler's eye attached to his glasses. Reminded me of Rod Steiger in that movie about a pawnbroker—Sol Nazerman had flashbacks about being persecuted as a Jew in Germany. Seeing the young clerk, I had flashbacks of my ex-lover, who was similar in appearance. Hot sex was about all we had going for us because we had a failure to communicate. I thought him temperamental— ninety percent temper and ten percent mental. But I tried to forget the past.

The snowy-haired pawnbroker nodded to his young assistant, who filled out the papers. I signed the loan agreement and he took the print of my right index finger. He gave me a C-note.

"Now I can get drunk and be somebody else."

He smiled. Sensuous lips I'd like to kiss. He made me hot. I cruised his basket.

"That's what I do on my day off," he said.

The old man returned to his office in the back.

"Care to join me for a drink when you get off work?" I said.

"Sure. Why not? I get off at five."

"How about meeting me at Wendy's on the corner?"

"See you then."

A customer came into the store and was looking at the watches in the glass display case. The clerk went over to help him. I left the store.

I wandered around downtown and looked in the store windows.
I was pretty horny after looking at the guy in the hock shop. I
could go back to my hotel and beat off. Maybe he wouldn't show
up. He looked butch and straight. Maybe he just wanted free drinks
at a bar since I invited him.

As it approached five o'clock I went into Wendy's. Got a Coke
and sat down by the window. Watched the people waiting for buses
after work. Looked at my watch. It was fifteen after five. He wasn't
going to show. Maybe he thought I was a queer and changed his
mind.

Just when I sucked the last of the Coke out of the cup and
chewed on some crushed ice, I spotted the guy from the pawnshop.
He came in and sat down beside me.

"Sorry I'm a little late. Got stuck with a customer who
couldn't make up his mind about which camera he wanted."

"Thirsty?"

"Not for a Coke."

"What's your drink?"

"Beer with whiskey, boilermakers."

"Jeez. Where to?"

"I usually buy the stuff at a liquor store. I like to tie one on,
but the money goes too fast in bars."

"I've got a hundred bucks," I said.

"But you don't want to spend it all on booze."

"No, maybe I'll save twenty bucks for food."

"What a guy!" He grinned.

"Let's go to my hotel room."

He nodded. "I'm Nelson."

"Bill."

I felt good about luring him to my room. There were possibilities, although it wasn't in the bag yet. He might know what I was
after, and then again he might not. I wasn't about to blow the
money on a stranger in a bar. I wasn't born yesterday.

I got us a fifth of Seagram's and a twelve-pack of Budweiser.
He insisted on paying for half of it, which surprised me.

In my fleabag hotel room, where I'd moved after splitting up with my lover, I threw the clothes off the chair and into the closet. Stacked the newspapers in the corner. Emptied the ashtrays.

I turned on the radio to some rock station that played oldies. "Sorry about the mess."

"My place looks the same way. Just a room to sleep in."

"How long have you been a pawnbroker?"

"Not really a pawnbroker. Just work there. Uh, about three months. After I got out of the Marines. I was going to reenlist. Still might. Haven't got a home. Folks are divorced, got different families now. Thought I'd try it as a civilian. The hock shop was the only job I could get. I hocked my watch so many times that the old-timer offered me a job."

"Bet you hear a lot of sad stories."

"That's for sure. Most of 'em are probably true, people down on their luck."

The whiskey made my tongue loose. I sipped on a beer after taking a slug. So did Nelson.

"I'm out of work but I'm not worried. Down but not out. I'll connect with something before long. I'm not lazy. I'll do any kind of honest work for a paycheck."

"Something'll break. It always does."

Looking into Nelson's big brown eyes, I thought he was either full of shit or a genuine nice guy.

"I've got a sad story," I said. "I've got this hard-on that won't quit."

He'd think I was drunk or crazy. He'd run or stick around to see what happens. "I get that way sometimes," he said.

"All I know to do is jack off. Don't mind, do you?"

He gave me a funny look when I whipped out my cock and stroked it. "No. Do your thing."

"Bet you got a big dick. I've seen short guys like you before. Macho and hung."

"Wanna see my cock? You must be queer."

"I like all kinds of sex."

That wasn't really true but it was enough to make Nelson

haul out his own tool. I was on the bed, he was on the chair beside it. His cock was about five inches soft.

"It gets big."

"Jack it, make it hard."

"What I really need is a blow job. Wanna blow me?"

I reached out and touched him, like the phone company says. It was a slab of hot meat. I fondled it and it got stiff right away.

"Go down on it, dude."

I reached in the drawer of the nightstand for a condom.

"You don't need that."

"I'm a cautious cocksucker. Don't take no risk with my health."

I stretched the rubber over his bullet-shaped cockhead and rolled it down the veiny shaft.

"Like my dick, don't you?"

"It's a big surprise. Beautiful piece of meat. Why don't you get undressed and show me the rest of you."

Nelson stripped naked. He was a real hunk. Light hair between the small nipples on his chest. Washboard belly and hairy legs.

I shed my own clothes and felt his eyes on me. I hadn't had a trick since breaking up with my lover. The ex-Marine pawnbroker was exactly what turned me on.

"Hot stuff, huh?" he teased.

I stretched him out on the bed with his huge prick that had to be nine inches of fat fuckmeat towering into the air, covered in latex. I crawled between his legs.

"Suck it," he moaned.

I held his cock by the thick base and licked up and down the sides, tasting the yucky rubber.

His eyes were dilated and glazed. I wanted to eat him alive. I started by licking his armpits, which surprised him. Tasting his sweat and inhaling his musk made my cock throb. I sucked on his small nipples until they were hard. I licked his inner belly button. His pubic bush was dense and I kissed it.

Holding his sheathed cock, I licked his ballsack.

"Suck my nuts."

I mouthed one, then the other. I got them both into my mouth and washed them with spit. Big, hard, succulent balls. I weirdly expected a pawnbroker to have three balls.

"Blow me, dude."

I sucked on his cockhead and took the shaft down my throat.

"Oh, yeah. Fuck, yeah. Suck me."

Nelson was such a beauty that I liked to look up at his chiseled features. He was handsome and manly.

When a guy really turns me on like Nelson I like to play with myself while I blow them. Turning into a sixty-nine position, I gobbled up his big cock and deepthroated it. All the while I frigged my cock.

He pushed my hand away and took over jacking me off. I liked that, the feel of his hot palm and strong fingers working my meat.

That left me with a free hand. Laying my head on his sinewy right thigh, I clutched the base of his cock with my left hand while I bobbed my head up and down. With my right hand I fondled his balls and squeezed them. Traveling downward, I fingered his hairy crack. He didn't stop me. I worked my middle finger into his pucker, which was real tight.

He got turned on by the ass play. I could tell because he thrust his pelvis upward while I fingered his hole and sucked his cock.

As much as I liked my finger in his hole, I wanted to put my dick in there, to feel his insides grasping it and feel the heat of his guts.

His cock was hard as a rock. I kept sucking it. He kept jacking me off. I could have come but I wanted to get him off first. That makes me even hotter.

He was breathing hard and I knew the moment was coming for his climax. I stopped sucking his dick although I kept my finger embedded in his hole. I snapped off the condom and watched him blow.

He shot a long strand of fuckjuice like a necklace of pearls that landed on his wiry pubic bush. I rubbed it into his hairy crotch until it glistened.

After shooting his wad he was determined to get me off. He roughly, furiously fisted my cock. I was at the edge. Then I blasted. Big gobs of cum shot off all over the bed.

"Oh, fuck. Oh, Nelson. Holy Christ!"

Looking up at him, I saw the shit-eating grin on his face. My own cock stayed bone-hard, like it was pumped full of air.

What occurred next had only happened in my wet dreams before. But it was happening now in front of my eyes. Nelson rolled over onto his belly. I looked at his hairy muscular ass globes and my cock was like a crowbar.

He wanted me to screw him. I'd always heard that Marines liked it up the ass. I thought that was only a put-down because of their emphasis on physical fitness. I'd never had a Marine before.

I got a condom out of the drawer and threaded it on my cock quickly, before Nelson could come to his senses or change his mind. I liked fucking ass, especially macho studs like him. My ex-lover was a bitch in bed, but butch as could be out of it. He was too young, too wild, too slutty for one guy to handle. I never did figure out exactly what went wrong.

I spread Nelson's buttcheeks. He looked over his shoulder. His sad brown eyes made me hesitate. I didn't want to hurt him but I definitely wanted to fuck him in his ass.

I stuck my finger in his hole again. It was all hot and juicy inside.

"Do it. Dick me."

I nudged my bloated cockhead inside his hole. The assring expanded and I was in like Flynn.

"Oh god, it hurts. It's so fucking big."

"Relax, baby. Let it go all the way in."

I slid the whole thing up inside his butt and waited for his hole to get used to the fleshy intruder.

"Fuck me. I want it."

That was enough for me. I lifted up and pounded his asshole with ass-stretching cockstrokes. He shoved his ass back.

"You got a hot ass. Real fucking tight."

"Keep fucking it. Yeah, harder!"

I slammed my cock in real deep, pulled way back, then plunged it home again. He took every hard inch of my latex-covered cock up his fuckhole.

He buried his face in the pillow and whimpered while I crammed his hole. I sat back on my heels and watched my cock slide in and out of the ex-Marine's bunghole.

"Do it, dude. Get off inside me. Cum up my ass. Cream my hole!"

I was dripping sweat on his taut body and groaning with pleasure. Lying prone on his body, I humped him. I bit his neck and corkscrewed his hole until he couldn't take it anymore.

"Oh shit, I'm cumming. Cumming with your cock up my ass. I've never done that before. Oh sweet Jesus. Motherfucker!"

His asshole shuddered, clamping on my cock, bringing me off while he shot his wad on the sheet.

"Here it comes. Take it, slut Marine sonuvabitch. Take my fucking load up your hiney!"

My balls crushed against his hairy asscheeks and I blasted a big wad of fiery jism that filled the rubber tip in his guts.

I panted and lay on top of him until my balls were drained. My cock softened and slid out of his hole with the condom intact.

He rolled over on his back and faced me.

"That was a good cum. The best ever."

I don't know if the devil made me do it or not, but I snapped off the condom and splashed the pearly white cum drops all over his chest and rubbed it in until the hair glistened like it did on his crotch.

I ran my fingers through his curly black hair and crushed my lips against his. He kissed me back.

Nelson and I partied all night long, gulping whiskey, chasing it down with beer. We did a hot sixty-nine. We jacked each other off. With the last condom, I suited up and plugged his hole with his legs up in the air.

I was in hock to Nelson the pawnbroker. But I took it out on his ass and got even.

I managed to find another job before my unemployment checks ran out. And Nelson decided to re-up in the Marines. I've got my diamond ring back—and one of these days I'm hoping like hell to get Nelson back, too.

LARS EIGHNER

TAU

DELT

I KNOW WHAT YOU THINK GOES ON IN A HOUSE like that: forty star jocks at close quarters, mystic rituals, secrecy, brotherhood. Stuff did happen at the Tau Delt house. But not so much as you might think.

Aside from a few legacies and some brains to keep up the grade point average, Tau Delt recruited jocks—not varsity athletes so much as guys who had been stars in high school. Everyone had an ego bigger than his biceps. But the main reason not so much stuff happened as you might think was that no one knew how to make the first move. Remember, we all had been stars, and until we got to the Tau Delt house, everything had come to us.

When I pledged, I moved into one of the attic rooms. The rooms were tiny, and it took a while—and a few bumps—to learn where all the rafters were. The rooms were so tiny we weren't expected to double up. There were five other pledges in five other rooms. Chip and Kip had the seventh room.

Picture a twenty-year-old, milk-fed surfer, light blond, blue-eyed, six foot three, a fat Polish sausage always having to be read-justed in his tight Speedos, a reddish tan, basically lean but with very muscular abs covered with sand-colored fur. That's Chip. Hold a mirror up to it, and that's Kip. They were always together. No one could tell them apart. To their faces and otherwise, we called them the Twins, as if that were their name.

Chip and Kip were actives. They could have had a much bigger room downstairs. But the attic was theirs. Cramming pledges in the attic, we were told, happened only in the fall. We would move downstairs as vacancies opened up—meaning as guys flunked out and depledged. Then the Twins would have the whole attic to themselves again.

In fact, it wasn't legal for anyone to live in the attic. According to the building code the spiral staircase was unsafe. But we weren't little old ladies, and the main problem with the staircase was that it was made of metal and whenever someone went up or down, it clanged and rang throughout the attic.

In the attic we took our cues from the Twins. They were actives; they had to be cool.

Downstairs, at least in the daytime, guys were supposed to be dressed. But in the attic the most the Twins wore was bikini briefs, which made their huge cocks seem even huger. So the rest of us ran around in our not-so-sexy skivvies. The Twins lay bareass on the deck. So we did too. Most guys downstairs didn't even know there was a deck on the roof. And we didn't tell them because then the spiral staircase would have been ringing all the time. They sunned in loungers by the pool and always had to wear swimsuits or shorts.

From the first night, the Twins organized bull sessions in a little sitting room, which was too small for all of us to sit down. We had been stars in high school. We were used to being the center of attention. So the point of most of the bull sessions was one guy saying, "I'm cool, the rest of you suck," and the next guy saying, "No, no, no, *I'm* cool. It's you all who suck." That's what it boiled down to.

But what we talked about was sex, sexual adventures starring us and our monstrous cocks. All of it was lies or exaggerations gross enough to be the same as lies. The Twins would start off. Their stories were usually pretty lame, and the only thing interesting was, according to the stories, they always did everything together.

That would start the ball rolling. After a session got started, the Twins seldom said anything, but they had a flask, and they passed it around while the other guys talked. The idea, of course, was for every story to top the one before.

The bullshit room—what we called it—would get hotter and hotter, and the shoulder of the guy next to you felt like a radiator. Guys started sweating. Their tits got hard. Their voices got husky. And everyone seemed to be breathless.

The Twins would throw boners. Their cocks just jumped out of their underwear. And we, as casually as possible, each got a good look.

I noticed Chip was circumcised, but Kip wasn't, or maybe it was the other way around. I made up the rhyme "Chip, clipped" to try to remember how to tell them apart. But I never could remember whether it wasn't "Kip, clipped," and I never needed to tell them apart except when we were downstairs, and then they would be dressed.

No one found it very surprising when the Twins' stiff cocks slipped out of their underwear. Everyone else got as stiff. And if our underwear had been as small as the Twins', our cocks would have got out too. So a couple of guys bought underwear like the Twins wore. It was a challenge, as much as storytelling—another way of bragging and sizing one another up. Guys who wore boxer shorts usually arranged little accidents. "Whoops, the mighty snake has escaped," was the saying.

I suppose some of the snakes were mightier than others. But snakes escaped only when they were at their mightiest, and except for the Twins, who were smugly confident they had nothing to fear from any comparisons, the mighty snakes escaped one at a time.

Then, just as the bullshit room was most like a furnace, when all our cocks were hard and our palms were beginning to itch, one of the Twins would say, "I guess it's about time to break this up." Everyone would dive for his own room.

The attic throbbed.

I could hear the squish of hand lotion from the next room—or was it spit or grease? I could hear the grunts and groans and the hardcomers bouncing on their bunks. Once I thought I heard the guy in the next room paste the wall, so sometimes I shot off on the wall and wondered if he could hear it.

To tell the truth I think the escaping of the sounds was no more accidental than the escaping of the mighty snakes. The message was, "I'm cool. Even when I jack off, I get off better than you."

The attic would stink of semen. Then guys peeked out of their doors to see if it was safe to take a shower.

I had discovered the dangers of the shower after the first bull session. Everyone had the chance to learn from my example.

The shower in the attic was only three by four and a half feet. But it was a two-header, and if another guy wanted in, there was no excuse not to let him. Of course, you bumped into each other every time you turned around, but usually the only problem was that jocks are mostly made of elbows and knees.

After that first bull session, I jacked off pretty quick, and as soon as my mighty snake had halfway relaxed, I grabbed a towel and headed for the showers. Abdul (that wasn't his name, just what we called him) had the room at the opposite end of the corridor, and we got to the shower at about the same time.

Abdul's a short guy, and his shoulders are almost as wide as he is tall. But mainly he's the hairiest eighteen-year-old you'll ever meet, like he's glued a black sheepskin to his chest.

I got in the shower first. I had to scoot over to let Abdul in. And he had to turn sideways to get his shoulders through the door. I noticed a couple of patches of creamy stuff in the hair of Abdul's chest.

This was after the very first bull session. I had gone right to my room to jack off. I hadn't listened for the sounds the others made. I hadn't thought the others were jacking off. I hadn't thought the others were not jacking off. All I had thought about was my cock.

It took me a second to think what the stuff on Abdul's chest was. I stared too long, and Abdul looked down to see what I was staring at. Our mighty serpents sprang to life at almost the same time.

I've got a pretty much standard blond-balled python. It's red-headed, a tad over eight inches, and its name is Pal. When it wakes up, it stands right against my belly, which is unfortunate, because unless I press it down with my thumb, it's a little difficult for other guys to appreciate how mighty and impressive Pal really is.

Abdul's mighty snake, however, juts right out from his thighs, so it makes a spectacular escape in a bull session. I don't know its name, but it's very thick and has the interesting feature of curving up sharply at its very tip, so all of the red meat ends up on top of the bone.

"You a homo?" Abdul asked. It was the ordinary thing to say when someone bumped into someone in the shower. But Abdul asked like it was a question.

So I said, "No," like it was an answer.

"Too bad," he said, like it really was too bad.

So we showered. Abdul washed the come off his chest. And we kept showering. And the mighty snakes did not calm down. Abdul turned his back and began washing his dick. He washed his dick with one hand and washed his balls with the other. I was waiting for him to leave the shower so I could wash my dick like that.

"So much came out the first time, I didn't think I'd have to wash my dick for a week," Abdul whispered, but it was as good as shouting in the tiny tile shower.

"Me neither," I whispered back.

"Oh, yeah? You washing your dick too?"

I had been planning to wait until he left the shower and I

had not consciously changed my mind. But I had been stroking my cock since Abdul turned his back. "I guess I am."

Abdul turned around. I pulled my mighty snake's head down to horizontal. Abdul could see how long it was.

At last he asked, "You wanna help me wash my cock?"

I pushed my cock out where he could have reached easily. "You gonna help me wash mine?"

I saw the answer was no before he realized he had decided. He turned his back again, and this time I turned too.

As soon as I faced the wall, I began to reconsider. If I'd put my hand on Abdul's cock first, I thought, he would have compromised pretty quick.

We bumped butts, like happens by accident all the time. But I didn't jump away and neither did he.

"Won't be too long," he whispered.

"Me too."

When he started shooting off, I could feel it through our butts, and when he lost control of his right leg, my mighty snake began to spit on the wall.

Abdul stood upright suddenly. I lost my balance. I hadn't realized I was leaning on him. "I can never face you again," he said.

"Bullshit," I said. "Nothing happened."

"Oh yeah," he said after a moment. "This never happened. We were just washing our cocks."

And so it might have been, except before we turned to the showerheads and washed off our cocks and fingers, someone—I don't know who—stuck his head in the showers and sized things up in a glance.

Before we were dry the whole attic had heard about Chas and Abdul 'moing off in the showers.

Believe it or not, that was as close to sex with another guy as I had been up to that time. I figured we had been 'moing in the shower, and Abdul and I were homos. I looked in the mirror in the morning, and there was a homo looking back at me.

But it was a fairly studly homo. His muscles didn't look any smaller. Maybe he even had a few more hairs on his chest. The mighty snake was mightier than ever. "You homo," I said. And the homo said, "So be it."

The problem seemed to be my reputation. That was saved in two ways. Apparently attic stories stayed in the attic. And in a week a couple of other guys were caught in the shower, but I think they really were 'moing on each other. Guys stopped talking about Abdul and me and in another week I forgot to think about being a homo.

Meanwhile I learned that there were a couple of official house homos. It was supposed to be the Twins, but the actives were supposed to be keeping it a secret so no one would freak out and depledge. But a word or two slipped out here and there. Among other things, the Twins were not twenty years old as they appeared. They were at least twenty-five. They had been in the house longer than anyone else.

"The world's oldest actives" they were called. It was hinted that they stayed young like vampires do, but what the Twins sucked wasn't blood, and it didn't come from guys' necks.

I didn't know what to believe. The Twins weren't 'moing anyone unless it was each other—and after my experience in the shower, I figured two guys in so small a space couldn't help 'moing on each other, if only by accident. But, come on, they were twins. That's like one person with two bodies. Whatever they did with each other wouldn't be like homos; it would be like jacking off.

True enough, because of the Twins the attic became more like a nudist colony every day. Guys who couldn't get their mighty snakes to escape by accident would go around naked at strategic times, ducking back in their rooms to revive their mighty serpents as necessary. And it was true the Twins did start the bull sessions and kept them well lubricated with firewater. But the Twins also broke up the sessions every time just about five minutes before the bull sessions would have turned into circle jerks. And they were always together, whereas one at a time they could have 'moed any guy in the attic they wanted.

It was a mystery.

One by one, vacancies opened up downstairs. Actives could move out of the house and a couple of them got apartments. A couple of guys depledged. After a while it was me and Abdul and another guy and the Twins in the attic.

Abdul hadn't spoken to me directly or looked me in the eye since the night in the showers, although it seemed like ages since anyone had given either of us a funny look. Bull sessions wore thin. Mighty snakes didn't escape so often, and when they did, it was usually a floppish sort of escape.

When the other guy moved downstairs the bull sessions stopped. I heard they had bull sessions downstairs, and I started going downstairs in the evenings. But the sessions downstairs were nothing like ours had been. The message was still, "I'm cool, the rest of you suck." But it was about cars and cameras and sports and stereos. Nothing of interest to the mighty snake.

One evening I didn't go downstairs. I went to an empty room across the corridor from mine. I think I meant to watch the sunset. But I just sat there for a long time.

The spiral staircase rang. Someone was going down. At the time I thought it must have been Abdul. It wasn't the Twins because they would have gone down together. Now I don't know who it was, but Abdul must have heard it too, and he must have figured it was me going downstairs.

After a while I noticed my mighty python was straining against my underwear. I stood and chucked my skivvies. In the attic it had got to be that being naked was no shame, so long as your cock was hard. I sat back facing the sunset. Absentmindedly, I began to handle myself.

I began to think I heard little gasps and squishy-squishies. I thought I felt familiar vibrations in the floor and walls. That was why the mighty snake had popped up. But I thought it couldn't be. The Twins' room was far down the corridor. Abdul's was even farther, and besides, I thought I heard him go downstairs.

I figured it was the horny crazies. But since I was going to jack off anyway, I decided to go to my room and do it right.

In three paces I was at my door. As I pushed open the door, I switched on my light. I don't know who jumped higher, Abdul or me. Abdul was kneeling by my bed.

His mighty snake was in his fist and something was in his mouth. He seemed a little relieved to see that it was me, that I was naked, and that my cock was hard. He raised a finger to his lips and then he tugged at the elastic straps in his mouth.

As soon as he got my jockstrap out of his mouth, he whispered, "Sh! They'll hear you." I guess he thought I was going to yell.

"Who?" I asked, although "they" could only mean the Twins.

"The Twins," he whispered, "but they aren't really twins."

"Of course they are. They're identical."

"No, they aren't. They're different in a hundred little ways. They're just guys who look alike. They dress alike. They get the same haircut. They say they're twins and everyone automatically confuses them. It's just what they want you to do. Haven't you noticed one of them's cut and the other isn't? Why do you think that is?"

"To tell them apart." That's what I'd always thought, but as soon as I put it in so many words I realized how stupid it was. Two brothers growing up, twins making the normal comparisons— no parents on earth could be so stupid or if they were, their physician would give them twenty psychosexual reasons not to do it. I guess a rabbi would want it to be both or none too. "But they've got the same name. They must be close to the same age."

"No," Abdul whispered. "I checked their transcripts. They changed their names before they came to college. They aren't even related. They're homos. They're lovers. I think no one else in the house suspects," he added. I guess he meant no one else suspected they weren't twins, because plenty of guys had other suspicions.

Was Abdul crazy? Was he lying about the transcripts? Maybe. But it seemed to me he had the right answer. It solved a lot of mysteries about the Twins, but it raised a lot of new questions. And speaking of questions, why was Abdul in my room?

"Because," he sighed, "I'm a homo."

"I know that," I said. "I am too." I'd stopped thinking about being a homo when the shower scandal died down, but I hadn't changed my opinion.

"You know, your dick," he said, "your dick." He indicated the soggy mess that had been my jockstrap before he chewed it up, as if he had explained something.

What with the surprise when I opened the door and the discussion of the Twins, our mighty serpents had become somewhat less mighty—Abdul's was more like a mighty turtle retired into its shell. "Let's get in the shower again," I said. "And let's get it right this time."

Who, after all, would catch us this time except the Twins, and I was pretty sure we had the goods on them.

In the showers our gargantuan boas soon revived until they were as stiff as they had been the first time. Abdul soaped his cock and kept soaping until foam was dripping off him in wads. But this time there was only one bar of soap. I stroked my cock gently. I'd never seen a man get so hot as Abdul got. Then it appeared to me he wasn't going to stop.

"Dick's so big," he gasped. "Great big snake. Big cock, so hard and stiff."

Then I realized he meant *my* cock, which, if you count only length, was a lot bigger than his.

"Why don't you put some soap on my dick?" I asked.

"No," he almost shouted. He shoved me against the wall so hard, I thought we were about to fight, and I could see how such a short guy could make an all-state tackle. His mouth pressed against my chest.

I reached into the mass of foam at Abdul's crotch. His cock was at least twice as fat as mine and hard as glass. His tongue circled my tit.

"I wanna suck your dick," he whispered.

My cock surged against the black hair of his belly. "Okay."

"Shoot off in my mouth, Chas, come in me."

"Yeah," I said. But nothing happened.

"I want you to shoot big wads into me like last time, like you shot on the wall. Big fucking dick. I want to suck your cock. I want that mighty snake in me . . ."

I let go of Abdul's dick. I don't think he had even noticed I'd been stroking it. I had tried to handle it the best I knew how—but I didn't know how. I'd never handled another man's cock before.

Abdul sucked on my tit, and when he came up for air he began again. "I gotta eat your dick, man. Please, Chas, please feed me your meat . . ."

I pressed down on his broad, hairy shoulders with both hands. Slowly, like I was molding wax, I pushed him downward. I couldn't see my mighty snake—only Abdul's curly black hair going lower and lower.

I felt his tongue first. Then his lips in a little circle like he'd made on my tit. Then he fell on it like a sword swallower onto a mighty steel blade. He took it all down.

It was the best thing my cock had ever felt, but mostly I was amazed. And then he started sucking.

It could have been sandpaper, it could have been velvet. It could have been ice, it could have been Tiger Balm. He could have been sucking my nuts out, he could have been ripping them off. It was all the same. I twisted and moaned. It was beyond pleasure—it was what had to be. He had to keep sucking, and I had to keep letting him.

There was a moment of calm. I opened my eyes and looked down. His eyes were rolled up toward mine. He'd taken his mouth off my dick. "Make muscles, Chas," he said.

"Oh yeah," I said. I raised my arms and slipped my fingers between the tile and back of my skull.

He slipped his mouth onto my cock. Slowly this time. I made muscles. Then it was the Furies again, scourging the mighty python.

One of Abdul's hands went under my balls and he grabbed a fistful of my butt. He squeezed until his finger began to quiver.

I looked down. I wanted to see it. See it, although it was the first time I would not see my wad fly. Abdul's head bobbed. Under the hair his shoulders were red. I held back through one stroke, and then another, and then I had to let go. I just let go.

The pattern in the tiles began to warp. I had to shut my eyes.

Now I've got to suck him off, I thought. The idea had appealed to me a whole lot more just a few minutes earlier. I couldn't think of a good excuse not to. I thought I'd never suck cock as good as Abdul. It would be much better if we waited until I could get hot again. But a homo's got to do what a homo's got to do.

First, I had to push Abdul's face off my cock because I couldn't stand it anymore.

Abdul sprang to his feet. His mighty snake was playing turtle again. There were creamy splotches all over his hairy belly and chest. "This didn't happen," he said.

I thought it was a joke about the first time in the shower, before we realized we were homos.

"It didn't happen," he said furiously. "We were just washing our cocks." He left the shower without even washing the come out of his hair.

I slept late. I was wrestling my mighty python before I even woke. I didn't wipe up. I didn't take a towel to the shower. I went with the fresh come on my mostly smooth chest, with drippy fingers, with my cock still red and trailing silver streamers.

The door of Abdul's room was open. The room was empty. I thought he'd got a chance to move downstairs.

Chip and Kip came out of the shower, drying each other's backs and eyeing the massive pools of semen on my manly pecs. They said Abdul had depledged.

I made muscles at the homo in the bathroom mirror. "Too bad about Abdul," I said. "Now what will you do, you homo?"

His biceps looked liked chiseled rock. His mighty python swung below his waist. "You're the homo," he said. "There're only forty jocks in this house. You'll think of something."

F . VALENTINE
HOOVEN, III
WRITING AS JACK WALDEN

BUSH

LEAGUE

YO, BOUDREAU, YOU IN HERE ALREADY?

Yeah.

What's with no lights?

It's cooler.

Oh. Did you get any, uh, you know?

Yeah.

Can I have a sip?

You can have all you want.

Yeah, well, a swallow'll do me. I never been much of a drinker, especially . . . Where's the damn bed—Ouch! Never mind.

Jeez, you're almost as clumsy off the field as on!

Don't start, Boudreau. I could of got my own room, y'know?

Yeah, right. With whose money?

49

I got money! I got—

You gonna get into the bed or what?

Christ, this's a lousy mattress. When're they gonna put us in a decent motel?

When we're first in the standings.

You wish! Okay, gimme!

Here. It's bourbon.

Here *where* here? I can't see a thing, it's so—Hey, you *naked*?

It's cooler.

. . . Oh. Um, thanks. Well, down the hatch!—Ugh! Ack! That's the worst bourbon I ever tasted!

It's cheap.

It oughta be!

Want some more?

Okay. Just lemme get my shoes off.

Take everything off. It's cooler.

Yeah, well . . . I always kinda sleep in my underwear, you know. It's more sanitary.

Hah! Never known you to be into cleanliness before.

You know what I mean . . . Okay—Mud in your eye! Ugh!

Have another shot. Go ahead.

Yeah . . . Phew! If Coach Strumpsky seen us now, he'd shit!

Aw, he's just assistant coach!

Maybe, but we won, didn't we? Boy, I didn't think we was gonna do it though, not until the eighth! Then, of all the guys on the team, ol' Pruitt pulled off that—

I don't wanna talk about the game.

Okay, what *do* you want to . . . C'mon, don't do that!

Jeez, at least take your T-shirt off!

I mean it, Boudreau!

Lift your arms. Come on. There we go, that's my boy! Damn, I love that hairy chest of yours!

You said we weren't gonna do none of this stuff again.

What stuff? Want another swallow?

Where is it?

Here. Gimme your hand . . .

Hey! Very funny! I meant the bottle!

Oh, you did? My mistake. Here.

... Ugh! This stuff tastes worse'n piss!

I didn't know you drink piss!

You're disgusting, Boudreau, you know that? I'm gonna go to sleep!

Whoa! No, you ain't!

Get your hand out of there! Boudreau! I'm totally serious!

I can *feel* you're totally serious! Jeez, you could hit a home run with this!

Give me a break!

Naw, I mean it! You gotta have the biggest dong on the team!

Naaaahh!

Yeah! Look at that—Both hands and there's still some left over for my mouth!

Boudreau!

Shh! You want Strumpsky in here?

No, but don't—Ah! ... Christ, that feels ... That's so ... Uh! ... Uh! ... Uh!

Thought you was going to sleep?

Do it some more.

Cheryl do that as good as me?

You kidding? Cheryl would never—Hey, look, I resent you saying stuff like that about—Ah, Christ! Ah! Yeah! Oh, yeah! Uh-huh! ... Pull the foreskin back so that—Oh, *yeah!* Oh, suck my cock! Uh-huh! Uh-huh! Uh-*huh!* I'm gonna ... I'm gonna shoot off! Stay on it! Come on, keep your mouth there! I wanna come in it! I'm gonna come! In your mouth, Boudreau! Down your throat, yeah! Swallow it! Swallow my load! Uh! Uhh! Uhhhhhhh! ... I love you, Boudreau.

Yeah. Right. Me too. G'night.

Hey, wait a minute! What're you doing?

What do you think I'm doing? You got your rocks—I need my beauty rest, okay? We got a game tomorrow!

Yeah, but, but—this's our last away game!

So?—I don't get you, Smitty!

Yes, you can! You can get me right now!

Jeez!—And you're the one won't even take off his underpants?
Oh, well, hey—There! Here! Feel me now!

C'mon, Smitty! It's after eleven o'clock and—

I'm totally bareass—feel! C'mon, put your hands on me! You said you like the way my ass feels.

I do.

Okay then—feel!

It's . . . It's nice.

. . . Feel here.

Holy—You're all greased up and everything!

I told you I love you.

Yeah, but—

I brung us some rubbers too. Lemme find my pants . . . Somewhere down here. Ah! I got the extra-longs 'cause you ain't exactly no pygmy yourself. Here. I got somethin' else for you, too. Lemme see if you learned me how to do it right!—

What're you doin'? I tol' you you don' have to—Jeez! Oh, jeez, your mouth is warm! . . . So *that's* what it feels like!

Wait a minute here. You sound like you never been sucked before?

Well . . .

What about Sanchez? You said you and him done the same as you and me! The Mainville away game last year, remember? You said he come four times!

Yeah, that's right! *He* come four times, not me!

He didn't even let you prong his butt?

Hell, no!

That shithead! Then it wasn't the same as with you and me, was it?

Truth is, Smitty, you're the only one *ever* paid me back.

All *right!*—And don' you forget it neither!

So . . . how'd it taste? Did you like it? Was it—Ah! Yeah! I guess that answers my question! Oh, yeah! . . . You keep doin' that like that and I'm gonna—

No, wait! I want to do like we done the other time.

Yeah? You liked having my dick up your ass, huh?

I ain't thought about anything else since.

Then why the hell'd you give me such a hard time earlier when I tried to get you to—

Well, you know, I had to be sure you were after the same thing as me.

I'm after it all right. Turn over.

No, wait. I want to do it this time on my back. With my legs up.

Like a girl?

Just do it, okay? Just get on top of me . . . Yeah.

I don't know. I don't think I can hold my weight up with my arms like this the whole time.

I thought you been doing it with Tiffany?

I have. I have!

Then do it the same way. Just lay on me; I ain't gonna break . . . Yeah. Now, stick it in the hole.

You do it for me.

Okay . . . Yeah, there we go! Now you just—Uhhn!—Easy!

Sorry!

Don't be in such a hurry! I ain't goin' nowhere. Just move a little bit, back and forth—Yeah—Just wiggle that ol' pecker of yours in and out till I get kinda used to it, till . . . Okay. *Now* give it to me!

Whole thing?

Yep, all of it—Uhhhhh!

Oh!—I hurt you?

I seen stars!

Sorry, but I—

Wonderful stars! Fuck me, Boudreau!

Yeah! Your ass! Oh, yeah! Your ass is even warmer than your mouth! Oh, man, take my dick!

So, what d'you think? You like it this way?

Hell yeah! You?

Uh-huh! And this way, you can kiss me while we—

Fuck you!

You are!

I mean, I ain't kissing no dude! No way!

I told you I love you!

Yeah, I love you too, but—

Okay, if you can fuck me, you can kiss me! You're gonna come, aren't you?

Yeah, but—

Then do it! C'mon, kiss me while you shoot!

But I don't—

You're gonna come; I can feel it! So kiss me!

But—uh—it ain't—uh—

Christ, I'm gonna come again too! C'mon, kiss me!

Men ain't s'pposed—

Kiss me! Fuck me!

Aw, jeez—

Kiss me, asshole!

Okay, goddammit, *okay!*

Mmmmmmm ... Mmmmmm ...

Mmmmmmmmmmmmmmm ...

... That was great! Thanks, Boudreau.

Smitty ... You know what this means, don't you?

What?

I think it means we're a couple of homos.

I know ... You know what else it means?

No, what?

Homos don't have to wait for away games.

Oh, yeah? ... Oh, *yeah!* How many more of them rubbers you got? It's your turn!

JOHN PRESTON

ABSOLUTION

MY LITTLE BROTHER KNEW HE WAS GOING TO have trouble out-butching me when he reached eighteen. That's when he finally realized he was always going to be ten years younger than me. He was always going to be inches short of my six feet two. He'd never have the hair on his chest that I have. He might get my build, but it was going to take a hell of a lot of work to catch up with the years I'd spent in the gym. His prick was always going to be shorter than mine and his balls would never hang as low. And he'd never wear leather the way I could. But he did try to live up to my example. Little Brother did the only thing that looked like it might work. He joined the Marines.

That made me proud. I never joined the military. I wasn't going to put up with some asshole trying to top me in boot camp. I checked the box rather than put up with that bullshit. But I liked the idea of Little Brother being put through his paces, even if I couldn't be the one who did it. He came back from Parris Island and showed me his new muscles and his close-cropped hair and we went out to have a beer together to celebrate.

Little Brother's Marine career offered us both some insights into the military mind. As I got to know his pals, I learned that most Marines thought they were violent. Really, they never trust their tempers. They are often guys who'd been in trouble in civilian life, high schoolers who were on the track to get a record. The Marines gave them the structure they needed to control themselves. Little Brother was like that. He'd been a hotshot kid. I gave him a lot, but he couldn't get anything more from our family. A bachelor gay brother isn't what a bad-tempered straight kid needed, not all the time, not in all ways. The Marines gave him a place to put his hostility and his rage and find some purpose for it.

Not only did he have a place where he could go and shoot off his testosterone, I had a new scout looking out for my benefit in that cesspool of repressed homosexuality—and masochism. Little Brother never had any misconceptions about my sexuality. When he was old enough to walk, I was bringing men around to the house. He got to first grade thinking it was normal for a big guy like me to have another hairy-chested man in my bed when he'd come in to wake me in the morning. Our parents weren't the most responsive people in the world, so most of his allegiances were with me. That I wanted a man was something he knew; that I wanted one who followed orders and rolled over when I snapped my fingers was easy for him to figure out.

We never had to talk about those things, at least not once he realized I didn't care about his sexuality. If he wanted a girl, that was his business and I didn't give a shit. So when he got out of boot camp and got assigned to a post near my house in Boston, he knew that he had a way to repay me for all the kindnesses of his childhood—all the Little League games I coached him for, all the advice I'd given him and the money I'd lent him.

He never made an overt offer and I never made a plain request, but little by little he began to bring me some of that hard young

Marine flesh. He'd bring home the guys he thought would tumble into bed with me, delivering them the way a happy puppy dog delivers a squirrel to his owner. Just a little payback for all that affection and love.

I had some hot numbers because of Little Brother. I usually got them when he'd bring a pal to the city and they'd stay in my apartment. It didn't take much for the one being introduced to catch on. He probably had been given some clue by Little Brother that there would be magazines and posters and that there were some things I kept in a trunk in my bedroom . . .

But those were only tricks, just little games I played with a couple guys Little Brother knew might like to experiment. The one really important one that I finally got through Little Brother was totally different. He was a whole other story.

It began when Little Brother invited me up to the town where he was stationed for a cookout. I didn't want to go, but he was insistent. My car was in the shop, so he came down to Boston to pick me up. He and a lot of his pals had off-base apartments. They were partial to new pseudo-condos that made them feel like they were grown up. They were all in their mid-twenties then, getting up in rank enough to afford something beside a bunk in a barracks.

I sat around and drank beer with them. The postadolescent bragging those guys do is pretty boring most of the time, but if you put your mind to it, it can be amusing. They were all boasting about the chicks they'd dicked and the times they'd been drunk. If the conversation was tedious, the talkers were interesting. At my age I've come to really appreciate tight, young flesh, the kind that reminds you of peach skin, no matter what the color. Most of the guys were standing around in shorts, their crotches bulging, their young legs tan and hard with muscles. A few had on jeans. I thought that was a shame. They all wore Marine T-shirts, par for the course. I wasn't going to complain. They showed off the hard chests, the flat pecs with nipples that had the smoothness of nature; a good top hadn't gotten to their tits to get them hard enough to push against the fabric. A couple guys wore tank tops that showed off their biceps even more, and gave a good peak at luxuriant armpit

hair as well. I shut off their talk and didn't listen at all. I just sat
there and drank my beer, letting them put on a fine soft-core porn
show for me. In my mind, I could smell their Jockey shorts, damp
with sweat, and I could taste the salt on their skin as they sweat
in the summer warmth.

Little Brother kept smiling at me, like he knew something
was up. I couldn't see it. I didn't have a clue, not until it was time
to call it a night and get back to the city.

"Mario's going into Boston tonight. Do you mind just catching
a ride with him? It would save me the long drive."

It looked like Little Brother had a plan. "Sure," I said, looking
at a shy-appearing jarhead standing beside him. "No problem."
Mario looked like he'd be as good a catch as any of them. He was
about twenty-five, only five nine. He had the usual buzzed hair and
clean-shaven face of a young Marine. He had a butt on him, too.
A nice high one, tight against his pants, too bad they were long-
legged denim. He was olive-skinned. There were slight wisps of
black hair over his bare arms, just enough to really look inviting,
not enough to make him appear nearly as masculine as he'd like. I
could taste garlic and tomato sauce from him, I could imagine a
fine Mediterranean sausage as the main course . . .

Mario led me to his car, one of those overpowered things that
young guys with too much money buy to balance their fear that
they don't have enough sperm. It was low, a two-door sports model
with an engine as powerful as a fleet of trucks. I climbed in and
ignored Mario as he turned the key and powered up.

Mario kept on trying to pick up conversation as he drove down
I-95 toward the city. All I gave him were some guttural sounds to
let him know I wasn't interested in mindless talk. If he wanted my
attention, he'd have to work harder for it.

He was shifting into overdrive on a straightaway when he finally
did say something worth hearing. "Your brother says you're gay."

I wasn't used to one of the jarheads saying something that
direct. I just said, yeah, I was. A little bit of me stood at attention
now; I wasn't sure where this little bastard was going and I wasn't
sure I wanted to hear it.

"I know about that."

This was more familiar ground. Many of the guys Little Brother had introduced me to had begun with a disclosure of some playing around in high school. They usually went from there to admitting a desire to repeat the performance.

"So?" I said. That was all the commitment he was going to get from me.

"Well, I never felt good about it, what happened."

"And what was that?"

Mario hadn't looked me in the eye during any of this. He'd been staring straight ahead. He had one arm on the top of the steering wheel, the other hand hanging down the side of his seat, like he'd watched too many James Dean movies. He kept up the pose.

"Some things happened when I was young. In Boston. Where I grew up. Where you live now."

"So tell me." He was going to anyway; I might as well take control of the conversation.

"I grew up in a tough part of town, the South End."

"Not so tough. That's where I live now."

"Yeah, I know. Your brother told me that. But I hung around with a gang then. We were all poor kids, mostly Hispanic, a few Portuguese like me. We never had any money. There was only one easy way to get it."

"You stole."

"Yeah." He didn't want to go on all of a sudden. He concentrated on his driving. "We stole from gay guys," he finally said.

I could feel something moving in my back, something was getting hard and mean. "How'd you do it?"

"My friends . . . we would go to the Fenway, you know the park where they all cruise? We'd go there and get some guy to go into the bushes and we'd roll him."

"Yeah, I bet you did." I flashed on all the guys I'd known who'd been caught like that. They'd foolishly go to the Fenway after the bars; too much booze and too hard a cock would make them take chances they otherwise would have known were stupid. Too often they paid for their foolishness.

"That's why I joined the Corps." Mario kept on going. "Because I could see what was going to happen to me."

"What was that?"

Mario was gripping the steering wheel now. I could see the white of his knuckles. He hadn't made this confession to many people before. Maybe never. I was trapped in the moment; I felt myself being dragged further into something that was going to be real. There was going to be a climax to this story. I was sure of that.

"One night . . . I was with some friends and they got a guy into the bushes. They got rough. The guy . . . My friends ended up in Walpole. Murder one."

"You got away?"

Mario nodded. There was a tear running down one of his cheeks. "I knew I was on the road to Walpole with them, if I didn't get out of it. The only thing that I could see that was strong enough was the Corps. I signed up . . ."

"As soon as you knew you weren't going to be charged," I accused him.

"I was never seen. No one knew I was there, except my friends. They wouldn't tell."

"And the faggot was dead, so he wasn't going to identify you, was he?" My voice got harsher. I got a picture of Tony, who got his handsome Greek face smashed in at the Fenway one night. And then there was Sal, a barber from out in Scituate who lost one of his balls after a gang of kids had kicked him when he was down, after he'd given them his week's salary. Those scum thought they could bash fags and get away with it. That Mario's pals had been caught was the only real surprise.

"You fucking little son of a bitch." That's all I said. Real soft. Real intense. I really meant it.

Mario sat up quickly, stiffening his own back, and probably his emotions. "I was young. I've made up for it . . ."

Not if you have to tell me now, years later, I thought. I let him drive on. The tear had been wiped away. The emotions seemed to subside. We were quiet for the last half hour of the drive.

Mario stopped in front of my place. He parked the car. He turned off the engine. "Come in. Get a beer," I said. I knew the tone of my voice wasn't welcoming, but I also knew he wanted to follow this one through. There was something we both knew had to happen.

Where there's confession, there has to be absolution.

Mario didn't say anything when I closed the door. He just went over and sat down on my couch, hanging his head and clasping his hands together in front of himself. I went and got a beer. Just one, just for me. I stood in the doorway to the living room and took a long draw on it while I looked at him in the faint light coming in from outside; I left the lights in the living room off. Then I started.

"You were the bait, weren't you?"

Mario nodded, just a little bit.

"You were the one they'd put in front of the bushes to get the fags to come to them, weren't you?"

He nodded again.

"A real pretty boy like you must have attracted a lot of guys."

He didn't like that; I could see him flush with anger. But he couldn't look at me, not even then.

"Stand up and show me how you did it." That got his attention. "I'm serious. I want to see how you did it. Stand up. Show me how you got the fags to come to you."

Wordlessly, Mario stood. He spread his legs. He tried to look at me. "I know you did more than that," I went on. My voice had that tone to it that only my most serious bottoms know, the kind of sound that means something mean is going to happen, and probably soon. "You aren't enough to attract anyone like that, like a limp pasta. You had to show them some dick. Let me see how you did it."

Mario moved a hand to his crotch. He kneaded himself, shyly at first, but then more lewdly. There began to be a fire in his eyes; a real flame started to come toward me. "That's right, Mario," I said, my voice lower, even more menacing, "show me how you did it. How you got those fags all hot and bothered."

The pouch of his pants began to expand. I could see a long length of flesh starting to develop down his right leg. As angry as I was, I could still be impressed. Mario had something to be proud of between his legs, something that would have attracted attention.

As he got harder, he also got cockier. It wasn't just his eyes, it was his posture, his whole way of being. There was heat coming from him now.

"Did you talk to them, Mario? What did you say? How did you get them interested in you?"

"Nothing, man, I said nothing. I didn't have to."

And he was right. His erection was at full attention now and I could just see the guys in the Fenway salivating. I could feel their desire for this young taste of Portugal. They'd walk toward him, quietly, full of hope, just the way I found myself walking toward him now.

I put my hand on his erection, cupping it hard with my palm pressing it up against his belly. "They do this to you, Mario? Did they touch you like this?"

Mario's head moved, but it wasn't the timid nod he'd used before, now he was being seductive, just like some Latin lover in a movie. "Yeah, they'd grab hold of my dick, they'd whisper in my ear what they wanted to do with it."

"What was that, Mario?"

"They wanted to suck my cock." He hissed it out, letting the words flow hotly against my face.

"And you wanted them to do it, didn't you, Mario?"

That broke the spell. He stepped back, tried to push against me. But I had hold of him and I wasn't going to give it up, no way. I squeezed the erection harder, getting a good handful of his balls in my grip at the same time. He let out a sharp cry of pain and then tried to make his move.

That was foolish. I know everything the Marine Corps ever taught him, and a lot more, a lot of it real dirty. The scuffle only lasted a couple seconds and when it was over Mario was on the floor, my knee up against his crotch, my elbow pressing down on his windpipe.

"You *loved* it, Mario, didn't you? You loved hearing that they wanted to suck you. You wanted it. Isn't that the real problem? Isn't that what really bothered you?"

He could claim that the tears in his eyes were from his pain, but the real ache was inside him. "How often did they get to swing on your prick, Mario? Did your gang give you grief for that? Did they sense that you really wanted it?"

"I was only a kid," Mario said, his voice soft because of the pressure on his voicebox. "I was just a kid."

"You were smart, Mario. You knew how to get it both ways. You could take your gang into the park and you could get your rocks off, and the rest of them wouldn't care. You could say you were only doing it for them, to get the fag into the bushes so they could roll him."

Mario's tears started to flow now. I had him. The nightmares he'd lived with were coming right to the surface and I had him by the balls. I knew he was going to be mine. I just knew it.

"Stand up, punk." I grabbed him by the shirt and lifted him to his feet. The shirt ripped from the strain, giving me a fine look at his chest, nicely chiseled, just as smooth as I'd hoped, with flat round circles for tits, nothing more to them than brown flesh.

"I want to see more, Mario. I don't just want to see how you acted when a guy came up to you in the Fenway, I want to see how you hoped he'd act. What did you really want to have happen, Mario?"

I stood back and let him catch his breath. He watched me carefully, diffidently. There was still an element of dare in his expression, but something else was coming to the surface. Mario began to rub his crotch again, provocatively this time. He got hard even more quickly. He cocked his head with a jaunty manner. The torn shirt was hanging from his shoulders in strips, letting me see even more of his torso. I liked the belly the most. It had nice lines to it, going down on either side, and the tightness of the stomach

promised there'd be some good abs there, nicely cut, ready to be
shown off, given the right position.

"Suck my dick," he said when he'd got his dick at full mast.
"Come and suck my fat dick."

I walked over to him and backhanded him across the mouth.
He nearly went down, but that Marine training came through. He
stood up, blood dripping from the side of his lips. He licked it
away with his tongue, making it look like one of the great seductive
moves of all time. He let the tip linger at the corner of his mouth.

"You want my cock," he said again, challenging me. "Come
and get it."

"No, kid, you got it wrong. I'm the one who's got your number. I don't want to chow down on you. You're the one that's got
the taste for my meat. You're the one who's getting down on his
knees, just the way you always dreamed of it."

He stopped working his cock then. He stood there, as though
he was petrified that someone finally saw the truth. I put my hands
on his shoulders and I shoved him onto the floor. When he resisted,
I got a foot behind his knee and he didn't have much choice.

His face was right at balls level. I pulled him in. I rubbed his
nose against the denim, letting the buttons on my fly scrape him.
"Did you ever suck those fags, Mario? Huh? Did you ever get down
in the mud of the Fenway and chew on one of their cocks?"

He couldn't answer, but I could feel his face moving back and
forth, no. "But you wanted to, didn't you, Mario? Didn't you always
want to taste a dick in your mouth?"

His head moved again, but in a different direction. I grabbed
the back of his neck and pulled him off my body. I reached down
and popped the buttons. I undid my belt. I pulled my jeans open
enough to let my half-hard flop out in front of his eyes. My wrinkled foreskin still covered the head, but it was being pulled more
tightly as my prick expanded with bloodlust. Mario's eyes looked
at it. I saw longing there. I saw lots of things in those eyes of his.

Before he could react, before it got too easy for him, I half
lifted him up and threw him face down on the couch. I whipped

my belt from its loops and wrapped it around my fist, leaving enough of it dangling—buckle out—to do what it needed. With my free hand, I reached in front of a now unresisting Mario and opened his own zipper and then yanked his pants down over his butt.

There was only moonlight and some reflection from the street lamps coming into the apartment. The shadowy light accentuated the whiteness of his briefs, as though they were fluorescent. The snowy cotton was stretched over that ass of his, the two mounds clearly separated by the deep crevice of his crack. I wanted to linger on the sight, just take it in, just enjoy it, but this wasn't the time.

I took hold of the elastic waistband and pulled hard enough to rip the shorts off him. He shuddered from the feel of the night air on his spread cheeks. I pushed on his neck with my free hand and then I began. The belt sang through the air, slamming hard on his butt, first one side, then the other, then the first one again. He howled with shock and pain and anger, but he couldn't move. His legs were trapped by his pants at his knees; my grip on his neck was too secure for him to escape. I whacked at his butt, taking out my fury at all the punks who victimize and persecute, pounding him with all of my rage . . . and with the righteousness that he needed this, that he wanted it.

I didn't stop until my arm began to hurt. I stood back and caught my breath. He was sobbing into the couch. His back was heaving with his tears. Even in the obscure light, I could see that his ass was covered with welts that were only going to become more obvious with time.

I was ready to make a speech, but I didn't have to. Mario moved, turning around on his knees slowly and painfully. He was still crying. He fell forward and stayed there. I thought at first it was an accident, that perhaps he was really too hurt to even move. But soon I saw that it was just inexperience. He was face down on the floor, his head against my boots, and there was the unmistakable pressure of a tongue moving against the leather.

He was licking his way up. He began at the toe and then

moved along my ankle. When his mouth got to the denim of my jeans, he moved more quickly, ascending the length of my leg until he was at my crotch again.

"I want to suck your cock," he said through his tears. "I want to suck your cock . . ."

I took hold of my hard prick and pointed it at him. I thought he'd be inexperienced and rough this first time, but I forgot to factor in the power of pure lust. He kissed the tip, where the foreskin was being spread tight again by my new hard-on. He just touched his lips to the flap and then used his tongue to move it aside so he could lick at the head of my dick. He licked around that and then down the shaft, nuzzling his nose in my balls.

There was another heaving in his chest, but it wasn't pain and it wasn't tears. It was twenty-five years of repression coming out to the surface. "I'm so sorry," he moaned. "I didn't mean to get them hurt. I just didn't know how to do this . . ."

His mouth worked on my balls, lifting them up with his lips, tonguing the surface. "You're learning real good, boy, real good."

I grabbed hold of my shaft then, I was rock-hard by now, and I aimed it at his mouth. I lunged forward. He gagged, thick viscous liquid pushed up his throat, only making it easier for my hard-on to slide its way down. I started to fuck his mouth, pulling my cock out just enough to let him get hold of his breathing, then shoving it back in, cutting off his air, forcing him to struggle to keep up with me. In and out, back and forth, my dick slid through the slime of his mouth, waiting for just the right time to explode a load of heavy come down his throat.

He tried to rebel at that first taste, but I held tight, pushing myself into him until I could feel the swallowing of my come.

He was exhausted after I was done. Another time, another place, he'd have wanted to jerk off, but Mario was done in. He slumped back on the floor. I thought there might be more tears, but there weren't. He said something, without even looking up at me: "Finally."

Mario didn't need the Marine Corps anymore. He was finished with them after that night. He applied for a discharge and got it.

The Marines don't fuck around with you if you convince them you're a fag.

A couple months later, Mario and Little Brother and I went down to Newport, Rhode Island. It's a Navy town and one of the major centers of tattooing in the United States. Little Brother wanted to get a Marine emblem put on his right biceps. I thought that was a good idea. I even paid for it. And the same shop did other work too. Mario got his own tattoo. My name on the right cheek of his ass.

When the three of us stood together and I paid the bill, having enjoyed watching both of them squirm under the needle, I noticed that Little Brother was eyeing Mario's now sore butt. I imagine he wondered just how the story got told, but he knew better than to ask. He just smiled all the way back to Massachusetts, like a pet that'd finally found the perfect way to please his master.

PART TWO

MASCULINE

RITUALS,

REALITY AS

PORNOGRAPHY

A major form of pornography is the confessional, the first-person narrative of the participant observer who insists on documenting his own part in the real-life pornographic act. After Stonewall, the historic event that's most often used to date the beginning of the modern gay movement, there was a great deal of pressure on gay men to become respectable. There was a belief that being homosexual had become a political act, but not just in the revolutionary sense. We were now players in electoral politics and, some said, we should clean up our image to make it more attractive to other members of society. While gay life might have been seen by pornographers like Gary Collins or Phil Andros as a purposeful violation of social and sexual mores, an individual statement that had truth on its side, the new gay activists wanted proper adherents to their cause—people who wouldn't talk about doing things that would scare away middle America.

To be outwardly sexual, to be what defined one as a homosexual, was a violation of this new order. Probably the most offensive thing that gay men did was to perform sexual acts in public. As Michael Bronski says in "How Sweet (and Sticky) It Was," "For most homosexuals [public sex] was the most flagrant of queer offenses." Rather than hide his participation in that crime, Bronski revels in it. His entrance into public sexual activity—he might say his liberation into it—came with his move to Boston years ago. In his essay Bronski not only describes his own experiences with public sex, but he also carefully documents the places where it happened—which park, what bar—showing himself as a careful archivist.

But the appeal of a public display of sexuality—a violating demonstration of one's homosexuality and of the place of pornography in one's life—is not limited to an older generation remembering back in time. Christopher Wittke followed Bronski's lead by moving to Boston, but it was at least a decade after Bronski committed the act. Wittke's introduction to anonymous sex came after AIDS had become a major restraint on gay sexuality. But as Wittke's memoir of his life in the tearooms of Boston shows, AIDS hasn't overcome gay imagination.

MICHAEL BRONSKI

HOW SWEET

(AND STICKY)

IT WAS

"DO YOU HAVE A PLACE TO GO?" WAS THE THIRD thing the man asked me over the din of the music in the bar. We had not even gotten to names yet.

"No." He understood that I had a lover, or a boyfriend, or a roommate at home. Or that my evening investment was for forty minutes, not two or three hours, or the night.

"Let's go out back. I know someplace."

We moved across darkened shadows in the unlit alley behind the bar. We came to a doorway half hidden by a trash tree. He pushed the broken wooden door open on one hinge and pulled me into a pitch-black room that smelled of dust and bleach, old tires and grease.

"Is this . . ."

He put a bottle of poppers beneath my nose and shoved his hand beneath my shirt, looking for my nipples. My hands were in his pants as

I pushed him up against the wall. I grasped at his hard-on, pulled his leather jacket off his shoulder, and pressed my face against his neck. Our bodies gave way to sweat as we inhaled the amyl and gasped between lust and balance. With our pants around our boots, our shirts ripped open and pushed down our leather-jacketed backs, we licked, chewed, and swallowed body parts, struggled and slapped one another, lost in the dark and floating in the void of desire and freedom. I held his face against the cool, dirty brick wall as I drove a second finger into his ass; his back arched as he struggled. He spread his legs as he furiously jerked off . . .

"Please. Please. Kiss me," he whispered.

As my mouth reached his, he jerked and shuddered, pushing his ass onto my hand. He shot all over the wall. Wet, tired, and unsure of our balance, we collapsed onto one another unable to separate breath from heart-beat, come from sweat. (Behind the Ramrod Bar, 1982)

It is easy to forget—these twenty-one years later—that the promise of Stonewall was (among other things) the promise of sex: free sex, better sex, lots of sex, sex without guilt, sex without repression, sex without harassment, sex at home and sex in the streets. "Why don't we do it in the road?" sang the Beatles the year before the Stonewall Riots, and many gay men had to smile to themselves because they were furtively doing it—if not *in* the road, certainly in the bushes *next* to the road, and in empty trucks *on* the road, and in subway bathrooms *under* the road. But the new pride and identity engendered by the Stonewall Riots changed all that. It is not as though gay men never had public sex—as it is disarmingly, although somewhat inaccurately, called—before Stonewall. *Au contraire,* tearooms, rest stops, and dark alleys were always busy with homos in pursuit of eros. (When Dick Cavett in 1976 asked Tennessee Williams on national television if he was a homosexual the playwright responded with Delphic wit, "I cover the waterfront.") The change that came after Stonewall was not that men *stopped* having public sex but that they stopped doing it furtively. They felt better about it, less guilty, and—most importantly— they felt that it was their right.

■ ● ■

Every night on visits to Manhattan I go to the darkened, decayed warehouses on the Hudson. Dangerous and mysterious, they were the realization of my childhood dreams of adventure; the creaky stairs and the breathless stillness that the Hardy Boys faced in The Sinister Signpost. *Except the reward here is not catching a criminal but being one. A man in a leather jacket stands braced against a half-fallen beam silhouetted against the night sky stroking his hard cock. I walk toward him and he holds up his hand. I stop. He leans his head back and I see that he has invited me to be the audience for his carefully arranged, meticulously directed performance. As the subdued noise of orgy sex drifts down from the other end of the building and merges with the lapping of the river fifty feet beneath us, I watch for almost an hour. This stranger shifts his hips, caresses his balls, and excites himself against a perfect blue-black night sky. His hands, cock, and torso are an aria of motion and lust, the jewel in some silent opera, as he brings himself to a sustained climax. I see his silver come appear and vanish against the indigo air. The Queen of the Night, as perfect as any imagined by Mozart. A smile and the readjustment of his cock precede his disappearing into the darkness. I am left with my hard dick and my admiration. Satisfied and ready to move back into the night.* (Pier 18, 1979)

Public sex has always been a contentious topic with both straights and gays. For most heterosexuals it was the most flagrant of queer offenses: blatant, bold, and ballsy, it was the persistent reminder that gay men existed and that they (or at least some of them) were not going to be intimidated into leading private, nonsexual, lives. For more conservative gays—who believed that homosexuals would be accepted if they acted like everyone else (i.e., straight, only without a sex life)—public sex signified the worst elements of obvious queerdom and was the bane of assimilation. But for many, many gay men—both within and without the movement—public sex was the public expression of their identity. Radicals argued that it increased gay visibility; that it broke down the stifling barriers between the private and the public, the personal and the political; and that it was a celebration of gay sexuality. Others, less rhetoric-oriented, found that it was quick, easy, cheap, and fun.

When I first moved to Boston in 1970 I had no experience of

public sex. Although openly gay for several years, I garnered boy-friends and tricks first from social, and then political, circles. "Public sex," I told myself, "is for those who have no other options." But being new in town, I soon discovered that social and political circles took time to build, that bar cruising had its drawbacks, and that my libido was none too happy. By that July I had discovered the joys of summering on the banks of the Charles—first in Cambridge in the bowers next to the Larz Anderson Bridge, and then in Boston in the coves of honeysuckle on the Esplanade. On these hot summer nights, surrounded by flowering bushes and trees, sex—in pairs or groups—felt idyllic: part porn movie, part *Maytime* with Jeanette MacDonald. It was a quick jump to the Fenway victory gardens—a veritable botanical Disney World of sex next to the more austerely landscaped Esplanade—and long, fragrant nights which ended when chirping birds signaled the onslaught of dawn. I remember one evening spent rolling about, fucking and sucking, with a long-haired country boy in a patch of wild *Mentha spicata* and coming home reeking of mint, wet grass, and come.

There must be fifteen men crammed into the unlit women's room at the back of the bar. I am against the back wall, nearly unable to breathe as my hands move from crotch to crotch looking for a half-opened zipper, a half-hard dick, some pubic hair. Hands roam over my pants as the smells of leather, poppers, and beer transform this mundane group grope into a trans-figured queer picnic. Lust coexists with breathing as we shift back and forth, moving almost as one, making small spaces to pull or pinch, probe or pummel. My body is crushed against the wall as the group shifts and reestablishes itself. Just as I catch my breath someone puts a bottle of poppers under my nose and for a second, maybe two, I am out of my body and suspended in the natural state of pure lust. (The Shed, 1974)

Once I had broken through the public sex barrier—should I or shouldn't I?—the possibilities seemed endless. In the mood for a fresh-air experience, one could always go to the Cambridge Bird Sanctuary as well as the Fenway and the Esplanade. For something a little more scholarly, Harvard presented endless venues: the base-

ment men's rooms in Paine Hall, any number of places in Widener
Library, the first floor at the now-defunct Burr Hall (rumored to
have been torn down because the tearoom action was simply *too*
notorious), as well as the recently infamous Science Center. But if
you were just passing through Harvard Square the basement bathroom at ZumZums (now the Ms. Coop) was always busy and presented a wide range of trick.

But Cambridge was a backwater of public sex next to Boston
proper. For something free during the day the men's room at the
Common Parking Garage was always the best place to go; not only
the local city boys turned up there, but men seemed to actually
drive in from the suburbs just to park their cars and use the facilities. The Boston Public Library men's room was also a popular
cruising spot until several police crackdowns in 1976. There were
demonstrations—several queens burned their library cards—and
when the cases came to court all of the arrested men were acquitted.
And of course the Trailways bus station—then in Park Square, now
moved over to South Station—allowed you to view and vamp not
only queens leaving town but those coming in. But not two blocks
away, on the corner of Washington and Essex, was the famous, and
fruitful, Jolar Cinema, which was open eighteen hours a day and
never, never disappointed. The Jolar was also the instigating site of
one of the most influential public-sex court rulings. In 1975 a local
gay liberationist and radio personality was arrested here—in a closed
booth—and charged with open and gross lewdness. He brought the
case to court and won by claiming that because they took place
behind closed doors in an establishment noted for its sexual activity,
his actions were private, not public. But by 1980 police harassment,
and a change in management, gradually made the Jolar uninhabi-
table. Of course besides the Jolar there were plenty of other peep
shows in the Combat Zone. Many of these were still around even
a year ago—you can see them boarded up if you walk down Washington Street—but some were demolished, victims of urban renewal
and the expansion of Tufts New England Medical. There was a
whole block of porn stores—which were basically gay male cruising
grounds—along Stuart Street from Tremont beyond Washington.

One could spend an entire afternoon perusing and cruising, never having to enter a store twice in one day.

Somehow I end up in the Jolar at ten in the morning. There are some men there but no one interesting. I lurk in the half-open doors of booths waiting. After forty minutes, a well-built redheaded man, not quite familiar, appears out of the shadows. Silently we go into a booth and I deposit quarters to get the movie going. He unzips and I begin blowing him. His prick is hard and insistent, his legs nervous and tight. He comes quickly and pushes his half-hard cock into his pants. As I stand up I realize that I've seen him on the other side of the peep show token booth earlier this morning. I begin to say something but he cuts in, "I have to go, if they find out I'm gay they'll fire me." (Jolar, 1979)

Of course if you wanted to sit down and settle in for a while there was always the State Theater and the Stuart. The State showed straight porn to a mostly gay male audience, more interested in who was sitting next to them than what was on the screen, and the Stuart specialized in third- and fourth-run Hollywood films. The booking for the Stuart seemed completely haphazard; you could catch *Last House on the Left* on a double bill with *Man of La Mancha* or a Neil Simon comedy like *The Prisoner of Second Avenue* doubled with *Shaft*. There were other Washington Street movie houses which screened not-very-recent Hollywood films, but the Stuart had a busy orchestra and an even busier men's room. Many of the peep booths featured gay male porn, but if you wanted to sit down and watch screen dick there was the ever-busy South Station Cinema I and II, Symphony Cinema (on Huntington Avenue), and the still open Art Cinema on Tremont Street. South Station was the premier porn palace—busy day and night. When it began as a gay screen in the early 1970s—booked by George Mansour and managed by John Mitzel—Cinema I showed porn and Cinema II campy Hollywood musicals. The mixed bills soon ended and both sides became porn houses. In 1983, when South Station closed, North Station I became a gay porn theater, but it had none of the charm of its predecessor and closed soon after. The Symphony Cinema was showing pop and art films—*Lady Sings the Blues* on one side, Bergman films on the other—before it became a classy gay porn house. In 1973 George Mansour booked Fred Halstead's high-toned classic *Sextool* here, and the Symphony continued for a while to show gay porn. The cruising was low-key, but certainly possible. The theater closed in 1979.

After a lazy afternoon of cruising the South Station Cinema toilets I finally make out with a good-looking number. We retire to the little utility room with the lockable door—a luxury on the sex circuit—and begin undressing one another. He has poppers, I have an extra cock ring, and in minutes we are mostly naked. I play hard with his tits, biting them and then taking handfuls of pectorals in my grip and slamming his body against the wall. He goes limp and then attacks my neck with his teeth. Between bouts of poppers and endless sweat we become quite delirious, almost transcendent as the play gets rougher and rougher and our joint consciousness less and less boundaried. Finally, in a flurry of orchestrated popper excitement, we both come: he across my face as I bring my teeth down on his balls and me spurting across the floor between his legs. He suddenly collapses on me and we bundle and pant on the floor, holding one another and gasping for breath. Gradually, as if in a dream, I become aware of music I know— slightly romantic, very sophisticated. Although I cannot place it, it is the perfect accompaniment to lying on a dirty floor with a stranger, covered in come and sweat, holding his limp dick in my hand and kissing the back of his neck. As my mind clears I realize that the music is the theme song from All About Eve—*a purloined soundtrack on a cheap porno movie set on Fire Island. Suddenly my life makes sense: sex, come, Bette Davis, elegant cocktail parties, small talk in toilets, stolen blow jobs in movie theaters, smart repartee, George Sanders sneering a witticism, and gasping for breath as I passionately kiss a man I've never seen before. There is, I think, a heaven and it is somewhere between a back lot on MGM and the filthy locked room at a porn palace.* (South Station Cinema, 1985)

If you wanted to linger in the Zone you could go for an afternoon cocktail at the Carnival (closed in 1978) or Playland (still there and still highly recommended). But these were busy watering holes and the chances for sex were close to nil. At the Champagne Lounge at 227 Tremont Street, however, if you slipped into the bathroom between your Pink Lady and your Golden Cadillac (it was a very elegant, queenly bar) a quickie was not impossible. Those with a taste for danger could also stop into the mostly straight, C&W Hillbilly Lounge—on Stuart Street close to Broadway—and *very* carefully cruise the truckers (real, faux, or fake) and the queens who lingered over their afternoon beers.

If you felt the need to freshen up during the long hours of cruising there was always the baths. The Liberty Tree Health Spa—which had a life of only a few years—was a few doors down from the Jolar and had a not inconsiderable afternoon trade. The Club Baths—in a lovely H. H. Richardson building on LaGrange Street (it was burned out in the early eighties)—featured a roof deck for nude sunbathing and a brisk, businessman's lunch following. I worked there for a little less than a year in 1978 and 1979. The Regency—on Otis Street, behind Jordan Marsh—was very quiet, and sometimes even closed during the day, but its boisterous dollar nights on Monday and beer and pizza fetes on Wednesday live on in memory; the Regency closed in the late seventies.

If pre-Stonewall public sex was always found in the unguarded, vacant nook or cranny, by the late 1970s some bars began to institutionalize sex space. The Stud, Mineshaft, Toilet, Anvil, and Strap were the most famous New York fuck bars, and Boston had several halfhearted attempts. For a while the basement at the Cowardly Lion (later Bienvenue)—in the alley next to the Colonial Theater—opened as a sex room, but since it was sort of a hustler bar (catering to the recently defunct Other Side crowd) with a disco beat no one was very interested. Quagmire—now the Eagle—in the South End had a moderately busy basement boff bin in 1980 or so, but the boys in blue from Area D (who were right across the street) soon put an end to it. This was the same fate met by The Loft on Stanhope Street—a private dance club that turned its back on what went on in some of the darker corners and was closed in 1984. There was even a movement afoot in 1981—rent was paid and licenses were secured—for an imitation Boston Mineshaft on Kingston Street but the deal fell through at the last minute. But while the organized, official sex spaces failed, there were two *very* active unofficial fuck forums in town. The Shed, across the street from Symphony Hall—for a while Boston's only leather bar—had a bathroom that wouldn't stop on almost every night of the week. Small, cramped, and often very smelly, it was a bit of heaven on Huntington Avenue. The Shed was popular from the early seventies to sometime later in the decade when Herbie's Ramrod—actually the upper floor of the popular piano chat bar 12 Carver—became *the* leather bar to frequent. Herbie's was a friendly, cruisy bar, but the most entrancing aspect of it was the large, super-spacious bathrooms on the landing between 12 Carver proper and the Ramrod. Easily accommodating sixty men, they were the salvation of many a slow Tuesday or Wednesday—or a busy Friday or Saturday—night out. In 1979, 12 Carver and Herbie's Ramrod (as well as the charming next-door restaurant, The Hound's Tooth, and the Hillbilly Ranch around the corner) were demolished to make way for the mammoth, ugly Transportation Building.

The toilet stall is slightly open when I go into the bathroom to piss. The bar is never very crowded during the afternoon, but it is occasionally cruisy. I go to the urinals, looking behind me to see what is happening in the booth, and the door slowly opens. In the dark I see a bearded man sitting, hunched over, peering out. He is stroking his dick in a hidden manner but when he sees my leather jacket he leans back and displays himself. I quickly enter the booth and watch him. He smiles and runs his hand across his belly, and then without taking his eyes from mine, he opens the right side of his flannel shirt to expose a pierced tit. This is no neat, doctor-done gold ring but a syringe needle—probably twenty-eight-gauge—pushed securely through the areola. He smiles. I smile. He pulls open the other side of his shirt to expose another pierced tit. His hands wander from his cock to his tits, inviting me to touch them, play with them. As I touch each one he moans. I rub my thumbs across the tough, bitten nipples and put the weight of my index finger on the piercer's plastic ends, forcing his flesh to move in concentric half-circles. I gently place two fingers behind each needle and pull them toward me while touching the sensitive tips of the nipples with my saliva-wet thumbs. Letting him rest a moment, I take a long piece of rawhide from my jacket pocket (this is still the time when you always come prepared for something—anything—on an afternoon stroll) and gently knot the ends behind each of the needles. His nipples lie there like pinned butterflies as I pull first one, then the other, then both away from his body. His hands fall from his dick and his torso lies against the back of the toilet as I pull and release, pull and release, using my own body as a counterweight. We remain there—connected only by ten inches of greasy rawhide— for twenty minutes or so. Our eye contact is intermittent but the sexual tension between us is as sharp as the syringes piercing his tits. Neither of us comes; our cocks are mostly soft, and in time I loosen my hold. He comes out of his dream state. He begins to undo the rawhide to give it to me and I motion for him to keep it. He smiles and leans forward and kisses my belly through my shirt. He kisses his hand and then places it to my face. We smile and I go back into the bar to finish my beer and get ready to go home for dinner. (Playland, 1984)

Looking back over the past twenty years, I realize that most of the places I have frequented and fucked in have been closed. Some that are still functioning—like the Fenway, the Bird Sanctuary, and the Science Center—feel unsafe. It is hard to pinpoint what has caused all the changes. Eight years of Reagan surely set a political and cultural tone for the last decade. And certainly the mainstream press has used AIDS to launch a vicious attack on gay sexuality, causing many men to react with fear and guilt rather than inventiveness of expression. And the AIDS hysteria promoted by the press has played no small role in the increase of homophobic violence against both gay men and lesbians. Urban renewal—if a monstrosity like the Transportation Building can be called renewal—has also played a part, and many of the bars, bookstores, and theaters where sex was easy and plentiful have been destroyed by developers. Some have argued that the advent of the VCR was the primary cause of the peep shows and porno houses closing. But this is untrue. These places existed not only so that men could watch the films but so that men could meet one another—socially and sexually. They were community gathering places.

I remember, in the summer of 1972, going to Sporters almost every night for three months and realizing for the first time that gay bars were not simply for cruising but that they were community centers, public meeting places, town squares, clotheslines people could hang over to gossip, and bulletin boards. There were no bar rags then or local gay papers. The bar was where you found your information: everything from who had been queer-bashed in the street the night before to whether or not Ken Russell's *The Music Lovers* really dealt with Tchaikovsky's homosexuality. And in much the same way, the peeps, the bus stations, the lobbies of porn theaters served the same function. But they were more than that. They were places to reaffirm—publicly reaffirm—and enjoy gay male sexuality.

It is a hot night and my lover Walta and I go for an after-dinner walk in the Victory Gardens. We do not plan to have sex but discover that the sight of two or three random coupling couples turns us on. At first we only neck but soon go down on one another, half hidden behind some scattered reeds close to the winding path that runs through the patchwork of gardens. I am on my knees balancing my hands on Walta's hips. A police car begins its slow, watchful ride through the cruising ground. I hear the other nocturnal lovers flee to the safer, more open ground of the sidewalk but have little impulse to move. Not only am I enjoying my lover's cock in my mouth, but in my erotic half-trance I do not see any illegality or even danger. After all, I would have told the police if questioned, this wasn't some illicit, promiscuous sexual encounter; this was my lover. (The Fenway, 1976)

With all the gains that the gay liberation movement has made over the past twenty-three years—and there have been many—there has also been a certain retreat. Not perhaps back into the traditional closet, but into a cultural mind-set which favors the notion of privacy over openness, of reticence over blatancy. This mind-set is not singular to the gay male or lesbian community, but pervades the whole culture: a rebellion against the relative freedom of the sixties and seventies. Its manifestations are myriad: warning stickers on rock records; protests against the Mapplethorpe exhibit; the ever-increasing hysteria about any sort of drug culture; the insistence that "romance" (a private notion if ever there was one) is better than a more open, free sexuality; the fight over NEA funding of homoerotic art; the medicalization and therapeutation of sexuality with the labels of "addiction" and "compulsion"; the fact that the police, backed up by these cultural mandates, feel unrestrained in their attacks on gay sexuality; the "just say no" mentality. Even George Bush's "thousand points of light" managed to privatize, and gut, the sixties ideal of working for the common good.

After Stonewall, I and many, many other men felt that we had an unquestioned right to our sex lives. It was a newly felt freedom and it was exhilarating. But over the past decade that feeling has become endangered, threatened. It is not gone, but it has to be constantly fought for, constantly brought back into focus. On some profound level the issue is not the "right" to have public sex but rather the ability to feel, to know, that any of us have a "right" to our sexuality at all.

We go to the Nickelodeon Theater a full half hour before the movie begins and smoke a joint in the car. The dope, the music on the radio, and the early-evening heat make me feel high and turned on. I suggest to Jim that we go to the end of Blanford Street and have sex beneath the turnpike overpass. It is dark and we are mostly hidden in shadows as I unbutton Jim's jeans and take out his dick. Stroking it, I get it hard and bend over and take it in my mouth. Soon I get down on my knees and begin working in earnest. Suddenly a car zooms along the turnpike and for split seconds its headlights flash through the supporting concrete pillars, illuminating us. Another car speeds past. Can they see us clearly or are we just blurs, phantom figures hidden in the crevices of a maze of steel and cement? I continue sucking Jim's cock and more cars whiz by, their headlights flickering across us as we have our private games. More headlights and our privacy is made, if only for split seconds, public. The cars rush past, and in my head our sex takes on a new dimension: public, private, public, private, public, private. The constant change blurs the very parameters of these notions—public private public private public private public private— until they become obscure, almost meaningless, in the reality of our hard dicks, our warmth, our feelings for one another. (The Mass Pike, 1982)

CHRISTOPHER WITTKE

JUST

DO IT

"I really got scared—Well, ex-
cited and scared. . . ."
STEPHEN SONDHEIM'S
"I KNOW THINGS NOW"
FROM INTO THE WOODS

THE CITY OF BOSTON WOULD LOVE TO BE RID OF
its "adult entertainment district," also known as the Combat Zone.
Located near the downtown business section and bordered by Chi-
natown, at its height the Zone featured countless strip and peep
shows and cinemas. In the early 1990s, few remnants of the Zone
remain. Among them is the Pilgrim Theater on Washington Street,
which (perhaps to the embarrassment of chamber of commerce
types) is the oldest continuously operated cinema in Boston.

Built in 1912 for the then staggering cost of more than $1
million, the Pilgrim was originally called the Olympia. Designed
by architect C. H. Blackall, the Olympia was the first deluxe theater
in the city dedicated to the screening of films, as opposed to vaude-
ville, burlesque, or "legitimate" theatrical productions. Its elaborate
architecture earned the place several nicknames from the moviegoing

public. The lobby escalator that whisked patrons up to its balconies caused folks to dub the Olympia "the House with the Moving Stairs," and the theater's two balconies were built at such a steep pitch that people referred to the theater as "the Matterhorn."

In an attempt to compete with other porn palaces in the seventies, the Pilgrim also featured strippers along with its hard-core features. It was in the Pilgrim that Representative Wilbur Mills had his notorious encounter with stripper Fanne Fox. Before long, however, the theater was back to a steady diet of adult cinema, no live shows.

Like many gorgeous old theaters that have lived on as porno houses, the Pilgrim is today a bit rough around its edges. Murals by Vesper George have long since been covered over by many coats of paint and grime. Clean queens and neatness freaks would probably be completely repulsed by the Pilgrim today, but those of us who can appreciate a diamond in the rough know just what a gem the Pilgrim theater is, as well as the other kinds of pleasures that can be found within it.

The first time I walked into the Pilgrim Theater, in 1987, my heart started racing and I almost turned around and walked out. Here's why: a large piece of posterboard was taped to the wall of the lobby, and on it was scrawled the message, "Attention! The Boston Police Vice Squad has now arrested patrons of this theater for engaging in sexual activity and indecent exposure."

There was something about the use of the word "now" that frightened me. As opposed to when? As in, that morning? That afternoon? Last week? Last month? Had a storm troop of baton-wielding behemoths dragged a whole slew of startled meat-beaters out of the largest straight porno theater in town mere minutes before my arrival? I calmed down enough to walk through the inner door to the darkened theater once I determined that the shaky Magic Marker lettering was rather faded; the last syllable of "Attention!" and "Vice Squad" ran together thanks to three long-ago drips of some sort of fluid. "Now" was probably more like then. Plus, I couldn't justify wasting the five bucks it cost to get into the place without finding out if it was a male-male passion pit. Nervousness be damned, I was heading in. I threw my backpack (with wallet buried in the side pocket amid dozens of loose papers and pens and zipped up tight as a drum) over my shoulder and confronted the Pilgrim.

A mixture of adrenalized fear and lust was really nothing new to my sex life. I was in my late twenties in 1987, and I had been cruising places like this for more than ten years. Growing up in a working-class Connecticut town, I found my earliest adventures in public rest rooms, parks, and (when I got a little older) straight porno theaters. (There are not now nor have there ever been gay porno theaters in Connecticut.) Of course, in such places there was always the fear of discovery or arrest, which some public cruisers consider part of the fun. For me, this fear dissipated once I came out to my friends and family. The lure of such activities in such locales never faded, however.

Some people, "experts" mostly, would call my attraction to the kind of public sex I pursue an "addiction" at worst or a "compulsion" at best. I prefer to consider it an ever-evolving fascination. I am captivated by what it is that men will do when men know that they can do it. Over the years, I've come to see the Pilgrim Theater as the zenith in the constellation of my cruising for hot public sex; a singular oasis in a city notable for its sexually repressed attitudes, even—surprisingly—within the gay community. But at the Pilgrim, my individual predilections for sweaty, almost wordless encounters with horny strangers in rest rooms, cinematic pornography, voyeurism, and exhibitionism intersect. I'm getting ahead of myself.

That first afternoon at the Pilgrim I walked through the inner lobby past the sixties-looking drink and candy machines toward the pitch-black auditorium. The only thing that told me where I was going was the huge onscreen image of a penis thrusting in and out of a vagina in vivid close-up. "Oh, oh, oh . . ." the actress acted in a breathy monotone. Having seen this scene in a hundred other films, I knew what would be next. The man would pull his dick out and ejaculate all over the buttocks and lower back of his costar, who would be so moved by the sensation that she would have a screaming orgasm. Or three. Do straight men really believe this stuff?

I felt my way along the theater's back wall, bumping into several men who were leaning against it. Although the lobby warning seemed ominous, at least it confirmed that people had fooled around in the theater at some point in its history. I was therefore, on some level, regretful that I had lived in Boston for almost two years before mustering up the courage to venture into the Pilgrim. I had tried out the half dozen or so other adult theaters in town (two of which were officially gay) and found some halfway decent action in a few and absolutely nothing in others. But the Pilgrim managed to intimidate me for a long time. Perhaps it was the size of its marquee, the flashing neon, the Open All Night sign. Whatever it was, I had managed to avoid what would turn out to be the sexual bonanza that was the Pilgrim for quite a while. But now I could make up for lost time.

As I leaned against the back wall, my eyes fixed on the screen and attempted to adjust themselves to the surrounding darkness. I was aware of figures moving all around me. As my vision got better I could see a veritable parade of men walking in a full circle from the back to the front of the theater, through what was once the orchestra section and back up toward the standing-room area from which I was observing. "It figures," I remember thinking. "Only in Beantown would this colossal straight movie theater be the epitome of gay cruising."

My thoughts were interrupted by the feeling of a man moving toward me and slowly pressing against my left side. His shoulder was probably six inches above mine, and his arm slowly brushed mine. It was big and hairy, two of my favorite adjectives for forearms. But I suddenly thought about the sign in the lobby and worried that maybe I was being set up; perhaps this was an undercover cop who would run me in as soon as I mentioned that I would like to lick every lock of his body hair. I could hear my heart pounding in my ears and the thought of this guy slapping the cuffs on me (although hot in other circumstances) scared me enough to walk away.

I decided to scope out the gigantic theater. Down a huge flight of stairs, through what once must have been a distinguished gentlemen's lounge, I found the men's room. Four stalls faced four urinals. The stalls were door-free (the better to see you with, my dear). There were redundant glory holes in each of the walls between the stalls, and three out of four of the stalls were occupied by men manipulating their respective erections. Although these were interesting sights, I wanted to get a real sense of my surroundings. Heading back out, I noticed a condom vending machine attached to the far wall, the likes of which had yet to make an appearance in the gay smut theater a few blocks away. Back upstairs, I joined the parade.

Down near the screen I could turn toward the entrance and clearly see the huge Pilgrim balconies. I would later find out that just the week before my first visit, management had boarded up the stairways to the balconies for the last time. Apparently things would get really wild up there and (my typical luck) I had just missed ever experiencing it. I walked back up to the standing-room section, feeling a little braver and wondering if the hairy, muscular forearm was still around.

Instead, I bumped into a different man entirely. He was also taller than me and on the thin side. He thrust his crotch toward my hand and when I gave his dick a squeeze it felt way above average in size and thickness. I reminded myself that pricks in pants often felt much bigger than they really were—heck, my own smack-in-the-statistical-middle average-sized dick gains about two inches when it's covered in denim. Still, I was getting horny; so was my new friend, and I was wondering what we could do about it.

"Let me suck it," I whispered hoarsely.

"Come on," he said, motioning me with a jerk of his head to follow him farther into the theater.

As he walked ahead of me I felt in my right pocket for my three-pack of rubbers. Had I remembered to take them out of my backpack? I found the condoms and pulled one out, breaking open its wrapper as we continued down the aisle. I wondered if the man was going to find a semisecluded seat somewhere, but he took a right toward one of the exit doors halfway down the stage-left wall of the building and then a left toward a doorway that led to complete darkness. I would later deduce that this nook (and the one exactly like it on the stage-right wall of the building) was once an entranceway to the loge seats of the lower balcony. But since management had closed the upper reaches they were now two small cul-de-sacs that perfectly duplicated the backroom experience of gay bars in the good old days.

As I entered the dark little makeshift love shack I couldn't see an inch in front of my face. There were men everywhere I moved. I felt a strong squeeze on my right shoulder and hoped it was the man I had followed. One grope of his genital area confirmed that it was he. I felt him unzip his pants and out popped his truly massive cock; the size had not been augmented by clothing at all. I would have to say, in retrospect, that this man's dick was at least nine thick inches long, and perhaps ten. All I know is my mouth was watering. I squatted down in front of him, my backpack bouncing off a few of the other loiterers. I deftly stretched and unrolled the rubber over his massive organ. I was glad it was dark and relatively quiet (except for the sounds of slurping and the occasional muffled groan) because it eliminated the need to "negotiate" safer sex, which was something we were constantly being told we had to do in the mid-eighties. I was free to just dive in head first, so to speak.

The man leaned against the wall and I eagerly worked his cock into my mouth. He arched his hips out a little and I took a deep breath through my nose as I sucked him into my throat. When my face was up against his body and I could feel his prick head throbbing somewhere below my Adam's apple, I realized that this was easily the biggest cock I had ever felt (since seeing was out of the question). I grew sweaty with the exertion, and the experience grew more surreal as I felt the hands of several strangers drifting over my back and shoulders. I could hear the distinct sound of a well-lubricated dick being beaten about half an inch away from my right ear and I wondered if I was about to be baptized in cum at any moment or if the guy would aim at the floor.

I ran my hands up over the chest of the man I was blowing, bumping into a few other men's hands along the way. One particularly pushy fellow moved his hand down to my friend's bush and tried to grab the base of his cock as it thrust in and out of my eager mouth. I thought this was rude but it's hard to argue etiquette with a mouthful of throbbing penis. Apparently someone was squatting down near my level, because I could feel him reaching under my butt and massaging my crotch and butthole through my jeans. For a split second I thought about my backpack and let my new special friend's cock pop out of my mouth, at which point the man who had been groping for his meat snatched a hold of it. I stood up slowly to give my knees a little respite, grabbing for my friend's cock as if it were a baseball bat and Mr. Opportunistic and I were choosing up sides. I could make out the outlines of several people and realized that there were probably ten or twelve of us crammed into this little cubicle. I also could sense that the man I was blowing enjoyed being the center of attention of two cocksuckers.

I kept a grip on the base of his cock while the other guy massaged the head. At this point I could feel him tugging on the reservoir tip of the condom as he pulled it off my soon-to-be-ex-friend's dick. I heard a faint splat as the stretched-out rubber hit the floor.

"Yeah," the blowee moaned as the other guy lowered his head to crotch level and sucked his unsheathed shaft into his mouth. "Oh yeah," he said, turning his back toward me. Because you don't have to go to Western Union to send me a message, I walked out of the dark room. I felt a little sad but thought the experience had been fun while it lasted. Of course, I do remember thinking that I hoped the guy who swiped Mr. Big Stuff from me choked on him.

I walked toward the dimly lit inner lobby to get a glimpse of my watch, acutely aware of the frozen-in-time quality of public sex scenes. Encounters that seem to take a minute and a half are sometimes hours long. When I turned around to look at the clock over the entranceway, I heard something fall out of the side pocket of my backpack. I looked down and saw a pen—one of my pens!—on the floor. I swung the pack off my shoulder to find that the side pocket was gaping open. Had I forgotten to zip it up when I came into the theater? I riffled through and most everything seemed to be in order, until I realized that my wallet was missing. My ATM card, all my identification, and what little cash I had to my name was gone. I ran to the box office and asked to borrow a flashlight, which the man inside reluctantly gave me. I went back to the sex nook and flashed on the light to find the room almost completely empty, save one man masturbating in the corner. Everyone else— and my wallet—was gone.

Getting ripped off on my first trip to the Pilgrim sort of soured me on the experience for a while. I felt ashamed for "allowing" myself to be victimized and I was too embarrassed to admit to anyone what had really happened to my wallet. I made up some unlikely story of discovering my backpack unzipped after a particularly crowded evening commute on the subway, which garnered sympathy from my friends.

But of course the call of the cruise eventually lured me back to the theater. Over the past five years I have become something of a fixture in the crowd of regulars who enjoy the Pilgrim's dilapidated splendor. Naturally, after my inaugural visit I made it a habit to tuck all valuables into my sock before entering.

Of course, as time has marched on the Pilgrim has undergone its share of changes. Since that first visit I've seen the switch from projecting 35mm films to big- (very big-) screen video; two hikes in admission price (currently $7); the fencing off of the sex nooks (so of course the guys just do what they did inside in the shadows outside); one noisy protest by Women Against Pornography (who broke one of the glass doors at the entrance and shouted into the theater, "We know who you are and we know what you do to women," um, no they don't); the removal of one of the four men's room stalls (which makes the three remaining toilets prime space); as well as the frequent rumor that the Pilgrim is about to go out of business at any moment. I also very quickly learned that three-packs of condoms would sometimes not be enough and switched to the more practical and economical twelve-packs.

I've actually managed to fetishize rubbers to the point of not seeing them as an intrusion. I like to suck lots of cock and I like to feel the shaft pulsing against my tongue as the cock spills its seed into the rubber. There are a lot of people in the world—and certainly many among my fellow Pilgrim-goers—who suck but don't swallow and do so without rubbers, and that is their choice to make. But when you suck as much prick as I do (it is not unheard of for me to go through two twelve-packs in a week) the safes seem like a great way to have a no-worry no-mess explosively sexual time in an otherwise worry-filled and messy era.

Over the past five years Boston has not become any more conducive to the kind of sexual activity I seek out. If anything it's gotten worse. The Combat Zone is now at best a Zonette, and the Pilgrim and the Art are the only two porn theaters that remain. There is only one peep show place left as a result of the city government's effort to "clean up" the Combat Zone.

The Art Cinema is Boston's last gay theater, and management patrols the place so heavily for fear of cop infiltration that there is almost no fun to be had within its confines. (When one of the place's most fanatical sex-stoppers gets off duty, he takes over a stall in the Pilgrim's men's room and blows dick after dick after dick: Boston's sexual attitude in a nutshell.)

So the Pilgrim is the last great hope for those of us who like a chance to find somebody and just do it with none of the pretense or game-playing of other venues for meeting sexual partners. Mutual attraction is the only requirement. Class and color barriers break down in group lust; the Pilgrim is the least segregated place I've ever been in Boston, an extremely segregated city. And because I frequent the Pilgrim so regularly, I've managed to accumulate many hot memories of things I've done there.

I got to the Pilgrim on a recent Monday afternoon at about twelve-thirty, just in time to have a few businessmen for lunch. I was lucky enough to snag one of the toilets in the men's room; it's so crowded you almost have to take a number sometimes. I dropped my pants and took my place at the toilet nearest the door. I stroked my dick so that passersby could figure out what I was up to.

I saw some guys I'd had sex with at the Pilgrim in the past and a couple seemed to want to come back for more. There were two men that day who happen to be a couple of the handsomest I've ever blown, both well hung to boot. Both of them showed up at the same time and were cruising each other, which seemed logical because to me they're both hot and desirable.

Only the handsomer of the two was interested in sex with me that day, but believe me, I'm not complaining. He's balding and has a mustache and that day he was wearing a gray pin-striped suit. He's got a nice smile and a hefty eight-inch cock. The backs of his hands, which I made him wrap around my head, are covered with dark brown hair, which reminded me of the hairy chest I had felt through his shirt the last time I blew him.

This time I made him plow my mouth and throat for an eternity. He smiled in recognition as I unfurled the rubber down his great big shaft (oh, how the times have changed!). I took both of his hands and placed them on the back of my head. He slowly started to hump his pecker into my mouth, his hips in a rhythmic swaying motion. All I could see was the undone zipper of his dress pants and a dark, thick bush advancing to and retreating from my face. The sound of my slurping was surely audible outside the stall. The man's hands drifted away from my head and floated up to the walls of the stall, which he gripped, all the while maintaining his humping action.

I glanced up with his shaft still poking in and out of my mouth. His eyes were almost shut and his mouth was slightly curled in a grin. I popped his prick out of my mouth. "How's it feel?" I asked. He answered by shoving his cock back in my throat and fucking it harder. After a few minutes of this he pulled out, explaining that he had just arrived at the theater and that he wanted to watch some of the movies. I told him to come back anytime, hoping that it would be later that same day, but knowing that if he didn't make it back I'd probably hook up with him again on another visit.

There was another guy in a suit, probably six feet, four inches tall, and I noticed he looked quite nervous. He kept walking by and staring at me as I beat my meat. But he never ventured into the stall. He was at the theater that day for as long as I was, but for quite some time he kept to the routine of just walking by me and looking in. As the day wore on, guys in the other stalls came and went, usually literally, their departures signaled by a flush of the toilet that alerted other cruisers to the imminent availability of a coveted seat.

By about three in the afternoon the construction workers started their daily end-of-shift arrival. There weren't as many—and they weren't as universally eager to get their cocks sucked off—as there have been on the Friday afternoons I've found myself in the theater. But I did manage to suck off one dark-haired, husky beauty. He had on a denim jacket and pants, work shirt, boots, and a wedding ring. He was one of those guys who's in a hurry, but I love a quickie. His cock was about the same length as mine, maybe a little thicker. He eagerly humped away at my mouth and throat until he let out a groan. At this point I had to readjust myself on the toilet—I was leaning so far forward I worried that I might fall off. But the construction worker must have thought I was going to pull away just at his magic moment. So he grabbed my head and held it there as he pushed his meat to the back of my throat. I had to tilt my head to the left to accommodate the onslaught and avoid choking. He kept pushing and then let out a groan. I could feel five strong pulsations on the underside of his cock. As he pulled out of my mouth I slipped the rubber off him and tied the end. I shoved it in my pocket as a souvenir to examine later.

A good deal of time went by; waiting for dick to suck can sometimes require the patience of a Buddhist monk. Unlike the time-flies-when-you're-having-sex nature of the actual encounters, the downtime can really drag. At some point close to dinnertime the guy who had been observing me and avoiding my invitations showed up again. He went into the center stall immediately to my left.

I watched through the glory hole in the wall as he pulled his dick out of his navy-blue dress pants and started playing with it. Obviously, hours of cruising and movie-watching upstairs had over-ridden his apparent shyness, and suddenly Mr. Timid became Mr. Show-off. The guy is one of those big-boned, large-featured types whose dick, not surprisingly, is also a large feature. I would estimate it at about eight and a half inches and rather thick, one of those meaty/spongy ones. He also had a real dark pubic bush that con-trasted beautifully with his light skin. After playing with his own dick for a few minutes and occasionally bending over to see if I was paying attention to his display (which, of course, I was), he stuffed it back into his pants and zipped up.

I figured it was my big chance as he walked past my stall again. When he looked in my direction I motioned for him to come in, but he looked panicked and kept walking. I pretty much gave up hope of any actual contact before he resurfaced about fifteen minutes later. I beckoned him with my right index finger and the best come-hither-I'll-do-anything look I could muster. Apparently feeling very horny or bold or both, he came in and stood in front of me. I tugged his tie so he would lower his ear to my mouth. I could tell he was made nervous by the thought of contact, so I said, "Why don't you take it out of your pants and show me what you were doing in the other stall?"

He looked really scared.

I said, "Come on, show it to me, man."

He pulled out his cock and started stroking furiously, not six inches away from my eager face. To my delight, his pecker got much bigger than it had appeared to be through the glory hole. I started blowing hot and cool air on his shaft and though I could tell he didn't want me to touch his prick, I really wanted it in my mouth. I kissed his balls lightly, which alternately disturbed and aroused him. After a few minutes of this I decided he was suffi-ciently turned on for me to interest him in something else. Plus, I figured I'd lose him when he had another panic attack.

I pulled a rubber out of my pocket and held it up to the light for him to see. When he focused on it and realized what it was (it probably went through his mind that it was a badge), he nodded. It's amazing how accommodating some guys are when they see a rubber, while others get all straight-acting and say things like, "I just don't feel anything with a rubber." Well, not this guy.

I unrolled the condom down his hardening shaft and swallowed his rod in one gulp. It's a good thing it wasn't the first cock of the day or I would never have been able to handle it and would have gagged like an amateur.

He groaned.

I took his hands and placed them on the back of my head. I wanted him to fuck my face. Hard. Why is it that you have to do so much work to convince people that you want to be treated roughly? Finally he got the idea and started vigorously thrusting his hips. Soon he was pounding away so hard that it seemed almost involuntary, like he couldn't stop if he wanted to. Personally, I love being on the receiving end of such an experience. It's as if you've become part of a well-oiled cocksucking machine set on perpetual motion.

After doing this for an extended time, I pulled his cock out of my mouth. I slowly masturbated his shaft with his dick head resting against my lips. He had a look of extreme frustration on his face. He wanted back in!

I tugged on his tie again, indicating that I wanted to whisper another message. I found myself fantasizing that I was a delivery boy getting his mouth reamed by a strapping and horny business-man. He impatiently bent down to listen to whatever impertinent thing I had to say to him. "Wouldn't it be great," I whispered hoarsely, "if you could bend me over your desk at work and fuck the shit out of my ass?"

He smiled and chuckled and shoved his dick back in my mouth. Of course, most men who cruise the theater don't want to engage in ass play right out in the open like that and I, Mr. Bold-As-Brass, had hardly ever done it. (Except for the two times with the hugely hung, hugely popular Boston radio personality whom I didn't recognize the first time despite his ornate Madonna tour jacket.) I only ever want to get fucked when I am extremely horny, which at this point I was.

He pounded my mouth for a few more minutes, and I mean pounded. My eyes were watering, my nose was running, and I even choked a couple of times, overstimulated by the whole experience. It was nice and rough. Then he pulled his cock out of my mouth. He grabbed me with one hand under my left armpit and reached around to my ass crack. He lifted me to my feet and spun me around. I couldn't believe what was happening. He really wanted to fuck me right then and there. Was this the same guy who didn't even want to walk into my stall originally? I was startled and unprepared, but I really had been asking for it.

I managed to gasp out, "Wait a minute," and fumbled through my pockets for the trial-size tube of Foreplay lubricant I toted around with me in the unlikely event that such an unlikely event ever happened to me. I even took out another condom and rolled it on top of the original one (just to be doubly safe, a little trick I first tried with that famous deejay). I slathered some grease on his double-covered dong and shoved some up my asshole with my right middle finger.

He placed his right hand on the back of my neck and bent me over the toilet and *Pop!* He shoved his huge hog about three-quarters of the way up my hole.

I get fucked maybe once or twice a year at the most, so I'm sure it was a tight little fit for his above-average schlong. It burned like hell for several seconds as he began his relentless thrusting. He found the same rhythm he'd been using on my throat and I knew there was going to be no stopping him this time.

But stop we did when his dick popped out. I was amazed that the condom looked pretty clean; as I mentioned, I hadn't planned on this so there was no telling what condition my canal was in. I gasped for breath and he started to remove the rubbers.

"Don't," I said heatedly, "not without sticking it in me one more time." He shoved me down roughly again and burst right in me. This time he plowed the entire way in and I was amazed that it didn't hurt at all. The thrusting started at a feverish pitch and only grew more intense. I was being fucked to nirvana. I could see stars around the perimeter of my field of vision; if I shut my eyes I saw even more stars. I could feel his hip bones bouncing off my ass cheeks as he held me roughly by my soaking-wet armpits. I could feel his bush scratching up against my crack with his every inward push. I could hardly wait for the throbbing sensation as his dick delivered billions of sperm into the rubber. It was heaven. I couldn't believe it. This was exactly what I wanted, exactly the way I wanted it.

I glanced over my right shoulder and gave him a lascivious smile to let him know how much I loved the feeling of his pecker in my hole. He smiled slightly at the corners of his mouth and then shoved me down closer to the toilet. It was hard to believe, but it seemed as if he was probing me even deeper. My head began bumping into the tiled rest-room wall with each of his rough plunges. But before he shot his load his dick popped out of my butt again, my asshole expanding and contracting in its absence, lube dripping down to my balls.

He had drilled so deeply that this time the rubber was a bit less than pristine, which made the guy look kind of nervous. So I carefully removed it myself (which is simple to do when you've got a clean condom under a dirty one). He looked relieved that he didn't have to touch anything he didn't want to touch, so I pulled him down to my ear again and said, "Why don't you stroke that thing like you were doing in the other stall? Only this time, why don't you do it right in my face?"

I moved my face as close to his uncovered cock as I could without getting smacked by his pounding fist. He pumped ferociously and after maybe twenty-five strokes he huffed a few times and then groaned real low and long. Squirt! The first splash blocked my left nostril. Squirt! The next glued my left eye shut. Squirt! Right on my mustache, dripping down over my lips and to my chin. Squirt! A direct hit to my lips. Squirt! One last stream to my lower lip, chin, and upper chest.

By the time I got a wad of tissue to my nostril and eye and

looked up, the guy was zipping up quickly. Mr. Jitters was back. He was out of the stall long before I had composed myself or finished cleaning up my face. As I sat on the toilet with my pants around my ankles and cum drenching my face, three guys who had apparently been watching our sex extravaganza burst into applause.

I bowed a little bow and wiped off my face with a wad of toilet paper, feeling some of the cum begin to dry on my chin beneath my beard. It left a lovely sperm scent on my face, which I was sure I would be able to smell for the entire subway ride home.

Two friends of mine were once driving from Boston to New Jersey on a hot summer evening when they pulled into a service station for a fillup. As they drove up to the pumps they noticed two mechanics and another employee working on a pickup truck in the open garage. All three of them had their shirts off, streaks of grease forming various patterns across their backs and muscular torsos. Chest hair gleamed with sweat and oil. Scuzzy, disheveled jeans bulged at the crotches. When the service station bell sounded, the three sweaty men glanced over at my friends.

"I feel like I'm in a Gage film," one of my friends said.

The other replied, "You know, porn films are never, ever like life. But every once in a while, life is like a porn film."

At Boston's Pilgrim Theater, my life has come closest to being like a porn film. And given that porn was the first thing that ever confirmed for me the fact that other gay men existed, I find a certain symmetry in that. Porn is also where I learned everything I know about sex, so what better place to perfect my technique? At the Pilgrim I've connected with the deejay, the businessmen, the priest, the construction workers, the married men, the daddies, the writer, the photographer, the model, the punk, the artist, the mechanic, and countless other hot strangers of all shapes and sizes and colors. Even if its days are numbered, my memories of the Pilgrim will never disappear.

PART THREE

PORN

VÉRITÉ:

HOW WE

TELL OUR

STORIES

When I began putting this collection together, one of the first people I contacted was "Dan Veen." I wasn't even sure he was alive. These are times when one doesn't count on gay men's longevity. Four of the contributors to the first volume of *Flesh and the Word* are already dead: Roy Wood, W. Delon Strode, John Wagenhauser, and T. R. Witomski.

But Dan Veen is still alive and well, he quickly informed me. He simply wasn't writing for public consumption anymore. I wasn't willing to let that go unanswered and wrote back, wanting to know why not. He had, he told me, a "situation" now, one in which he couldn't offer his writing for publication.

Eventually, I convinced him that the existence of his situation was precisely the kind of material I would want for this book. "The Stories of V: An Essay" is fascinating for many reasons. It certainly is a remarkable piece of obsessive writing. Here the author is totally swept up in what he is creating, and the audience for whom he is creating it.

But "The Stories of V" contains another element of intrigue. It fits a classic form of pornography but resists classification as fiction. Note the shrewd subtitle: "An Essay." Is this a short story by an otherwise retired writer? Or is it what's really happening to him?

Anaïs Nin, after all, created a whole body of work by writing erotica for a man at a dollar a page. Couldn't Dan Veen be doing the same, or is he simply stealing Nin's scenario? The ending, especially, seems too farfetched, or is it just that it's too far for our imaginations to follow, entering into the arena where, rather than having a college-educated adult writing for another consenting adult, we have the sudden intrusion of economic coercion?

If the end is difficult to believe, because we don't want to believe it, certainly the harshness of the writer's life is factual. Dan Veen has captured just what it's like to try to earn a living as a pornographer. Far from being the lucrative employment that many seem to think it must be—certainly there should be monetary rewards for doing something so dirty, you can hear them say—it's often difficult and discouraging. Dan Veen's descriptions of payments he received and the agreements he made in the time before he found his situation are highly accurate.

John W. Rowberry, best known for his editing skills, first at *Drummer* and now at *Stallion* and *Inches,* enters into the same realm where fact and fiction blur, but in a different way. Clearly these "Travelers' Tales" are fiction, but they are deliberately written so that they might be the oral history of the characters as real people. The attempt in these selections from a much longer work is to present the vernacular experience of gay men as they find one another and sex in their day-to-day lives. Like William Cozad's, these characters aren't going to make it onto the society pages, but there's the definite feeling that Rowberry wouldn't ever want them to be there.

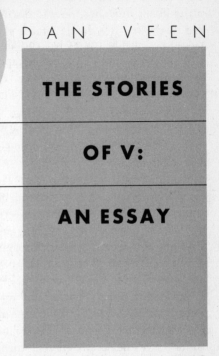

DAN VEEN

THE STORIES

OF V:

AN ESSAY

V'S LETTER ARRIVED WHEN I WAS CONTEMPLATING selling a kidney. Already a weekly blood bank depositor, I was best friends with the winos who habitually replaced their blood with Old Crow.

The winos put me on to the kidney idea. They also told me about the sperm bank, which paid fifty dollars per load. Problem was, you couldn't have an ejaculation for two days prior to your donation. And then there were these dirty stories I wrote, the ones V inquired about. My stories made regular deposits at the sperm bank even harder to achieve.

It was no joke about the kidney. I was dead serious. People needed kidneys all the time, didn't they? Hell, they had waiting lists for the damn things. I had a spare. Surely some wealthy father would pay a mint to get his son off dialysis. Before the advent of

V, I researched the kidney business in medical libraries, queried organ donor programs, only to discover such get-rich-quick schemes had in the last decade been made illegal. If it had not been for V's letter, I probably would have pursued Project Kidney through the medical underworld, ending up under a scalpel in Tijuana.

> *Mr Veen:*
> *I like your work. I like your style. It is disarming. I am a lover*
> *of literature. Would you please mail me any of your unpublished*
> *materials. I would be pleased to reimburse you for your trouble.*
> *Cordially,*

Well, wasn't V pure fucking business?

Unpublished? Just about everything I wrote got published— one way or another. I'm not bragging. When a story gets rejected, I rework it, I revamp it, twist it, tighten it. Let's see, in this context is the word "moan" sexier than the word "groan"? Hm, does this character have a "cock"? or a "prick"? or a "dick"? Or maybe it's a "schlong." "Prong"?—no, only on special occasions. And I've always been partial to the Southernism "peter." Asslips? Asshole? Or is it butthole? Is cum hornier-sounding than cream? Only sometimes. Give the screws another turn with every rejection—until it sells.

V (not his real initial) was unknown to me. Where he had read me, what he liked about me, how he got my name (not my real name), and my address, and how long he had been following my career, were complete mysteries.

Did V know my first porno sold to a now-defunct nudist monthly when I was sixteen? No *Saturday Evening Post* Poetry Contest for this kid.

I stole this nudist magazine from a pharmacy on Castro Street in San Francisco. I jerked off in the company of Denny, a fellow street waif who enjoyed trying on me some of the fancy footwork he read about in the magazine. Denny'd see a picture of a boy sucking himself off while another kid fucked the upended butt and say, "Hey, let's do this!" And I would gladly double myself over dick first. Though Denny was older, it was I who first seduced him, giving him ideas with the magazines.

It was always a comfort to mouth Denny's throat-filling peter while he lay back and read the magazines I swiped for him. His was a comfortable peter. It made itself right at home in my mouth. It could sprawl out along the couch of my tongue, loafing for hours like that, its puffed marshmallow head like a throw pillow, propping his soft balls on my lower lip.

Denny read me cocksucker stories while I chowed down on his meat. I loved cocksucker stories, especially when he read the part about sucking cocks. Sometimes he'd read aloud, quoting all the tough talk he learned, giving my head an absentminded push just to keep the suction up.

In the midst of all this puppy lust I wondered at the miraculous ability of words to connect so instantaneously with the flesh, to vibrate from cortex to crotch.

Denny read aloud to his cock, and to me, its devoted sucker. My nerve-sensitive palate could palpate which words prompted a throb of his meat. Denny's cock had favorite stories, too, surefire cum stories Denny would haul out and read to us. Denny's cock and I always got doubly excited when he started reading one which we knew produced an extra-thick load for me to suck down.

Sucking and reading. Fucking and reading. We practically majored in it. What more wholesome way for two hotblooded American boys to spend Saturday afternoon? What better memories could a kid have?

To this day Denny sends me Xeroxes of stories that turn him on. He mails them to me sometimes with a knotted rubber filled with his cum (the contents of one of which I am savoring as I type this).

Denny underlines the passages he fixes on while he masturbates. The provocative sentences. The heated phrases. The *mots justes*. Knowing that this is the line where Denny came to a boil, lovingly stroking his pudgy-dumb peter to climax, brings back memories and hard-ons.

In fact Denny once mailed me a copy of a story that, unknown

to him, was one I had written as Dan Veen. A rubber full of cum
was enclosed. I drank that one like champagne of a vintage year.
Nice to know I still have the touch with you, Denny.

I composed my first story for our favorite purloined magazine,
our hustler's *Kama Sutra*, based loosely on some of the things Denny
and I did. I was sixteen at the time, but magazines require an age
statement only from their readers, not their writers.

My next youthful stories for other magazines were surprisingly
successful send-ups, drawn from the vast and cultured literary
sources of childhood.

The "Adventures of the Hard Boys" featured intrepid boy
sleuths, Frank and Joe Hard, two adolescent brothers whose teenage
detective high jinks found them investigating each others' teenage
cocks and their teenage friends' teenage cocks, as well as some other
cocks. Their nicely well-endowed buddy Chet would join our thrill-
seeking duo in many a daring yet satisfying escapade. The series
sold well on the underground circuit. The so-called mysteries of our
adventurous brothers never got solved. No reader ever complained.
Or noticed. For that reason alone, I consider the erotic stories were
successful in their purpose.

Words and sex, thanks to you, Denny, are inextricable. To this
day I love fucking guttermouth guys who turn the air blue with
expletives, spluttering obscenities like cum over rubber bedsheets.
Words, for me, have replaced amyl nitrate as the requisite heady
oblivion that makes good sex so good.

I wrote porno regularly over the next decade under a dozen
arch names. Not obsessively. For folding money mostly. But always
for money. Much as I loved literature, Art never came into it. Art
was what professors found in Shakespeare a hundred years after he
died. Shakespeare worried about the mortgage on Stratford-on-Avon.
My *nom de plaisir* of Dan Veen was, however, a backhanded *hommage*
to the literature of Vladimir Nabokov. Dan Veen is a peripheral
character in one of Nabokov's books. *His* Dan Veen was a shady
roué who could plausibly take up writing Victorian erotica for a
sideline. Was our V, our lover of literature, connoisseur enough to
catch this inside joke?

■ ● ■

Which of all my *oeuvre* had V read? What did he mean by that "disarming"? Can you be disarming on demand?

Dan Veen wrote back to V asking if V had any connection with any federal, state, or local law enforcement agency. (Entrapment is always a possibility in this country, where the public taste for freedom varies with the president in office.)

Yet I was audacious enough to forward a story already written. Magazines had thus far rejected it as too savage. Magazine guidelines, like consciences and hemlines, change to fit the fashion of the time. My tale trucked with such salacious topics as bondage, mutilation, young men of undetermined legal status, piss, and—that constant menace to the moral tissue of this nation—shit. I was in the process of toning down this fable when V's letter arrived. Lover of literature, huh? Okay, I said, love *this*.

One week later I received a check from V in the amount of $200. To my surprise, it did not bounce.

My integrity was getting a pretty fair price. Maybe I could keep both kidneys after all.

I tested V with another story floating around in my desk.

This story a magazine shied away from because the theme was a little too offbeat to beat off to. It was a love story, really, between a middle-aged guy and a retarded boy just coming of age.

They were right, of course. Mr. Average Reader might never find sex with the mentally handicapped appealing. Yet I liked the subject and retackled it for V. Henry James, another mentor who wrote much about sex without ever mentioning the word, always complained: "A writer must be allowed his subject. There should be no question of what is permissible. The question is only that of quality, of how that subject is treated, whether the skill be good or ill."

With that quotation tacked over my WP, I did my best with the love story. Three days after it was posted, I received a check for $175.

Screw those rich kids on dialysis. Immediately I mined other ideas heretofore consigned to small paper scraps, working simultane-

ously on previously aborted stories. Suddenly I was free to explore
back alleyways of eroticism that had always intrigued me. No more
piss-and-shit restrictions. No more pussyfooting around mild bondage scenes for Peoria's sake. No softpedaling the S&M trips to get
into the mainstream mags. No more "Payment will be made 60
days after publication, or 260 days after notice of acceptance."

A letter from V arrived about this time. There's no remembering exactly when. That first year of working for V was a hurried
daze of self-harassment.

> *I require from you and your product absolute exclusivity. I reserve
> the right to first rejection of any story. Acceptance of story implies
> that the story will never be used by you for publication in any
> form whatsoever, in return for which you will be amply remuner-
> ated. Violation of these terms shall be grounds for cancellation
> of this agreement.*

Sounded very lawyerish. The tone a touch snippier than last
time. Anal-retentive type? Some passive-aggressive CEO of IBM you
wouldn't even suspect would hoard pornography? Then one day he
unexpectedly dies. Authorities discover collections of perversity dat-
ing back to the days of the Emperor Tiberius's dementia. Albums
of erotic tintypes. Baron von Gloeden's Sardinian youths posed like
Theocritan goatherds. Manuscripts of Edith Wharton's erotica. My
stories.

Just who the hell was this V? Did he oversee a stable of writers
grinding out stories for him? Did there exist a network of silent
unpublished scriveners paid just to send their personal "products"
to V's P.O. box? I picture him having bound in calf's hide all the
stories I've dished out to him over the years, the pages deckled or
marbleized, and maintained alongside the ribald eighteenth-century
etchings of Thomas Rowlandson and the erotic lantern slides from
the court of Louis XIV.

Past or present, who is any audience a pornographer reaches?
Are they at all the same people when they are not "appreciating"
his work? How much is it ever possible to know about them? Why

should I care? I was, after all, doing it for money, wasn't I? And money, after all, was what I was getting, wasn't it? The remuneration, V's legalese went, *was* ample.

I wrote to V constantly after that. Faithfully, loyally wrote to him, lover-like. Spinning fantastic tales of cum and compassion. My work ranged from the viscerally crude to circumlocutions that Henry James might've blushed over, if he'd caught on.

I've never written so much in my life as in the first months of my engagement with V. There was no pausing to think what V might be like. It didn't matter. I wrote lightning-quick. Who knows when this gift horse might suddenly give a few snorts and gallop off to spread his manure in someone else's pasture?

You didn't dare look too closely at a Mephistophelean deal like this. Most of the time I'd be too busy cadging hot phrases from rap music for V. There was no questioning where all this was headed, or where my weekly, twice-weekly, or thrice-weekly stories were ending up. I eavesdropped on schoolkids at bus stops. Kids' lingo is always the freshest, filthiest, and most colorful. A few words from them could inspire whole stories. Or I'd sneak into college lavatories, scribble down graffiti from the stalls like an earnest social researcher. There is nothing like a muscle-bound freshman insecure about his masculinity for coming up with trenchant sexual squibs.

Yes, I did my share of stories for V about college freshmen and streetsurfers and construction workers and delivery boys. (V seemed to like them just as well as the more exotic locales.) After all, delivery boys *are* a part of life, they *will* sometimes let you fuck them, and their lively bodies have become as much of a convention to the porno story as the dead body is to the detective story.

For my own diversion, and to test V's limits (if any), I would venture into less vanilla tastes, sampling the neapolitan flavors of sexuality. Migrant workers; astronauts; Republican senators; whores who charged each other for sex just on principle; skinheads; piercing parties; a Vietnam veteran who could only get it up by sucking on a loaded gun; cavemen; an Arab sheik with an all-boy harem the size of the Vienna Boys' Choir comprised of virgins from every country in the world; voodoo rituals with exotic love elixirs that will make the imbiber do whatever he is told; Eskimos; Cajun crawfishermen.

All of which I sweated to make realistic as possible.

Rapid-fire as I worked, I couldn't let go a piece unless it had a feel of workmanship about it, holding one back a day, to double-check whether I had done my "subject" justice no matter how wild it was. Test-driving the piece, as it were, for its coarse power.

There was sex with the ghosts of lovers who'd died of terminal illness; sex during an out-of-body experience (bird's-eye voyeurism). Bisexual encounters with an ex-wife and her boyfriend and his boyfriend. Paratroopers. Science-fiction sex never excited me, but that was the challenge: to *make* it excite me. Ringling Bros. came to town one week, inspiring two stories, one about acrobats, and another about clown-sex. *"This time, Pepe, won't you please leave those big ol' shoes on, just once, for me?"*

As I say, I was testing V's limits as well as my own.

Rarely would I break from my marathon eroticizing, only seldom mumbling through the bookstores, paging the trade literature, scanning for a story remotely similar to any of the slew of stories I assembled for V.

That was my chief suspicion of V:

V was buying my stories and, for perverse reasons of his own, reselling them to magazines under his own name. There could be no profit in this. Most magazines' rates were well below V's. I never had any proof of this. As far as I can tell V is guarding everything I have written, though I still check the bookstores from time to time.

The other angle to this setup is that I *am* furnishing V with fantasies. But these fantasies are only superficially sexual ones. Underneath they are fantasies of creativity. Having bought the manuscript, one enjoys the feeling that one has created the writing. This happens all the time in the marketplace of visual art. Art consumers derive such a feeling of identity through ownership; through the finical selection of the proper masterpiece, they come to feel they fostered its actual creation.

In looking at my records just now I find I managed to knock

out thirty stories for the month of February. More than one a day. I have no memory of that period. I dropped out of sight. I spoke to few, except to explain the truth when they asked why I had disappeared.

"Sort of a literary 976 number, isn't it?" a friend joked. After that I never said anything more about it. This little duel was just between me and V. I tried to wear out V's sanguine interests. To see if his attention would flag and the $200/$175 checks would falter. If he would just return something with comments and suggestions. Reject something outright. Be appalled. Be shocked. Might he have a few scenarios he would like to suggest to his author? Be disgusted. Revulsed. Call me a bad boy. Gimme a hint. Spank me. What fancied his tickle?

Orders for ephemeral goods shot up. Had I been a factory I would've had to hire armies of new employees. With V, market saturation never peaked. My desk had been devastated by V's blitz-krieg. There was no longer any resort to the raw materials of the commonplace book where I once warehoused ideas, false starts, non sequitur dreams. Notebooks were gutted. Everything had been cobbled together for the sideshow. Everything turned fantasy-fodder. I ran on high-octane inspiration, desire at full steam. I mailed him a modified homo-epic poem I'd been toying with for years based on the Biblical Song of Solomon, titled *Song for a Green-Eyed Sailor*. I deconstructed an abandoned erotic novel written when I was seventeen, sending a reworked chapter to V every week. The astonishing inventiveness of the jailbait pornographer who was me at seventeen was almost Rabelaisian. Footfucking. Slaveboxing. Prince Alberts. Also featured in this serial was a Victorian mansion where rows of young Olympic athletes were hooked up to diabolical electronic milking machines. Their accumulated cum emptied into a swim-ming-pool–size vat where the material got converted into more re-tail uses than George Washington Carver found for the peanut. Cosmetics. Soaps. Hamburger patty protein additive. Carbonated strawberry soda. Sort of a queer *Willy Wonka and the Chocolate Factory,* come to think of it. Nothing was sacred. Our hero, a young man just turned eighteen, puts the diabolical vat of cum to use by

swimming in it and fucking a certain Mr. Rosco, a large and black
Ubangi. Every kid's wet dream. The book's installments were regu-
larly accepted. (Some chapters of the same novel received $200 from
V, while some netted $175.)

Whether or not I invented gerbiling, my teeming brain was
certainly desperate enough to use it. From there, other varieties of
bestiality were but a step. Chimpanzee or dog, I made sure the
animal was always a male and was always a willing partner in the
consensual act. The SPCA has not called me up before the House
Un-American Committee—yet.

Was nothing inhuman alien to V? Was there anything I could
not write about? Anything he would not buy? Why buy them and
bury them? Was he storing them up in fireproof vaults? Compiling
this weird legacy of distorted social studies? That initial year was
a challenge. Every time I mailed a story, there was a check waiting
in the mailbox. In one day I'd polish off a story and—*bam!*—back
came the check pronto. V's nymphomaniac appetite was greater
than my capacity to sate. Larger than my own greed. Flexible as
my writing facility became—and it poured forth from brain to
fingers to keyboard to screen in uninterrupted flow—some weeks I
can barely remember rising from the PC. My desk remained littered
with Chinese take-out cartons. Satisfying the maw of V's post office
box was my full-time preoccupation. No Casanova endites such love
letters as I to a more voracious pricktease. After a year I was sure
my output already rivaled what the Marquis de Sade wrote during
his Bastille days. *120 Nights of Sodom. Justine. The Boudoir Conversa-*
tions. God knows I resorted to these classics for juxtapositions I'd
not yet utilized. *My Secret Life. Fanny, the Memoirs of a Woman of*
Pleasure. Autobiography of a Flea, Vols. 1–3. The entire Catholic *li-*
brorum prohibitorum got pilfered.

Especially for Valentine's Day I sent V a story I was particularly pleased with. I wrote him a note telling him so, adding that
it was a gift. I received a check for it anyway. That felt almost
insulting. Like a god refusing an offering. I made V another gift
of a story on the anniversary of the first story I wrote him. For
some reason, this was to V a $175 story.

If I neglected the care and feeding of my poor prick it was only because I now suffered from an obsession with these vicarious thrills. Greed and flattery had a lot to do with it, too. I developed satyriasis of the pen. My mind seemed to be the major sexual organ of the body. It was what I fucked with. It was what swelled with blood when it got excited. I had but to caress it with an idea and it would pour forth a copious flow of words. My dick, forgive this pun, was another story. When I noticed it at all, this long-suffering penis seemed an atrophied thing between my legs.

When I sought out the privacy of my own fantasies, there was V, reminding me that I was not giving my all, that I had obviously reserved something from him. I had held back. Just what was this filthy pamphlet tucked under the dustbunnies of my mind in a plain brown wrapper, hm? A memory? This was tantamount to employee theft!

Caught red-handed dredging up childhood memories of, say, losing my virginity, I found that V was there to intercept the residue.

That moment in the woods when my brother and his friend showed me the *Playboy*s they had hidden in a Tupperware container. How they were explaining to me how a woman's nipples got hard. How that showed she wanted to get fucked. *And when a man's dick gets hard, that shows he wants to fuck her. Hey, let's see, your titties are sticking out, that means you want to get fucked like a woman. Yeah.* They take out their dicks and show me how big and how hard their dicks are. *Sure you can take it. See how it's going in. Just relax and let it. There. Just relax and let it. Okay I will. But go slow.* This time I take notes for V, a paying participant now in every memory. He is the Internal Revenue Service ready to tax buried treasure found in my backyard.

Denny's high-set haunches and deep-planted butthole writhed through several of V's stories. I plagiarized Denny's fetish for having me suck my own toes while he fucked me. Even the cowlick of hair that flapped in front of Denny's eyes whenever he was hunkered over me and fucking industriously.

The freckles from Ron's back appeared in a romantically stylized story. Ron was transmogrified into a sort of atmosphere piece depicting a pleasant one-night stand. In reality we met frequently for more than a year.

Here I thought I'd had our fling safely tucked away in a bad poem, but V's demands retrieved Ron from my past. The day after I mailed in my story, I ran into my former fuckbuddy at the mall. My recently composed words had obviously conjured him up.

Ron had changed his mind about who he was. He was no longer the Ron of the private story I'd written for V.

I don't know if I had anything to do with it, but Ron had since converted to the heterosexual faith—as evidenced by the presence of his wife and newborn child.

She must have thought this nice man cooing over their child was a high school chum of Ron's. Looking at his child, I felt . . . related. The drool on the baby's chin recalled the brine-rich lotiony quality of its father's cum. How I would suck it all down as it came spouting out of his dick. Ron liked me to make smacking-slurping sounds when he came, like a child nursing, and that milked his cum out even more. I could see his balls close up. Bobbing deliriously in a sort of cum fit.

We'd play games with his cum because he always shot so much of the stuff. I wrote of this to V, telling him every detail of the tale as if we did it all in one rainy night, the balcony doors of Ron's bachelor apartment open to the wetness outside and fusion jazz toodling on the late-night radio. That is how I mostly remember our nights together. We smeared his cum all over his belly. I wrote my name in it. I'd rub my cock in that man-milked lubricant, tickling it against the feather-feeling hairs of his chest. Then he'd do me again. Or he'd dump it all in my mouth. I'd save it for when we were face to face. We'd swap his cum back and forth till both our tongues were mucky-pasty with it. Once we recycled it afterward in the shower as a shampoo. A thousand and one uses.

So there was no looking at Ron's child without thinking of Ron's cum. Both child and cum so creamy white. It had flowed so abundantly yet fruitlessly into every receptacle of my body. For a moment, looking at the child, I twinged with an anthropophagous *nausée* in my stomach, which had swallowed so much of Ron's live seed. You mean that stuff did that?

But the moment was not my own. V was right there with me, measuring the possibilities, gauging the fantasy potential. "What about a story of two boyhood lovers who make a pact to initiate each other's sons into male sex. I could only entrust my son to my best friend. . . ." Great copy. Even my present didn't belong to me, dammit. It was like working in a health-food store and being malnourished. There was no time for one-night stands, much less any more devoted relationships than the distant one I had with V. The sperm bank was a welcome—my only—relief.

A more antiseptically cheerful place my "Fertility Clinic" could not have been. While I waited my turn to jerk off, I dutifully inspired my sperm by fantasizing about the private university freshmen, usually medical students, waiting alongside me. The Chronic Pornographer in me already noted physical details of the WASP lad beside me, the boy with desirable genes. We boys in stud never speak. Our mission is just too personal a thing. *"I'll sell ya a spoonful of cum for the mizzus, mister!"* Stud service. DNA will out. Bashful as we were together, these kids would waltz out of their private powder rooms brandishing their hot cuppa cum like it was the Olympic torch.

Now it was my turn. V, omnipresent, nudged me.

I entered a small room wallpapered with sunny floral patterns. Birds and bees. A spice rack opposite the cot held heterosexual smut. Luckily, I always bring my own spices.

Most magazines with slick color photos of big beefdicks don't turn me on—much. No. My tastes are for rawer, amateur-style photos. The stuff found in older porno magazines sold when buying them meant a surreptitious foray into the cheating side of town. I often wish magazines would deliberately imitate this raw footage again, backing away from the impossible Ken dolls. Even Ken dolls are more appetizing when it looks like somebody sweet-talked the local high school quarterback to step into the trailer for a few Polaroid snapshots of what is known locally as Cheerleader's Deelite.

For this old reliable style I thumb to the back of the magazine. There the pictures of men fucking are near-microscopic, but these tiny blurred images sprout a cord of wood in my pants that would fire up any winter night. In the middle of tapping my sap for the propagation of more middle-class rug rats, I am aware of V standing over my shoulder. Get away from me. Approving or disapproving of my fantasies. Paying me or not paying me. I look afresh at my sprawled-out hustlers, naked apes. Doing my damnedest to ignore V. Is this a $200 fantasy, or is this a $175? And what's the difference, for chrissake? I have popper flashbacks, out-of-body insights on this web of monetary power and bodily desire. How monkey-like, how ridiculous every photo suddenly looks. What is flesh? What is man? *It is so thin between skeleton and skin, oh how does anything else fit in?* an old gospel hymn goes. These professional punks are somebody's lost children. The economically deformed court jesters of the nation, funneled by social conditions to strip for the privy delectation of the economically well-endowed. Yet I admire them as I ravish them. Latter-day Huck Finns. They have the Thoreauvian freedom to make their living from exactly what God bequeathed them. No accessories and trappings. No bullshit degrees, no club memberships. Their accidental religion doesn't believe in underwear, much less a three-piece business suit. Rousseau's Noble Savage shaking his moneymaker on Forty-second Street. I want to redeem them for V. Make him feel better about them.

V wears that tacky Hawaiian shirt I've hated him in so often. Tourist. He smokes a cigar and leers at me in my preposterous groveling position, like catching me sitting on the john. Sightseer. Get out, goddammit! Voyeur. This is *not* for you! Can't you for one goddamn minute leave me in peace! What do you think I'm doing, writing Malcolm Forbes's goddamn *pillowbook?* Who do you think I am—*Scheherafuckingzade??* My bloodstiff penile tissue looks for a flash like an evolutionary remnant. Might as well be an appendix.

The clinic attendants remark on the noise I made in there. Are you okay? Do you need to rest?

Honey, if you only knew. I've racked up so much frequent-flyer mileage in head trips that I deserve one free orgy of reality.

In the three years we have been together V and I have, like many couples, come to an understanding. Sometimes I need to get away.

The airfare to Veracruz is cheap. From there I take a bus into the mountains to Popocatépetl, where I stay at a *finca* owned by a friend who now lives in New York. The farmhouse is deserted except for a few cowhands who aren't sexy, and Aztec housegirls. The housegirls polish the floor by wrapping dustcloths on their feet and skating around the rooms. They scatter eucalyptus branches beneath the beds—superstition or pest control.

After two days I miss V. I wonder if V's accountant misses me. The girl brings in the blank paper I ultimately ask for. The love letters continue.

For the rest of the month I will write. Nowadays I pace myself. Somewhere between need and greed and art. I take breaks. Go out. Play tourist. Sightseer.

The Popo marketplace is crowded on Saturdays, so I find what I want. A boy. I haggle with his mother over the price. Sometimes the mothers come with them. Riding in the back of the truck all the way to the farmhouse.

The housegirls know to avoid my room while I write. The boy, Javier today, is over there naked on the bed. He is chewing the bubble gum I bought him at the marketplace. I write for a while and then I fuck him. His mother sits patiently outside the bedroom door all day long while I fuck her son. I write several pages and then I fuck her son. She must be thinking, *Crazy gringos, gringos are crazy.* I keep writing until almost suppertime, and then I fuck her son some more.

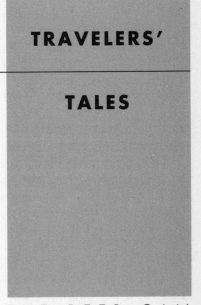

JOHN W. ROWBERRY

TRAVELERS'

TALES

THE BEER CAN

THE BIGGEST COCK I'VE EVER HAD (OR SEEN) WASN'T all that long, maybe about eight inches, but was as big around as a beer can. I had heard about this guy for a couple of months before I ever met him. He hung out at the same neighborhood bar I did, and the regulars had a joke about him—they never said it in front of him—when they'd order a beer. If they wanted a Bud in a can, they'd say to the bartender, "Give me Tom's dick" or "I want Tom's dick."

The first time I heard that and saw the bartender give the guy who said it a Bud in a can, I didn't get it. But I heard this guy I know laugh one time when someone said, "Give me Tom's dick," so I asked him what it was supposed to mean. He told me about this guy, Tom, who had a dick as big around as a beer can. I didn't believe it.

One night my friend pointed Tom out to me. He looked very normal, and I could see his crotch, which had a bulge but also looked pretty normal. My friend asked me if I wanted to meet Tom. I was a little bashful about it, because I thought if anyone was introduced to the guy, then they probably had been told about his dick, and he probably knew they had been told. I didn't want the guy to think I only wanted to meet him because of the size of his dick. It was true, because I would never have even noticed him otherwise, but I didn't want him to think that. So, I passed on being introduced. I decided I would find some real natural way to meet him. But I wasn't sure just how that might come about.

Providence made the introduction. One night, in the parking lot, as I pulled in, I noticed that this car had its hood raised. I stopped and walked over—it was Tom. His battery was dead. I introduced myself and offered to jump his battery so he could get to a gas station. I did. I said I'd follow him just in case it died again on the way. He was grateful, thanked me for taking the trouble, and gave me a real sincere smile.

I hung around the gas station while he had a new battery installed, talked with him about batteries, and suggested he might like to have a cup of coffee afterward—at my place. Either he figured it was the way to repay my kindness or he really was interested in getting it on. Either way, he said yes and we drove to my house. I went into the kitchen and made coffee and he stood around, watching me, talking a bit.

We took our coffee into the living room. I turned on the radio. We sat down on the sofa. He said he thought he had seen me at the bar. I told him I went there about once every two weeks, but only stayed for a beer or two. I told him I had seen him before, but that he was always with someone.

There was one of those long pauses, like when one of you is getting ready to make a pass at the other one, but no one does anything for a minute or two.

Finally, I just blurted it out, "Is it true you have a dick as thick as a beer can?"

He grinned at me. "Yeah," he said. "You want to see it?"

"Sure."

He stood up in front of me and unbuckled his pants, slipped them down a little, and slipped his briefs down. Out flopped this fat, fat dick, the head about the size of a crab apple. It looked about five inches long, but it was still soft. It was real thick; it looked like it might—just might—fill up the coffee mug in my hand. I leaned forward and took it in my hand, then sucked the head into my mouth. It was fat and fleshy, and it filled up my mouth. I thought I might go down on all of it while it was still soft, but it started growing right away, and I never got all the way down. It was actually stretching my jaws, and I backed off. I held it and looked at it and stroked it while it grew to its full length— about eight inches, like I said—and swelled up so big I couldn't get my hand around it. I was a little embarrassed. I had got this guy home, got his dick out, and I couldn't suck him off. I tried. I could get the head in my mouth, but that was all. I figured that was probably what he was used to, guys sucking on the head . . . but I was in for a surprise.

"Can I fuck you?"

He said it real low; I almost didn't hear him. I backed off and looked at it some more.

"It's not so hard to take, I'll go real slow so it won't hurt."

I really felt bad. I just don't get fucked, that's all there is to it. There was nothing else to do but tell the truth. So I did. He understood. If I didn't like getting fucked, then his dick wouldn't be anything but a big pain in the ass. And he said he wouldn't enjoy it either if I wasn't enjoying it.

He told me that if I wanted to suck it I could, but he couldn't come that way. He sat down next to me and I continued to play with it.

We talked a little more, and his dick started getting soft. He said perhaps he should hit the road, and I said that was fine, that I was sorry I couldn't give him what he wanted. He said not to worry about it, but that if I ever changed my mind, to let him know. We laughed.

I've seen Tom a few times in the bar, and we say hello, but that's too much dick for my ass.

COASTAL COCKSUCKER

Years ago, during World War II in fact, I used to hang out at a popular beach north of Los Angeles. I lived close to the beach and would spend my weekends there soaking up rays (as they call it now) and sucking off whatever stumbled into my lair.

I discovered, completely by accident, that there were some small caves carved into the cliffs above the beach. One day I was climbing up the cliffs, which was not really difficult to do but which one did not do casually, when I noticed a young man about my own age. He was squatting down in the opening to a small cave. At first I thought he was taking a crap, so I started climbing in a different direction, so as not to embarrass him. I happened to glance back and saw that he was stroking an erection that stuck down between his legs.

I came to a complete stop. I had on a pair of baggy trunks, so I pulled up on the leg and let the head of my meat hang out.

By the way, it was an old trick among guys in the know to buy a pair of swim trunks with a built-in supporter and remove the "ball brassiere," as they were called. That way your rod would swing against the cloth when you walked and guys on the prowl would get the idea that what you had swinging might be available.

He raised his head for a better look and I started getting hard. He ran his tongue across his lower lip and I headed in his direction.

I walked up and pulled my trunks down midway to my knee-caps and my dick leaped toward his face. He opened his mouth and I buried it to the hilt, then started fucking his face. He was a good cocksucker and took it in long, slow strokes: all the way out to the corona, then all the way in to the bush.

There's something about getting your dick sucked on the beach that makes it special when you blow your load. I steadied myself by grabbing hold of his shoulders and gave him my first, thick load of the day. He gulped it down in appreciation. I looked down between his legs and saw he was shooting his own load onto the rocks.

I pulled up my trunks and said "Thanks," then started down the cliffs. That's how I like cocksucking—if I'm getting it or giving it—no conversation, just good throat and stiff dick.

I went back the next day to the same place but it was deserted. I didn't know if I had lucked out or what the day before. But I figured if that cocksucker knew about this place, then others must know about it, too.

I had a plan. I took off my trunks and settled back so that I could catch the sunlight. I put my trunks between my legs in case the wrong person started climbing up. I discovered I had the best vantage point and could see anyone approaching before they could see me, or see all of me. I pulled out a Lucky and figured I'd know in a couple of hours if this was going to be a hot spot. And if not, well, I'd be working on my tan.

I probably sat there for a half hour before I saw anyone begin climbing up the cliffs. He looked to be about thirty, casually dressed but not in swim trunks, dark hair, possibly Italian. My cock was half hard and hanging down between my legs. I saw him look my way, then begin to move in my direction.

Back in those days, pants were much fuller-cut than they are now. So when I say that I could see a sausage hanging down his pant leg, you can believe this man had some meat. He reached my level of the cliff and didn't seem at all fazed that I was sitting there with my cock jutting out.

He gave a little grin and asked if I had a smoke, which I offered him. That let me get up on my knees so that I was facing his crotch. He bent down for the light, then straightened up and took a drag. The sausage in front of me jumped a jig in the khaki pants. It was all the encouragement I needed. I reached up and pulled down the zipper, fishing the fat tube out of his boxer shorts.

He just spread his legs apart a little while I worked his cock and balls out through his zipper.

I've seen a lot of big meat in my time but this was one I would have liked to marry! It was about half hard and already as fat as a salami, a smooth, long tube of skin that ended in a fat, skin-covered head. I held it in front of me, both hands holding it, looking at the opening of his skin and the dark red head peeking out.

I figured this to be a real throat-ripper, but it snaked its way down my throat as smooth as silk. It actually didn't get much bigger, just harder—and not completely hard; it always felt a little soft in my mouth.

And it sure tasted good! I've always preferred Mediterranean cock, both the uncut and the cut variety. There's something about that olive-hued meat that tastes extra nice.

I swallowed as much of his pole as I could, but I couldn't get all of it in my mouth. Nonetheless, I think I took more than he was used to having in a guy's mouth, because he really had a pleasant look of surprise on his face while I was sucking him.

At one point, he closed his eyes and started grinding his hips, like he was fucking standing up. I stayed with him, his thick cock sloshing in and out of my jaw. I wondered if he was thinking about some sweetheart.

He gasped; then the cum started pouring out of his cock, rich and thick and sweet. I swallowed it down like a champ, sucking and tonguing his cockhead and foreskin, balancing his low-hanging balls in my hand.

A lot of uncut guys pull away right after they come. I always figured it was because their cockheads are sensitive and the continued sucking after they shoot is irritating. But not this guy, he just stood there and let me work on it all I wanted. Long enough to start getting hard again.

After a while, he pulled it out. "I gotta go to work now, buddy. See you 'round."

I had a lot of hot times at that beach that year, until I moved to the East, but I never saw the Dago again.

THE BROTHERS

Once upon a time I was visiting an old friend in New York. It was my first trip to the Big Apple, and my friend had promised to show me the sights. Back in Little Rock, where I live, you can count the sights on the fingers of one hand and still have enough room left to hold a cocktail glass and a canapé.

My friend had promised that he would take me someplace where I could suck all the dick I wanted, to make up for the ongoing drought in Little Rock. There's dicks in Little Rock to suck, but believe me, you wouldn't bother with most of them.

The place we went to was a porno theater called the Cinema Art Palace. They had live shows. I thought the idea of live shows was nice—there's nothing better than seeing a hot man with a big dick shaking it in my face, unless he's shoving it down my throat.

We sat down in the front row. The show started with a muscular young black guy who was dressed as a construction worker dancing to a Village People's song. When he stripped off, he had a big black hose of a dick that swayed when he walked and nice nuts. He got it hard real fast and waved it right in my face. I looked over at my friend, who was grinning from ear to ear. This man's dick was about two inches from my mouth.

He danced over to another section of the front row and waved it in another guy's face; that guy leaned forward and sucked on the head. The dancer climbed up with one foot on each of the armrests and fucked the guy in the mouth a few quick strokes, then jumped back on the stage. I couldn't believe my eyes!

The black dancer stayed on the stage after that, but kept coming up to the front as he jacked his dick. Time flies when you're fascinated; he shot his load all over the stage and bowed and smiled and turned around and was gone before I knew it.

"This place is wild!" I told my friend, who now had his dick out of his pants.

The next guy who came onstage was a skinny youth with stringy hair who looked like he needed a good meal. Just the sort of stuff Little Rock is full of! All I can remember about him was that he couldn't get it up and he finally just bowed and left the stage.

Two guys came out next, and I thought my heart would stop. Two Puerto Ricans, both tall and lean and very sexy-looking. They weren't twins, but they did favor each other, and they could easily have been brothers.

Their act was very slow and quite sexy. They would undress a little, pose a little, one would look at the other; they would undress some more, pose some more, until they were both naked.

Such hunks! Beautiful olive skin without a flaw. Black, curly hair. Dark, deep eyes with long lashes. And their dicks—each one a perfect sausage hanging down a good seven inches. I've always been a softy for Latinos, and these two young men could have convinced me to try and walk on water.

By the time they were hard, so was I. I didn't take my dick out like my friend did—but it was hard as a rock all the same. These two beautiful young men stood facing each other on the stage and jacked off in unison, stroke for stroke. And they shot at the same time, their loads splattering against each other's stomach. The audience was making such a noise you almost couldn't hear the disco music blaring away in the theater. They got a lot of applause, and they really stole my heart!

The best is yet to come. After another dancer came on (another stringy-haired type) I decided I wanted to get up and walk around, so I told my friend I was going to pee and to get a cup of coffee. The men's room was behind the stage. I was just about to go in when I heard a sexy voice laugh and say something in Spanish from behind this other door, right next to the men's room. I had a sneaking suspicion it might be the dressing room for the dancers. I knocked very lightly. The conversation stopped. I tried the handle and opened the door and walked right in. There they both were— one sitting in a chair, his swollen dick hanging down between his legs, and the other standing in front of a mirror, wiping the sweat off his body with a hand towel. They both looked at me, but they didn't throw me out, so I closed the door and started telling them how wonderful their show was, and how beautiful they were, and hot, and how I was so glad I had come to this theater and seen them perform—anything I could think of to just keep talking.

They weren't the least bit apprehensive, and they smiled as if they understood every word I said, although I'm positive all they understood was that I liked them.

The one in the chair started scratching his balls and, of course, I had to stare. I stopped talking and just watched him scratch those beautiful brown globes. The other one said something to him in Spanish and he smiled at me and picked up his long cock in his hand and sort of motioned with his head. I didn't bat an eye, I just walked over, squatted down, and took that dark, smooth pipe in my mouth.

I've never tasted silk, but this young man's cock tasted like silk. It slid down my throat and he shoved his butt forward and spread his legs so I got every inch in my mouth. It started growing and I started sucking. Such a smooth, perfectly proportioned piece of meat!

The other guy was talking real low, and the guy I was sucking was moaning real low. His cock got rock-hard and he put his hands on my shoulders to guide my head up and down on it. He groaned again and unloaded a stream of sweet come down the back of my throat. I just held on, his dick buried in me, while he finished shooting.

I sucked on it until it started getting soft again, then looked up at him—he was still smiling. He motioned with his head toward the other guy, who had come over and was standing next to us. I turned and reached up and met his cock on its way to my face. I still had one hand grasped around the smooth, soft cock in the chair, and deep-throated the standing one. Such slender, muscular thighs! I reached up with my free hand and held on to his butt while he fucked my face with his long, straight cock.

The one in the chair was holding the back of my head, pushing it forward on his friend's stiff cock; in almost no time it, too, was pouring its load down my throat. They started talking to each other while I was still drinking come.

I stood up a little wobbly from being bent-kneed for so long, and said thank you first to one and then the other, nodding a little each time. They both smiled. I hated to leave, and I stood there for a minute, just letting my eyes drink in these two beautiful men, their swollen cocks hanging down, smiles on their faces—what a vision!

My friend was standing outside the dressing room door when I came out. He was positively grinning from ear to ear. But he never told me if he had set this up, or if I had simply stumbled into paradise for a few minutes.

PART FOUR

VIDEO:

HOW WE

LOOK AT

SEX

The single major change in the world of pornography—gay or any other kind—in the past decade has been the advent of video. Suddenly visual pornography was something that could be brought into the home. The viewer had fairly easy access to the technology—new stores opened up that rented not only the tapes, but also the VCRs necessary to play them.

It used to be that people had to enter an adult theater to see pornography. They had to be willing to be witnessed as consumers of porn. The theaters were never well kept; they were most often, in fact, places where, as Michael Bronski and Christopher Wittke have written, sex was going to happen in dark corners and men's rooms, not just on the screen. An adult theater was not a place for the squeamish, nor was it a place for people who were intent on having sex with one another. The theaters could be a meeting ground for anonymous sex, but they weren't conducive to any form of privacy.

The video changed all that. Now only an understanding clerk at the rental store need know what you're going to watch, and you can watch in privacy by yourself or, if you choose, with a partner or partners.

Such a massive explosion of technology has to change the way we view things. The video has certainly altered how many gay men perceive themselves and their sexuality. Norman Shapiro is a fascinating artist whose works have, until now, been contained in chapbooks and other self-published forms and circulated only through private channels, most often through art dealers.

Shapiro is a retired high school art teacher. When he left teaching he was faced with a new freedom. His income was secure, and his art could exist for its own sake, he decided. He wanted to be a pornographer and to be one who broke rules. He wanted to free himself, in fact, from the idea of creating art and, as he says in the introduction to his story, simply create pornography. He began this process as a self-described straight man. He has ended it, by his own admission, as someone who has become "a little bit gay" as a result of his erotic exploration.

Dave Kinnick is a Los Angeles journalist for such publications as *The Advocate*. His beat is the new porn industry, and especially its stars, the new icons of gay male sexuality. He views all of them with a certain critical distance, but takes the actors and their producers on their own terms, as performers and entrepreneurs.

In "Slaveboy Weekend" Kinnick has written about an outgrowth of the porn video industry. As if to prove that there must always be obfuscation between reality and fiction, Kinnick has reported on a new phenomenon, the video weekend.

People who will be the eventual purchasers of video porn are now invited to come to the actual taping of the films. For a very considerable sum, producers not only allow the customers on the set, but arrange for the stars to be nude waiters at privately catered meals and to be available for private photo sessions. (One result, video lovers tell me, is that now there is often a distracting noise in the background of many videos. It's the sound of the private clients' cameras clicking away during the taping.)

If the video set can actually be a place where pornographic fantasies can be lived out, then the video store, the marketplace for these ideas and images, must also be a spot where sex becomes available. Larry Duplechan, an accomplished gay novelist, has used a video store as the scene for a short story. Duplechan has, like many gay authors, found ways to put sex into his novels. His gay characters have used sex to find themselves and their lovers all along. But this is one of the first times he's set out to write a purely pornographic story, one that could be included in this book. He has accomplished his goal like the professional he is.

NORMAN SHAPIRO

SCENARIO

FOR A

PORN

FLICK

THIS STORY APPEARED IN ONE OF MY ARTIST'S
books called There's More to a Book Than Its Cover. *I dovetailed
excerpts from a comic strip,* Working Out, *I drew along with it. Some
were on acetate sheets. The effect was bold line illustrations overlaying the
printed text. The acetate itself suggested "film." As one reads the book, one
notices that the scale of the printed text varies from page to page. The
mimicry or equivalent is of images made by a camera pulling back and
zooming in. I chose to overlap or repeat sections of the text on consecutive
pages, hoping the reader sees the text as a continuum similar to frames on
film. The overlap suggests not stills but a movie projector sending a flow of
moving images onto a screen.*

*So reading a book designed in this mode would be like seeing a movie!
I think of it as a cubist kind of thing. It's not so much that it's illusionistic
or realistic as that it works one medium to give us equivalences: indelible*

images but in another medium. For me, as an artist, authenticity and realism are really secondary. I am essentially interested in its being pornographic.

We're dealing in imagination, prurience, archetypal (or stereotypical) imagery of a kind to stimulate my own gonads. The version presented here has been modified for this anthology. I did so to compensate for its having none of the aforementioned effects. I hope this version can stand up as presented here.

SCENARIO FOR A PORN FLICK: He's a boy of about eighteen. Good build. His face still hasn't had its first shave. We see him coming out of the breaking surf. His wet undershorts cling revealingly to his crotch and asscheeks. The guy behind him is in his late thirties. He's completely nude. His body hair lies flat and slick on his gleaming sunburned torso. He runs past the boy, playfully shoving him. He knocks him off balance and the two fall together into the shallow, rolling surf.

They're laughing, rolling in a tangle toward the shore. The man tugs the boy's shorts down off his pelvis. The boy wrestles to hold onto them. They struggle till the man gets the shorts down around the boy's calves. The grinning boy gains his footing as the garment slips to shore on its own. The boy picks up his garment and chases after his companion.

They tumble together onto a blanket spread out at the edge of a grassy ridge. We see the boy's face up close. He's still laughing. We see his expression change. His eyes close.

There's a low-level shot of the boy, and a back view of the guy cradling him. The camera moves up and around from behind. We see the guy making head. The overhead shot takes in the boy, and how his hands are grappling with the guy.

BOY: No fair. Please, Jack, ya gotta stop.

But Jack won't quit. The boy's rubbery cock goes way into Jack's mouth. He slides one hand under the boy; the other hand has his balls.

The boy's breathing hard. His mouth is wide open. His arms lift up around his head. No resistance now.

The camera draws back. A wide shot is taken of the pristine, empty beach in front of the two figures on the grassy ridge.

Fade and cut.

The same boy's smiling face is seen close up. He's under the shower spray. We see him soaping his torso. Jack comes in through the curtains and joins him. They kiss. It's a sultry embrace.

Jack runs his hands all over the boy's bod. Then he takes hold of the boy's stiff cock. The boy clings, his arms wrapped around Jack. He masturbates the cock to stand-up hard-on.

JACK: This is so right, Gary. You know it. It's got to be the whole way. I want you, Gary.

Gary nods dreamily.

GARY: I'm so hot, Jack. You make me hot. I'll do anything you want. Honest. Anything you say.

They kiss some more. Jack eases Gary down. The boy is on his knees. He starts making Jack's dark-skinned cock. Jack clasps Gary. He humps, shoves his stiffening cockshaft farther into the boy's mouth.

The view is from above the showerhead for a shot looking down on the two. Jack, head tilted back, looks exultant. The camera zooms in to study the pleasure expressed on his cruel but handsome face. He arches. The spray spatters his well-formed pecs.

Cut.

Gary is sprawled face down, asleep. Jack lies beside him, the man's forearm draped across his back. Jack's asleep also. The camera takes a slow tour of Jack, then Gary. The tour of Jack ends at his dark, glossy cock.

The boy stirs. The camera starts on him. The tour accents the boy's androgyny, catches a shot of his firm asscheeks streaked with glossy lube.

New scene:

A convertible sports car is making sixty on a straight stretch of scenic road. The boy, Gary, is behind the wheel. We see him in profile.

(Jack's voice:)
Blackstar is one of those re-creations, an alpine castle. It's owned by a man named Morgen LeFey. I'm sending you there to be with him. You're the promise I made, Gary. I know he won't be disappointed. The castle is way up there. It's at the top of this mountain. You'll love it. You won't be the only boy there. You've all been specially selected.

We hear this as the car winds its way up and up the mountain road. The sequence ends with a spectacular view of the Blackstar castle.

Cut.

HAROLD: Mr. LeFey will be here tomorrow. Your room is just at the head of the stairs. Please follow me.

We see Gary following a bald, broad-shouldered man in his mid-forties. He is without his jacket, but looking very much like a butler. He leads Gary up an impressive staircase. The interior seems cavernous. Huge Gothic windows situated high on the walls cast slanting beams of light onto the ornately decorated interior. He is led to a room that is quite small.

HAROLD: You can see, sir, why in medieval days this was called a closet. You will be meeting the other young gentlemen after you've had a chance to freshen up. Your costumes are in the top drawer of this bureau.

The man leaves. Gary sits briefly on the four-poster bed. He gets up to look at a door. It opens on a bathroom. Gary strips. The camera savors the slow strip. Gary, once naked, caresses himself, grips his cock and asscheeks. He falls back onto the bed. His cock is all of twelve inches.

A ghostly Jack is in bed with him. His hand and Gary's play over his torso. Gary shuts his eyes.

His eyes come suddenly open, surprise on his features. A blond boy sits at the foot of the bed. He looks to be sixteen, maybe younger.

THE BLOND: I'm Lee. Harold sent me to fetch you down.

The boy draws closer, leans and stretches to kiss the tip of Gary's rubbery cock. He signs him to silence. The camera gets a good angle on him making a bit of head.

The boy's cock-naked too, only he's wearing thigh-length stockings and a see-through tank top. Lee suddenly slips back off the bed. He moves rapidly to the bureau. He gets out of the top drawer a similar see-through top and thigh-length stockings. The stockings have a harlequin pattern. Gary grabs Lee to him. The boy begins to resist. They kiss. Just as Gary gropes for his cute cock, the boy gets away from him.

LEE: You'd better put this on and come on down with me. Harold's
waiting for us.

The next scene:

They're descending the magnificent stairway together, Gary in costume. Lee leads him to a pair of heavy doors at the foot of the
steps. He opens one of them and ushers Gary inside.

It's a dark high-ceilinged room. A huge fireplace dominates one
wall. Illumination is mainly from its flaming embers. Four boys in
costume crouch, asscheeks high, on red-cushioned stools. Harold
stands at a long table. He's naked, his legs sheathed in leather
leggings. We see him with Gary's eyes, scan his torso, his impressive hairiness, his muscularity. The black pubic hair is oily, glistening over a dark glistening cock.

HAROLD: Take your place, Lee. (Then to Gary) Welcome, Gary. At
least one of these young men will be exercised. You've come
in time to witness the pleasure he achieves.

Lee takes up a stool and sets it next to the end boy on the right.
He crouches, asshole up like the others.

Harold selects a long blunt instrument from the table. He hands
it to Gary. One end is a handle. It fits neatly in Gary's hand. The
rest is unmistakably cock. Gary follows Harold, who picks up a
similar instrument. They walk behind the row of crouching boys.
Harold stops. He aims the cock end at the uptilted asshole. The
boy is seen to grit his teeth. Harold shoves the full length of it
into the boy.

HAROLD: Pleasure relies on two things, Gary. A boy's horny need,
and a man's talent in providing for that need.

Harold lets the instrument go. The camera zooms in on it and the asscheeks of the boy. The boy has it quiver and wag. We see him arch, crouch lower, spread his legs wider. His pink cock rubs agitatedly along the cushion's edge.

HAROLD: Please grasp Tim's dildo, Gary. I'm sure Tim would greatly appreciate it.

The boy sobs, grabs his ass as Gary delicately takes hold of the handle.

HAROLD: Remember to be compassionate. You wouldn't want to hurt Tim, would you?

Gary's eyes glaze over, his mouth turns down. He begins the boy's fucking.

Cut.

The last boy leaves the room. Only Harold and Gary remain. A tall bearded man appears in the doorway, wearing a white hip-length toga.

CHALMERS: Is he Jack's?

HAROLD: Yes, Professor Chalmers. He's been promised to Mr. LeFey. We expect him tomorrow.

CHALMERS: Has LeFey given you any restrictive instructions regarding him?

Gary's eyes fasten curiously on the newcomer. His face betrays confusion and frustration.

HAROLD: None whatever, sir.

CHALMERS: Then he'll come with me. Come, boy, I'm sure Harold
can spare you for the time being.

Gary and Harold exchange looks of longing and disappointment.

The next scene is a book-lined study. The bearded man has seated
himself on a high-backed spindly stool. Professor Chalmers separates
his robe to give the boy a view of his hairy crotch and thighs.

CHALMERS: Stand beside me, Gary. I want your cock within reach
of my hand. Three years ago, your sponsor, Jack, stood here
with me. He was older than you at the time. But I must say,
not braver or more handsome.

Nostrils quivering, body tense, the boy places himself within reach
of the older man.

CHALMERS: Yes, lovely. (as he caresses Gary's cock) You are well
endowed. Kneel for me. Now.

The boy frowns. He hesitates before descending to his knees. He
stares at the floor. Chalmers tilts the boy's chin till his eyes are
level with Chalmers's stiffening cock.

CHALMERS: Put my cock to your lips, Gary. Has it been very long
since you've had cock?

His hands grasp Gary. He fondles his scalp, gathers locks of his
auburn hair. He presses Gary to rub his lips along the whole of his
enormous erection.

CHALMERS: It's always too long between times, isn't it? Don't be
shy, greedy boy.

Gary draws the cock between his lips, suctions it, fills his mouth,
and presses his face to the man's gray-flecked bush.

CHALMERS: Greedy boy! That will do for now. I want you to lie face down, Gary, across that desk.

Gary's cock is now every bit as stiff as the professor's. He bends across the desk, spreads out his arms, and grips the edges. Chalmers plays his hands on Gary's ass. He traces the crack with his fingertips.

The camera circles overhead as he kneels behind Gary and puts his face to the boy's ass. We see his tongue flicker. He washes up and down, then presses to delve deeper. Gary quivers, spreads his legs.

After some extensive tight close-ups, the camera eases back to see Chalmers shrug off his robe. He gathers the unresisting boy off the desk and down onto the floor.

Glassy-eyed, Gary takes hold of the professor's cock. He straddles, aims it to his ass. The professor fastens to the boy's right nipple as the hot boy arches, seats his cock.

The camera gets to the floor, low, showing us the cock-splayed asscheeks. The huge cock undulates, fills the asshole. The fucking is steady.

The man tilts Gary. He eases him over on his side. The fucking becomes vigorous, the thrusts like blows socking the buttocks. The boy gasps and lifts both arms above his head. The agony and the rapture are written on his agonized face.

The cocksman slips off. Gary does not move. He lies, breathing hard as Chalmers gathers his legs, aligns with his asshole again.

One leg is up, draped over Chalmers's right shoulder. Chalmers's cock wedges deep. Hilting his cock, he presses and locks the boy till rapture and release are written in the cocksman's face. The boy's semen spills.

The scene closes with Chalmers making head, his fist wedged between the boy's rosy buns.

New scene: Long shadows. Light comes from the hearth, throwing sensual shadows. Making the shadows are two men and two boys. Off to the side, more in the gloom, are three more figures. Three boys. Two on one. The boy between is Gary.

Cut.

Bright sky; the sun is below the western rim. Gary walks alone on the parapets. The style of his hair is different from what it was. His lips are painted red. He has on striped leggings and a black toga. He fixes his mascaraed eyes on the spectacular vista.

Harold comes out of a nearby passageway. Gary smiles upon seeing him. They kiss. The embrace is passionate. When Harold breaks it, Gary is guided down to his huge cock. The camera lifts skyward.

Cut.

(The subsequent action sequences of Gary with Harold, and his subjugation to dildos of various shapes and sizes, have been deleted in this version.)

The awaited Morgan LeFey is a man in his late fifties, of medium height. His chiseled features are crowned by a huge shock of the whitest hair. A monocle glints over one eye on his brown rugged face. He appears to be wearing a normal white suit. But his cock is conspicuously displayed below his open jacket.

LEFEY: So you are Jack's boy. I'm sorry our meeting has been so delayed. I'm certain your stay at Blackstar has been a pleasant one. So glad you could come. You will address me as Mr. LeFey. You know why you are here.

GARY: Jack promised me to you. I'm here for you, Mr. LeFey.

LEFEY: Yes. That's right. I am so glad you understand.

The man extends his hand to the completely naked Gary. He leads
Gary away from the attending entourage of men and boys. They
proceed down a winding stairway. They come into a mirrored chamber. Dominating the room is a gleaming contraption of chrome,
ropes, pulleys, chains, netting, and manacles. LeFey leads the boy
to it.

LEFEY: This was made for me in Heidelberg.

He takes Gary's wrists and secures them to leather manacles, urging
him to step and lean so that the machine might do the rest. Knees
here, a leaning in this direction. The naked boy is literally captured
by the leverage of his own weight. The old man tugs at one rope
and then another, maneuvering Gary like a mannequin.

Gary hangs in space. He stares at the profusion of images of himself
in the mirrors. The old man slips a condom-like sheath on the boy's
cock. It weights it, tugs it vertically.

LEFEY: Jack promised you to me some three years ago. Can you believe
    I've waited for you for that long, Gary? He served and lived. He
    showed fear. But not you. And that makes it so perfect. It makes
    everything permissible. That is as it should be.

(The camera maintains its ongoing tour of Gary in bondage.)
    Does this arouse you? (His hand slides along Gary's pectoral,
    massages his nipple.) I am aroused. My cock cannot dissemble.
    Look at it, boy. In this, we are no different.

LeFey turns away. He dips his right hand into a jar of blue lubricant. He returns to Gary and works his fingers between his uptilted
buns.

The boy shudders, struggles in the harness wildly. LeFey grips Gary's cock forcibly. He plunges his fingers and fucks vigorously with his dripping hand.

The finger-fucking and masturbating is inexorable. Gary comes.

Released by LeFey, his body lax and motionless, he sways in the harness.

The pederast's monocle catches the light. LeFey's face is flushed, eyes aglow, demonic. He works the chains to align his cock with the boy's face. Gary stares expressionlessly at LeFey's sparsely haired pubis. The gnarled uncut cock tilts, brushes his face. LeFey has to clasp the boy's scalp. He offers him his scrotum with its single low-hung ball. LeFey waits. Moments pass. He smiles beatifically.

Cut.

We are treated to a collage sequence of the several ways Gary is sodomized.

LEFEY: Perfect. You're all Jack said you'd be.

LeFey lets Gary slip down out of the harness. He draws him to his feet. They kiss, this time with no reluctance. He leads the subdued boy to a red circular seat. Gary lies across it.

Screen credits flow up as Gary matches with LeFey's cock. They're eating, sixty-nine. The credits continue up the screen. LeFey, dildo in one hand and a needle-like instrument in the other, licks at Gary's bone-stiff cock. The boy becomes intensely passionate. The last of the credits slide up the screen. LeFey has eased away. Gary lies very still, torso twisted, prone on the cushion, his mouth agape, arms akimbo, legs lax, his wide eyes sightless.

Finis.

DAVE KINNICK

SLAVEBOY

WEEKEND

HOW COULD ANY RED-BLOODED JOURNALIST AND pornographic connoisseur pass up a weekend of gourmet food, naked slave boys, and videotape? The brochure arrived in my office in May and promised all this and more, in a weekend-long seminar conducted by Washington, D.C.-based fetish video producer Bob Jones. For three days in July, Bob would gather three dozen curious paying guests at a gay resort located in one of the more obscure parts of the country for the first in a series of events that would walk a thin line between art and obscenity—not to mention between tourism and tribalism.

In attendance would be a dozen "stars" of gay video, acting as models, waiters, and all around good-time fellas. At Jones's invitation, I flew out from L.A. to watch and observe. What follows is a relatively unedited journal of my experiences, written on a laptop computer that, in the high humidity of the weekend, kicked in and out intermittently. It was not all easy, but it felt mighty real at the time.

Thursday, July 18
7:40 a.m.
I arrive at LAX and meet young porn star Trey Tempest, who is to accompany me on Delta Flight 100 to Atlanta and adventures beyond. We ask the curbside skycap to check our bags through to the Tri-Cities Airport in Tennessee. He's never heard of it, and has to write it in on a generic luggage tag. Even our luggage doesn't know where we're going.

9:30 a.m.
The plane takes off fifty minutes late. The in-flight movie stars Charlton Heston, my favorite actor. We ignore it. The food arrives an hour late. Trey is the last passenger on our L1011 to be fed. He does not give me the cherry on his fruit plate. He looks over my shoulder as I write this and says, "All you had to do was ask for it." Later, he tells me he is now directing videos as well as performing in them. He's just completed one that he thinks will be called *Trey Does Thailand*.

6:00 p.m.
After a harried connection at Atlanta, our plane comes in for a landing at the small airport. Trey wonders out loud what the state we've been flying over is. His best guess is Oregon. Okay, so for a bright kid, his geography ain't all that great. We're picked up in a van by Alex, a Bob Jones model whom I recognize from *Boot Slaves in Bondage*. We meet up with Vivid model Brad Chase, just in from Chicago; Troy Kidwell, a *Playgirl* model from Florida; and Mark Carson, a toothsome but sweet working boy from Boston. The ride to the lodge takes thirty minutes. All the buildings we pass look like they were ordered from the Sears catalog's garden shed section. Every other one is a church.

7:05 p.m.
We arrive at the Timberfell compound. The whole area lies in a heavily wooded canyon with a creek running down the center. The first structure you see when you drive in is a somewhat dilapidated barn that houses about a dozen guests in bunks. Nearby is a newly completed pool, indoor Jacuzzi, and pool house with showers and sauna. The main lodge is a quarter mile up a gravel road.

7:30 p.m.
Dinner is served in the main lodge. It's a sit-down affair for twenty-three guests and staff that provides my first chance to see the naked slave boys. "Michael" serves the salad course, dressed in a stunning chain collar and chrome cock ring. The salad is dressed in oil, vinegar, and herbs. "Scott," boasting hugely distended nipples, keeps our water glasses full. The third nude and becollared waiter is named Guy Fox, and I can't describe how he is garnished because he is too beautiful to look at below the neck. His mouth hangs open tantalizingly throughout the serving of the meal. I will later discover that it is always this way. The dinner is pork sautéed in brandy and mushrooms, with fresh peas, and potatoes au gratin. The coffee after dinner is flavored with vanilla. The guests are not.

8:15 p.m.
I walk back to the barn via a path through trees and creek. The sounds of crickets are everywhere. Apart from certain young porn stars, I have never heard anything so loud. I see my first fireflies apart from the audioanimatronic ones at Disneyland's Pirates of the Caribbean ride. The fact that I am now in the South in a major way starts to sink in.

9:40 p.m.
Jody Hanvey, a stunning blond thirty-year-old from Atlanta (and winner of the 1988 Mr. Gay America title), drags me up to his room to show me something. It's a videotape that he has taken of himself, nude, earlier this afternoon. He has planned a still photo shoot for

tomorrow for a series of safe-sex art pieces he wants to distribute free through AIDS organizations in Georgia. He solicits my aid.

10:07 p.m.
Some of the guests come down to the pool area and mingle with the boys. Everyone here is selling something or someone. The trick is to discover what the commodity of the hour is.

Friday, July 19
2:00 a.m.
It would be nice to go to sleep. My berth for this night is on the floor of the barn. Unfortunately, the floor of the barn is occupied by a middle-aged man with a German accent interrogating a youngish masochist who is upside down on a rack being yanked around by his balls while Guy (the most beautiful boy in the world) makes like Carol Merrill with the torture implements. It's the first of Bob's video shoots for the weekend. Staff and off-duty slave boys quickly form a peanut gallery on one side. I retreat to the Jacuzzi and a six-pack. The bubble noises partially mask the highly cinematic screams of pain from the barn.

3:50 a.m.
Sometimes the term "clothing optional" also means "good taste optional."

4:15 a.m.
The scene now over, the search for beds commences. The lucky boys have found patrons and spend the night in the lodge. The press is offered a junket in Brad Chase's top bunk in Room 2 over the barn. He accepts, only Brad abandons his post and is molested by three men as he sprawls on a lower bunk. Lesson for the evening is: seek high ground in sleeping accommodations, and if you don't want It fooled with, don't leave Its luscious naked roundness lying out where people can get to It.

8:15 a.m.
I awake and notice three things. One is that there is a big black

dog under the bed. His name is Max. Also under the bed is Max's owner, a young nudist with a spacious mustache and a shaved crotch that is very eye-catching for various reasons. In addition to the dog, a leather ball stretcher and a flashlight swim into focus. Useful things to have in the dark, no doubt.

11:15 a.m.
The lodge's principal owner, David Yoder, takes me on a tour of the facilities. The rooms in the lodge are small but tastefully appointed. Some have slings under the bed that can be hung in seconds from hooks in the ceiling. Yoder obviously takes great pride in the place and his enthusiasm is infectious.

1:30 p.m.
Jody of Atlanta takes me on the photo shoot with three of the other boys. The most beautiful boy in the world asks me to help arrange the chains trailing across his thighs and butt.

4:00 p.m.
I pitch my first tent, which is to be my home for the next two days. It is a nonsexual experience.

8:00 p.m.
Dinner over, I hurry back to the barn area, steal a pool float, and drag it to my tent. Inside the tent, it is very hot and very humid. I strip to my underwear, dripping with sweat, and watch the sunset over the distant hills. I try reading a copy of *The Advocate* before falling asleep, but it is too damp. Note to Liberation Publications: get crisper paper.

10:15 p.m.
I wake up from a nap to find the world changed. A fog has come up. The temperature has dropped ten degrees. A stage has been built at one end of the pool and lights on long extension cords from the pool house play eerily over the stage for the "Meet the Performers" portion of the program. Each boy comes out, strips,

and does a little dance. Guests sit around in the dark on lawn chairs, snapping video and still pictures and commenting on the gamboling boyflesh. Kenny, the armed-to-the-teeth security guard for the weekend, is in charge of handing out play money, which the guests use to tip the boys. I wonder what the exchange rate is.

11:45 p.m.
Scott Fox, Guy's ersatz but equally lovely "brother," scores big in the tips department—he walks away from the pool with $160 in Monopoly money sticking out of his drawers.

2:30 a.m.
Someone, presumably a redneck homophobe, rams a car through the front gate and sets fire to a bale of hay out front. Not smart. The hay belongs to the mayor of the local town. The Greene County sheriff's department pledges to send a car tomorrow night to watch the gate. The attitude of the local politicos is very supportive of the lodge, which brings a lot of money into the region.

Saturday, July 20
11:30 a.m.
After a light breakfast at the lodge, a bridge up the hill from the barn is dressed with naked slave boys for the taping of *Bound Boys in Slave Hollow.* It is the major photo op of the trip. Trey, Brad, Mark, and Mike are tied to the bridge railing by guest bondage person Larry Townsend of *Drummer* magazine. Bob explains his conceptualization of the scene. The camera fades in on a shot of the beautiful green Tennessee hillside and, as the titles roll, tilts down to reveal the boys struggling against their ropes. As Bob admits, we the audience do not know why or how the boys got there. That's not important. The Fox brothers, Guy and Scott, then enter the scene from stage left to do some tormenting of the helpless boys. The stillness of the early afternoon is interrupted for ninety minutes by the noise of cicadas and autowinders.

1:30 p.m.
I come up with this great idea for a Bob Jones movie and hasten

to the pool house to write it down. Two boys are on a camping trip in the woods. They sit by the campfire. The sounds of the night are soothing. In the light of the flames, they begin to kiss and fondle each other. Suddenly the stillness of the night is disturbed by a horrible noise—half scream, half growl. It is answered by a second shriek. They discuss the matter, but finally turn in and suck each other's feet before going to sleep.

The next day on the trail, they come upon a pair of exhibitionist Sasquatches, humping each other. Both shocked and strangely intrigued, the boys watch from a distance and finally join in, discovering that the giant creatures especially enjoy a good spanking. Later, they shave the bigfoot creatures from head to toe, return to California with them, and pass the two anthropological throwbacks off as their uncles from New York.

5:20 p.m.
I play a one-on-one game of water polo with Trey Tempest. We miss the ball a lot and half drown, our best volley being seven contiguous shots. Afterwards, in the shower, a man makes arrangements with Trey to do a private photo shoot after dinner. I feel a little left out.

6:15 p.m.
Alex takes a swim. Alex has made fourteen foot-fetish videos. Bob says he has the most photographed feet in gay America. He's a six-foot-tall Kentucky boy with a pair of beautifully arched size twelves. He tells me that a man in North Carolina regularly pays $35 for his toenail clippings. I am impressed.

11:00 p.m.
The big event of the weekend commences poolside: the slave auction. The twelve boys come out one by one and are worked over by two leathermen while one of the guests, Marty, talks about their teeth and their sexual peccadillos. Twenty percent of the high bids go to local AIDS charities, and the winner gets the company of the boy for one hour, commencing immediately. The bidding for each,

again with play money, starts at $50. Jody sings a blond Elvis song and goes for $190. Trey goes for an even $100 due to a temporary lack of high-rollers in the audience. Brad Chase is up next. Who will buy?

11:48 p.m.
Brad goes for $375. The buyer announces that the entire amount will go to charity. The event raises a neat $1,000.

Sunday, July 21
9:30 a.m.
Another night in the tent, in which it rains occasionally as condensation collects on the three-foot-high roof and slides off onto my face. A squirrel attacks the tent just before daybreak. I fend it off with my half-awake whimpering noises. My electronic alarm clock seems to be on its last legs.

11:00 a.m.
Some of the guests are leaving. There is talk of some of the staff and boys driving over to Dollywood for the afternoon. It's about thirty minutes away. I don't think I could bear it. Back in L.A., I'd never say that an afternoon spent at a movie star's monument to self-aggrandizement would be difficult to swallow, but right now it sounds a bit like sorghum. Maybe the woods are having an effect on me.

11:45 a.m.
The foot fetishists have taken to hiding the boys' shoes in hard-to-find places. Jody enlists my aid in looking for one of his pairs of sneakers.

2:00 p.m.
One of the guests, Paul of Rhode Island, agrees to take Trey and Brad and me off the compound for lunch at the local truck stop. This plan calls for no small amount of moxie. And my, do we get looks. Perhaps it was me in my combat boots, multicolored drawstring

surfer pants, low-cut black Lycra tank top, and demi-mohawk. And
that is conservative compared to Brad's apparel, which makes him look
like a citified version of Daisy from *The Dukes of Hazzard*.

The accents peppering the Union 76 Davy Crockett truck stop
hit me like a redneck's baseball bat. I have heard very little of this
sort of thing at the lodge, even from the Southerners among the
staff and guests. For a moment, I remember where we really are,
and at the same time, how extraordinary it is that a place like
Timberfell can thrive in this community.

11:35 p.m.

One of the younger guests puts together an impromptu little
demonstration in the barn that blows me away. He owns an old-
fashioned acu-jac. One of the big, bruising models of years back
that comes in a wooden case with large steel knobs on it to control
the pressure and speed of the sucking action. Wearing a wetsuit
with an opening for his penis, he inserts his penis in the clear
plastic tube, which also has a vibrating hand sander (sans sandpaper)
attached to a leather harness and strapped to it. While the thing
"sucks" him, the other thing vibrates madly and makes a satisfying
racket. He does this standing spread-eagled in the barn, his arms
tied over his head with ropes passed through eyelets set in the old
building's uprights.

Now the really advanced part. While all this is going on, he
pisses in the tube, flooding the compartment and sending a clear
stream up the hose. Then, giving instructions to his curious onlookers, he has the suction in the tube suddenly reversed, and the fluid
is pumped back down the tube and into his wetsuit, giving him
an orgasm. American ingenuity at its best.

Monday, July 22
3:00 a.m.

I've been given an air-conditioned room on the top floor of the barn
for my last night. Unfortunately, the entire floor vibrates and shakes
with some ferocity. As a Californian, I rate this quake as about a
3.8. It seems to go on forever, though, and is in fact merely a small

orgy in progress two rooms over. At one point it stops, and there is some applause from the staff trying to sleep next door. Then it starts in again. What libertines! I have difficulty sleeping. At one point, the vibrations take on a different character—a new harmonic. This would be someone in the sling downstairs. I have no idea when I'll be able to sleep.

9:20 a.m.
I somehow wake up unassisted by my once-faithful little Casio alarm clock, which is so frizzed out now that it just reads "0L2 AL" in the digital window and makes pathetic bleating noises when I push the button to reset it. It is a clear, beautiful day—the most perfect since I've been here, and you would never know that anything untoward had been going on in the wee hours. At the lodge, there are hot coffee, tasty scrambled eggs with herbs, sausage, and muffins. Most everyone looks chipper. How do they do it?

11:40 a.m.
Goodbyes are said in the hot gravel parking lot near the barn. Too many goodbyes are said. We have something like forty minutes to make our plane. That does not stop certain boys from pulling the van over at the local bank so that they can cash their paychecks. Though the amounts are in the four-figure range, they take it in small bills. It's a cash industry. We make the plane with several seconds to spare. There is always time enough for twenties.

Even as we jet back to L.A., Jones's parting words echo in my head. "You've been such a good sport," he said. "You really are a true journalist." I am flattered. Perhaps now I am ready for the big assignments: slumber parties of the stars, Hollywood's favorite douche products, celebrity shrimp-jobs—the list of possibilities seems overwhelming. When I arrive home, a brochure awaits me describing the next Bob Jones event at the lodge. This September weekend will have a crime and punishment theme. It will feature customized manhunts, abductions by secret police, and the very best in arrest and interrogation fantasies. Once again, there will be naked slaves and gourmet food. This time, I won't pack a tie.

LARRY DUPLECHAN

VIDEO

X-PRESS

JESSE SHOVED THE DOOR OPEN AND THE MUSIC
blasted out so hard he could have sworn he could feel it against his
skin like a gust of wind: Billy Idol singing "Mony Mony" through
an audible sneer, the volume so high the bass line made the metal
door handle vibrate beneath Jesse's palm, made the floor throb un-
derfoot like a drumhead. A man, heavyset and balding, approached
the door just as Jesse opened it, coming out as Jesse was heading
in. Jesse held the door open for the older man, who stopped in the
open doorway for a moment to give Jesse an obvious once-over in
the yellowish mix of light coming from the neon Video X-Press
sign blinking over the door and the fluorescent light pouring out
with the Billy Idol boom-boom music.

Jesse watched the man's eyes flicker over him, taking in the
physique he'd worked so hard to build: his big pecs, the muscles

rippling beneath the smooth, brown skin of his arms and shoulders, the hard ridges of his belly that showed in clear relief under the tight red tank top he wore. Jesse noted how the man's eyes paused at the protuberant crotch of his grey cotton-and-spandex shorts, then moved down to his thick thighs, then back up to his crotch again, before finally looking up into Jesse's face.

"Thank you," the man said, his voice breathy. Jesse smiled, his teeth even and very white against the milk-chocolate color of his face. "No prob," he said.

The man opened his mouth as if to say something else, but then didn't, and hurried away. Jesse entered Video X-Press with an extra backbeat in his walk, striding in rock rhythm toward the checkout counter, swinging the long plastic bag containing one videotape. His full lips silently formed the words of the Billy Idol record as he went: "Ride ya poh-neh! Mo-ny Mow-neh!" Struck by the sudden temperature change from the warm, dry Santa Ana—blowing L.A. night outside Video X-Press to the air-conditioned inside, Jesse felt his nipples pucker beneath the thin material of his shirt, felt tiny goose bumps rise and fall on his bare thighs. He rubbed the palm of his free hand over his chest—once to warm his chilled nipples, then again just because he liked the way it felt.

He could only see one other customer in the store—an extremely tall person standing at the counter (from behind, Jesse couldn't tell if the person was male or female), dressed entirely in black, with spiked, Easter-egg-purple hair. Jesse glanced up at the twin nineteen-inch video monitors which hung from the ceiling about four feet above the counter. The monitors were showing *Mary Poppins* with the sound off. Jesse smiled as Julie Andrews floated down from a Walt Disney sky to the incongruous Billy Idol accompaniment.

Jesse couldn't see over or around the big black-clad figure at the counter, so he couldn't tell who was working the register until the person turned away and started toward the door. Jesse's smile grew wider when he saw The Kid standing behind the counter, wearing a very tight white T-shirt and a smile of his own. Jesse

approached the register, smiling every step of the way, dropped his
bag and then his elbows onto the counter, and stood practically
smile to smile with The Kid.

The Kid's smile was one of the things Jesse liked best about
him—and there was a lot to like about The Kid. His lips in repose
(they seemed almost always to be just slightly parted) or when
speaking were full and ruddy and infinitely suggestive of kissing.
When The Kid smiled, exposing his slight overbite and the one
long, deep dimple which indented his practically beardless right
cheek . . . well, at the moment it required most of Jesse's restraint
to keep him from clambering over the checkout counter. The Kid's
sandy blond crewcut looked freshly mown, and his T-shirt looked
as if he must have had it since he was a few years younger and a
good deal smaller: it was threadbare in spots (in particular, over
The Kid's left nipple) and seemed barely able to contain his broad,
angular shoulders.

Jesse generally thought of this kid as The Kid, even though
he knew the kid's name was Corey: he'd spoken with Corey dozens
of times and besides, the hand-lettered name tag pinned just above
The Kid's nearly exposed left nipple said COREY. Jesse sucked in a
breath through his mouth while he imagined sucking the nipple
that poked against the thin cotton of The Kid's T-shirt, brown and
enticing beneath the nearly translucent white. He could have sworn
he saw that sweet-looking tit pucker and point as he did.

Jesse knew Corey was the son of the man who owned and
managed Video X-Press—a solidly built man of fifty or so who
called himself Mac. He also knew Corey was on the gymnastics
team at UCLA, where he was a sophomore, which made him about
nineteen years old. Which seemed awfully young to Jesse, who'd
be thirty-six on his next birthday. Even safe in the knowledge that
he was youthful and good-looking and in damned good physical
shape—not a wrinkle, not a gray hair, not enough fat on his body
to fry an egg—thirty-six still seemed light-years away from nineteen; college felt like lifetimes ago.

"What's up?" Corey said, raising his voice to be heard over
Billy Idol's.

"Up?" Jesse repeated, still smiling. He glanced quickly down toward his crotch and said, "Nothing yet. How about yourself?"

Corey smiled through the blush he could feel creeping up around his ears. The fact was, the sight of Jesse's muscular, veiny arms and big chest in that tank top and the well-packed basket between Jesse's legs had gotten Corey better than half hard. He felt the head of his excitable teenage dick poking upward against the inside of his sawed-off sweatpants, and Corey was for the moment glad he was standing behind the counter where Jesse couldn't see. Corey had been harboring a secret crush on the handsome, older black guy for weeks. He knew Jesse was gay—he rented a lot of X-rated gay videos; and he was pretty sure Jesse liked him, too. He could tell by the way Jesse looked at him, joked around with him, the way Jesse's deep brown eyes connected with his own.

He also knew Jesse's full name (Jesse B. DuBois), his home address, and both his phone numbers (home and business) from the customer files on the computer. He'd even gone so far as to copy the information down on a scrap of paper and tuck it into his wallet, but he hadn't been able to make himself call.

"Could we turn Billy down just a *hair*?" Jesse said, yelling louder than necessary for effect.

"Sure," Corey said, and, reaching for the stereo tuner behind him, he turned down the volume of "White Wedding" by about half.

"Thanks," Jesse said.

"Anything for you," Corey answered with a little smile.

"Yeah, I'll bet," said Jesse. "Returning," he said, indicating the bag on the counter.

"Right," Corey said, pulling the videotape from the bag: the latest Matt Sterling suck-and-fuck epic. Jesse had kept the video for three consecutive nights: it had taken him several sessions to get through the entire eighty-five minutes. Corey smiled, raised an eyebrow. "This is a good one," he said.

"You've seen it?" Jesse asked.

"Oh, yeah," said Corey, though he actually hadn't.

"Oh, yeah?" said Jesse.

"Sure, why not?" Corey said, looking Jesse right in the eyes while running a light pen over the bar-coded spine of the videotape.

Since the first time he'd met The Kid, he'd been wondering if maybe Corey was gay, or bi, or at least young and randy and willing to experiment. At first, Jesse assumed it was just the wishful thinking of a dirty, relatively old man. But then The Kid began to say things to him when Mac was out of earshot, look at him in a way that made Jesse lick his lips and shift his weight, in a way that made him wonder. Of course, it could all have been just a cute, smart-ass kid teasing an older gay man. But now it seemed The Kid was a gay smut fan. Well . . .

"So where's Daddy tonight?" Jesse asked. He usually called Mac "Daddy" when talking to Corey; he usually called Corey "The Kid" when addressing Mac.

"Home," Corey said, tossing the empty plastic bag over his shoulder and into the big cardboard box used for recycling. "Threw out his back yesterday lifting a box of videos. Been flat on his back all day. It's just me tonight." And he gave Jesse one of those looks.

"I see," said Jesse, wondering if that look could mean anything like what he hoped it meant. Nah, he said to himself; probably not; when suddenly Corey was tracing Jesse's right bicep with his finger. The unexpected physical contact raised the hair on the back of Jesse's neck. He looked into Corey's smiling green eyes.

"These are nice," Corey said calmly, still looking into Jesse's eyes. "You work out every day?"

"Three or four times a week," Jesse said, his voice suddenly higher than usual. "What do I owe you?"

"For what?" Corey said, still fingering Jesse's arm.

"For the video."

Corey shrugged. "On the house."

"Really?" Jesse asked. "Why?"

Corey didn't answer. He raised his arms up over his head and stretched like a big pussycat. Jesse watched Corey's T-shirt rise, exposing the deep indentation of his navel and the dusting of light brown hair that started there and disappeared into his low-hanging homemade sweatshorts. Was it his imagination, Jesse wondered, or was The Kid getting a hard-on? He felt the unmistakable swelling in his own shorts: when Jesse got hard, it wasn't an easy thing to hide; and in a few seconds, he was going to be very hard. "I gotta close now," Corey said, still in midstretch.

"Well," said Jesse, "I guess I better go, then." He turned away quickly, hoping to hide the rapidly growing lump of his crotch.

"No," Corey said. "Why doncha hang around." He hoped he looked and sounded a hell of a lot cooler than he actually felt. He'd never tried anything like this before with a customer—he'd never had the chance, for one thing—and now that he'd gone this far, now that it all seemed so close, he found he had to press his palms against the top of the counter to keep from trembling. He'd done just about everything he dared to: he'd stroked Jesse's arm, he hadn't charged him for the three nights of rental. And now he'd invited the guy to stay around while he closed up.

It was up to Jesse now. Corey'd seen the bulge in Jesse's shorts, and it made him pretty confident Jesse might stay. Watching Jesse's thick back and high, round ass, he licked his lips, hoping Jesse really wanted him like he wanted Jesse, hoping the hot black man would stay and share the fantasy Corey'd been replaying in his mind for weeks. Jesse didn't turn to face Corey, but he didn't seem to be leaving, either.

Jesse turned toward the nearest rack of videos—the children's section—and now made a show of browsing casually, while his dick throbbed within the close confines of his shorts; while Corey locked the cash register, drew the shades over the front windows and doors. Jesse could see Corey in the corner of his eye, locking the front door. Jesse picked up a video box and glanced at it absently, wondering exactly what this boy might have in mind, when Corey called, "Hey, Jesse," making him drop a rental copy of *A Smurf Christmas* to the floor with a clatter.

Jesse turned to find Corey standing right next to him, so close he could smell the ripe scent of day-old boysweat on The Kid's skin. Corey inclined his head toward the video screens up over the counter. "Seen this one?" Corey asked. Twin images showed on the screens: on each one a huge, hard cock, shiny and slick, pushing slowly past the opening sphincter of a man's asshole—pink and vulnerable-looking, yet opening, willing, wanting penetration. *Mary Poppins* it wasn't.

Jesse felt his dick swell further, rendering his shorts painfully tight. He had scarcely managed to look back into Corey's smiling face (the smile was both mischievous and sexy) before Corey raised himself slightly on tiptoe, touched his palms to Jesse's shoulders, and kissed Jesse's mouth, first meeting Jesse's full, parted lips with his own, then slipping the tip of his tongue between Jesse's lips for a quick trip around his gums, and finally taking Jesse's lower lip between his teeth, giving it a playful little bite.

Corey lowered onto his heels and expelled a long breath. "I've been wanting to do that for a long time," he said. Jesse opened his mouth, tried to speak, but couldn't. Nearly smiled, but didn't. Finally, he said, "Jeez, Kid: I'm old enough to be your father." Corey leaned in and licked a stripe up the side of Jesse's neck. He spoke into Jesse's ear, "You're not my father."

Jesse smiled. The Kid had a point. He took Corey by the shoulders, pulled the boy against him, and kissed him hard. Jesse spread his legs a bit to even out their heights, and they kissed, lips pressing and sucking, tongues licking and tickling and tasting one another. Jesse took Corey's head into his hands and fingered the crisp blades of his hair; Corey stroked and squeezed Jesse's big back and high, hard butt. Jesse caught Corey's earlobe between his lips and sucked it a little bit, then wiggled the tip of his tongue into Corey's ear, making Corey's breath catch, making Corey's dick jump in his pants.

They held each other close, four strong arms squeezing tight; grinding their hips, each man rubbing the hardness in his own shorts against the hardness in the other's, stiff cock bumping against stiff cock. Jess grabbed Corey's ass, a firm cheek in each hand, and squeezed, moaning low in his throat. The way Corey's body felt against his own, the smell of him, the way he whimpered when Jesse licked his ear again—he wanted The Kid, bad. He wanted to take him home and fuck him long and sweet. He removed his mouth from Corey's ear and kissed his smooth face, his forehead,

his eyelids, then his lips again, softly, before he pulled back, pushing Corey away from him, holding him at arm's length. Jesse's
breath came in audible heaves. Corey smiled with slightly swollen
lips. He glanced down at himself and then at Jesse, then looked up
again, still smiling.

"Look what you do to me," Corey said. Jesse looked down to
the stretched-out front of Corey's pants, where his hard, bobbing
dick had left a dollar-size wet stain. Jesse's own cock, unable to
push through the waistband of his shorts, had bloated sideways,
where it pressed painfully into his hip. Jesse was going to suggest
he take Corey home with him, but then Corey's hands were tugging
at Jesse's shorts, sliding them down his hips. "Let me help you
with these," he said. It was then that Jesse realized that whatever
he and Corey might end up doing together, Corey meant for them
to do it right there in the store.

Corey pulled Jesse's shorts down over his full, round ass, then
in front, freeing his cock, which sprang up and slapped his hard
belly, then stood out and up. "Ooh, yum!" Corey said at the sight
of Jesse's cock, long and thick, darker brown than the rest of him,
arching its bloated head back toward Jesse's navel. Corey lowered
to his knees, dragging Jesse's shorts down toward his ankles. As
Jesse stepped out of his shorts, Corey leaned forward, burying his
face in Jesse's naked crotch, sucking in the smell of it, a strong,
musky scent that Corey loved immediately.

Corey moaned softly behind his closed lips, humming on one
long note as he ran his hands up the backs of Jesse's long, solid
legs, kneading his meaty ass, and then down again; all the while
rubbing his face—nose, lips, cheeks—against the warm, smooth
skin of Jesse's low-slung sac of balls; at first so lost in the delicious
feelings and smells of Jesse's lower body that he didn't at first notice
just how smooth Jesse's scrotum was. When it did occur to him,
Corey reached up and palmed Jesse's big nuts, then moved his hand
up and around the thick base of Jesse's cock—the black guy's crotch
was as hairless and smooth as a baby's.

Corey looked up, still quietly caressing Jesse's balls. "Shaved,"
he said. "I like." Then he began licking Jesse's balls with long

tongue-strokes. He tried to take one big ball into his mouth but it was an uncomfortable fit, and he contented himself with lapping Jesse's unnaturally smooth ballsac with the flat of his tongue. Licking and nibbling and sniffing between Jesse's legs, Corey untied the drawstring of his sweats and pulled out his cock—rigid and hot and sweetly familiar, and wet with sweat and precum leakage—and moved his hand slowly up and down the shaft of it.

Jesse watched the blond head between his legs, enjoying the feeling of The Kid's sweet mouth on his balls. He spread his legs a bit more (releasing more of that smell Corey couldn't seem to get enough of), reached down, and gently stroked the back of Corey's head with his fingers. Jesse's knees nearly buckled when Corey began licking the underside of his overly excited cock. Jesse's dick was engorged nearly to the point of pain, and he knew it would take very little handling before he'd come. Jesse enjoyed and endured the nearly painful pleasure of Corey's tongue on his dick for a minute or two, his eyes darting around the room looking for something that might distract him from the intensity of the feelings emanating from between his thighs and coursing through his body like electricity. But on the video monitors a pretty Latino boy was down on all fours across a bed, taking a blond boy's long, hard cock up his ass, his body lurching forward and back as the fair-haired boy slammed into his upturned rump, fast and hard, again and again. Jesse closed his eyes, bit down on his lower lip.

Corey wrapped a spit-slippery hand around Jesse's cock and stroked it up and down. Jesse felt his balls lift in their sac, felt the sweet-and-sour feeling of his cum gathering and rising up his bloated cockshaft, preparing to shoot. "No," he said, grabbing Corey's shoulders and pulling him to his feet.

"What's the matter?" Corey asked as he stood up.

"You're about to make me come," Jesse said, his voice low and breathy.

"That was the idea." Corey smiled and kissed Jesse a wet and sloppy kiss involving excitedly watering mouths, allowing Jesse to taste his own crotch on Corey's tongue.

"Don't want to come yet," Jesse said, and licked Corey's chin.

"You're right," said Corey, wrapping his hand around the shaft of Jesse's swollen dick. "I want to feel this thing inside me first." Jesse felt his cock throb at Corey's touch, and then again at his words, and he was afraid he might come all over The Kid's hand. He took a couple of deep breaths and said, "Sounds good by me. But you're going to have to take those pants off first."

He reached for Corey's cock (jutting out from over the top of his sweats), wrapped his fingers around it, and gave it a little tug. It was a pretty thing: not long but thick and juicy-looking, with a slightly oversized red noggin, its long, puckered pisshole drooling a steady flow of clear, sticky stuff. Jesse rubbed his thumb around and around the head of Corey's cock, sending a shudder through the boy's entire body, like a sudden chill.

"Shit," Corey said.

The black guy smiled one of those sexy smiles of his, reached for the top of Corey's pants and said, "Let me help you with these." With only the slightest nudge, the loose-fitting pants fell to the floor, and Corey stepped out of them, kicking them aside. He allowed Jesse to push his T-shirt up toward his armpits and lifted his arms so Jesse could pull the shirt up over his head, leaving him in only his dirty high-top Converse All-Stars. Jesse stroked up and down Corey's sharply defined chest and hard, flat belly with his big palms. "You're beautiful, Corey," he said. Jesse tugged at Corey's nipples, making The Kid tremble, making him stutter as he said, "S-so are you."

Arms collided as Corey reached for Jesse's shirt.

"What?" Jesse said.

"Shit," said Corey.

"No prob." Jesse pulled his tank top up and over his head with one quick motion, tossing it somewhere near Corey's pants. "Okay?" he said, completely naked except for his Nikes.

"Shit yeah," said Corey, looking Jesse over: his big arms, muscular chest, rippled belly, fat, hard cock. He wanted to touch the sexy black man all over, wanted to kiss and lick and sniff him all over. He wanted Jesse to hold him some more and kiss him. And fuck him. Corey could feel his asshole contract at the thought of

Jesse's big cock pushing its way up inside him, but then Jesse was leaning in close again.

Jesse bent slightly at the knees, tilted his head to the right, and took Corey's left nipple between his lips. He felt the sensitive nubbin react immediately, felt it harden and lengthen like a little erection, as he flicked it with the tip of his tongue. Corey sucked air in through his teeth, and his back involuntarily arched as the tingling in his titty seemed to send tingles all the way down to his cock and balls. Jesse released Corey's left tit and moved to the right one, at the same time moving one hand down to play with Corey's genitals; caressing his balls, stroking his oozing dick, then back up to that left nipple to pinch it almost hard enough to hurt, exactly hard enough to make Corey crazy.

Corey, his head back, eyes half shut, could barely see the cute Latino guy on the monitors getting royally fucked. The sight of that, along with what Jesse was doing to his tits and balls and cock (and the driving beat of Billy Idol dancing with himself), suddenly brought Corey dangerously close to orgasm. He took Jesse's head in his hands, flexed his fingers in the black man's short, woolly hair, and gently removed Jesse's face from his chest. Jesse looked up, his lush lips parted, and said, "What?" He straightened his knees, rising to full height. "You don't like it?"

"I love it," Corey said, reaching out to touch Jesse's long, muscular arms, tracing his fingers down the outsized biceps, following the distended veins that ran the length of his forearms. "I love your arms."

"Take 'em," said Jesse, stretching his arms out toward Corey. "They're yours."

Corey wondered if he should ask. Would Jesse laugh or think he was weird or something? "Would you do something for me?"

"Ask."

"Flex," Corey said. "Make a muscle."

Jesse laughed, just a little, then curled his right fist and flexed the arm, making his biceps bunch and rise. He tensed his arm again, and the upper head of his biceps separated clearly, forming a sharp peak at the top of the bulge of muscle.

"Shit," Corey whispered and reaching for Jesse's arm, he stroked the hard, high-peaked muscle with both hands. "When I fantasize about you," he said softly, "I always think about your arms."

Jesse felt his cock throb and jump at the thought that this lovely boy fantasized about him, his body. He suddenly felt a surge of warm, sweet feeling for the boy and he leaned his head forward, meaning to nuzzle Corey's hair, when Corey leaned down and licked Jesse's bicep with the flat of his tongue—once, then again—a little hum barely audible in his throat; then opened his mouth wide and sucked the peak of the muscle with his lips. The look of it, the feeling of it made Jesse's breath catch, made his heart race, made his legs weaken so that when Corey removed his mouth from Jesse's arm (making a wet, slurpy sound) and whispered, "Please fuck me," it was all Jesse could do to nod his head, Yes.

Jesse had never bought any rubbers at Video X-Press, but he was suddenly very glad the store stocked a variety of condoms (there was a small display behind the counter between the candy bars and cigarettes), as he leaned back against the checkout counter watching Corey kneeling in front of him, slowly unrolling a slick, lubricated condom over the engorged head of his cock. "So big," Corey said to himself as he eased the rubber down the length of Jesse's dick. Corey stood up (catching a glimpse of the Latino guy taking a big cock up his ass and one in his mouth), leaned forward against the counter. He spread his legs wide and arched his back, directing his firm little ass out and up. "Do it, Jesse," he said. "Fuck my ass."

Jesse stood close behind Corey for a moment, just looking at the beautiful boy who offered his sweet ass so willingly, flanked by dual images of wild fucking from the video monitors. He only hoped he wouldn't come before he got all the way inside The Kid. He stroked the small of Corey's back, wrapped his fingers around the boy's tiny waist, rubbed his hard asscheeks. He reached down between Corey's legs and palmed his knotted ballsac, tugging it gently away from his body. He trailed his middle finger up and down the deep crack of Corey's ass, pushed at the tight pucker of

Corey's anus with his fingertip. Wondered: would he even be able to enter him with so little lubrication?

Jesse positioned the head of his cock firmly against Corey's hole, his breath heaving, his entire body trembling. "I don't want to hurt you," he said.

"Hurt me," said Corey. He could feel the heat of Jesse's big cockhead against his asshole through the condom. He'd never taken a cock as big as Jesse's inside him before, and he was sure it wouldn't be easy getting all that meat up into him; still, he knew he wanted it, even if it hurt at first. He concentrated on opening, loosening his sphincter muscle, at the same time moving his ass back just slightly, pushing against the rubbery head. He looked up at the video monitors, where the Latino guy was now squatting down on two big hard cocks at one time, and he felt a stab of pain as the head of Jesse's cock popped into his hole. He could feel his sphincter spasm around the rim of that big cockhead, and it hurt, but he knew it was going to be good—God, so good—from there on.

Jesse stood as still as he could and gave Corey a few seconds to get used to the big-headed intruder. He stroked Corey's back and shoulders, sides and flanks and said, "You okay, Baby?"

"Okay," Corey said and pushed back farther, past the cockhead, taking another fraction of an inch of thick cock into him, and then another. A low noise rumbled down in his throat as he pushed back farther, slowly, until finally he felt Jesse's crotch, smooth and warm, against his ass. Corey said, "Ooooh, Jesse!" and Billy Idol sang "Have mercy!" and Corey could feel that cockhead of Jesse's way up inside of him, jammed up against his distended prostate, and it felt like it was all the way up into his belly, and his own cock felt fat and tight, like it might burst its own skin.

Jesse breathed deeply and slowly: the feeling of Corey's bowel clutching at his cock, the sight of the boy's beautiful back arching his pale, perfect ass up against him, and his own cock disappearing into Corey's asshole was almost more than he could stand. His dick felt huge and hypersensitive (even with the condom on it): he was going to have to take it slow. He stood still while Corey dipped and arched his lower back just slightly, moving his ass up and down, back and forth, slowly. Corey moaned softly and continually as he stirred his own insides with Jesse's cock, fucking himself with it; feeling his balls jump each time the cock punched at his prostate, feeling his asshole relax and loosen, and then moaning louder as he felt Jesse begin to move.

Jesse pulled slowly away from Corey's butt, until only the head of his cock was left inside the boy, clutched by his tight hole, and then pushed just as slowly back in, relishing the delicious sensations shooting up through his dick and throughout his body. He moved his hips back again, then forward, and then back again, his hands gripping Corey's hipbones, dicking him long and slow, not wanting to come before he'd sufficiently pleasured both himself and The Kid. He reached around the boy and rubbed his chest and belly, tweaked his hard nipples; he grabbed Corey's balls and rolled them in his palm: he could feel Corey's hole twitch and tighten when he yanked on The Kid's hard, slimy cock.

He rotated his hips around and around, fucking Corey in and out from side to side, and Corey growled and gurgled and shoved his ass hard against Jesse's dick, and he was moving forward and back, meeting Jesse's thrusts with his own. Billy Idol shouted, but Corey and Jesse didn't hear it, and on the video screens the Latino boy did fast, deep squats on two big cocks, but Jesse and Corey weren't watching: they were lost in the fuck. Jesse's hips seemed to move without his permission, slamming his cock into Corey harder and faster than Jesse thought he really wanted to. He wrapped his arms around Corey's chest and leaned in close against his back and pummeled his ass with hard, quick strokes.

Corey was nearly delirious with fucking; his body and mind and everything centered at his asshole, around the big, black cock that slammed into him again and again. "Oh!" he cried, "fuck me, Jesse! Fuck me!" And he repeated it over and over, a nasty mantra in rhythm with Jesse's hips: "Fuck me fuck me fuck me," and then, as Jesse moved even faster, he was all but inaudible as he chanted "Fuck fuck fuck fuck." And then Corey's lips went slack, and his eyes opened wide without really seeing anything and he roared like some kind of animal, and his balls rammed up against him as if they'd been slapped upward and he came: his cock flew up and slapped against his belly, then surged forward and shot without being touched, splattering the front of the checkout counter with hot boycum, moving up and down like a firehose out of control, spewing fat strings of sticky stuff, thick as pudding and hitting the counter with a slapping sound.

The spasming of Corey's asshole shoved Jesse over the edge and he growled so loud and hard he hurt his throat as his hips lurched forward, planting his cock so hard and deep into Corey's butt that the boy screamed, and he felt the pounding behind his balls and the explosion at the head of his dick as he came, pumping what felt like quarts of hot spunk into the condom up Corey's ass.

He might have been coming for minutes or hours or days, and when the spasms finally subsided and his cock was slowly dripping a tiny puddle of cum onto the floor in front of him, Corey found his legs almost too weak to hold him up. He leaned hard against the counter, moving just slightly away from Jesse's dick, just enough to send a last little shudder through him. Jesse leaned forward against Corey, his stickywet chest making a damp farting sound against Corey's back. The Billy Idol CD had finished: the only sounds in the store were the heavy breathing of the two spent fuckers, and the juicy noises of wet skin on wet skin.

Corey glanced up at the video monitors: the fuck film was over, too. Both screens were filled with static snow.

"Good movie," Corey said with a weary little smile.

Jesse laughed, which hurt his tired stomach muscles a little and made his still hard dick stir in Corey's hole. "Yeah," he said, his voice a little raspy. "Real good movie."

PART FIVE

ROMANCE:

WHAT SOME OF

US ARE STILL

LOOKING FOR

The romantic urge is so much a part of gay life that it is a part of our pornographic literature.

In some cases, such as playwright Robert Patrick's "Kit," the romance is a question of the sweet memory of a past lover. Kit is not just someone who exists in Patrick's recollection, he's also, in a way, an ideal, like the adolescent ideal that crops up in so much gay writing. There is a time of innocence, when a love exists that's not part of either the politics or the day-to-day hassles of our lives. It's always a fond memory, and it's sometimes easier to stay in love with the image of someone who was once here than it is to maintain a relationship with the person beside us.

What's particularly wonderful in Patrick's story about Kit is the language. Here is a playwright in full command of the words as he presents us with a nearly complete lexicon of the gay vernacular. People do not just fuck in Patrick's story, they have a literary adventure.

The realities of gay life provide for a kind of wistful romantic remembrance as well. There are always the dark strangers of Tennessee Williams in gay life, men who come in and leave, perhaps to return, perhaps not. It's partly because gay life is still so borderline, with so many pressures on us, that those who want a monogamous relationship discover that it's even more difficult to sustain one because of the stress that our marginalization brings with it.

Leigh Rutledge is best known for his work in documenting the gay existence in books like *The Gay Decades*. He's also been a major literary influence on gay erotica. Often dealing with issues of alienation and aloneness, the stuff of romance, Rutledge's best work sometimes takes on an air of regret, regret for the love not won, for the person who's gone away. "Fatherless" is a fine example of his work.

"Herzschmerz" is a totally different example of romantic prose. It originally appeared as a column in *Christopher Street*. It has the best attributes of the letters I receive from its author, Andrew Holleran, and of his novels. Holleran has always loved the baths; he's described them as a place he might like to live. Even when traveling in Europe and taking part in its culture, there's a call to the sexual for him. Inevitably for him, as for so many gay men, the call becomes romantic. It's not enough that there be a strong handsome stranger; the stranger must become the lover, until reality intrudes and once more defeats even the strongest romantic craving.

ROBERT PATRICK

KIT

I WANT TO TELL YOU ABOUT KIT, THE CHICAGO
lighting man who shared the brief flare of my fame. "Kit" was
short for Cristofo. His Italian family held a big dinner in my honor
so that all could come ogle and approve me before I carted their
Kit away to bop till we dropped.

How he loved to bop—and to drop. I'd be doing phone business and he'd kneel to unzip and ingest me while I talked tougher
and tougher. I'd be writing at my desk and he'd crawl under to
hump my shin like a puppy while he sucked seed through me like
a straw. He tried to juice me even on the john, but that was too
advanced for romantic me. On a dare he ate me in the backseat of
an airport bus. Out of boredom, he lapped me under a lapful of
overcoats in an off-off-Broadway dive. Despite protests, he once rav-

aged me orally too early and got paid with a firehose-force faceful of semen *cum* piss.

But much as he loved cock-teething, it was nothing next to his passion for getting packed. Witty and wily when conversing in any company, he'd lose his smile at the smell of a swell in my jeans, and turn surly till we were where he could bend and get boned. He loved to lie loose and be bounced on like a trampoline, or he'd cross his thin legs and then tense, locking me in, and I'd trap his Achilles tendons between my toes, his wrists in my fists, and do my sawing-the-lad-in-half trick. Other times he'd flail on his back with his shanks rubbing blisters on my shoulders, clutching the edges of the mattress as his head banged the resonating headboard and he howled rodeo jokes. One night he'd lie supine, pretending to read a music magazine, and make a big "M" for "mystery-maze" with his legs, so my poor blind pig would get linen burns truffle-snuffling across taut sheets for the hard-to-hit hole concealed among squashed haunches. The next night I'd come back from an interview to find all lights out but a gooseneck bedlamp craned to spotlight the hole he'd cut in a black blanket draped over his giggle-jiggling buns.

He was burdened with a heaven handle which he played hell getting erect without a dork in his fork. More than once I found him on his back, slapping his stomach with his limp lump, no do-it-yourself Kit, only to see me and cry in exasperation, "Thank God! Bob, help me up!" And he'd hoist his hindparts for me to fall onto him, into him, whereupon we'd both with gratified sighs watch his flower tower to Beardsleyan bulk. He'd hold his prize in two hands and say, "I could never have done it without you little people." Then he'd look into my aching eyes, hit my belly with his bully like a gavel, and say, "Make a motion."

Not that Kit wasn't active. There's nothing so active as a tail out to get tolled. He'd drop suitcases any-old-where, fall face down across a hotel bed, roll down his jeans, tuck his knees up under, and pucker his hiney-hole liplike as he ventriloquized in a squeaky voice, "Dick! Quick! Dick! Those bumpy Boston streets got me so hot!"

He would apologize for interrupting me at my work to show me an article about New Wave rock. I would scan it rudely, turn to hand him the magazine, and find my nose in a Vaselined crevasse. At such times he liked being taken quickly and quietly, with no more moves on my part than standing, skinning, driving, drumming, withdrawing, wiping, and zipping back into my routine.

On other occasions he wanted to be gotten drunk, fondled, flattered, kissed wetly while my five fingers walked one by one into his web, then used like a much-drunker sailor and left on the floor with five bucks poked up his person.

There was no end to the ways he would be wadded. Over-a-sofa was welcome, before-a-fire a treat, on-a-kitchen-counter a wacky novelty. In-the-shower was of course a free-for-all, especially hotel showers with odd extra bars bolted into the walls (towel holders for tiny tots? Antigrav grips for geriatrics?), which afforded more positions, making Kit feel "like a brand-new bride moving the furniture around," as he put it to me as I put it to him.

He liked new places: in the light booth of a theater, poking his head out a peephole to watch my show while I, pants tangling my ankles, manually rolled his globes around my scepter; in line for a urinal at a busy intermission, brand-new oversize raincoats and Manhattan men's room indifference actually letting us get away with it, him inching forward tugging-chugging me by my bitten button, both of us coming instead of going when he achieved the bowl; in cabs, of course, Kit on my lap and writhing while drivers adjusted their mirrors for a better view; in a pew in Saint Patrick's Cathedral, him sitting turned away as if grieving, me tight beside/behind him offering urgent comfort; standing at the window of an apartment we briefly sublet, Kit in nothing but his brand-new leather jacket, mightily rubbing his lamp as I aligned our legs for leverage and pumped him till his spout spat, less for pleasure than for the frustration of the naked man in the window across the courtyard waving scrawled signs that read, "Street number? Apartment number? Name? Phone number? Please?"

His own king-size kong fascinated him, but so did any extended male flesh, or, in fact, just any long, firm form. I surprised him betraying me with a broom handle, a cucumber, and once a frankfurter, which I churned him with till he burned, then ate out of him as he squeezed it into my mouth and chuckled.

The few times he ventured out venally during our affair, he ran home with show-and-tell reenactments of his defections to make me hot.

He didn't need them. I need only know I'm wanted to make me wanton. The availability of the playing field makes me instantly athletic. Just as he had only to see me uppin' to make him open, I had only to think of his hole and my pole vaulted. He, with his potency problem, thought me with my third leg a world-wonder, though it was, ironically, precisely his monotheism about my monolith that kept it rock around the clock. I succeeded where others failed in arousing his much-sought but seldom-sated bush baby simply because the existence of his anus kept me walking bowlegged around a hard-on.

And what hard-ons! I was steeled to have Kit lay cracks as well as crack about my only-average endowment, but he never had cause. I was never bigger with any man. I hardly recognized myself, so hard, so long, so long. He gave me, and I gave back to him, every species of tumescence: your standard stiffy, the everyday competitive diving-board; the porn-prompted glass-prod, hard-edged and inflexible; the lazy-day bulbous baseball bat sheathed in sponge rubber; that triumph of masturbatory lubrication, the Art Deco ice cream cone, perfect cylinder topped by perfect dome; the unexpected spare-time turkey-neck, skinny and rigid and slow to flow; the suck-off sweet potato, hot and homey; the midnight tender tube, touchy, even ticklish; the showdown switchblade, skinny and lethal; the Jockey-shorts bellywhopper, flexing elastic and spilling pre-cum in the navel; the bunched-up blackjack, as hard as the bellywhopper, but for some reason swinging loosely from the bush, suitable for beating lovers in the face; the babyfinger, stiff enough to suck, but not tough enough to get up anything; the warhead, when the *glans penis* swells like a thundercloud; the sugar-shaker, a fat shaft whose head stays tiny and wrinkled and apparently indifferent to the congested zeppelin beneath; the hot rod, rubbed too smooth too long down a pants leg and adolescently aching to sneeze the moment it's seized; the trigger, the tiger, the dagger, the digger, the dug, and the raging red tom-whallager, maximally distended in every direction, painful at the base, so raw it makes you fear you've got a rare tropical disease and so gorgeous the two of you touch it and talk about it and almost forget what it's for—these and all other variations any man who masturbates can catalog, I shoved into that willing, thrilling sheath, my earthy Kit.

So consistently was I mushroomed in his presence that it was in at least our second or third moon of rooming and roaming that he came out of the shower to find me shaving and said, "Bob, babe, I didn't know you ever got soft; how have I failed you?" And he grabbed my grub, instantly inching upright under his thumb, and we watched in the mirror as I did everything in his mouth but melt, and at last even that.

Our anatomies were to us Tinkertoys, teddy bears, water pistols, pinball machines, kid jokes, finger traps, joy buzzers, dribble glasses, whoopee cushions, Silly Putty, Slinkies, Slime. We'd flex our erections and see who could flip Milk Duds farther. Since he was too big for me to blow, I'd wait till he'd spunked and shrunk, then hold him down and suck him soft, which any man knows is murder if you've just come; Kit was my only trick who ever loved it. When I, doggy-fucking him in a hallway, curled my arms around his thighs and stood, still impaling him, then lowered him onto the floor on his shoulders, then slowly fell forward on him, gently fucking and with each stroke adding weight to curl his crotch down to his gaping mouth until bit by bit he was being force-face-fucked by his own full fuse, letting him for the first time test his own jaw to taste his own bone and his own fresh spume, he licked his smiling lips and asked if that was patented or could he try it on the next guy when I threw him out. That grin on his face came to be as important to me as my groin in his base. Once when I was housing my hose in classical fashion, what he called "the stapler position," him prone, me doing push-ups reaming his recess, he said, "Ho-hum." Challenged, I pondered what invention I could introduce without pulling out (I liked it where I was). I told him to lie very still and very stiff, and then I slowly spun like a compass needle, using my prick as a pivot, until I was licking his heels, my dick pulled back a hundred and eighty degrees, painfully-but-not-painfully reverse-fucking him. He'd never had it at that angle; he had one of those driveling, snickering, prostatic-massage oozy orgasms from the unusual pressure. I got the grin I wanted. "Next time I feel like yawning," he said, smearing his shmarm over us both, "I'll do it at the other end."

And speaking of bending your dick, one night I laid him on his back and tucked his log between his legs, closed his thighs tightly over it, then got atop him, bent mine back, and diddled him in the improvised cunt, the tops of our dicks sliding on each other, the tips snapping like fingers, each glans glancing off the other rubberily, flicking like Bics. He sputtered into a fluttering spasm that spilled come-slick under his knees. "You fucked my dick!" he kept saying after, "I don't believe that you literally fucked my dick!"

As you would expect, dramatic games came into play. My favorite was Captain Kirk and the new ensign, in which I had to summon him to my private starry quarters to explain that there were certain favors we fellas did for each other while we were off on these five-year galactic cruises. His was to pretend we were college dorm-mates, him a virgin begging me, a veteran, to tell him, and finally show him, how he should handle his first girl. This involved alcohol and jockstraps and an awful lot of clambering around while I muttered, "Now you do it to me and see if you got it straight," and was one of the few ways of getting his wand in my wound. Another was to pretend I was him and he me; this worked only once but surprised the hell out of him. After putting himself through some of the Herculean exertions he regularly expected of me, he fell off the head of the bed (where the particular distortion he'd decided on had necessitated his perching) and landed astride me, huffing, "No more of that, man; that's too much like *work!*"

Despite his appreciation of artistry, Kit didn't really mind how we did it, or when, or where. Though basically he liked his sex,

like his dicks, long and hard, he was amenable to the well-since-
you're-bent-over-doing-the-breakfast-dishes pop-top quickie, the
lazy-afternooner of lounging and lunging, wallowing and swallowing, with pauses for cigarettes and popcorn; or the all-night
experimental orgy-for-two, which could take place anywhere but
seemed to flourish in borrowed or rented burrows, which, with my
lifestyle as it was right then, was our usual habitat.

A guest house in Canada had plushly carpeted spiral stairs.
We engaged in baroque sculptural compositions after pink Kit slid
down the greased banister onto my newel.

Crossing the Midwest by train, I tamped him in a cramped
bunk with a ceiling too low for the requisite ramming. Then I
discovered that if I but relaxed, the bumpety-bump of the train on
the tracks bobbed Bob and did the fucking for me. The resultant
rhythm was so rib-tickling he hankered to experience it. He slid
out from under over onto and into me and bored aboard me through
a capital city whose inhabitants reading and rocking in their lit
windows knew nothing of what was Bob-bobbing behind our dark
one in the night.

"Jesus, it was hot in there," he said afterwards, lying on me
like a wet blanket and fingering the cavity in question. "Am I that
hot?"

I told him to lick my wick quick after I vexed him next and
see. And he smiled, he smiled, he smiled.

We had, of course, as Hercules and Hylas, Merlin and Arthur,
Butch Cassidy and Sundance must have had, certain elements of set
bedroom ritual. No matter what excesses we'd explored in private
or public that day, when beddy-bye beckoned we'd stake out our
own sides of the bed (his right, mine left), and begin digitally
fidgeting each other's controls. When his loaf came to life, I'd slither
down to salivate his gland, which by itself crowded my craw. When
his resultant humming thrummed down into basso, he'd stretch out
a tentacle to tug on my tool, and I, still feasting, would sidewind
around on my knees to deliver my own myth into his moth-mouth.
This mutual mastication continued until his swollen spoke threatened to choke me. Then I'd slather my tongue down his tong like

a snail, from the raw rose down the veined underside, flick back his bothersome balls, take a deep pungent breath, and with a long lingum begin to worm wide, warm wide, the hole that was our hearth. For a time we two lay in trance-state stupidly sucking pole and hole like boozy babes in boyland, ears muffed from the wails of the world by the other guy's thighs, my tongue in his bung and my rung halfway down to his lungs. But eventually something in us suggested that these twin intrusions were mere symbols for the one true act, and I would begin numbly humping his gorged gorge, and he would longingly spread his legs like a wishbone, and our nervous systems would chime it was time for the adult stuff. We hugged one another's butts and I rolled over on my back, tumbling him on top of me. After a few last laps at my apse, he would sit back onto my face, masturbating us, and I'd take a few last tasty tours of the fault my staff would soon stuff, then I'd shove my slick love down my torso, till he landed on the arrow that would split his apple. We both took sharp breaths as his wet warm crook first clasped my hot hard hook. His back to me so I could observe the operation, he rose on his knees, my suppressed mass rising to follow his scent. He hovered above, a spaceship over my south pole. Then he'd lower my lover onto my lever, taking the time for our wired nerves to record and applaud each frame of the event: the quiver when the dick touched dock; the initial annoying, clawing, cloying coyness of his sphincter; the slight snagging of the remnants of my prepuce; our sighs like seas as all elements yielded and my pearl popped into his water lily, a moment of strange suspended peace, and then the millimeter-by-millimeter melodrama as he drew me as far past his fur as flesh can go. His lean loins permitted deeper intrusion than entries more abundantly bunned. He nudged his limbs around until he was squatting on his feet, the better to spread his interfering cheeks and try how much more of my rude rod he could get in his gut. I lay stunned and still; let him be the gauge of the gouge. He pressed down; I stood firm. By the time our scrota intermingled like adventurers' parachutes, I was wrought right to the root in his rut. He flexed and made me flinch, to show what he could do. I thrust, nearly making him bust, to show I could, too. Then, slower than Uranus, he revolved, wrenching his ring and certainly wringing my wrench, gradually revealing his dew-topped ivory tusk. Kit looked like a giant cock himself, rising slim in my groin, his veined neck and uptilted chin shining like the tip of the dick lost now in his warm wet velvet. And out of Kit-the-cock grew the cock of Kit, which he now began to shine with its own skin as I pulled my pud in and out of him like something prehistoric stuck in mud. Digging for friction, I said, "Jesus Christ, I wish you were hairy clear inside," and bending down to kiss me, he said, "And I wish I had taste buds up my ass." And this, with gradual exaggerations and casual variations, we continued, groaning and grinning, humming and humping, working and jerking, demeaning, demanding, conversing, convulsing, mounting, surmounting, him performing prodigious upright acrobatics with his automatic which he could never have balanced to do was he not on my roll, me buckling and chuckling, slapping my nuts against thumping nates, trying to kill him with my column while he tried to murder me with his mortar, him holding me down with one hand to buttress himself as he attempted to achieve blast-off with his other while stamping his rump on my stump trying to force my cock up his, me grasping his hips and brutally revolving him as he went up and down on me and simultaneously my own wrestly pelvis rotated the opposite directions, an overloaded carousel, the consequential conflicting rhythms of our wrangling not independently resolvable because of the groin-join where we ground energy into and out of each other, generating unintelligible tangles of tonus until at the peak of tectonic upheaval the ultimate earthquake possessed the tumultuous bed and Kit lashing hair from his eyes cried, "Huh?" and I, glimpsing his goad in his hand and, between flashing descents of his bowels and his balls, my god in his hind, crowed, "Uh *huh!*" and he clamped himself tight, and, hands flickering faster than piranhas, stabbed his balls with his inflamed sword until like virgin blood he shot hot snot at our streaming faces while every spurt pinched his gut shut, detonating each clinched inch of me to blow deep into his moist mush my replenishing come.

That was your average run-of-the-mile Bob-and-Kit couple-fuck. Then he'd lie back, a mask of semen and sweat, and say, "I like you. Let's us have sex sometime." And smile.

About the smiles: I read him Blake's lines,

"What is it men in women do require?
The lineaments of Gratified Desire.
What is it women do in men require?
The lineaments of Gratified Desire."

and he pretty much agreed with me that that was what it was all about, that silly smile on the face of the other guy. "I like sex so much," he said, "because when you feel a guy come in you, you know he loves you. You can't fake a fuck." I said I, too, liked more than anything to hear a body-buddy let go of that long breath of uncertainty and tension that you don't even know you've been holding until you lie stuck together by your own body products. That certain sigh. "Yes," Kit agreed. "We are certainly both sighs queens." He would occasionally say things like that, mimicking certain excesses of my verbal style. Once he held a hand mirror behind him to watch me insert my quirt and quipped, "Thank God, I see it, too." I fucked da punk up his queer ass for dat.

I think he liked best the third or fourth time of a night, when I was no use for juice, just a staid stud he could cajole into manipulating his thin limbs into monkey puzzles, and then into assuming among them postures reminiscent of samurais, paramedics, cowboys, tarantulas, so as to massage insensibly with my pale pole the insatiable cells of his undersoul, which, as the dawn reddened our horizon, had swelled beyond recognition into a raw, pitiful, puffy, manly mound, which I lay by and licked until I slept like a grateful dog.

It was hard not to feel grateful all the time, hard to remember that this one wanted me, too; I had been alone in love so long. Kit and I could not, by several million astronomical units, love one another as Jack and I, Ted and I, could have done, but we loved each other in fact and not in theory, and we loved each other fully as much as we could.

He gave me those things we must stop pretending are unimportant, without which nothing else is of any import. He eventually left my centerless life to take root with a wife, but he was fine and loving and lovely and he made me sane.

And yet there was never a night in our gymnastic history, no matter how joking or close, as I held him to keep my climax from blasting him away, that I did not for at least a poised moment say in my soul, "I should be giving this to Jack. Ted should be getting this. I should be giving this to theater, to my culture, to my country, to my world."

But the world isn't mine and mostly doesn't want me. We live in a time when body and mind have been split and we can only hold ourselves together. What Kit could reach was healed, and the rest withheld, and I've been one of the luckiest modern men.

FATHERLESS

RICK IS NINETEEN, HIS FATHER WAS KILLED IN A helicopter crash in Vietnam, and his mother, who remarried a psychiatrist, is hooked on Valium. Rick thinks this last part—about his mother and the Valium—is pretty funny; it's as if she's gotten her just deserts for marrying the psychiatrist. Rick hates his stepfather.

He tells me all this in a breezy, disinterested manner, as if to suggest that none of these things has the power to wound him—the manner of all boys who, stepping uncertainly into adulthood, want to convince the world that they are invulnerable (or at least imperturbable), especially in matters of the heart.

He is standing in the middle of the whirlpool at the gym where we both work out. The steam from the churning water slowly rises around his lean, naked hips and broad, sunburned shoulders.

His body is tall and compact, well muscled, and touchable like a vivid bas-relief whose sculpted, sensuous forms tempt one's fingers. His eyes rarely stray from the image of himself in the mirrors surrounding the pool. Studying his reflection, he takes a handful of water and slowly—almost ceremoniously—pours it over his pecs, which are full and wide, rather square, with small, alert nipples. The water washes down over his gut muscles and flattens the dark amber pubic hair on his lower belly before flowing back into the pool.

His father's name is on the Vietnam War Memorial in Washington, D.C., and he hopes to get back there someday soon to see it. He doesn't remember much about his father—a shirt that smelled funny in the rain, a stuffed animal sent from boot camp in Texas—but he's impressed that his father's name is on a public monument, especially a monument that has been at the center of so much controversy and intense national emotion. His father, he tells me proudly (and with just an edge of defensiveness), was a war hero.

Of course, it's easy to suspect Rick of lying about all this: he's breathtakingly pretty but dishonest, you can see that immediately. His pale gray eyes are fervent, watchful, and full of deception, and he has the voluptuous, demanding face of a hustler. His father may actually have died in Vietnam; or he may still be alive, an ordinary man—an insurance adjuster, or a car salesman living in some place like Duluth—a man who got tired of married life and just one day walked out on a wife and son . . .

Rick reaches behind and soothingly rubs his bare ass with both hands. He has one of those incredibly small, sweetly plump asses set high atop long legs. His pale buttcheeks are so tiny they barely fill the palms of his hands, and the nearly translucent flesh is so smooth it almost looks shaved: there isn't a hair anywhere in sight on his little butt. What's more, the small of his back curves in with distinctive charm—almost like a swaybacked pony—giving his ass even more of a provocative, fuckable look.

He flexes his arm muscles—which are dripping with sweat and steam—relaxes them, then flexes them again, as if trying to drive out the lingering "burn" from his afternoon workout on the Nautilus machines. There's a small dark scar on his right bicep, and he touches it thoughtfully, with curiosity, as if it symbolizes something important to him. He sees me looking at him, smiles coyly, and says simply, tapping the scar, "A go-cart race when I was twelve . . ."

It goes without saying that he's a cockteaser—even though he'd fiercely (and sincerely) deny that he's gay. He's constantly touching and feeling himself: small, casual, crude gestures that, in the end, seem premeditatively seductive. He reminds me of certain women one sometimes sees lying alone around motel pools in the middle of summer: rarely relaxed or at ease, they're always midway through some anxious performance inspired by the admiring glances of nearby men. The way Rick's standing in the whirlpool, the surface of the water just barely covers his dick; even through the foam and the steam and the ripples, I can see his sizable cock flopping from one side to the other with the currents of water. He occasionally reaches down to finger it—idly, instinctively, protectively.

After a moment, he steps out of the whirlpool. Water streams glistening down the sides of his torso and the insides of his husky thighs, and drips from his hands and his ass and from the head of his cock; it forms small, somehow alluring puddles around his big bare feet. He suddenly looks over his shoulder at me, flashes a winning grin, and says, with no particular emphasis in his voice, "Looking pretty good, huh?" Then he walks around to his locker to towel himself off.

Even the act of drying himself is exhibitionistic. He plants one leg on the bench in front of his locker, the other on the floor, and then leans over to towel his feet and ankles. His bare ass sticks out prominently, intruding deeply into the aisle as other guys walk by.

"Yeah, my mother and the shrink," he says, taking a long time to dry his legs. "I think they have three-ways and shit like that. He's into free love and open marriages and all that kind of crap." He straightens up and reaches for his underwear. A second later, he pulls the tight white briefs up over his ass, and adjusts them with a quick yank to his crotch. "I wish she had married a real man, not some lousy doctor. I mean, the guy's a shrink, right? But the one time I tried to talk to him about my problems, he just kind of glared at me and said, 'Hey, I'm not into that.' What's that supposed to mean? Aw, he's a phony. He's some kind of faggot."

I watch him pull on his jeans: his butt looks so good in them, and his cock and balls fill out the fly perfectly. He takes a lot of time tucking his shirt into his pants, especially around the back, where he fusses and lingers as if trying to call even more attention to his rear end. He suddenly adds, after a long pause, "My real dad's name was Ed, by the way." He stares at me a second too long before slamming his locker door shut.

In the end, he looks at me as he looks at all men: something of the way a traveling salesman studies his potential clients, face by face, appraising their weaknesses, instantly calculating what he might be able to get out of them; as if he were demanding approval from them, demanding that they take him seriously, but also as if he wished, desperately, that they'd admire him and care about him. He isn't actually a hustler, but he always looks at me—at all men—with a violently expectant expression.

Finally, he throws his towel over his shoulder and—with a deeply masculine "See ya 'round"—walks out of the gym: one of those elusive, needy straight boys who, one intuitively senses, long to get fucked by another man, but can't bring themselves to acknowledge the need, let alone how deeply it runs through their emotions.

ANDREW HOLLERAN

HERZSCHMERZ

WE ARE SITTING IN ERLANGEN, GERMANY, A UNI-
versity town about twenty minutes' drive from Nuremberg (the
Jewel of the Reich in the thirties), on the small patio of a small
Italian restaurant on a small street opposite the formal gardens of
a palace which is now owned by the university. Everything in Erlangen is small, or rather, on a human scale—one of those German
towns you've never heard of that, it always seems (so spread out
was political power, so broken up into numerous small centers of
church and state), all have their own palace or castle or cathedral.

We are talking about the handsome young waiter, who has
left the top two buttons of his white shirt unfastened, and is joking
in German with my host, a professor of American and Caribbean
literature. The professor likes to flirt. He tells me, among other
things, that Thomas Mann's diaries have just been published, and

in one entry, the elderly Mann wonders whether the way a beautiful young waiter put his plate down indicated a sexual interest in him; that, even at an advanced age, Mann was still fixated on male beauty. (Mann also regarded homosexuality as chaos; hence his choice of a stable married life—like Cheever, whose diaries have also just been published, I tell the professor.)

From this, we move on to the subject of middle and old age. American gay men, the professor says, from what he sees, do not age gracefully; perhaps, I say, that's because our culture is so obsessed with youth—has youth as part of its historical self-image, uses youth in a daily barrage of advertising to sell products—does not much honor history or old age as other cultures do. I nod, and agree, and wonder, as I'm sitting there, if in this light it is obvious that I have just dyed my hair for the first time—for this trip, in fact. I'm going to Berlin, I tell him. I'd like to go to the baths in Nuremberg—there are two—but have not had the opportunity to get away. Berlin is a time bomb, he says. A high rate of AIDS. A hunky blond student pulls up on his bicycle beside our patio and rings a doorbell. We ogle his Rubenesque flesh. The men in Germany are so handsome, I say. They're statuesque, like blacks. Is that the reason for the Germans' interest in African-Americans? He doesn't know.

Riding the train from Nuremberg to Berlin the next day, I have plenty of time to think about whether American men do or do not age gracefully; it's true that the number of television commercials for hair coloring seems to increase with each passing month—the products must be selling; I now suspect every man my age of coloring his hair, finding, at the same time, men with gray hair exceedingly handsome. I feel guilty for having dyed my hair. A friend said, years ago, before I understood what he meant, that one feels guilty for growing old. He was right. I go around now avoiding mirrors, which suddenly seem cruel, ubiquitous—waiting to ambush you on the pillars of supermarkets, along the walls of gymnasiums and bathhouses. In the locker room at the baths, I walk with my head turned slightly away, avoiding my own reflection. Head down, eyes averted: clearly a posture of shame. Shame for what? For growing old.

I am also trying to forget someone on this trip—someone twelve years younger than I—whose very youth seems to me a perfectly valid reason that he would not want to see me again. The two ways to forget someone who has rejected you, everyone says, are: (a) passage of time, (b) sleeping with other people. A third they do not mention, a method the nineteenth century held in high regard: travel. Change your surroundings. The man in Florida I am trying to forget, however, has a German surname, and at the castle in Nuremberg, my first day, we enter a shop to buy gifts for friends back home, and to my horror, the young man who waits on us, between the counter and shelves stacked with boxes of gingerbread, has my heartbreaker's hands—huge, handsome, German hands—and powerful forearms. Listening to the clerk explain the various kinds of gingerbread for sale, I stare at his hands—B's hands—and think: It's because B has German blood, that's where he got the hands, the arms, the beautiful dick, the balls that flow down the inside of his thighs like a waterfall. The salesclerk is charming, too, like B, has a sweet smile, an affability, a vulnerability which, in the case of B, I learned to regret, is only a mask for an iron will.

(All the clichés rose up full-blown my first day in Nuremberg. In the streets of the old town later on, voluptuous blonds in pairs walked past—Hitler Youth—and I had to ask myself later that afternoon: Why do we insist on standing, two Jews and I, on the platform where Hitler stood reviewing the parade at the rally-ground now used for rock concerts? Because we romanticize things, even this, and there is no country more romantic than Germany.)

Even the former German Democratic Republic seems romantic to me, and I expect, when we cross the former, invisible border, a deep radical change in what I see. Instead, I merely find the same small towns, with unpainted houses, the gray cement stucco deeply depressing after a while. The forest, however, looks deeper and lusher in Thuringia than anywhere else. On the way are towns I planned to stop at—Dresden, Leipzig, Weimar—but I have so little time, I stay on the train. Leipzig is marked, at first, by a vast row of Stalinist-modern apartment buildings on its outskirts, and, in the center, by a wonderful cast-iron train station that evokes every movie you've seen set in the thirties. By the time we reach Berlin, it is nightfall, and the train stops not at the Zoo, where my friend is waiting with the keys to the apartment I can stay in, but the Bahnhof. I grab a cab to the Zoo station, can't find my friend, and, after consultation with my taxi driver, decide to be dropped off at the baths.

There are two baths in Berlin; the Apollo Sauna is the one I go to. I've had little sleep the past three nights, but the minute I find myself inside, I feel a return of ecstatic energy. I don't live here, I know no one, the lighting is soft, I'm traveling, it's late, I can drop all the guilt and worry and apologies at the door; I can just swim again, through the dim red hallways, through all the pale white flesh.

I go, the next day, to the Schloss Charlottenburg; I walk up and down the graveled paths lined with wooden tubs of oleander and plumbago; I see the bust of Nefertiti across the street; I take the train out to Potsdam, and see Sans Souci. But the minute I enter the gardens of the palace there, I see a shirtless young gardener digging up the edge of a portion of lawn in the hazy sunlight, and I think: All I care about is this. Thank God, then, for the baths.

It is hard to generalize, but if one had to, one would say: The Apollo is the glitzy baths, the Steam Sauna more S&M. At the Apollo there's a pool, a luxurious bar and lounge, and walking down the narrow halls one might be on a passenger ship looking for one's cabin (like Vivien Leigh in *Ship of Fools*). The crowd is eclectic, and good-looking. Disco is played all the time. At the Steam Sauna, there is also a nice bar and lounge, but only one floor of rooms, a darker, quieter, more Spartan atmosphere, and bigger, more middle-aged, more muscular men; though this crowd is eclectic, too. When a friend told me the Tom's Bar crowd goes to the Steam Sauna, it only confirmed my impression of the place: that there was something more serious in the mood here, more somber, more silent. The more I go, the more intimidated I get, in fact, and spend my last visit there just sitting in a chair at the end of a corridor watching people walk by. My friend was back at the apartment, waiting for me to call; when I did, I said there was really nothing more I wanted to do in the way of museums, so I called every two hours and kept extending my stay at the Steam Sauna. All I wanted to do, I realized, was look at these men.

In Munich, I had gone on the advice of a friend to the Glyptothek, the museum devoted to Greek and Roman sculpture. Athletes and gods, Roman emperors—that's what I was looking at, though they seemed to me taller than the Greeks or Romans ever were. Some of the young men at the Steam Sauna are as tall as basketball players; and they wear the same haircuts, too, the haircuts favored by black urban youth—shaved around the sides, with just a flat cap of thicker hair like a plate on top of the skull. They are huge, gangling youths, with long arms and legs; six feet, six or seven inches tall. Some wear little leather straps around their necks. They seem as angular as giraffes. I'm feeling short now—I who in my generation was tall—and as I sit in the chair at the rear of the corridor, I'm shrinking, like Alice, in self-esteem. I don't even think I can try to sleep with any of these people. They're too handsome, too muscular, too hung, too big. It's all too serious, too German, too S&M.

Or so I imagine; in truth I can see—thousands of miles from the baths in Florida—the same expressions, the same behavior, the same moods that I recognize so well in Jacksonville. The odd distance that, I think, AIDS has created: a moat of indifference, or wariness, on top of the usual boredom, the tired search for the men who will give them attention, if not ecstasy. The feeling that one has been here too much, knows everyone else, will probably go home without doing anything. There is an extraordinary patience, and a resignation, at the baths now. A reserve, a distance, a depression. The first man I see on entering—spread out on a mattress in one of the rooms—attracts me immediately; he sees the expression on my face and stares back; but then, taking my time, seeing him in the hall later, I decide the face is too sharp, too wolverine, not what I want, and I spend the rest of the afternoon mystifying him by not acting on the desire he saw written on my visage when I first came in. The baths have their timetables. Their languors. In Jacksonville it all seems too casual. Here a certain murkiness prevails. The big, young, beautiful, godlike blond who takes the chair next to mine is only one of two or three beauties who seem to find no one they want. It is a Sunday afternoon; for some, the dregs of a weekend. Who knows what mood these people are in? Though I could stay here forever, I'm afraid to find out—to do anything more than look; I'm afraid to cross the threshold, to pierce the membrane, to test the visual fantasy against reality. Reality is what I'm here to forget.

The luxury of being a tourist on vacation—the luxury of Berlin itself—is deepened by the fact that the Steam Sauna and the Apollo are on the same street: the Kurfürstenstrasse. Not the Kurfürstendam, the famous avenue lined with smart shops and glass display cases holding purses, scarves, china, and, beside them, when I walk home late at night, prostitutes in hip-high boots who all seem to be doing what I was just doing at the baths. The Kurfürstenstrasse is on the other side of Europa Center, the central square of West Berlin, where the bombed church and modern spire that the Berliners call the Lipstick and the Compact stand. You can walk from one to the other sauna in about four minutes. So on my last day in Berlin, this delicious Sunday, I leave the Steam Sauna, have dinner at a Greek restaurant with friends, and then go to the Apollo. The Apollo, which used to intimidate, is, after the Steam Sauna, a relief; more glitzy, yes, but more cheerful, more heterogeneous, less somber and S&M.

Which means I want to find someone here—all the inhibition, the intimidation, the stimuli of the past week, the attempt to forget B, have mounted to form a certain desire for release. Yet what a curious mix of self-esteem, and lack of self-esteem, selecting an object entails: the confidence to think one can obtain this person; the feeling that this person is worth one's abasement. We bring things to the baths that grow ever more complicated, and delicate, as we age. We bring aging itself. Its guilt, its vulnerability, its sense of masquerade. Everything is poured into one intense performance, one unconditional adoration, with no encore. Before I left on this trip, I was having sex with almost anyone who showed up at the men's room of a local state park; now I am all discrimination. Wait for the connection. Wait till there is someone who calls up enthusiasm. Because, when you're older, rejection and acceptance are both more intensely felt.

The person this time comes up and stands beside me for just a moment as I watch a film in the porn room; he then leaves and sits down in a chair in the hall, where I stand, a few doors down, behind two men gossiping, so that I can see parts of his body, without his being aware of my interest. He's smaller than I am—about five foot eight. He's smooth, and has short brown hair, and skin that is either naturally olive-toned, or burnished by the sun. He sits in the chair, somber, reserved, like a Mexican sculpture, a Toltec god, beneath a pinlight. I follow him when he gets up and goes downstairs, and there, on the staircase, he looks up and sees I am intent on him, sees what he has snagged, as I follow him down to the next floor, where he disappears, until I see him five minutes later, lying in his room with the door open.

Heartache, obsession, aging, the men at the Steam Sauna, the men in the streets of Nuremberg, the men in the streets of Berlin, in the gloomy green paths of the Tiergarten, where they cruise, speechless, somber, slow, the force of a desire which crystallizes less frequently but is deeper when it does, the whole long Sunday, all coalesce on his body—his nipples; which I take into my mouth and tongue for a long, long time. Nipples are always a surprise; some men feel nothing, others are like pianos being tuned. This man has shaved his chest and groin; the former, I can tell, has the faintest stubble, as I move my face down its smooth surface. The best sex is mutual; he does to you, you do to him. I haven't had that sort of sex in a long time, I don't know why; it hasn't been my luck; more and more, I seem to raid people—to plunder their bodies, enact an adoration which might be, I've thought, boring to the recipient, since I suspect most of us want to adore. I lick this man all over. His penis is perfect. Soft, meaty, a cylinder of dough, easy to swallow. His balls I can hold in my mouth. The insides of his thighs are smooth. We pause to reach for a rubber. He seems to me like a courtesan—someone who shaves himself, who perfumes himself, who prepares himself for a pleasure he values highly. His face, when I glance up, has a serious, almost pained expression. He seems to me Europe itself: the respect for pleasure. When we are through, I slip off the bunk and kneel down on the floor beside him and stare at his body in profile. I've seen the Glyptothek, the bust of Nefertiti, the Guido Reni painting in the Alte Pinakotek of Apollo and Marsyas, but this is what lies behind them. He smiles gently at the depth of my emotion, and tells me I have been eating garlic.

PART SIX

HISTORICAL

FANTASY

One way to deal with the harshness of contemporary life is to retreat into historical fantasy. In another time, in another place, our lives could be different. Or, even more luxurious to contemplate, perhaps they *were* different and we simply haven't been told about what really happened.

Randy Boyd has captured that sense in "The King and His Virgin Boy." Here is the same insurgent belief in a different reality that Gary Collins has written about in his Clay Caldwell novels. There is the king, yes, and he is married and performs his duty as consort and ruler, but he has a more important secret life, one that is more romantic, more fulfilling, and more important to him than all the honors in the world.

The kings of other times, Boyd seems to be saying, had their own lives, much like ours. They were not as offensive as they might have been—the king waits in this story until his virgin boy is of a decent age—so the danger of duress isn't dealt with head-on. The fantasy is that even the kidnapped boy discovers romance and contentment in the fantasy world that so few others know about. Not that the implication of pederasty is ignored; in fact, one of its attractions is highlighted: that through the love of a youth, an old man will stay young forever. Romance was never a stranger to that idea.

"If New Orleans Were Paris" is another historical fantasy that seems to deal with a social issue that's too harsh to face in our time: the love between two black men, one who might disown his lover by "passing," an ultimate betrayal. We find in Jamoo's story the belief that there was a period when love itself could rule, a place like Paris where happiness could be achieved, no matter what today's realities are.

THE KING

AND HIS

VIRGIN

BOY

IN A FARAWAY LAND UNTOUCHED BY MACHINES, where camels and oxen labored through the sprawling village, where peasants bartered in teeming streets and slept in mud-based huts, where the merciless sun baked the earth brown and crackling dry every day of every year, a king sat high on his throne in the palace, watching his little offspring frolic amongst the statues, discussing the state of his gold with the wise men of the kingdom, accepting the parade of gifts from neighboring leaders terrified of his army.

He was a handsome king, with long sinewy muscles and dark cocoa skin as shiny as the sun-drenched sea that bordered the kingdom and as smooth as the bushels of silk his explorers brought back to him from the East. From the day he was born prince, not one hair had ever emerged from his head, and men from lands near and far spun tales of the good fortune they encountered after seeing their reflection in the King's skull.

The King seemed ageless, but the elders of the palace knew him to be near the end of his fourth decade on earth; and this meant that one day very soon, when the sun was at its apex, the King would rise from his throne and lead a hand-picked procession of the wisest men into the village, searching.

The King would not pick the day. The day would pick the King. He would feel the passage of time as never before, and the ancestors of his heart would sing to him a song of passion, reverberating without end through the chasms of his soul. And he would know: the time had come. To do as his father had, as his father's father had, as had every king since the first ruler of the land, his great-grandfather eighteen times. It was the kingdom's oldest ritual, the King's most revered and respected right, that once he had tamed the world with his iron fist, he could explore the deepest, most forbidden desire of the land.

Thus, on the seventh day of a spell when the sun had all but set fire to the earth, the King declared he had heard the song in his soul and set out for the village.

In the glaring light of day the streets were filled with merchants and peasants shouting loudly, children and geese running wild, smoke from kettles coating the air. The village was so chaotic, at first no one noticed the King in his long robe of red with gold trimming, flanked on all sides by the twelve wise men with their solemn black robes and thinning white hair. But then, as the procession wandered deeper into the masses, the crowd began to part like the sea. Many bowed as they saw the King, although it wasn't the law. Others sought the sight of their reflection on the side of his head. But the King paid no attention to his fawning subjects. Instead he traveled purposefully through the streets, face emotionless, eyes steady, looking to the right, then the left, always down toward the legs of the adults.

By a large steaming kettle, amidst a sea of taller bodies, a young boy was playing with a short stick that had a small ball attached via a string. He was a light-skinned boy, perhaps seven, with straight, jet-black hair and haunting, sky-blue eyes that were consumed in trying to land the ball atop the stick. Eagerly, the wise men looked to the King. Barely moving, the King shook his head and looked away.

On the other side of the street a dark-haired brown boy of ten was straddling a mammoth oxen, whipping it with a tree branch, admonishing the stubborn beast to move while his tiny sister pushed at the animal's ass from the ground. For a moment the King studied the boy, whose too-large shirt hung loosely on his narrow frame and whose exposed brown thighs were made meaty by their pressing against the oxen. Tempting, but the King glanced away and continued on.

Under one of the merchants' tents five young Arabian brothers were hawking garments for their rotund father, who was busy bickering with an elderly woman just outside the tent. The King's eyes swept over all five boys, who seemed to be lined up from oldest to youngest. The oldest was around eleven, with a tall lanky body that moved with stilted self-consciousness. The next one had buckteeth and anxious black eyes. Then came two seven-year-old freckle-faced twins, each lazily resting an arm on the other's shoulders. The youngest was a sobbing four-year-old with chubby cheeks made even chubbier by his tears. The wise men eyed each other expectantly, thinking surely one of these might do. But the King made note of them all, then proceeded.

Underneath a tent flap blowing in the wind was a pure black boy who looked to be twelve. He was bony, and because he was shirtless, his ribs showed through his flat torso as he raised his arms high above his head, offering a freshly caught fish to the crowd. His hair was nappy and still wet from the sea, and sun-filled droplets of water speckled his smooth ebony shoulders like glistening pearls of sweat. Trying to be heard above the rumble of the village, he cried out loudly about the fish, his voice alternately high and coarse, the change from boy to man only just beginning. From a distance of ten paces, the King looked the boy over, his still hairless underarms, his skinny but toned legs lost in his baggy khaki shorts, which were also still wet and clinging to his hiked-up butt. Seeing the

King's prolonged glance, the wise men stepped toward the boy, but suddenly the King turned away. The village was full of young boys of many origins with sprouting bodies, healthy heads of hair, and golden auras, but legend dictated that only the boy who unquestionably harnessed the desire reverberating in the King's soul would live at the palace. The fisher-boy was not the one.

Next to a bountiful vegetable cart, a weathered, dark-complected woman with graying hair was arguing with an equally weathered merchant about his prices. Behind her, tugging at her drab brown dress, was a wide-eyed boy of mixed origins, younger than the fisher-boy by three, perhaps four, perhaps even five years. His skin seemed pale but for a deep, rich caramel coating the sun had permanently poured into his pores, and his upper lip turned upward, suggesting a hunger for experience. His eyes were green and blue at once, and atop his head he possessed big, overgrown curls that collected the sun's rays like tiny little magnets and rendered his hair as blond as the desert sand beyond the village. Yet he was neither light like the tribes to the far north nor dark like the people of the King's region. Nor was he the color of yolk as if from the East. He was all of them and he was none of them. He was his own breed of boy.

As the King laid eyes on him, the boy stopped tugging at his mother and glanced upward, not at the King, who was twenty paces away, but at the boisterous bodies surrounding him, looking around as if to take in this daily sight of life in the village. Though he could see him only through a maze of bodies, the King became immediately drawn to the boy, the flawlessness of his caramel skin, the promise of life and energy in his lean, developing body, the purity of his eyes, vacant of malice but ripe with curiosity.

The King's head lifted ever so slightly and his eyes widened with barely detectable anticipation. And the wise men knew the search was over. The King turned away and began walking in the direction of the palace while the wise men slipped through the crowd toward the chosen boy. Catching the suddenly sober reflection in the merchant's eyes, the mother turned around, just in time to see the twelve wise men standing over her son, who regarded them unassumingly. Then, in the distance, she saw the back of the King moving away, and instantly she knew what was expected of her.

The eldest of the wise men extended his hand in front of the boy, who looked up to his mother out of confusion. As an answer, she returned glassy, stoic eyes, saying nothing but nodding once and offering encouragement with a forced, bittersweet smile. The boy then turned back around, contemplated the hand before him, and began walking, not understanding why but realizing that these were the most important servants to the most important man of the land.

The wise men formed a colonnade on either side of the boy, who marched slowly and solemnly through the parting crowd, following the King, who marched alone fifty paces ahead. Several times the boy looked back to his mother, who fought back tears filled with pride that her son had been chosen and sorrow that her boy was being taken away from her.

At the palace the boy was told he would be living with the King now and was shown his room by the wise men. It was a vast room—second only to the King's in size—with plush sofas made of the finest velvet and a huge canopied bed draped in silk and covered with gigantic pillows that loomed like small mountains. The bed alone was as big as the tent the boy used to call home, and upon his request, it would be surrounded by servants to fan him when the palace became too hot.

And every night, in his own bed, at the opposite end of the palace, the King would stroke his massive cock, swirling and writhing, hands roaming over his body for hours on end, drowning himself in a sea of sweat and cum, dreaming of the virgin boy he had chosen, the tenderness of his chiseled jawline, the rosiness of his sun-baked cheeks, the supple muscularity of the curve in his back, the petite, cuppable nature of his perfectly round, hairless butt. Everything about him was pure and untouched, captivating the King's senses every night for most of the night. His boy, his smooth, innocent virgin boy, the King would think over and over, stroking, throbbing, pulsating, praying for the day when he was finally ready . . .

The boy's daily schedule was exact. He was given the best teachers in the land, the best philosophers, the best athletes, the best warriors, the best thinkers. In the palace's hallowed halls of learning, he was taught arithmetic and the secrets of the galaxies. He boxed with champion fighters and hurled spears with the most renowned soldiers of the King's army. He learned how to scale the palace walls and conquer the swiftest of horses. He was taught the history of all lands and lifted sacks of gold twice his weight for strength.

From time to time, the King observed these lessons, not in the boy's presence, but from behind hidden holes in the stone walls, sitting in the darkness of the elaborate series of catacombs that ran though the palace and were forbidden to all but the King. And what he saw of the boy and his lessons rendered the King numb with desire.

At mealtimes the boy was given everything to eat his growing body cried out for. Tray upon tray filled with the land's best meats, breads, vegetables, and desserts were placed before his eyes, which never failed to widen with awe and delight. Dinner was a great feast at the palace, conducted in a huge, ceremonious hall draped with flags of every color and attended by fifty of the King's most privileged guests. At one end of the long dining table sat the boy, flanked on either side by his teachers. In the middle sat the King's wives and his many children, and at the other end was the King himself, surrounded by the twelve wise men and visiting dignitaries.

But neither the King nor the boy paid as much attention to the royal guests as they did to each other. The King couldn't help studying his virgin boy's roving, curious eyes as they surveyed the feast and his soft, full lips as they engulfed the fruits of the village; and because the highest man in the land kept casting his gaze on the boy, the boy found himself perpetually glancing at the solemn-faced King in the distance, mesmerized and mystified every time their stares interlocked. But stare was all either could do, at dinnertime or any other time, for legend dictated: for now, the King did not speak to the boy and the boy was not allowed to speak to the King.

As the seasons passed, the boy grew stronger and stronger. His thin, cable-like legs became thicker, his buttocks rounder and fuller.

Where a flat chest once lay, hills and valleys began to take shape, and his shoulders strained to expand like wings. His hair began to straighten and brown, retaining its sheen with streaks of gold caused by the sun; but elsewhere on his body, he remained hairless and pure, his skin as smooth as the day he was born, his blue-green eyes still full of life and wonder.

When he was a little older, the elite of the land came dressed in their most regal attire and lined the courtyard ten deep to see the King's virgin boy match skills with the other boys of the village in the palace warrior games. Naked but for loincloths made of oxen skin, the boys wrestled, boxed, and clashed with spears twice their height; and in each and every one of his contests, the King's boy emerged triumphant, rising proudly over the defeated boy, basking in the glorious roar of the onlookers. And no one was prouder than the King, who sat upon his courtyard throne atop a velvet-covered stage, barely containing his grin. To think that his boy was succeeding in becoming the fiercest warrior of the land!

After each day of courtyard conquests, the virgin boy would collapse behind the silk draperies of his canopied bed and fall fast asleep amongst the mountains of pillows, as peaceful as a baby, with his cheek thrust against the pillow and his lips barely open, effortlessly omitting a small steady breath. And sitting quietly on the other side of the wall in one of the dark catacombs the King would watch him, peering hypnotically through a small rectangular hole cut in the stone wall.

And every night, in his own bed, at the opposite end of the palace, the King would stroke his massive cock, swirling and writhing, hands roaming over his body for hours on end, drowning himself in a sea of sweat and cum, dreaming of the virgin boy he had chosen, replaying his unparalleled athletic feats, savoring the way his soft, miniature muscles moved as he leaped and soared and wrestled the other boys down to the dirt, the way his solid little thighs tensed as he lunged forward, the crease between his jutted-out shoulder blades as he raised his spear high above his head, the way his buttocks spread like two perfect melons when he got down on all fours, straddling his soon-to-be-defeated opponent, the way his hair moistened with sweat from the unrelenting heat of the desert sun, the way his eyes widened as he went in for the kill, then shyly glanced toward the King after each conquest, anxious for approval that was only forthcoming by way of a slight nod and an even slighter grin.

The King dreamed of these things every night, brandishing his cock with both hands, tossing his head from side to side, arching his back until he was offering himself to the gods, moaning and writhing until his cock blasted the juice that bore his love for the virgin boy. And the King devoured the juice, imagining it to be the boy's, knowing that that day could not come soon enough . . .

With each season, the boy became bigger and more strapping, so much so that he burst from his britches often, sending the royal tailor into a frenzy trying to keep up with his growth. No other boy, older or younger, could beat him in the warrior games, and none of the beasts brought in from the wild for a ferocious challenge stood a chance against his mighty spear. He treasured the physical labor around the fields of the palace, sweating away days at a time under the sun, lifting boulders and felling trees, harnessing his boundless energy in a way that only made his limbs stronger. He was growing by leaps and bounds, his enthusiasm for the life he'd come to know unmatched by his teachers and the other boys brought into the palace to play with him.

So great was his thirst for life, he was never motionless. At night, when all others were asleep, he roamed the palace alone, searching for clues to the biggest mystery in his life, the King, a man with whom he had never exchanged words. Somehow he realized their destinies were intertwined. He knew not how or why, but understood that his presence in the palace was due to His Majesty and relished putting a smile on the King's face, whether it was at the warrior games or in the great dining hall, where the King reacted with amusement to the boy's swift and furious devouring of meals. The boy admired the King in ways he couldn't articulate and savored even the briefest chance to glimpse the most important man in the land holding court, receiving other royalty, or dispatching his army.

The boy became obsessed with the King, and one night, during his secret explorations of the palace, he stumbled upon the catacombs forbidden to all but His Majesty. Curiosity won out over fear. The boy snaked his way through the pitch-black corridors and eventually found a faint light emanating from a small rectangular hole cut through the stone at his waist. As he bent over to peer through the opening, his heart leaped into his throat: he saw for the first time the King's candlelit bedroom. And in the canopied bed—a larger replica of the boy's own—the King was wide awake, seemingly wrestling with himself with the covers torn off.

The boy squatted down and watched in amazement at what he saw upon a more careful look. The King was handling his dick in a way the boy had never thought of, never imagined, grabbing onto it with both hands, pumping it into his fists. It was ten times the size of the boy's, or so it seemed, and the boy looked on with eyes as wide as the desert, his breath taken away, his senses reeling, unable to take his gaze off the King and his dick and the way the King was stroking it and the strange, almost pained look on the King's face.

Outwardly the boy was frozen. Inwardly he was shaking from the magnitude of his discovery and the fear of being found. Then instinct forced him to look down. Underneath his white bloomers his own dick had popped upward with such force it was aching and he thought it would fall off. It had hardened before, but never like this. In a panic he looked back through the hole, as if the King might suddenly spot him and his aching dick and erupt with anger. But in the next instant, he saw that the King's hands had stopped their motion and now His Majesty's dick was peeing, peeing milky white pee all over the King's face and bed and chest and hands. The boy almost fainted from shock, but instead stumbled backward, away from the hole. Then he hastily crawled down the corridor, and when he was a safe distance away, he rose and sprinted all the way back to his own room, diving into his bed and burying his head underneath the mountain of pillows, his whole conception of life and the King suddenly cast chaotically into the wind.

Every night after that, the boy ventured back through the catacombs to watch the King perform his ritual; and when the King's big dick peed the white milk, the boy ran back to his own bed and stayed up half the night, replaying what he had just witnessed. Not a spare moment went by that the boy didn't think of the King and what he did with his dick, and one night, in the moonlit darkness of his own room, he summoned up the courage to give in to his desire to try the King's ritual for himself.

He felt pleasure immediately, but was disappointed when his dick failed to pee the white milk as the King's had. Must be something only kings can do, he concluded, but repeated the ritual night after night anyway, always eventually giving up the quest to produce his own milk and falling asleep with his dick in his hand. Many times while he stroked himself, he imagined he was the King, pleasing his royal dick by pumping it into his huge, manly fists. Other times he fantasized he was lying next to the King in the royal bed, both of them handling their dicks until they wanted to shout out loud.

So began the boy's own nightly ritual, watching the King and repeating the act, and after a few more seasons passed, milk finally erupted from within the boy. He was overjoyed to be just like the King, and from then on, he practiced the ritual as many times as he could during the course of the day, all the while thinking of the King.

The wise men, who periodically monitored the boy through their own private viewing holes, saw that he could now ejaculate, and as legend dictated, they watched and waited for his cum to be lily-white, thick, and plentiful every time without fail before informing the King. The suns and moons came and went, the boy practiced his favorite new activity over and over, and soon his orgasms became as potent as geysers. Thus, on a day when the King was on his throne holding court, the wise men whispered the news in his ear. Wordlessly, the King smiled, a gradually evolving grin that had been years in the making.

For the rest of the day, the King canceled all business and did nothing but bathe and sauna and tone his muscles. Then, at nightfall, he dressed in his finest, shiny gold pantaloons and white, frilly shirt, and all of the palace was dismissed into the village. The boy was to be dressed by his teachers in white britches and nothing else, and told to wait at his bedside to formally meet His Majesty.

The boy knew not what to say to the King or how to act, and once his teachers left him alone and waiting, he trembled with thoughts of meeting the mythical figure whom his day and night had come to revolve around. Visions of the King's nightly ritual and his own nightly reaction danced a furious dance in his head, and every piercing look the King had ever given him came flooding back in his memory. The boy had no inkling what to expect, but every part of his soul told him that tonight, their rituals would merge into one.

The King entered the room and walked deliberately toward the boy, who sat on the bed. Then, standing over him, the King extended his hand. Nervous, the boy looked up, eyes darting back and forth, not knowing what to do. "Be not shy, be not afraid," said the King in a soft but commanding voice, his first words ever uttered to the boy. With trepidation, the boy placed his hand in the King's, and even though he had grown and was still growing, his hand was much smaller than that of the man towering over him.

With a firm grip, the King drew the boy up from the bed, then gently scooped him up in his arms and carried him out of the bedroom, past the sky-high stone walls, past the statues and the great halls, up the long, sweeping staircase to the King's wing and the King's bedroom. At the royal bed, the King set the boy down on the floor and they stood a breath apart, the boy barely reaching the King's shoulders.

Soundlessly, the King peeled off the boy's white britches, leaving the boy naked with his cock reaching upward like a bowsprit. His was a long but skinny cock—still budding, just like the boy himself—with a light-colored swirl of pubic hair forming a small wreath around the base. After pausing to drink in the sight of the tender flesh before him, the King also stripped nude, then placed two fingers into the mouth of the boy, who stood there agape, still trembling with uncertainty. With his other hand, the King took the boy's shaking hand and placed it on the King's chest. The boy felt it on his own, astonished at being able to touch a man's chest, so much bigger and harder than his.

Slipping his fingers out of the boy's mouth, the King ran his hands down either side of the boy's torso, so narrow and lean. Then, as the King's hands reached lower, the underside of his forearm brushed against the boy's cock and discovered a wetness. The boy had come already, shooting a healthy load on his stomach just above his blossoming pubic hair. Immediately the boy's face flushed red. The King smiled to put him at ease, then went down on his knees and kissed the boy's waning erection and licked his taut, bald stomach, lapping up his fresh, white cream, as sweet as any delicacy in the kingdom. Then, with a full mouth, he stood up and kissed the boy, the taste of the warm juice lingering on both their tongues. The boy kissed him back, so hard their teeth collided, and when the King brought their bodies together, he found the boy's dick was stiff as stone once again. The kiss grew harder. Their arms wrapped around each other, holding each other prisoner. The boy began running his hands all over the King's arms and backside, as if finally he was able to explore a body, like his own in that it was a male's, but unlike his own in that the King was a man, and the man was the King.

The King's hands went to the boy's butt, caressing his firm yet soft cheeks, sliding his fingers into the crack, feeling warmth and dampness within. Their bodies swayed against each other, the King's cock lodged against the boy's stomach, the boy's breath becoming shorter and shorter. He was on the verge of coming again.

The King drew back to stop him and set the boy on the bed, easing him down on his back and straddling his face, then guiding the boy's head upward as the boy's mouth opened, taking in the King's cock. At first the boy's lips remained motionless, simply satisfied to be encased around the King's swollen head. Then he started to swallow the King's cock, then retreat for air, then swallow some more, then retreat, then swallow, and soon he got the hang of going up and down with his soft pink lips and hot watery mouth, sucking till the King feared he himself would come.

The King twisted around so that he was facing the opposite direction and, while the boy still sucked on his dick, he bent over and nuzzled his face in the boy's crotch, inhaling the fresh musk of the tiny patch of pubic hair, eyeing the boy's quivering dick, which rose above his nose like a small tree trunk and would surely explode again at a touch. So instead of reaching for the narrow little tree trunk, the King played with the boy's balls and burrowed his nose toward his ass. Then, without warning, he scooped the boy up by the small of his back and turned the two of them over, putting the King on his back with the boy over him; and while the boy became more and more adept at devouring the King's dick, the King planted his face in the boy's butt, flattening his tongue and running up and down the length of the crack several times before stopping at the pinkest of pink holes. At first the King merely stared and admired it, its softness, its rosiness. Then he gently kissed the slightly puckered lips. Then, unable to contain himself any longer, he dove in, burying himself deep within the dark tunnel of the boy's butthole, caressing the whiskerless outer cheeks with his hands and massaging the silky-smooth inner walls with his tongue till the smell and taste and quite literally the boy's ass became another layer of skin on his face.

As if the sensation he felt on his anus was completely unexpected, the boy arched up in ecstasy, squatting even farther down on the King's face, moaning a moan that was somewhere between an exalted cry and a helpless whimper. The King plunged even deeper into the boy's ass, eating away as if it were his last act on earth, and the boy began gyrating in sync with the wondrous tingling swimming from his butthole to the rest of his entire body.

Helpless at the hysteria every nerve and muscle was experiencing, the boy bent down to eat the King, his cock, his balls, his ass, sliding over the King's lower body like a puppy frantically lapping up water. The boy's reaction only encouraged the King to make a meal of his ass that much more, and the two of them began grinding their slippery torsos against one another, the King eating and fingering the boy's butt, the boy slurping on the King's balls and ass and jacking off the King's cock while humping his chest. They became one feverish mass of flesh and heat, skin rubbing on skin, sweat dripping on sweat, spit cascading in rivers, their bodies frenzied and frantic and pumping and gyrating till the King blasted his cum high in the air and, moments later, the boy drowned both of their torsos with his own white milk.

The two collapsed side by side, facing opposite directions, panting for their lives. When conscious thought returned to the King, he lay still and quiet, waiting for the boy to recover, knowing they'd do it again and again and he would show the boy a thousand more things they could do with each other, that night and every night for the rest of their lives. And the King would rule his kingdom, his wives would set protocol for the women of the palace, his oldest prince would be groomed to someday rule the world, his other children would vie for other prominent roles in the village, and the King would be forever young with his boy by his side.

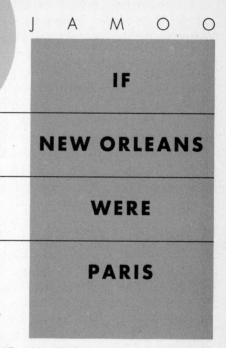

JAMOO

IF

NEW ORLEANS

WERE

PARIS

ARMAND SLEPT BY THE WINDOW WHENEVER IT
rained. It always seemed strange to me to sleep there in his big
arms, my head resting on his massive, hairy chest. The warm furry
curls in his armpit pressed against my shoulder as he held me and
slept in a dream. I waited impatiently for him to wake. On mornings after it had rained, Armand always seemed to possess a strange
power. On those mornings, he always worked me, murmuring in
French while kissing my nipples. And then he'd fuck me like a
stallion, leaving me sore and longing for it to rain every night, all
year long.

It was humid that summer of 1888. Thirsting Louisiana mos-
quitoes buzzed hungrily outside the netting over the bed. We lay
naked, sleepy and satiated on the warm mattress, our bodies hot
enough to set the bed aflame.

Armand lay sleeping in the early-morning light, lying on his back with his long, brown, hair-covered legs spread apart. His big cock and balls nestled between his powerful thighs. His fingers were resting in the delicious patch of black pubic hair around his long, slender organ. He played with himself as he slept, a smile upon his handsome face. His other powerfully muscled arm was thrown back on the pillow. As he stirred, I leaned over and rubbed my nose into the thick patch of hair in his exposed armpit, glistening with sweat. I smelled his musky, manly scent. My tongue lapped as my cock hardened and slipped out of my foreskin. I reached down and cupped his silky balls—large, loose-hanging, and covered in hundreds of tiny black curly coils. He groaned and jerked open his eyes. He squinted in the bright sunshine streaming through the window.

"Benjamin, let me sleep," he whispered, reaching up to stroke my face lovingly.

"Turn over," I whispered back, giving him a push. He rolled his huge body over with a groan and lay still. I ran my eager fingers over the muscles in his back and down to the soft patch of hair growing there. The patch spread out to cover his buttocks, growing even thicker in the cleft. I grasped each muscled globe of soft flesh and began to lick between them. Pulling them apart, I flicked my tongue against the wet, twitching brown bud hidden under the curls. Armand groaned, thrusting his buttocks into the air. His heavy balls seemed to swell as he humped the mattress. I wasted no time in taking those balls, one at a time, into my mouth and sucking them, feeling the soft, squishy flesh and knowing that they were full of hot come.

I rubbed my nose against the crack of his ass. I slid my middle finger into the hot wetness where my young cock had been buried the night before. He twitched and shivered, his asshole tightening hungrily. Armand rolled over. With one swift motion, he grabbed my shoulders and pulled me up onto his body, chest to chest, cock to cock, our bodies against one another. We rubbed together, feeling our sticky precome oozing out onto each other's bellies. He grinned, the tiny lines around his large green eyes crinkling.

"*Mon Dieu!* What am I to do with you, little Benjamin? Will you let me have no sleep? You are worse than a satyr!" he laughed, rubbing my smooth back as I lay on his barrel chest. I licked his face like a puppy eager for attention. He squeezed my ass and cupped the rounded globes. He worked his finger into my tight anus. He held me tightly to him. The bed smelled of sweat, cologne, and men's bodies; I wanted it always to smell that sweet.

"Armand, please do it again?" I begged. "Make love to me. Fuck me, please?"

"*Mon bébé!* But of course, my work is never done till my boy is happy." He grinned.

I sat up straight and arched my back. The curly hairs between my asscheeks rubbed against the sensitive tip of his brown-gold cock. The thick, bunched-up foreskin began to withdraw. His bright pink, wrist-thick cockhead was wet and shiny in the sunlight streaming through the mosquito netting.

Armand locked his big hands on my waist and pulled me, in one motion, right down onto his erect cock. The greasy hot pecker was buried deep in my gut. I wiggled, moving up and down, the ring of my sphincter contracting tightly around it. He groaned and gritted his teeth. As I rode his cock, his forehead wrinkled and the veins in his thick neck bulged. His fingers dug into my waist and I rode him as hard as I could, his big body trembling beneath me.

Then, as he was getting close, I reached down and grabbed his massive pectorals, covered in a thick blanket of salt-and-pepper hair. I squeezed the copper-colored buttons of his nipples, twisting and teasing them.

Poor Armand! He was dripping with sweat and moaning. I felt his cock pulse as his hot essence pumped into my sweet ass. He moaned in a deep voice over and over again.

"Was it good, Papa?" I teased, knowing it was. I leaned down, licking his sweaty nipples and causing him to twitch. His now spongy cock slipped from my slick hole with a popping sound and flopped against his thighs.

"What does my Papa want?"

I loved him. It was hard for me to believe that he had already lived half a century, had seen and been born into slavery. Long before freedom would come to rest, Armand's white father had set him free and set him up as a blacksmith. He thrived in New Orleans among all the rich, free mulatto and quadroon men. He was accepted and respected in his craft by all and had won his place in society.

A beautiful man, Armand had been blessed with a perfect body, handsome face, a huge horse-sized, golden-brown mulatto cock, and heavy balls. Sometimes he looked closer to thirty-five than fifty. A few gray hairs mixed in with his beautiful long curly hair and in his sideburns, adding to his dashing appearance. The soft, luxuriant hair on his flat belly and the hair of his crotch and underarms remained black.

Through years of experience, Armand had learned well how to please his lovers with every part of his body. He still worked at his blacksmith shop and his muscles were well-toned, bulging in his arms and legs. His waist was narrow, his back broad, and his hairy chest huge and hard as rock. Yet he felt soft and warm as a blanket as I nestled against him every night.

I lifted his legs over my shoulders and pressed my cock against his hot brown asshole. My cockhead popped in, past the tight ring of his sphincter. I shivered with delight, sliding into what felt like heaven, pure heaven.

Armand contracted his ass muscles around my cock like some living glove. I fucked him as if my salvation depended upon it. He reached up and tugged at my little yellow nipples. I came, sweating and crying, and collapsed on top of him.

Armand kissed me and gave a little laugh as I rolled off him and onto the mattress. I watched him rise and cross the room.

"It's like a few seconds in the hands of God when I'm inside of you," I said softly.

"And I see stars when I come inside you, *mon petit*," answered Armand. "Do you know, I wonder, how angelic you look, lying there?"

He filled the washbasin with cool water and dipped a cloth into it. I played lightly with myself as I watched him washing his body. Droplets of water glistened on his golden pectorals, his biceps, his dangling foreskin. He looked at me with a knowing grin on his handsome face as he reached around, washing between the perfect cheeks of his ass, putting on a show for me.

He changed the water in the basin and carried it over to the bed with a fresh cloth. I pulled the mosquito netting aside for him, then lay back against the pillows, my hands behind my head, my legs stretched apart. Gently as a lover can, Armand washed me. My twenty-year-old body, still so sensitized from coming, shook at his touch. He looked at me lovingly, with a touch of sadness. He washed me carefully, as if he were caring for the finest thing in his life. It embarrassed me to be treated with such unexpected reverence; it pleased me nonetheless.

He dried my chest and cock, then rolled me over and washed my back, paying extra attention to my asshole.

Now we were both clean, but the unbearable morning humidity soon had us sweating again. I rolled onto my back. Armand climbed onto me to suck my cock while dangling his hefty cock and balls in my face. We took each other's cocks into our hungry mouths. We sucked on each other's balls and licked at the hot, twitching assholes before our eyes. I moistened two fingers with spit and slid them into him. He reciprocated with three fat fingers and began milking my cock with his other fist.

"Come, Benjamin," he urged, "be a good boy and shoot all over the face of your Papa!"

I could only groan in response. My toes curled. Clots of thick, white come shot up onto his face and neck. He slid my dick completely down into his throat and sucked as hard as he could to catch every drop I'd left to give.

He groaned and his powerful body went taut. My mouth flooded with his hot sperm and I gulped it down greedily.

Armand and I lay exhausted, once again sweat-drenched. He hugged my dripping body and I nuzzled into him.

"Ooh, you are so sweet, my child," he sighed, sadly again. "You are almost too sweet, almost too much like an angel." He looked as deeply into my eyes as I dared let him.

"I love you so much," he confessed.

"And I love you, Armand. You are like the papa I never had," I said, knowing that he was better than my own papa had been.

My white father had loved me and given me everything I'd wanted. He lavished gifts upon my quadroon mother, too. But all we would ever be to him were two things: his mistress and his bastard son. Being one-eighth black, I would never be accepted as his son.

Seeing that there was no future for me on the rapidly declining plantation, I fled to New Orleans. I appealed to Armand for work, and he took me in. Though I wanted him to, he didn't touch me at all in the beginning, preferring simply to give me direction and affection. Only after I'd begged and cried real tears did he let me into his bed, and then only to hug and comfort me.

Until that point, all the men in my life had been unlike me and had eyes only for women. But Armand was like me, he liked men; he wanted only men. He made no attempt to hide it. He had friends and lovers of all colors. Now, I was the one lucky enough to lie in his bed—but only to sleep.

Finally I could stand it no longer and, one morning, he awoke with my mouth on his cock. He made no move to stop me, but began running his rough, callused hands over my soft, light-skinned body. It was the beginning of what felt like paradise on Earth to me. Now, all mornings were as full of delight as this one, almost. But mornings when it had rained the night before—these were the best.

Now we lay there, smiling into each other's eyes. But again Armand's sadness returned.

"One of these days," he sighed, curling my wavy hair around his finger, "one of these days my son is going to leave me for someone else; a rich man, perhaps a white man?"

"I'll leave my Papa for no man," I protested, "be he black, white, or high yellow."

"I think you will, Benjamin. I've seen you passing before. Why do you do it—why do you pass for white?"

"Because I can," I answered, feeling terrible to have saddened him so.

"As you say, Benjamin, you can. But I cannot and this thing will destroy our happiness."

"No, Papa, there is always Paris! We can go there and you will be accepted as a man despite being mulatto. But whether we go there or stay here in New Orleans, I'll never leave you, ever!"

"Even when I am old and gray?" he asked.

"But Papa," I needled him, "you already are!"

He looked at me as if he couldn't decide whether to strike me or kiss me. Then he laughed and his green eyes lit up. He smiled and hugged me tightly.

"*Oui,* Papa," I said, "even then."

"We shall see," he said. "Come, it is time for work."

Armand was the one I loved most in my heart. And, though it did not come for many years after that morning, I remained with him until the end. He will always be part of me.

PART SEVEN

VIOLENT

LUST

History is a way to deal with the violence of our lusts. There can be a kind of historical reconstruction that performs the exact opposite of the fantasies in Part VI. History can be used as a filter through which the savagery of our desire can be examined, but at a step away, a step that takes that ferocity far enough from our present that we can examine it, even if it is upsetting.

Aaron Travis is the pseudonym used by Steven Saylor for most of his erotic work. Saylor is best known now for his detective novels set in classical Rome, most recently *Arms of Nemesis*. He began his professional writing career with pornography. Just as he would use his fascination with Roman life to construct his mainstream novels, that same absorption by the images of Roman gladiators, cruel masters, and tormented slaves fills his erotic stories.

"Slave" is a near-epic story of the cruelty of one Roman master over his handsome slave. It is an S&M classic, a story that evokes some of the strongest reactions possible in the reader. It is distressing for many people to discover themselves responding sexually to the afflictions that Jonah suffers.

It's part of the convention that Jonah is rewarded for his endurance. The pornographic sense in gay erotica doesn't often encourage anything else. After all, it is the masculine rite of passage that the character is going through during all this violence, proving himself to another in some way that involves perseverance and fortitude. A reward is expected after such a trial.

If not a reward, then at least a retelling of the story in a new fashion. What is violence to the perpetrator is not necessarily violence to the victim, or so many gay pornographers write. "Party Meat" is a fine example. It is another example of a rite of passage. Take note of the last sentence and see who the nurturing figure is.

"Baby Love" transforms a violent encounter in the same way. For many gay men, acting out the brutal scripts in the society around them is a way to overcome fear. Savagery may be a reality for black men in America's cities, but the pornographic imagination can take that force and alter it in the erotic lives of the men who live it.

The ritualization of violence in the world of S&M attracts many gay readers and writers. It is a method that we have used to take the mythology of being men and create stories for ourselves in our modern lives.

Gavin Geoffrey Dillard has expressed the gay pornographic imagination for years. He began as a film actor, the star in the classic *Track Meet*. He's moved on, becoming involved in all kinds of iconoclastic art, visual and literary. "Race" is an excerpt from his autobiography that tells of his decision to learn about the ways of S&M from a master, a man whom he had identified as someone who could teach him, and someone whom he could trust.

STEVEN SAYLOR
WRITING AS AARON TRAVIS

SLAVE

"*The unfortunate human being was exhibited exactly as horses are now, and could be stripped, handled, trotted about, and treated with every kind of indignity. . . . He had no rights as a human being, but was himself simply a piece of property. The law left him absolutely at the disposal of his master, who had the power of life and death over him, and could punish him with chastisement and bonds, and use him for any purpose he pleased.*"

—W. WARDE FOWLER, *Social Life at Rome* (1909)

ONE

THE ROOM IS CIRCULAR, HIGH, SPACIOUS, AND airy, with delicate diaphanous curtains drawn against the blistering noonday sun. Bright yellow light seeps through the curtains. An occasional breeze, warm and dry, causes them to ripple and part in places, revealing long slitted glimpses of the pastoral farmland outside—rolling hills and vineyards, faraway vistas of hazy blue mountains.

The columns supporting the high domed roof are of fluted white marble, the best Grecian handiwork that silver can buy. The floor is perfect black marble without veins or impurities, so finely polished it reflects like a mirror the body of the young slave who stands in the center of the room with his head bowed and his hands tied behind his back.

Except for a filthy scrap of rag tied about his loins, Jonah ben-Aden is naked. He might be posing for a statue, or be a statue come to life, so sublime are the proportions and the symmetry of Jonah's physique. His body is short, broad, massively muscular. His shoulders are as square as bricks. His wide, deep chest is as sleek and hairless as a boy's. His pectorals are enormously developed, square and slab-like with a shadowed cleft between, two massive protrusions of flesh overhanging the scalloped ridges of his belly. His forearms are bound together behind his back; his upper arms flex forward, showing off biceps swollen like wineskins.

Jonah's body is a badge of shame. No citizen would ever need such strength. No gladiator or acrobat would ever allow his physique to become so encumbered with muscle. No free laborer would ever work so hard. Jonah's body is the body of a slave.

His legs are the legs of a draft animal, a beast of burden, hardened and grown big from long days of plowing, pushing, heaving, pulling. Strong, shapely calves. Sturdy knees. Stout thighs etched with tendons and plated with muscle, broad and flat behind, melding upward without a crease into his massively developed buttocks. The thin, sweat-stained rag about his hips stretches taut across the twin loaves, molded to the dimples on either side, dipping into the deep cleavage between.

Jonah's hair is cut very short, a tight cap of crisp black curls. His features are large and sensuously molded, his forehead and cheeks smooth and unblemished. His eyes are hazel green flecked with chestnut. They glitter with fear in the soft light.

His skin is dark olive, burnished by the sun and made even darker by the filth that covers his flesh, an accumulation of many days of dirt and sweat dusted with tiny bits of grass and smudged with grease. A constellation of freckles is spangled across the bridge of his nose, and another across the massive arch of his back.

Sweat makes him glisten in the soft yellow light. Jonah sweats now, standing meekly in the center of the room, head bowed, shivering as if he were chilled or feverish. A nervous sweat, the sweat of fear, trickles down his broad back. It gathers in the deep dimples at the base of his spine and spills down the crack of his ass. Beads of sweat erupt across his broad forehead and run down the bridge of his long wide nose. Sweat washes down his naked chest, collecting at the tips of his plump brown nipples, and drips with a quiet patter onto the mirror-like sea of black marble at his feet.

Suddenly there are voices beyond the wall, from deeper within the house. They draw nearer. A door opens and shuts, accompanied by the soft tread of sandal-clad feet.

Jonah gives a start. He shuts his eyes and bites his tongue, too late to stop himself from letting out a strange, high-pitched squeal of dread. The sound, so odd coming from such a massive body, is met with a deep-throated laugh.

"So, Laertus, what has the slave done this time?" The voice is deep, knowing, cruel. The very sound of it causes Jonah to feel a sudden dizziness, a tightness in his groin, an unwanted loosening in his bowels. He makes the noise again. The two men laugh. Jonah bites his tongue and trembles.

"The usual, Master, the usual!" Laertus's voice is high and hoarse—the grating, wheedling voice of a toady. He hobbles toward Jonah, dragging at his crippled leg to make it keep up. "Touching himself! Touching his smooth, pretty flesh in places where he oughtn't, places where the Master forbids it!" He clutches a short whip in his fist. He pokes it against Jonah's chin. "Raise your pretty face, pig! Let the master see your guilty face."

Jonah looks up. Briefly from the corner of his eye he sees the hunchback beneath him, leering up at him and poking at him with the whip. Then his eyes meet those of his master.

Fabius Metellus Maximus is dressed this morning in a simple gray tunic embroidered with blue, cinched at the waist with a broad leather belt. He wears a band of blue cloth about his forehead: his lank black curls are damp with sweat. When Laertus came running to inform him of Jonah's crime, he was busy plowing the ass of his new favorite, the young Greek wrestler from Alexandria.

At the age of thirty-five, thanks to the early death of his father and his own ruthless ambition, Fabius is the master of many estates. Friends and foes alike admit, and no one knows better than his slaves, that Fabius is a perfect specimen of Roman virtue: in love with wealth and power, totally unscrupulous, selfish, unforgiving, harsh, and demanding. He is a man of strong appetites and no compassion, contemptuous to everyone and everything that is not Roman.

Physically, Fabius embodies the raw strength and stature admired by his countrymen, who consider the fluid, graceful ideal of the Greeks too refined and effeminate; a body too beautiful is an unmanly body, fit only to be enslaved, tormented, and raped. No one has ever called Fabius beautiful, though there are those who grudgingly find him handsome in a crude way, with his broad face and piercing gray eyes, his fleshy nose and square, jutting chin. His smile is unnerving, a knowing, smug leer, as threatening as a clenched fist. He stands at least a head taller than Jonah and looms even broader in the shoulders, dwarfing him as he steps closer, drawing by his very presence the line between them as man and youth, master and slave, owner and object.

As Fabius approaches, dread settles over Jonah like a heavy blanket. He no longer trembles. Punishment will come, no matter what he does. The tightness in his groin becomes a knot. His bowels go slack; try as he might, he cannot clench them shut. Against his will, his body prepares to submit. He parts his lips and lets out a moan—not a squeal of panic as before, but a sigh full of shame and defeat, a sound of utter submission and surrender.

Fabius touches his face. Jonah shivers. He feels a sudden urge to lick the man's palm, to kiss his master's hand. He swallows and bites his own lip instead.

"Touching himself?" Fabius growls in mock-wonder, his eyes narrow and heavy-lidded. "Touching himself where?" He runs his fingers down the boy's throat and over the throbbing vein below his ear. He caresses with his fingertips the broad, swelling expanse of the boy's pectorals, flushed with heat and slick with sweat. "Here?" He pinches a nipple between forefinger and thumb, sawing his manicured nails deep into the tender flesh, tugging at the very tip, rolling the nub between his fingers until it burns. Tears gather in Jonah's eyes.

"No, Master, not there!" Laertus wheezes and fingers his whip with excitement.

"Then where, Laertus? Show me."

The hunchback cackles with joy. He seizes the rag at Jonah's waist, raking his broken fingernails against the boy's hipbone, making him wince. The rotten cloth comes apart with a shriek.

Jonah ben-Aden stands nude before his master—exposed, vulnerable, humiliated, his head bowed and his arms tied behind his back. He thought he had conquered his dread. Now, remembering all the other times that Fabius has summoned him for punishment, he knows that the torment has only begun. His heartbeat pounds in his throat. His chest heaves out of control. He begins to sweat again, filling the room with the acrid odor of fear. Unchecked now by the rag, the sweat washes down his belly to gather at the base of his cock, stinging his shaved pubis, trickling down the thickening shaft to dribble like watery semen from the snout.

"Here? Is this what he touched?" Fabius's voice is low and menacing. He runs his forefinger down the circumcised shaft, following the trickle of sweat. The touch sends a shiver through every part of Jonah's body. His penis abruptly swells and thickens. In less than a heartbeat it stands fully erect, jutting nude and achingly hard from his denuded groin.

"Yes, there, there!" Laertus sways back and forth in a frenzy. "I saw him! I caught him while he did it! At daybreak I took ten slaves to work the northern field, and I watched him every minute, just as you tell me to. Then not an hour ago he comes to me and says a tether has snapped on his plow and shouldn't he run to the smithy for another, and I let him go, but then I said to myself: Jonah thinks he's so clever, but I know how he works. Sooner or later he gets himself into trouble again. So I followed a few minutes later, and sure enough I caught him, hiding in the shadows behind the smithy, his fist wrapped around the big dirty thing, stroking it and squeezing it, his eyes rolled back in his head and his mouth hanging open. His big ugly thing was almost ready to spit, I could tell, but I stopped him just in time. With this!"

The hunchback holds out his whip. Fabius looks down at the fresh whip marks about the boy's upper thighs and groin. One mottled welt slices across the head of his cock.

Fabius licks his hand and takes hold of Jonah's shaft. The youth shudders and gasps as Fabius begins to stroke, very slowly, very deliberately. He winces whenever the man's hand rubs over the welt on his cock. The pleasure is so intense his legs begin to tremble, then to wobble, like the wildly exaggerated quiver of a bowstring, as if he were doing an absurd dance. Fabius laughs. Laertus cackles.

"Is this true, Jonah, what Laertus says? Is it true that you disobeyed me—again?"

Jonah bites his lips, tries to open his eyes, blinks them shut. His heart pounds, flooding his cock with warmth. His cock is the center of the universe. Neglected for so long, the simplest touch racks him with spasms of ecstasy. Fabius's hand controls him utterly. Jonah opens his mouth to answer, but instead a strange noise comes out, like the whinny of a horse.

Fabius lowers his voice to a whisper—low, seductive, chilling. "Tell me the truth, Jonah. Did you touch yourself, as I'm touching you now?"

A premature dollop of semen squirts from the tip of Jonah's cock and falls to the floor with a liquid slap. He clenches his teeth and lets out a hiss. "Yes, Master! Forgive me!"

Suddenly the pleasure turns to pain as Fabius bends the boy's cock double. He holds it that way for a moment, then gives it a wrenching twist. Jonah squeals. Fabius releases him. He lowers his hand and swings upward, delivering a hard open-handed slap to the boy's dangling scrotum. Jonah gasps and bends over. Fabius clutches the boy's neck, viselike, and forces him downward onto his knees until Jonah's lips kiss the cold marble floor.

Fabius stands and places his foot squarely on Jonah's neck. The nude slave boy crouches beneath him, his knees drawn up to his chest, his hard cock pressed between his thighs, his arms tied behind him, his bare buttocks rearing high in the air.

"You disobeyed me again, Jonah. You know I've forbidden you to give yourself pleasure. Your body belongs to me. Pain and suffering are your lot, Jonah, and hard, endless labor to keep your body strong and beautiful. No pleasure for you, Jonah. How long since the last time he touched himself, Laertus?"

"Thirty-two days, Master."

"Then for thirty-two days the slave has been bound in his bunk at night, flat on his back, his arms above his head, unable to touch himself? And for thirty-two days you've worked him in the fields, keeping your eye on him, never letting him touch himself even when he empties his bladder?"

"Yes, Master, just as you order. A few times there's scum on his belly in the morning—wet-dreams such as little boys have, it can't be helped. But I never let him touch the big ugly thing, oh no, I see that he keeps his hands clean."

"Then it's been thirty-two days since he was punished. He's getting better. Before that he lasted only twenty days, and before that barely ten. Perhaps we should make the punishment more severe this time."

Jonah trembles. His cock jabs up against his belly as hard and heavy as a stone. He feels his sphincter open and shut in a sudden spasm of desire. His nipples tingle. His mouth fills with saliva.

"You've made a mess on the floor, slave." With his foot, Fabius pushes Jonah's face into the pool of warm semen. "Lick it up."

Fabius steps back. He takes the whip from Laertus. While Jonah laps at the floor, Fabius dangles the lash against the boy's upraised ass. Jonah gives a shiver and a start. A sob catches in his throat. Fabius laughs.

"Tomorrow—we'll begin his punishment tomorrow. Right now I have business to finish with the little Greek I bought in Rome the other day." Fabius smiles a dreamy smile. "Wrestling is not his only skill. The boy has a throat like honey."

Fabius returns the whip to Laertus. He plants his foot on Jonah's backside and sends him sprawling across the floor. "Meanwhile, take this disobedient slave back to the fields to finish his work. Give him water to drink tonight, but no food. Bind him in his bed as usual. In the morning shave his pubis with a fresh blade and clean out his bowels with a few wineskins of mineral water. Then . . . but I have a very special punishment in store for Jonah. A surprise I've been preparing for a long time. Until then, let him think about the price for his disobedience, and sleep if he can. Jonah's suffering begins at sunrise."

Night falls. In the slave quarters, Jonah squirms wide awake on his hard pallet. His cock lies stiff against his belly, throbbing in time with his heartbeat. His scrotum hangs smooth and heavy between his thighs, bloated with unspent seed. He listens to the soft breathing of the others, who sleep soundly after the hard day's labor, thankful for the oblivion of night. But for Jonah there is no oblivion, only a long miserable night of fear and dread, bitter memories and regret . . .

Far away in the great house, Fabius dozes naked on his divan, his head settled against pillows stuffed with goose down, his powerful legs splayed open. Nestled between his thighs is the young Greek wrestler, who nurses sleepily at his master's cock. The boy has already drained it twice tonight. Now he will hold it safely in his mouth until morning, keeping it luxuriously warm and comfortable, allowing Fabius to dispense with any need to rise during the night. Fabius smiles in his sleep, thinking of Jonah cringing and naked, of tomorrow's punishment, of their first meeting two years ago . . .

It was below the decks of his private galley, the *Fury,* that Fabius first saw Jonah.

The *Fury* was used chiefly for transporting grain and goods, but every two years Fabius commandeered it for a trip to Alexandria. This was partly to transact business, and partly for the pleasure of visiting the city's notorious slave markets, those great arenas of degradation and shame where every species of human beauty might be fondled and admired, every imaginable monstrosity might be gawked at, and either might be purchased for whatever private uses one might desire.

The *Fury* set sail from Ostia and entered the open sea. Fabius spent the morning and afternoon reviewing consignments in his small private cabin, or walking the deck, examining the various repairs and alterations since his last journey. It was not until late that night that he had time to descend below the deck into the netherworld of the galley slaves.

If there existed a hell on earth it was surely here, amid the churning heat of hundreds of close-packed bodies in constant motion, the stench of their sweat and vomit and excreta awash in the bilge. Their wretchedness and anguish were played out against the maniacal never-ending pulse of the great oars, plunging forward and back through the waves like parts of a giant unstoppable engine. For that engine the slaves were merely fuel, to be consumed, drained, and discarded with hardly a thought.

There was a desperate beauty about the galley slaves. Constant, heavy labor carved their tortured bodies into godlike forms even as it doomed them to a harsh and early death. Every one of them was a convict; and of all the cruel sentences of death that could be meted out to a man, slavery in the galley was considered by all to be the cruelest, even more crushing and dehumanizing than the bloody arena or the dreaded mines. In the galleys a man was reduced to a status lower than the animals, utterly without hope or even identity, a tiny cog in a great engine, instantly disposed of if he should falter, easily replaced if he should fail. A sentence to the galleys inevitably meant death, but not before the last measure of strength had been squeezed from a man's body and the last vestige of his dignity had been annihilated by suffering and despair.

The labor of the rowers never ceased. The great oars were kept

in constant motion, day and night. Fabius did not bother to wonder
when and how they slept; it was no concern of his. Instead a fever
seized him, warm and dreamlike, as he walked down the long central aisle between the naked slaves, his nostrils filled with the smell
of their flesh, his skin awash in the humid heat of their straining
bodies, his eyes roving among the great congregation of agony constantly asway in the darkness. Here and there a bit of moonlight
found its way into the dim hold, shining silver blue on the sweat-
glazed arms and shoulders of the rowers, glinting upon the manacles
that kept their hands locked in place upon the oars. The dull beat
of the drum was slow and steady, setting an easy nocturnal pace,
its constant rhythm as hypnotic as the hissing murmur of the waves
sluicing against the prow.

The day had been long and tiresome. Fabius would have numerous opportunities in the coming days to amuse himself with the
galley slaves; for now, he needed sleep. He was making his return
up the walkway when his eye was drawn to one of the rowers along
the aisle. A beam of moonlight illuminated the slave's face.

Fabius paused for a long moment. Despite his massive shoulders and chest, the slave could hardly be more than a boy. Along
with the filth that smudged his cheeks and the suffering in his
eyes, there was a strange look of innocence about him. His dark
features were strikingly handsome, his prominent nose and mouth
and wide dark eyes suggestive of the sensuous East. As Fabius studied him in the moonlight, the beautiful young slave dared to look
back at him and then actually smiled—a sad, pathetic smile, tentative and fearful, longing to trust.

Fabius smiled back at him. He brushed his hand against the
boy's smooth cheek. The slave closed his eyes, sighed, and stroked
his cheek against Fabius's palm. But when Fabius ran his fingertips
over the slave's lips, pressing his middle finger into the warm moist-
ness of his mouth, the boy abruptly stiffened and turned his face
away.

Fabius drew back. His smile became brittle. He walked quickly
up the aisle and ascended the stairs into moonlight.

The next day he pointed the boy out to the whipmaster.

"Oh yes, that one," the burly giant nodded. "You mean the slave in place seventy-six. A strong rower. Been with us a long time."

"He wasn't here on my last journey."

"Let me think—no, probably not. Reckon he showed up just after, which would put him here for nearly two years now. Holding up well, ain't he? Most of them really start to show it after a couple of years, but he still looks fresh somehow. Of course he was just a kid when they brought him, youngest of the lot. Never thought he'd last. Healthy enough to start with, but not all that big, not back then. Didn't look strong enough to do his share in the galley— though you wouldn't have any doubts to see him now. Looks like a little studbull, don't he?"

"What was his crime?"

"No crime, not exactly. Politics, rebellion, something to do with the Jewish revolt—Masada and tearing down their precious temple and all that. I don't keep up much with news from outside, but I remember we got three or four shipments of new slaves from Palestine all around the same time, while Titus was wrapping up the war."

The whipmaster turned his head and spat. Fabius watched the thick spittle land smack in the face of a rower. It spattered against the slave's forehead and trickled down his nose. The man gritted his teeth and never stopped rowing.

The whipmaster narrowed his eyes and scratched his chin. "If I remember it right, the kid was some sort of scholar, the intellectual type, not a fighter at all. But his father was some big-time Jerusalem troublemaker. So Titus chops off the old man's head, rapes his wife and daughters, and ships the sons off to the galleys and mines. A book-learner, that's what the boy was, awful haughty when he first got here, you could tell by the way he looked down his nose at all the others. A little of *this* put him into line pretty quick." The big man slapped the handle of his whip against his palm and smiled. "A lot of good his book-learning does him here, eh? Now he's got muscles like an ox instead. Should last another five years, maybe even more if he don't get sick."

"What's his name?"

The whipmaster shrugged. "How should I know? He's number seventy-six to me."

Fabius walked slowly down the aisle in time with the steady, dull beat of the drum. The rowers kept their eyes averted, but in their faces Fabius saw the lurking fear and hatred and envy of the man who owned them.

Alone of all the rowers, the young slave in place seventy-six looked him in the eye as he approached. Fabius smiled at the boy's boldness. The slave blushed and looked away. Fabius stopped beside him, staring down at the boy's massive bare shoulders, at the rippling undulations of the muscles in his arms and back.

"Look up at me, number seventy-six."

Rowing in steady stride, the slave turned his eyes up to Fabius. "Do you know who I am?"

"The Master," the boy said, lowering his eyes.

Fabius nodded. "*Your* master. I own you, number seventy-six. You are my slave. Your body belongs to me, which is why you row, whether you like it or not—because it pleases me that you should row. What was your name before you became my property?"

"Jonah." The boy's voice caught in his throat. "My name is Jonah ben-Aden, Master."

Fabius crouched beside him and brought his lips to Jonah's ear. "Last night you smiled at me in the moonlight, Jonah ben-Aden. Do you remember?" Fabius placed his hand lightly on the back of the boy's neck, studying the workings of the muscles beneath the flesh as the slave continued to row. The smooth skin turn to gooseflesh.

Jonah kept his eyes straight ahead. "Yes, Master. I remember."

"Good. Because last night, after you smiled at me, I had a dream. A dream about you, Jonah. In my dream, you were no longer a galley slave. Imagine that—that would be a fine thing, wouldn't it? Instead of these manacles you wore a necklace of gold, and your flesh was glistening and sweet with fragrant oil. And that was all you wore. Because in my dream you were naked, Jonah. Naked in my bed. You were sucking my cock."

Jonah narrowed his eyes and seemed to purse his lips in pain, even as he strained to offer his neck to Fabius's caress.

"Of course, it was only a dream. But I'm a powerful man, Jonah. It's not unusual for my dreams to come true." With his other hand, Fabius brushed his knuckles against the boy's nipples, feeling them grow erect at his touch. He opened his fist and cupped the boy's massive pectorals in his palm, one at a time, feeling them heavy and sleek and firm in his hand.

"You have a beautiful body, Jonah. A beautiful mouth." Fabius fondled the boy's hair and plucked at his nipples. "I like you, Jonah. I think you like me."

Jonah opened his eyes and gave him a strange wild look of longing and dread. "Of course," he whispered. "Of course I like you, Master. I like you very much."

"Good. That's as it should be, number seventy-six. A slave should like his master. Should respect him, love him, worship him. Yes, as a mortal man worships a god, so a slave should worship the man who owns him. I think I'll reward you with a gift. Would you like that, Jonah? A token of my fondness for you." Fabius tenderly kissed the boy's ear, gave his nipples a playful pinch, then stood up. As he turned away he glanced down between the slave's legs. Jonah's large, circumcised cock stood up stiffly from his lap.

Fabius conferred with the whipmaster, who conferred with the drumbeater. Then he walked to the prow and took a seat on the high throne facing the rowers.

Immediately the drum began to beat faster. The rowers groaned and followed the tempo. The whipmaster stepped out of the shadows at the far end of the hold and swaggered up the aisle. He cracked his whip in the air, loosening his arm. The rowers cringed. The drumbeat accelerated. He exchanged a sour smile with Fabius, who smiled back and nodded.

The beat grew faster. The rowers at the outer edges of the ship were able to stay in their seats, but those along the aisle, like Jonah, were abruptly driven to their feet by the heightened motion of the oars, scrambling to keep up, stretching their arms high in the air to keep the gyrating oars under control. They had no choice. Their hands were manacled to the wood.

The beat accelerated even more, beyond any normal maximum, to such a tempo as would only be used if the ship were pursued by pirates or a sudden storm. The vast machine was at full throttle now. The oars moved in great circles at a mad tempo. The slaves pumped with all their might. Fabius studied their grimacing faces—jaws clenched, eyes burning with fear and confusion. He nodded to the whipmaster, who drew back his arm and took aim.

There was a loud snap and a crack, as if one of the great oars had suddenly split asunder. Jonah threw back his head. His mouth wrenched open in a silent howl.

The whipmaster raised his arm again. The lash slithered through the air. Jonah shrieked as the scalding pain struck square across his naked buttocks. He faltered against the oar, tripping on the catwalk. For a long moment he hung suspended from the manacles around his wrists as he was dragged forward, backward, and up again. As he hung from the highest point, desperately trying to find his balance, the whip lashed between his thighs and snapped against his dangling scrotum.

Jonah screamed, convulsed, and fell again. The oar carried him for another revolution. He somehow found his grip and joined in the effort, every muscle straining. The drumbeat blasted in his ears even louder and faster than his own heartbeat. For an instant he caught Fabius's eye and saw that his master smiled.

The lash struck again. Through the scalding pain Jonah understood. This was his gift.

The drumbeat boomed. The whip rose and fell. Squealing and gasping from the pain, Jonah danced like a spastic. His huge muscles convulsed at the whipmaster's rhythm, out of time with the great machine. His face was contorted in agony. He cried like a child. The whipmaster struck him again and again.

Fabius watched, no longer smiling. He pressed his palm to his groin, then slid back the folds of cloth that covered his sex. Out of the noisy chaos there was a sudden hush among the slaves. In their slack-jawed faces he saw envy, hatred, desire, hunger. While the slaves desperately rowed, while Jonah danced and sang shrieking for his amusement, Fabius held his naked erection in one hand and gently caressed it with the other.

Fabius looked between the slave's legs and gave a sigh of astonishment. Jonah, too, was still erect; his thick, scarred penis slapped against his belly and thighs. So it was, Fabius had come to understand, with slaves unable to pleasure themselves in any normal way, especially the young and virile. Once erect they remained that way, even in the midst of torment and exhaustion. Jonah was not the only one. There were others among the rowers who stared hungrily at Fabius, lusting for him and all he stood for—domination, power, pleasure—envious of the simple freedom to touch himself at will. Naked, drooling, erect, straining madly at their manacles, they watched as Fabius brazenly slid lower in his chair and masturbated, drawing on their suffering for his own excitement.

The whip snapped. Jonah convulsed and squealed. With a single voice the rowers groaned, like a tragic chorus. Fabius squeezed his cock with both hands, rapidly stroking in time with the booming drum.

He felt like a man in a dream watching other men in a nightmare. He stared into Jonah's eyes and saw the boy struggle to move his lips, unable even to beg. The pleasure between his legs was suddenly too exquisite to bear any longer.

Fabius raised one hand in the air. The drumbeat abruptly stopped. There was a final whiplash, followed by a scream from Jonah. Then all was still. The silence was broken only by the lapping of waves against the ship, the creak of wood, and the hoarse, gasping breath of the rowers.

Fabius staggered up from his chair, clutching his shaft tightly in his fist. He walked down the aisle carrying his sex before him as if it were a heavy bar of lead bending him bowlegged from its tingling weight. Jonah lay collapsed atop his oar. Gasping, eyes narrowed, Fabius stared down at the slave boy's broad, muscle-scalloped back, crisscrossed with welts and racked with sobbing.

"Did you enjoy your gift, slave?" Fabius seized the boy's hair and pulled his head back. "Answer me, seventy-six!"

Jonah's mouth was twisted with exhaustion and pain, his eyes blurred with confusion. He moved his lips but seemed unable to speak.

Fabius pushed his face away and stepped behind him onto the narrow catwalk. With his knees he pushed Jonah's legs wide apart. Using his fist to steer himself, he pushed into the slave's ass with a single thrust.

Jonah squealed, convulsed, and went rigid beneath him. Fabius exploded with ecstasy, feeling his sex quiver and spit inside the boy's tight rectum. Once spent, he paused only long enough to catch his breath, then roughly withdrew. He turned away, covering himself as he stepped onto the gangway, and hurriedly departed without a word.

TWO

A cock crows in the stillness of the night.

Jonah gives a start. Was he sleeping, or was he somehow dreaming with his eyes wide open—staring into the darkness above but watching his memories instead? He frantically glances about, dreading the passing of the night. But the cock is premature. Night still lies heavy and dark on the land. Dawn is hours away. It is not yet time for Jonah's suffering to begin. He turns his face to one side, wishing he could hide it against the bed; the bindings at his ankles and wrists hold him rigid. He begins to softly weep.

In the great house, Fabius hears only a faraway echo of the cock's crow, translated by his dreaming into the call of a seagull circling about the Fury *on an evening long ago. He smiles and turns in his sleep. His shaft abruptly thickens. The young Greek gags on the sudden mass in his throat and blinks his sleepy eyes, then swallows hard and accommodates the swollen flesh, nursing at it gently like a baby sucking at a nipple.*

Fabius moans with pleasure, remembering Jonah in his dreams, and their first night together beneath a full moon on the open sea. . . .

On the morning after the whipping, two slaves came for Jonah. The whipmaster unlocked his manacles. The slaves helped him from the seat. They walked him down the aisle and up the stairway. His body was stiff with pain, his eyes blinded by the sunlight. The smell of the fresh sea air was so sweet he began to weep.

The slaves were very young, with soft, girlish features. One was blond with blue eyes and red lips. The other was a Nubian with skin like coal. Together they made Jonah stand naked beneath the central mast while they bathed him. The ship's crew passed by, leering and laughing as the slaves expertly rinsed him with precious fresh water and lathered him with a sweet soap that seemed to soothe his wounds. They cooed as they ran their slick hands over his broad back and across his massive chest. They scrubbed his arms and legs, sudsing him between his fingers and toes. They told him to bend over and shamelessly cleaned his sphincter, scrubbing it with a coarse rag before reaching deep inside with soap-slick fingers. They made his stand straight again and laughed behind their hands at the stiff erection jutting up from his groin. They cleaned that as well, taking turns stroking it with soapy hands until Jonah began to bleat with pleasure.

He was on the very verge of orgasm when they drew their hands away and doused him with a tub of icy water. The master had given them strict instructions that the slave should not be allowed to spill his seed.

They washed his hair as well, then had him sit in the sun while they combed the knots from his tight black curls and clipped them short. They scraped the thin boyish beard from his cheeks. Simply to sit in the sun, smelling the fresh sea breeze, feeling the touch of other hands on his body while he did nothing, was like a dream of ecstasy to Jonah after two years of unrelenting torment below the deck.

His cock remained swollen and tingling the whole time. He tried to touch it, but the slaves batted his hand away and he docilely obeyed, even though they themselves occasionally reached down to squeeze it. The least touch anywhere in the vicinity of his sex caused his penis to rear up, achingly erect and dribbling from the tip. More than once they looked about to see if anyone was watching, then took turns bending down to swallow him for just an instant, licking his shaft and nuzzling his balls. In this way they teased him throughout the morning and Jonah was kept in a perpetual state of arousal.

At length they took him to the side of the ship and told him to bend over. While a snickering group of sailors watched, they inserted the nozzle of a large wineskin into his sphincter and filled him with a mixture of warm water and wine. Such a thing had never been done to him before. At first it was pleasant; then the sudden, urgent pressure began. He scrambled toward the railing, but the slaves stood in his way, playfully restraining him and grabbing at his swollen cock. At last Jonah pushed his way through. He squatted over the rail and loudly emptied his bowels into the ocean. The sailors laughed. The slaves tittered. Jonah blushed with shame.

Afterward they scrubbed him clean again between his buttocks. The Nubian even bent down to lick at the rim of his hole.

They trimmed his nails. They scrubbed his callused feet and hands with pumice stones. They anointed him with fragrance behind his ears and between his legs. They massaged him with a warm oil that made his pale, naked flesh shimmer like alabaster in the sunlight. They fed him a meal of delicacies such as he had never seen before, food so rich he could take only a taste from each dish. They took him to a small cabin with a soft bed and allowed him to sleep for hours.

That night the slaves returned. Lit by lamplight, standing before a tall mirror, they dressed him to be presented to his master. First they oiled his flesh again, this time with a heavy coating of a richly scented oil that made him shimmer as if his flesh were polished gold. They placed a silver collar around his throat, and silver clasps around his massive biceps. They tied a thin leather cord about the base of his genitals, so tightly it disappeared into the flesh and made his already stiff cock and heavy balls turn bright scarlet and swell up even more. They tied a loose string of pearls about his hips below the navel, to accentuate his nudity. Over his shoulders they threw a white robe made of a material so sheer it was almost transparent, parted down the front so that nothing was concealed.

By the light of a flickering lamp they led him to another room deeper within the ship. They opened the door, guided him inside, and then departed.

The master's cabin was small and intimate, but filled with luxury. Polished wood, intricate hangings, objects of gold and silver surrounded him. Plush cushions were strewn about, and his feet stood upon a thick rug of Eastern design. For an instant the pattern reminded him of his homeland, his boyhood and family. He closed his eyes against the memories, too painful to bear.

"Look at me, number seventy-six."

In a chair against the far wall, dressed in a long gown of red linen, his master sat watching him. The man who had touched his face so gently the night before. The man who had ordered him to be brutally whipped while he looked on and masturbated from the pleasure of watching. The man who had pierced him with a single stroke while he lay exhausted and racked with pain. Jonah cringed with fear.

"Step closer, slave. Now stop, there in the lamplight."

It seemed to Jonah that he stood motionless for a very long time while his master stared and sipped wine from a hammered-silver goblet.

"Let the robe drop from your shoulders."

Jonah hesitated for a moment, then rolled his shoulders back. The sheer cloth rustled and fell in a pool about his ankles. Though the cloth had concealed nothing, it had given him the illusion of being clothed. Without it he suddenly felt an acute shame. Jonah ben-Aden had been raised to conceal his flesh from all eyes and to keep himself pure from unholy lusts. Now he stood nude before his master, blushing and painfully erect. A tear rolled down his cheek.

"Why do you weep, Jonah? Haven't you enjoyed the day I've given you? Or had you rather have spent it below the decks, rowing with the rest of the slaves?"

The hellish image of the galley rose in Jonah's mind and he answered without hesitation. "No, Master. Thank you, Master."

Fabius smiled. "I'm a rich man, Jonah. A powerful man. There are many gifts I can give you. Like the one I gave you today."

Fabius took a sip of wine. He gazed up at Jonah with a glint in his eyes. "Or like the gift I gave you last night."

Jonah shuddered.

"You haven't yet thanked me for that gift, Jonah. I had you whipped. I watched you scream and dance. That amused me. It made me hard between the legs. It made me ache to pierce you with my cock. I gave you the privilege of amusing your Roman master and the honor of giving pleasure to a Roman cock. I planted precious Roman seed in your bowels. And yet you haven't given me one word of gratitude." Fabius lowered his goblet. His eyes narrowed. His face hardened.

Jonah's eyes glittered with a sudden passion, a last flicker of defiance. Fear and shame were stronger. His eyes grew dark and he bowed his head. "Thank you," he whispered. "Thank you, Master."

"For what? For raping you? Or for having you whipped?"

Jonah bit his lip. He swallowed, and the lump in his throat seemed to quiver and burn. "For both, Master."

Fabius's smile vanished as he slowly shook his head. "No, slave. You'll have to do much better than that. Down, Jonah, on your hands and knees like an animal." Fabius took a long draught of wine. "Now crawl to me, number seventy-six. Spread your knees and your hands far apart, let your face graze the floor and crawl to me like a worm."

The rug was thick and soft under Jonah's hands. His lips were so close to the floor that his own breath was like a warm mist about his face. The tip of his hard cock caught against the rug and slapped back against his belly. He pressed himself still lower, spreading his knees, so that his cock was pressed between the rug and his belly, grazing the tufted wool like a plow against the earth. The lamplight seemed not to penetrate to the floor of the cabin. He crept through dim shadows and felt somehow safe and protected, wriggling nude across the floor to his master.

Fabius looked down between his legs, beyond the bulge beginning to swell at his groin. Jonah's curls glittered in the lamplight, lustrous and blue black. His oiled shoulders were like marble hewn from a single massive block, shaped and smoothed and polished, pale white that glinted amber in the flamelight, lacerated with welts from yesterday's whipping. Beyond his shoulders Jonah's body narrowed to lean hips, cinched by the string of pearls. Fabius gazed down at the slave boy's naked buttocks, sleek with muscle, mottled with bruises from the whip and dusted with beads of sweat.

"Now show me your gratitude, Jonah. Thank me for putting my Roman seed in you. Lick my feet." From between his legs Fabius heard a sob and a boyish whimper. Then he felt warm breath against his toes and the hot slick moisture of the slave's tongue against his feet, licking between his toes, kissing them, taking them into his mouth and shamelessly sucking at them. For the first time, Jonah ben-Aden groveled naked at his master's feet.

"Enough, Jonah. Raise your head."

Jonah slowly lifted his eyes. He drew in a shuddering breath and released a groan mixed of dread and desire.

The thing hung suspended above his face, arching outward from between Fabius's widespread thighs—the shaft that had penetrated him the day before, when he was weak and helpless from the whipping. He had felt it in his bruised bowels for hours afterward. Now it loomed above him like a battering ram made of flesh, crudely shaped, huge and primeval, a Titan's cock.

There was nothing beautiful about the thing between Fabius's legs, unless raw power and grotesque size have their own beauty. The thick slab of flesh drooped half-erect above Jonah's face, as broad as a man's forearm, sheathed in a wrinkled mass of foreskin corrugated with thick veins. Great masses of foreskin hung from the core in draperies of thin, translucent flesh. Beneath the hood the plump head was visible, glinting wetly and dribbling a long suspended thread of milky fluid. Hanging from the base of the trunk, Fabius's scrotum lay nestled on the seat between his legs, a spreading pool of silky flesh that spilled over the edge.

"Kiss it, slave. Open your lips and nuzzle them against the crown. Lay the tip of your tongue against the portal."

Jonah reeled, breathing in the odor of the man's sex. He drew closer, feeling its warmth on his cheeks, not quite touching it with his lips. From far below, through the timber of the planks, he felt the vibration of the great oars and the beat of the drum pounding in time with the pulse of blood through his own cock, spearing rigid and untouched between his thighs. He settled back on his haunches. His balls brushed against the plush rug, heavy with semen and hanging like ripe fruit between his legs. Jonah closed his eyes and submitted.

He pressed his lips to the sleek crown and slid them over the ridge, pushing back the foreskin in delicate folds. His mouth was filled with warm, smooth flesh. He pressed his tongue to the slit and was amazed at how far he could slip inside. Above him Fabius gave a low moan. A warm trickle of fluid flowed into his mouth, thick and musky. The smell and the flavor overwhelmed him.

For a long time Jonah held the crown of his master's sex between his lips, letting the warm seepings from the portal fill his mouth before he swallowed, then letting them fill his mouth again. He rolled his eyes up and saw that Fabius stared down at him with a stern frown. He closed his eyes and pushed his face forward, swallowing more of the cock, suddenly craving all of it in his mouth, wanting it to fill his throat.

Fabius pushed him back. The cock slipped from his lips and sprang up rigidly erect, glistening with spit in the lamplight.

"You want to suck it, don't you, Jonah?"

Jonah stared at the thing, awed by its size, transfixed by a crude ugliness that was somehow so beautiful he could look at nothing else. He leaned forward to kiss it.

"Answer me, slave." Fabius held him back with a fist in his hair, and with his other hand he clutched the base of his shaft, waving it back and forth while the boy's eyes followed, pointing it at his face and brushing the moist tip against his lips. "You want to suck it, don't you?"

"Yes!" Jonah wept, because it was the truth.

"You want to pleasure me with your mouth. You want to please your Roman master. Don't you, slave?"

"Yes!"

Fabius raised his legs and rolled back. He spread his thighs far apart. He gazed down at Jonah beyond the upstanding column

of his sex. With one hand he held his cock aside. With the other
he pointed with his middle finger. "Kiss me here, slave. Yes, here.
Open your lips and press your mouth to the hole. Ah, yes! Now
use your tongue. Lick the hole. Suck at it, as if you were trying to
draw something thick and sweet from inside. Now harden your
tongue and push it deep inside . . ."

With a groan that vibrated into the depths of Fabius's bowels,
Jonah obeyed.

The *Fury* sailed on into the stillness of the night. For a time a
thick band of silvery clouds obscured the moon, but after midnight
a faint wind arose and dispelled them like tatters turned to ash.
The sea was calm. The face of the moon was bright on the waters.
All was silent except for the low, unending murmur of the sea.
Even the galley slaves were allowed to sleep for an hour. Within
Fabius's private quarters the lamps burned low, casting a soft glim-
mer across the silky flesh of the nude slave suspended upright in
the middle of the room.

Jonah's wrists were lashed together and tied to a hook above
his head; the lamp that normally hung from the hook now sat upon
the floor. Its candles flashed a wavering light upon his straining
muscles and lit the underside of his upright sex, casting a shadow
that stretched all the way to his throat. To touch the floor he had
to hold his feet together, toes extended, flexing the knotted muscles
of his calves. An occasional shudder of the ship caused his feet to
slip, pulling with agonizing pain at the stretched muscles of his
upright shoulders, making him grit his teeth and whimper.

Despite the strain and discomfort, at moments Jonah felt as if
he floated. Locked for months in the galley, his body responded
acutely to every sensation, whether of pleasure or pain; yet at the
same time he felt somehow distant from the torments that Fabius
inflicted on him. He shivered with exhaustion. A fresh sheen of
sweat erupted from his pores, washed down over his back and chest,
and trickled into the recesses of his buttocks and groin.

He closed his eyes and swallowed, and swallowed again, but
he could not wash the flavor of Fabius from his mouth. The man's

strong, bitter semen coated his tongue, clogged his throat, dripped from the corners of his lips. The same fluid seeped from the hole between Jonah's legs, trickling moist and slick between his buttocks. Fresh bruises marred the alabaster perfection of his thighs. His nipples and the tip of his penis were raw and swollen from being pinched and bitten. The roots of his freshly cropped curls throbbed with a dull ache; Fabius had used his hair like a rein to hold him in place while he fucked him about the room—standing, kneeling, bending him backward like a bow so that Fabius could reach around to cruelly pluck at his nipples and slap his balls even as he rammed his iron into Jonah's bowels. . . .

Suddenly a hand slick with oil wrapped itself around his cock. Jonah gave a start and opened his eyes. Fabius smiled at him and lazily pulled at his shaft, squeezing it, milking it, twisting it gently in his hand. Jonah bleated from the exquisite agony of suspense. He felt the blood gather in his groin. The balls jostled in his scrotum and drew upward. He tensed every muscle—and Fabius abruptly drew his hand away.

Fabius had been playing with him in this way for hours, ever since he had satisfied himself in Jonah's mouth and ass and had begun the interrogation, calling in two soldiers to help him hoist Jonah upright onto the hook. The soldiers had departed, but while their hands were on him Jonah had blushed with a shame that was almost unbearable. Perhaps Fabius had seen how strongly Jonah reacted to the soldiers, how deeply they frightened him; or perhaps he already knew Jonah's history. From the first he knew the questions to ask.

"Tell me again," he was saying, pinching one of Jonah's nipples between the polished nails of his thumb and middle finger. "Why did they arrest you?"

Again Jonah told the story of his father's arrest, of how the Roman soldiers came one day and beat down the door of their house in Jerusalem; how the terrified family huddled together and watched as the soldiers overturned tables and chairs, pulled hangings from the walls, heedlessly broke heirlooms handed down from centuries

before. In the atrium they made a bonfire and into it they threw
the forty volumes of his father's library. Jonah's father flew at the
soldiers in a rage and was repulsed with a single blow across the
face that sent him reeling to the floor with a fractured jaw. Jonah
and his four brothers broke past the guards and were repulsed as
easily as if they were children. Armed with shields, swords, and
clubs, the Romans were invincible.

While the brothers watched, bruised and battered and hemmed
in by a circle of spears at their throats, Jonah's mother and his five
sisters and sisters-in-law were stripped naked. Their fine gowns were
tossed into the bonfire. The Romans ripped the jewelry from their
throats and wrists. And then, while the men of the family watched,
the Romans took their pleasure with the women, laughing and
calling in reinforcements from the street. The rape was vicious,
relentless, appalling. One of Jonah's brothers, unable to bear the
sight of his young bride being raped by three soldiers at once,
pushed his throat onto a spearpoint and died, covering Jonah with
blood. Forever afterward Jonah felt ashamed that he had not had
the courage to do the same.

Finally they were herded into the street. The Romans sacked
everything of value—jewelry, gold, coins—then set fire to the house.
The women, naked and chained neck to neck, their legs and faces
glazed with semen, were driven toward the slave market wailing
with grief. The men were shackled and driven at spearpoint into a cart,
then taken to the Roman garrison. Each was thrown into a separate
cell deep in the bowels of the prison.

Jonah never again saw his brothers, but he did have a final
glimpse of his father's face. That very night the commander of the
garrison dropped by to show him the old man's head. He tossed it
at Jonah like a ball and gave a drunken laugh when Jonah turned
away and began to vomit. . . .

The ship gave a sudden lurch. Jonah swayed uncertainly from
his bonds, his feet for an agonizing instant suspended in space.
Then Fabius's hands were upon him, molded to his pectorals and
running down his flanks, as if he could capture the boy's moan

where it began at his diaphragm. Fabius drew close to him for an instant, breathing against his face, then drew away and circled him, brushing his knuckles over the hard muscles of Jonah's rump.

"And then they beat you, didn't they, Jonah? Your Roman captors?"

Jonah bit his lip and tried not to weep, remembering. That night the prison guards had crowded into his cell, as many as the tiny room would hold. They took turns holding him in place and pummeling him with their fists, joking and laughing and swilling wine the whole time.

Fabius nodded. "Good. It's only right that an enemy of the Empire should be beaten by her guardians. I hope they punished you long and hard. I hope they made you weep with suffering and shame. I'm sure they gave you a beating you'll never forget— Romans are good at that." Fabius lowered his voice and brought his lips close to Jonah's ear. "And then they raped you, didn't they, slave?"

Jonah shuddered. Fabius stepped around to smile at him, but Jonah averted his face.

"Don't try to gloss over it, Jonah. Don't lie to me. You were even younger then, and though you were not as strong and finely made, you must have been at least as beautiful as you are now. Completely helpless and alone, a young troublemaker at the mercy of a roomful of drunken Roman soldiers—oh yes, they raped you. Didn't they, Jonah?"

Jonah writhed in his bonds as if his muscles would suddenly erupt from his flesh. His face twisted with pain. At the same instant Fabius reached down and clutched the slave's erection firmly in his fist.

"Yes, Master!"

"How many?"

"I don't know."

Fabius squeezed his shaft with one hand and slapped it with the other. "How many, Jonah? How many Roman cocks had their way with you that night?"

"I don't know! Please, Master, a dozen, maybe more. Yes, I'm sure it was more. It was always changing. They came and went, always more of them—"

"Yes, I'm sure every soldier in the garrison had his way with you. And of course you couldn't see very well, could you, bent over with your face pressed into a Roman soldier's groin. Your eyes filled with tears from the pain and humiliation. Your throat stuffed with cock."

Jonah began to weep, even as a sudden thrill of ecstasy shot through him from the pressure of Fabius's fist on his erection.

"They began with your mouth, didn't they, Jonah? They spilled their semen in your throat and made you swallow, until your belly was bursting with it."

"Yes, Master."

"And they raped you between the legs as well. Used you like a woman, like a slave. Raped you the way you saw your mother and sisters raped."

"Please, Master, I beg you!"

"And you squealed like a girl, didn't you? I can tell; you're a strong boy, Jonah, but not strong enough to take a Roman cock in silence. You squealed while they raped you, just as you squealed when I had you whipped last night."

Fabius leaned closer, dropping his voice to a whisper. "You come from a chaste people. You were a virgin, Jonah, weren't you, before the Roman soldiers took you?"

Jonah blushed. "Yes, Master!"

Fabius drew back, his face flushed with excitement. "So they were the first, the garrison at Jerusalem. Good! Roman cock was the first that you served. Roman cock broke you. Roman cock took your manhood and made a woman of you. So it should be, that a young rebel, a virgin boy, a wealthy scholar's son reduced to rags and slavery for his impertinence against the Empire, should be raped by a gang of Roman soldiers." Fabius removed his hand from Jonah's cock and began to pleasure himself instead, using his other hand to caress the slave's hard clefted chest and smooth belly. "How long did they use you, Jonah? Romans are famous for stamina. They must have fucked you all night." Without waiting for an answer he circled behind Jonah and thrust two fingers into the boy's already ravaged hole. Jonah whimpered in response and danced on his toes.

"Each one of them taking his turn between your legs while the others held you down and watched, then making you clean it with your mouth and taking another turn in your throat. Then lining up for another round. Pumping you full of Roman seed all through the night. How long were you kept at the garrison?"

"Three days. Three nights." Jonah's voice broke.

Fabius laughed. "I know Roman soldiers. They beat you during the day and raped you at night. Working while the sun was up, saving their pleasure for the darkness."

"Yes." Jonah wept.

"For three days they tortured you. For three nights they raped you. Over and over. Why are you weeping? You should be proud, Jonah ben-Aden. Think of the Roman seed they spilled in your barren hole. They could have been out raping your women, spreading precious Roman blood among your people. Instead they spent themselves in you. You should be honored that they condescended to waste their seed in your hole, that they gave you rich Roman semen to drink. You should be proud that you could give so much pleasure to a lusty group of Roman men. Proud and honored that your virginity was stolen from you by Roman cock."

Fabius looked down at the boy's shaft to find it as hard as ever. With the tip of his middle finger he stroked its underside from scrotum to tip. The shaft gave a tiny jerk and dribbled a stream of pearly fluid.

"And since then, Jonah? Who has taken you since they sent you to serve on the *Fury*? Who do you pleasure here with your mouth and your ass?"

Jonah blushed an even more furious red. He drew his eyebrows together, whether from some new shame or from the taunting pleasure in his cock Fabius could not tell. "No one, Master."

The boy had no skill at lying. Fabius gave his shaft a hard slap and grabbed him by the balls, lifting him clear off the floor. Jonah stiffened and flailed his legs, but the motion only increased his pain. He hung suspended from the hook above and from the fist that clutched his scrotum. Fabius gazed at him in the lamplight, speechless for a moment before the tortured beauty of Jonah's body.

"Answer me again, slave." He gave the balls a half-turn and watched Jonah contort into a new spasm of beauty. "And this time, the truth."

The interrogation lasted through the night. When it was done, Fabius had wrung from Jonah every secret shame of his life as a captive and slave.

After his confinement in Jerusalem he had been driven overland to the state slave market at Antioch. Apparently he had not been molested on the way. Perhaps the marks of what the Romans had done to him in the garrison moved the slavedrivers to pity, though Fabius doubted it; more likely his filthiness and the bruises on his face and body had served as a kind of temporary disguise for his beauty, camouflaging him from the eyes of the slavedrivers, who were notorious for despoiling their goods on the way to market.

In Antioch the slaves were divided into groups of twenty, mixing the young and the old, the weak and the strong, and sold by the lot. One of Fabius's agents, seeking slaves for the *Fury,* purchased Jonah's lot with only a cursory glance to make sure there were no idiots or cripples in the group. The slaves were herded down to the wharf and doused with seawater. For a few moments they were unshackled before being led aboard, and Jonah was almost raped.

Another slave who had been watching him with lust all the way from Jerusalem saw his opportunity and tried to seize it. He knocked Jonah to the ground and began to mount him, and was almost inside when the guards pulled him off. The man was marked as a troublemaker and condemned on the spot; the agent, hating to waste a slave for nothing, decided the man could at least be used to make an example to the new galley slaves. The man was first hung by his heels and whipped, and afterward a heavy stone was tied around his throat. The guards cut his feet free and dropped him off the wharf, where he plunged into the sea and vanished without a trace.

Once on the *Fury,* Jonah had given his favors to only one man. This was the slave who sat beside him, a gray-templed Bedouin who had been arrested on the Eastern border for looting a temple. For many months, in quiet moments, Jonah had been pleasuring the man with his mouth, leaning over as far as his manacles allowed to nuzzle the man's groin and swallow his sex. The Bedouin had never reciprocated and gave him no friendship or even acknowledgment, but only taunted him with obscenities whenever Jonah served him. Such a man would never show tenderness, Fabius knew; reduced to a slave, the only pride that remained to him was to dominate, as best he could, another slave.

The whipmaster had never raped Jonah. This was not too surprising, as many ship's captains made a policy of hiring slavehandlers with no particular taste for boys; otherwise a youth as handsome as Jonah could make no end of trouble.

Fabius smiled as Jonah came to the end of his confession. Miraculous as it seemed, between the soldiers at Jerusalem and Fabius himself, no other man had been inside the boy's ass. No barbarian had fouled his hole.

Just before sunrise Fabius took Jonah down from the hook. He left his hands bound. For an hour or more he took his pleasure with the boy, using his mouth and his ass interchangeably, inflicting punishments on the most sensitive parts of his body for the simple cruelty of it. When he was through with him he sent Jonah back to the galleys. Long afterward Fabius treasured the sight of the slave boy as he was escorted out by the snickering soldiers—red-faced, naked, stiff and bowlegged from being fucked, his jaw slick with semen, a look of utter bewilderment and disappointment in his eyes.

Fabius did not use him again on the journey to Alexandria or on the way back; he did not even visit Jonah below deck, but intentionally avoided the sight of him. His only action in regard to Jonah was an order that the Bedouin be removed from his seat and replaced by the oldest, most wizened convict in the galley. Occasionally he daydreamed of Jonah nude and chained on his tier, sweating and suffering, bereft of all hope, and Fabius smiled. It was only as the *Fury* was at last pulling into dock at Ostia that Fabius gave orders that the slave in place seventy-six was to be taken ashore and transported to his villa outside Rome.

Jonah's fate was not to die of exhaustion and despair in the galley of the *Fury*. Instead he was doomed to serve as the pleasure slave of Fabius Metellus Maximus.

THREE

Fabius Metellus Maximus stands before the window of his bedroom on the second floor of his country villa. The vantage point allows a wide view of the rolling hills and vineyards that surround the house, field after field in an ever-widening circle that finally disappears in the hazy vista of faraway mountains.

Fabius stands naked at the window. His body is still warm from the bed, his muscles loose and relaxed. He takes a deep breath of fresh morning air and begins to urinate into the mouth of the Greek slave at his feet.

The young Greek gazes up at him with a look of mingled fear and adoration. The Greek is new to Fabius's household; the privilege of serving in the master's bed is a high one, and he has done his best to accommodate all of Fabius's demands, no matter how humiliating or painful. The task is relentless and exhausting. The Greek is hardly a virgin, but he has never encountered a man as tireless as Fabius, or as big between the legs.

The Greek was trained to be a wrestler. Fabius saw him at an exhibition in the city and immediately began negotiating with the boy's trainer to purchase him. But Fabius did not buy the Greek to wrestle; he bought him for the use of his mouth and ass, and for the enjoyment of his compact and superbly muscled physique. Fabius has had the boy punished only once, on his first day at the villa, simply to show him the consequences of disobedience or surliness. The Greek has not forgotten the hours he spent hanging by his ankles from a tree in Fabius's garden, or the kiss of the whip

wielded against his tender flesh by the spiteful hunchback called
Laertus. The Greek strives very hard to please his Roman master.

His enthusiasm is not driven by fear alone. Fabius is an easy
man to worship. His broad-shouldered, muscular body exudes the
crude mystique of raw manhood; his face has a harsh, rough hand-
someness that commands respect. His sex is like an inexhaustible
engine giving out pain and pleasure in equal parts. There is something in Fabius that casts a spell over the Greek, as it has over all
the young slaves who have served as his pleasure toys over the years.
Kneeling now between the man's powerful legs, holding his thick,
meaty shaft in his throat, gazing up at his massive chest and shoulders in the red morning sunlight, the Greek feels a sudden overwhelming urge to debase himself, to submit completely to his
master's power. It is not enough simply to allow the man to use
his belly as a toilet. The Greek swallows greedily, clutching at
Fabius's thighs, rolling up his eyes to stare pleadingly into Fabius's
stern, impassive face.

The warm flow lessens and stops. The shaft thickens and grows
stiff in the slave's mouth. The Greek moans at the sudden fullness
in his throat and reaches up to gently caress and fondle Fabius's
balls against his throat, all the while staring up submissively into
Fabius's eyes.

Fabius rewards him with a faint smile, and for a moment basks
in the pleasure between his legs. Then a movement in the valley
below catches his eye. The slaveherders are taking Jonah from the
slave quarters to begin his punishment. Fabius stares at the spectacle
with parted lips and narrowed eyes and forgets the Greek
completely.

Yesterday Jonah touched himself in defiance of Fabius's decree;
the vindictive hunchback Laertus caught him red-handed, secretly
masturbating behind a shed. Today Jonah will be punished.

Fabius watches as the slaveherders, six of them, drag the naked
boy across the vineyard nearest to the house. Jonah seems to resist,
but only because the herders clutch him with cruel tightness and
the sharp stones hurt his feet. The herders seem to enjoy the task.
Fabius cannot hear their words but he can see from their gestures

that they talk about Jonah and the long day of punishment ahead—they sneer at the boy and make faces of mock pity, wink at each other, leer at his naked body, jab at his buttocks and slap his cock. Jonah's cock is painfully red and erect. He has been denied release for so long that even the jeering touch of the slaveherders excites him.

On the hillside above the vineyard they push Jonah onto his back. The hillside is rough and rocky; Fabius chose the spot himself, seeing exactly how the jagged stones would jab into the boy's shoulders and spine. Pulling his arms and legs far apart, the herders reach for the iron stakes and the iron manacles already laid out. They snap his wrists and ankles into the shackles and pin him down with the stakes, passing the hammer from man to man, pretending to miss and making Jonah twitch for fear of his fingers and toes. Watching the game, Fabius chuckles, and then gasps with pleasure. The Greek has brought him to the very pitch of orgasm. The sensation is exquisite, but Fabius is already spent from the long night's debauch and looks forward to the delights Jonah will bring him in the hours ahead. He roughly pushes the hungry mouth from his shaft, the way a man might push a cur from a meal too good for it.

Across the narrow valley, Jonah lies naked and vulnerable beneath the rising sun. From this distance the details of his exquisite body are only a suggestion and the suffering on his darkly beautiful face is barely visible. The slaveherders draw around him in a circle, nudging one another, laughing, and groping themselves. One by one they hitch up their tunics and wave their cocks lewdly in the air, and then all together, like soldiers around a campfire, they relieve themselves on Jonah's face. Their laughter is so loud and raucous Fabius can hear it even from his window.

Meanwhile he feels the Greek's slavering tongue against his flesh. Denied his master's sex, the boy licks his strong thighs instead, then grovels at his feet, lapping them like a dog. He crawls behind Fabius, kisses his ankles, licks the backs of his calves and thighs in broad strokes. Finally he presses his face between Fabius's buttocks, groaning and whimpering in desperation to debase himself

for his master's amusement. For a moment Fabius clenches his buttocks tight, hard as stone; then he relents to feel the Greek's downy
cheeks sink into the cleft, and the sudden shocking delight of the
boy's tongue pressed hot and moist into the opening no man's cock
has ever penetrated.

Fabius prepares for the day. First he sends the young Greek to fetch
his barber. The Greek scrambles to his feet and begins to slip into
his loincloth, but Fabius knocks the scrap of linen from his hands.

"I ordered you to bring Kalides, not to dress."

"But, Master—"

"Go as you are. Quick, unless you want me to let Laertus beat
you."

The boy departs with a hot blush across his face and chest.
His sleek, taut buttocks jiggle and his small, hard cock slaps up
against his belly as he runs from the room. Fabius looks after him
and laughs softly. The bud of his anus still tingles from the touch
of the slave boy's tongue.

Kalides arrives with a basin of warm water, sponges, a stigil,
and a razor. The man is stooped and gray; he has been attending
to the care of Fabius's body since his master was a boy. He sponges
the sweat and saliva from Fabius's flesh and scrapes him clean with
the stigil, helps him into a simple gray tunic, massages his scalp
with oil and brushes his tight black curls, then tenderly moistens
and shaves the stubble across his jaw. All the while, Fabius deliberately keeps his gaze away from the window and the sight of Jonah's
suffering, knowing that a pleasure briefly delayed is all the sweeter.
But he cannot keep his thoughts from straying to the punishments
he has devised for Jonah in the past. Lying back in the divan,
feeling the scrape of the razor against his jaw, Fabius contemplates
the vast accumulation of pain and humiliation he has forced onto
the helpless slave for no other purpose than his own enjoyment. . . .

Once he ordered the field slaves to dig a narrow pit and buried
Jonah to the neck. For two days and nights he kept him that way.
Fabius had his carpenters build a prop for his back and sat for hours
with Jonah's face trapped in the crook between his legs, cramming

his cock and balls into the boy's mouth and playfully pinching his nose closed for minutes at a time, anointing his lips and nostrils with burning peppers, forcing him to eat grapes and olives from his rectum. At first there seemed to be no end to the torments that might be devised in such a circumstance, but Fabius eventually explored them all. When he at last ordered the slaves to dig Jonah from the pit, the boy had been as wobbly as a newborn colt, barely able to stand.

At parties of selected friends, Fabius has subjected Jonah to public torments and humiliations, allowing the most grotesque of Rome's elite, men aged, wrinkled, fat and toothless, to poke the boy and call him to heel, to shove their fingers up his ass while he grovels like a maggot before them, all the while forcing Jonah to praise them aloud for their Roman virtue and to beg them against his will for more abuse.

In his spare time Fabius creates new designs for racks and systems of restraint, as well as all manner of devices for torture— clamps, irons, vises, weights, specula, brands. All of these he tests first on Jonah. The chief of the Emperor's secret police once took an interest in this work, and paid a brief visit to see Fabius's inventions put to use. The man brought his own prisoners for testing the fatal devices; Jonah was used to demonstrate those which merely induced torment. The spymaster had been impressed, both by the devices and by Jonah. He had requested of Fabius the use of the slave for the night, and Fabius had assented, passing a sleepless night of excitement in the chamber next door listening through the thin walls to the sounds of Jonah being used by another man as cruel as himself.

Perhaps his favorite means for punishing Jonah is the device which Laertus calls the pony cart—not really a cart at all, but simply a long wooden pole set atop two central wheels three feet high. At each end of the pole a handle curves straight up from the end. Each handle is seven inches high and as thick as a man's wrist with a rounded knob at the end. On one of the handles Fabius mounts Jonah, tilting it down to the ground and forcing the slave boy to squat low and impale himself on the thick handle. Pushing down on the opposite end forces Jonah to his feet. Pushing forward forces him to stagger ahead with the handle lodged up his ass. The device is simple, insidious, and endlessly humiliating. Best of all is the contrast between Jonah's wretched exertions and the simple movement of a wrist to control him. Grasping the handle and walking at a steady pace, Fabius can drive Jonah naked across roads and fields, steering wherever he wishes. Simply by pressing down on the handle he can force Jonah to his tiptoes; using the full strength of his arm he can suspend him panic-stricken in midair. For hours Fabius has delighted in driving Jonah barefoot and naked about his estate, parading him before the other slaves, propelling him now faster and now more slowly, listening to the various bleating noises he makes on the various surfaces as the hard handle jabs and rattles against his delicate insides.

Occasionally, as a reward, he allows Laertus to drive the pony cart himself. The little hunchback sits astraddle the driving end and cracks his whip against Jonah's shoulders and buttocks, forcing him to trot on tiptoe in circles around their laughing master. Fucking the boy is always a special joy afterward. The torment of the wooden handle tenderizes his bowels and rubs his sphincter raw, so that the least movement of Fabius's cock inside him produces an agony of gasping and pleading. . . .

From the contemplation of these torments Fabius drifts to the contemplation of Jonah's beauty. Fabius had never tired of it. The boy's face might have been molded by the finest Greek sculptor. Each feature—mouth, eyes, nose, forehead, jaw—is outstanding for its bold sensuality, yet altogether they merge into a single thing of beauty. His body was astonishingly beautiful when Fabius first saw him on the slave galley; since then it has become even more impressive, shaped by hard daily labor to a pinnacle of massive development, softened by the youthful silkiness of Jonah's sleek amber flesh and the downy blush across his buttocks and cheeks. As much as Fabius enjoys festooning the boy with straps of leather or strands of pearl or bands of gold and silver, there is no real way to enhance perfection; Jonah is best seen naked, stripped even of the silky pelt at his pubis, denuded of anything that might stand between the eye of the beholder and the perfection of his bare flesh.

Even the boy's shaft is a thing of beauty—meaty and thick and perpetually erect. Perpetually nude as well, for like all his people Jonah is circumcised, his sex stripped bare, mutilated and vulnerable, unlike Fabius's own proud, shielded Roman sword. It pleases him that Jonah is big between the legs. Sometimes Fabius prefers a slave with a tiny cock, like the Greek. Such a boy can be manipulated and humiliated through his cock, made to feel inadequate and girlish. But sometimes he prefers a slave with a meatier shaft—a cock substantial enough to be played with in elaborate ways, bound up and twisted, pinched, clamped, whipped. A well-hung slave like Jonah can easily be controlled through his penis, brought low by the irony of a large, potent cock rendered useless for any purpose but torment, perverted into a tool to give its owner not pleasure but pain, a weapon turned against its wielder.

It was to mark Jonah's last punishment, thirty-three days ago, that Fabius devised the most exquisite torments for Jonah's cock. For the crime of having given himself an orgasm without permission, Jonah was bound upright to a whipping post. While Jonah watched in dread, Fabius wrapped the boy's swollen, denuded genitals in broad leaves of stinging nettles. The effect was spectacular. For hours Jonah kept up a rigorous dance, heaving against the post, unable to stop thrashing his hips uselessly against the air as the poison-tipped nettles stung him over and over again.

Afterward Fabius produced a vial of blue glass containing a stinging beetle from the Nile. The shimmering beetle was a thing of insidious beauty, blue black and as long as a man's forefinger with a snout half again as long. Its maddening bites were said to be a foretaste of hell. Fabius himself had once been stung by a Nile beetle; the single welt on the back of his knee had itched furiously for days and had made sleep impossible.

Fabius smiles, remembering the sight of Jonah hanging helpless in his chains and the quiet slithering of the beetle in the vial. Wherever he placed the tiny opening against Jonah's flesh the beetle eagerly jabbed its long, slender snout into the skin—all over Jonah's scrotum, in a circle around his anus, on his nipples, on the moist lips of his penis and in double rings around the crown and circumcision scar. The welts began to rise almost instantly.

Afterward Jonah was of course forbidden to touch himself, even to scratch. At night he was bound face up on his pallet so that he could not rub against the mattress for relief. Night after night the other slaves were kept awake by his sobbing. The punishment had succeeded; Jonah had remained wretchedly chaste and docile for the longest period yet.

But for tonight's punishment, Fabius has devised something truly spectacular. He conceived of the plan long ago; it has taken months and masses of silver to bring it to fruition. During the day he will inflict the usual punishments—tying Jonah spread-eagled beneath the searing sun, denying him any moisture except that which he can suck from Fabius's body, tormenting him in a hundred tiny ways. But tonight will be different. Tonight, his long day in the sun ended, Jonah will be invited to a very special party in his honor. The villa will be alive with music, food, and light, and with a very select group of special guests. . . .

Fabius smiles, contemplating Jonah's surprise, imagining the look on his face. Kalides finishes shaving his beard and holds up a burnished mirror. In his reflection Fabius sees the face of an ideal Roman—cruel, vain, handsome, supremely confident. And having seen himself, he at last can wait no longer to look upon his opposite. What shall he do to Jonah first? He turns to the window to see how the boy is holding up.

Fabius's eyes grow hard and his jaw stiffens. If he could see himself in the mirror now, he would know the true face of Rome—implacable rage, naked scorn. He bares his teeth in anger. The hillside across the vineyard is bare. The stakes have been pulled from the earth. The manacles lie open and empty.

Jonah is gone.

In a shed behind the smithy he found an old pair of sandals and a leather cloth to wrap around his waist. The sandals allow him to run across rocks and broken ground. The cloth allows him to flee through fields of high, sharp-bladed grass. The day is still young. The earth smells of dew. Jonah feels a sudden burst of elation such as he has not experienced for years, not since he was a boy in Jerusalem.

He runs without thinking. If he pauses to think, the whole world will come to a frozen halt, and him along with it. If he lets himself think, he will instantly know that running is useless, that escape is impossible. He will be captured, sooner or later, and probably sooner; and after his capture will come the punishment. For an instant the image of Fabius's smiling face flashes through his head. Jonah gasps for breath. He grits his teeth, and when the image of Fabius refuses to depart he stares straight into the rising sun to burn it from his eyes.

Jonah runs. Running is everything. Running is the world, and nothing else exists. He feels the pounding of the blood in his ears and the pounding of the earth against his feet. The high grass slithers against the leather skirt; a few tall blades whip against his bare stomach. He winces at the stinging cuts and runs on.

He comes to a fence, hurdles it, and finds himself in an open field. He runs straight across, into the rising sun. The cattle stare at him in drowsy alarm, never having seen a human run so fast. They stir themselves and scatter, braying with displeasure at being disturbed so early in the day.

He crosses the field and descends abruptly to a narrow creekbed shaded by oaks. The sight of the water makes him realize his thirst. For a brief instant he pauses in the stream, bends to splash the stench of the slaveherders from his face, and scoops handfuls of water into his gaping mouth. Then he runs on.

Jonah comes to a vineyard. The workers are not yet in the fields. He flies between the long rows of vines, stretching his legs as far as he can, taking giant leaps. He hammers his fists against his chest, flexing his biceps to keep them loose. He breathes deep, barely aware of the burning in his chest. His massive pectorals bounce up and down as he pounds against the hard earth, flinging beads of sweat from his nipples.

Jonah enters the oakwood. The wood is well groomed with trees spaced well apart, easy to run through. The understory of acorn shells and leaves crackles beneath his feet. The shadowy air is cooler here; he suddenly feels chilled. He runs faster to warm himself.

The air whistles and roars in his ears. For a long time it is all he can hear. Then he hears the horses.

Not the neighing of horses, but the drumbeat of their hooves against the earth. First distant, then less distant. The image of Fabius flashes through his mind. Not his master's face, but his master's cock, fully engorged and slick with mucus from Jonah's ass, dripping semen, held before his face like a delicacy to be devoured. Jonah grits his teeth and tightly shuts his eyes for just an instant to blot out the image. An unseen branch strikes him square in the belly and Jonah tumbles head over heels.

For a long moment the world is black. Then Jonah revives, dizzy, confused, and breathless. He cannot stop to think of where he is or where he's going. He gets to his feet and breaks into a desperate run. In only moments he seems to be coming to the far edge of the wood. Then Jonah realizes he's running the wrong way, back to where he came from.

When he stops to turn around he clearly hears the pounding of the horses' hooves, much louder than before. They must be in the vineyard, at the very edge of the wood. It is over now; it was over before it began. But a voice in his head screams, *No!* and forbids him to think. Thinking is useless. He can only run, run, run.

The land begins to rise. The understory becomes more and more rocky and the trees grow closer together. Jonah scrambles madly up the hill, thinking to himself that no horse could be as nimble. A horse would break its leg in such terrain. But above the pounding of his heart he can still hear the hoofbeats behind him.

Louder. Closer. Then, as suddenly as a candle is extinguished by the wind, Jonah feels his energy vanish. He still runs but he no longer feels the perfect rhythm of his body. His arms and legs begin to flail like parts of an engine spinning out of control. He hears the neighing of horses. And now he hears men shouting behind him. One of the voices could be that of Fabius—but no, Jonah cannot allow himself even to think of it, not until it actually happens, not until the very instant that he hears them shouting above his head to one another and the net drops over him—

The world becomes a spinning blur. The earth is hard and littered with stones that cut and bruise. Jonah struggles against the burning strands of rope, not with any hope of escape but simply because he cannot stop moving, not yet, because once he grows still he will have to begin thinking again. As long as he moves and screams he can blot out the future. But the net draws tighter and Jonah suddenly knows how it must feel to be a fish pulled from the sea.

He struggles against the net with his last ounce of strength and then collapses, so exhausted that the rise and fall of his chest are almost too much to bear. Voices shout overhead. Footsteps rustle about him. Dappled sunlight falls across his eyes and then is blotted out by the looming silhouette of a tall man with powerful shoulders. Suddenly a whip falls across him, stinging him even through the net. Laertus stands at his feet, raising the whip for another blow, but the silhouette reaches out and stays the hunchback's hand.

The sun blinds him as the silhouette stoops beside him, then vanishes again behind the halo of black curls surrounding Fabius's grimly smiling face. With a knife he cuts a hole in the net and lifts Jonah's head in one hand.

His voice is unexpectedly soft, almost tender. "Wherever did you think you were going?" For an instant, gazing into his eyes, Jonah thinks that the man is about to kiss him. The very idea makes him feel suddenly weak and submissive. He feels Fabius's breath against his face and the touch of his fingers on his neck. Jonah parts his lips, hungry to feel the man's mouth and taste his warm breath.

Instead Fabius stands and puts his hands on his hips, looking at something farther down the hill. "Good," he says. "The slave-herders are already here with the pony cart. Time to drive this one back where he belongs."

■ ● ■

"Higher, higher!"

Jonah struggles to lift one foot after the other. The handle rattles inside his ass. The whip cracks against his flexing buttocks.

"Lift your knees higher! Prance for me, pony!"

The sun is already blisteringly hot. The goatpath is narrow and rutted. Fabius decided they would take the long route home, up and across the southern ridge, down beside the lake, across the fallow vineyards. Laertus drives the cart, steering with one hand and using his whip with the other. Fabius rides alongside on horseback, observing, approving, modulating the hunchback's abuse. Laertus may crack the whip only once every twenty paces. The pace is not quick enough for Laertus. He screams at Jonah to quicken his step. Twelve, thirteen, fourteen . . . eighteen, nineteen—twenty! The whip lashes out and smacks Jonah's right flank with a searing kiss.

"Faster!" Laertus shrieks. "Faster!"

Jonah is naked. His feet are bare. Fabius took the sandals from him, ripped them apart, and used the straps to tie his hands behind his back. Jonah quickens his pace. His chest heaves. The sun burns his freckled shoulders. His sleek, massive pectorals jiggle in time with each step. The hard pole up his ass presses relentlessly against the pleasure spot inside him, making him feel like a woman between the legs. His cock is stiff and red and bounces in a circle with each jolting step, slapping with a sweaty crack against the belly and thighs.

He tries to keep count of his steps, to know when the next lash will strike. But the sun beating on his back, the pole up his ass, the sweat running down his face, the throbbing and tingling in his cock keep him confused and dazed. Seven, eight, nine . . . his right foot lands on a clod of earth that crumbles and gives way. The pole gives a jerk in his ass and he feels himself stumbling. Ten, eleven—fourteen? He struggles to right himself. The pole suddenly starts jabbing in and out of his ass like a hard cock fucking him—Laertus is doing it on purpose, banging his fist against his end of the cart. Fabius rides up and grabs Jonah by the hair, pulling him upright and helping to balance him. Jonah glances up, and just as their eyes meet the whip stings him like a wasp across both buttocks.

Jonah gives a yelp and staggers forward. As he turns his face ahead he cannot help catching a glimpse of the hard truncheon of flesh standing up between the gathered folds of Fabius's tunic. Beads of opal dribble from the tip and run down the shaft, making it glisten in the sunlight. Fabius touches it with one finger only, gently stroking the underbelly. On his face is a sigh of pure contentment.

The ordeal goes on forever. Jonah loses all sense of time. He cannot judge by the sun, for like a spectator claiming the finest seat the sun has found a perch straight above and hangs there, blinding the world with unending noon. He sweats. He struggles. The pole brutally fucks his ass. Laertus laughs. The whip stings his shoulders and buttocks and occasionally Laertus lands a lucky shot that wraps all the way around to nip at his bouncing cock and balls, compelling Jonah to scream. Fabius canters alongside; his erection pokes straight up from his saddle like a horn. The slaveherders follow along behind, happy for the holiday, making Jonah's ordeal into a parade. The slaves they pass on the hillside, in the fields and beside the lake show no pity at all. Some of them smirk, some show outright anger—they would pelt him with stones if the master allowed it. Some of them gaze at him with open lust, slack-jawed and stiff between the legs.

At last they reach the villa. In the outer court Jonah is made to stand in place, still impaled on the handle. At Fabius's command a slave fetches a bucket of water and splashes it over his sunburned, sweat-drenched body. A slight breeze stirs in the courtyard and Jonah's skin turns to gooseflesh, his nipples crinkle, but his cock stays hard as a bone.

Fabius calls for the six slaveherders whose carelessness allowed Jonah to escape. The wretches are stripped naked, then manacled wrist to wrist and neck to neck and made to stand in a row.

"Whip them," Fabius tells Laertus. "Start with the man on the right and whip him until he cannot stand, then begin on the next man. When you've whipped them all, begin again with the first. You needn't hold back. Whip them as long as you wish. I'll be getting rid of the lot tomorrow, and not one of them will fetch a decent price at market. Useless scum." The remaining slaveherders look with blood-drained faces. The sound of a whiplash cracks the air as Laertus begins the punishment.

"And this one." Fabius turns to Jonah and gently caresses his cheek. "Tonight," he says softly. "Tonight I have a very special surprise for you, Jonah. A dinner party with you as the guest of honor. What a shame if you had run away and spoiled it." He places his hands on Jonah's hips and with strong arms lifts him straight off the handle. The slick wooden pole exits Jonah's ass with a lewd sucking noise. The boy whimpers and staggers against Fabius's chest. Fabius's hands linger on his sleek naked thighs; his lips brush Jonah's forehead. Then he moves his hands to Jonah's shoulders and pushes him to his knees.

Fabius lifts the hem of his tunic. The thick, heavy truncheon slips free and slaps Jonah's face. Jonah closes his eyes and takes the club of flesh into his mouth. The shaft is slick with Fabius's droolings. The flavor is bitter and strong. Fabius tilts his head back and gazes through narrow eyes at a distant white cloud alone in all the blue sky. Jonah sucks like the most expensive whore in Alexandria, swallowing him to the root, pressing his lips into the wiry hair at the base of Fabius's cock and caressing the balls with his chin. Punishment has taught him to always give his very best. Even better than the little Greek. . . .

Laertus cackles. The whip slashes through the hot, still air. The errant slaveherders shriek and moan. Fabius abruptly feels his climax swell and steps back, pulling his shaft from Jonah's throat. He gazes down at it, proud of its massive size, bewitched by the way it bobs and jerks obscenely in the air as it spits streamers of white slag onto Jonah's wretched face and into the thirsty boy's wide-open mouth.

Fabius groans with pleasure and steps forward to feel himself swallowed by the clutching furnace of Jonah's throat. He basks in the warmth for a long moment, gazing at Jonah's face and then at

the solitary cloud. Then he pulls himself free and drops his tunic.
He pulls the boy to his feet by his nipples, spits in both hands,
and begins to stroke Jonah's cock.

Jonah bleats like a lamb at the unexpected pleasure, so sharp
and sudden it pierces him like a flame between his legs. In seconds
Fabius has him close to orgasm. Jonah whimpers and goes weak in
the knees. Fabius laughs, releases his cock, and slaps it painfully
back and forth until the pleasure subsides, then begins again. The
ordeal is maddening, yet Jonah craves it. He bites his lips and
pleads with his eyes. He stands bowlegged, gyrating his hips, never
minding that every slave in the courtyard can see his humiliation.
His cock begins to drool; Fabius uses the stuff for a lubricant,
making the pleasure all the more sharp and exquisite. Fabius brings
him close, cruelly slaps his cock, and brings him close again, over
and over in quick succession. Jonah begins to bleat with pleasure
and to weep at the same time.

Fabius abruptly lets go of him and walks toward the house,
shouting over his shoulder at the cringing slaveherders.

"Take him back to his place on the hillside. This time make
sure the stakes are driven into solid ground."

The slaveherders cringe and bow, then seize Jonah and drag
him to the hillside. His spit-glazed cock bobs between his legs,
slapping his belly and thighs. They untie his hands and pull him
spread-eagled on the stony ground, snap the manacles on his wrists,
and drive the stakes into the ground. Two of the herders linger
beneath the trees nearby to make sure nothing goes awry, afraid to
share the fate of their fellows being whipped in the valley below.

The sun leaves its perch and slowly descends. Jonah shuts his
eyes against the brightness. His head is filled with the sound of the
slaveherders' punishment. The slash of the whip. The echo of Laertus's laughter. The scream of the careless herders. Sometimes the
sounds fade and vanish, and it seems the punishment is done. Then
they begin again.

Then a new series of sounds begins. The sun has sunk low
enough to allow Jonah to open his eyes. From his place on the
hillside he can look down beyond his own feet and see the courtyard

in front of the villa. The slaveherders lie prostrate and quivering
on the flagstones. Laertus methodically moves from man to man,
wielding his whip, occasionally rubbing his tired right arm with
his left but never ceasing. Meanwhile a series of guests begins to
arrive at Fabius's door. They are of both sexes. Some, mostly in
military garb, come on horseback. Some come in wagons with es-
corts of bodyguards. Some arrive in litters borne on the backs of
slaves. All of them pause to gaze up at Jonah and at the punishment
in the yard. Fabius himself greets each guest at the door, dressed
now in his formal toga, smiling and nodding, gesturing to Jonah
and to the slaveherders and giving an explanation Jonah cannot
hear. The guests often laugh in response, and cast lingering glances
at Jonah's nakedness.

The sun sinks low, casting a red haze across the valley. Jonah
lies exhausted, almost asleep despite the pain of his whipped buttocks against the rocky ground. The taste of his master's semen
lingers in his mouth. From the great house come the faint sounds
of a dinner party—the peal of laughter, the clink of metal and glass,
a murmur of contented voices. As the red haze fades to twilight and
darkens to blue, the lamps are lit and the windows of Fabius's house
emit a soft yellow glow.

Jonah hears footsteps nearby and low, gruff voices. The slaveherders surround him and kneel, pulling the stakes from the earth.
They douse him with water and lead him shivering down the hillside, across the courtyard, and into the house.

The room is circular, high, spacious, and airy—the very room where
yesterday Jonah stood in abject misery awaiting the judgment of
his master.

Jonah is led into the room through a secret passageway, to
find himself in a dark recessed area concealed by a high curtain.
The herders chain his hands and feet and shove him to the ground.
Jonah gazes about him in confusion. Though he knows where he
must be in the great house, the surroundings are all wrong. Some
strange trick is being played—in place of black marble, the floor
seems to be made of common flagstones. In place of pillars he finds

himself surrounded by dank, grimy walls set with manacles like a dungeon. They remind him of another place, and a flash of forgotten dread causes him to tremble. Dazed and weak, Jonah cannot place the memory; he has tried to blot it from his mind so many times.

From beyond the curtain he hears the sounds of the dinner party. The voices are desultory, quiet, restive—the hush that comes at the end of a long Roman dinner, when the bloated guests are sleepy and stuffed and ready to be entertained.

The curtain rises. The cavernous room is dark, lit only by a single small lamp set above Jonah. He can barely make out the vague shapes of the diners lounging on their divans. Titters of feminine laughter and masculine guffaws merge together into a single noise of scorn. Jonah instinctively tries to cover himself. The chain chafes against his wrists and the small of his back.

Fabius steps out of the darkness. He slowly approaches Jonah and stops a few paces away, his face barely visible in the gloom. "My gift to you, Jonah," he says, loud enough for all to hear, gesturing to the dungeon that fills the alcove. "You are a virgin boy again."

Jonah looks at him with knitted brows, confused. His skin is hot, flushed with shame. He feels the eyes of every person in the room on his naked body.

"You heard me, Jonah. You are a virgin again. Because I say you are. Because tonight I have returned you in time and space to the city of Jerusalem, to the garrison filled with rebels rotting in their cells. Look around you, behind you. Don't you recognize the place?"

Jonah stares in horror at the grimy walls and floor, the dangling chains, the iron bolts. Exactly the same. The cell where the Roman soldiers took him after they burned his house and arrested his family. His heart beats like a hammer.

The heavy iron-bolted door behind him opens, creaking on its hinges—exactly as it opened then. A Roman soldier ducks his head and steps through, followed by another and another. One of them carries a torch that he sets into a mount on the wall, casting the craggy walls into lurid relief. They wear the red tunics of garrison soldiers, stripped of their armor. The leader has an ugly pockmarked face. He carries a broad strap of leather that he snaps between his fists. He stares at Jonah like a hungry wolf and gives him a nasty grin, looking not at Jonah's face but at his naked body. Jonah recognizes the man instantly. How could he ever forget him?

Jonah spins his head around. Fabius has disappeared, melting back into the unseen audience. The brightness of the torch blinds him; Jonah can see nothing beyond the dungeon.

More soldiers crowd through the door. Jonah remembers every face; they are all burned in his memory. He squeals in panic and desperately tries to back away, but the garrison commander stops him by catching his heel on the chain between his ankles.

"Beautiful," says one of the men. The way he says it makes the word sound ugly.

"More meat on him now."

"Right. A regular little Hercules. But just as scared as he was then."

"Remember how we—"

"Why talk about it? Here he is, ready to play . . ."

Fabius watches in the darkness, lounging on his divan. His toga is unwound and his tunic is pulled up to his chest. The little Greek kneels beside him on the black marble floor, slowly and gently sucking his cock. One of the guests, a handsome young legionnaire, has crept through the darkness to lie beside him; he nuzzles Fabius's chest, sucking at his nipples and pulling at his own cock. Meanwhile Fabius watches the spectacle unfolding and smiles.

It was not easy tracing the soldiers who had taken part in Jonah's rape in Jerusalem, but Fabius has high connections in the capital; one of the Emperor's personal friends, who lounges at the next divan, was able to round them all up. Fabius transported them to Rome at his own expense; the reconstruction of Jonah's cell was more costly, but a worthwhile investment. The look on the boy's face when he realized . . .

Fabius pushes the Greek from his crotch and shoves the soldier's face between his legs. The young legionnaire seems to hesitate for a moment, then hungrily swallows him, moaning in the darkness. The Greek slave, meanwhile, begins to kiss and lick Fabius's feet between the straps of his sandals.

On the stage, the soldiers have chained Jonah to the wall. The commander has just finished beating him with the strap. Jonah's backside glows vivid red. The soldiers crowd around, laughing and poking at him. The commander shoves them aside. He slips the strap around Jonah's hips, then winds the two ends of the strap around his right fist. He pulls Jonah away from the wall until the naked boy stands on his toes, his arms lifted to the iron bolt above as if he were praying. With his other hand the commander hitches up his tunic to reveal his short, stout erection, as thick as a man's forearm. He guides it between Jonah's whipped buttocks, snaps his hips forward, and gives a grunt of pleasure.

Jonah stiffens and throws his head back. His cock is as stiff as iron. One of the soldiers spits on it in contempt and gives it a hard backhanded downward slap. The commander begins to bang his hips brutally against Jonah's buttocks, making the wail that comes from the boy's lips broken and breathless as Jonah helplessly begins to climax, spraying his semen in great bolts against the gray dungeon wall.

The audience lets out a collective gasp of surprise and delight. "How clever of the boy," drawls one wag, "putting the climax at the *beginning* of the drama!" There are scattered laughs, mostly from the women, but Fabius hears nothing. For a frozen instant all goes black as he clenches his fists and gasps, abruptly giving the soldier between his legs a mouthful of warm, bitter semen, the first of many to follow through the long evening ahead.

Jonah wakens very slowly.

He lies on his back. Above him a high marble dome arches upward to a circular skylight filled with radiant blue. For an instant, still half-dreaming, he imagines he stares into the vault of heaven, and that the circle of blue is the eye of Jehovah himself staring back at him. Then Jonah moves his limbs, and knows that he is still trapped in the only world he knows.

Every muscle in his body is stiff. His jaw is sore and his lips are cracked from so many cocks using his mouth. His throat feels swollen and bruised inside. The hole between his legs is split and stinging and he feels a deep throbbing ache inside. For nine hours the soldiers raped him without ceasing. Toward the end Fabius joined them and managed somehow to fuck him along with the commander, both of them putting their cocks in Jonah's ass together.

Jonah realizes suddenly that the dome above is the ceiling of the banquet hall. Jonah has never seen it before, having always kept his eyes cast downward in the house of his master.

He does not lie on cold marble; some sort of cushion is spread beneath his back. His body is naked, but his limbs are unchained. He rolls onto his side, groaning at the pain. Across the room a group of slaves is dismantling the set which recreated the dungeon in Jerusalem; it was their noise which woke him. Teams of three or four push the stone slabs apart and carry them out into the courtyard. One of the slaves notices that Jonah is awake. Soon all of them pause to glance at him without expression before continuing their work.

Lying beside him on the floor, neatly folded, are a simple tunic and toga, and beside them a pair of sandals and a small leather pouch. Jonah stares at the pouch for a long time before he reaches out and pulls open the strings. Inside is a handful of gold coins amid a larger handful of silver ones. Then he notices the ring on his finger, a simple gold band with a brief inscription in Latin. Jonah has always had to struggle with the Roman alphabet; he is just piecing together the first word when a noise startles him. Fabius stands before him.

Jonah's heart begins to hammer in his chest. Against his will the ache between his buttocks turns into a yawning hunger—he can actually feel the hole open and begin to throb. His skin turns hot. His mouth turns dry and then abruptly fills with so much saliva that it drools from the corner of his mouth. His cock, withered and small for the first time in months, begins to fill with blood until it pokes up stiff against his belly; the taut flesh is mottled with fresh welts and whipmarks. Jonah bows his head and struggles to catch his breath.

He can feel Fabius's eyes on him. The slaves go about their business. Jonah stares at the floor, afraid to look up. At last Fabius speaks.

"Do you see the ring on your finger, Jonah?"

Jonah looks at his hand and nods.

"Do you know what it means?"

Jonah stares blankly at the ring, hardly seeing it. He shakes his head.

"Then read it. You can still read Latin, can't you?"

Jonah bites his lip. His breath catches in his throat. He can hardly speak the first word. "Freed ... by ..."

Fabius interrupts him. "Freed by F. Metellus Maximus," he says impatiently. "And there you see the date. It's called a ring of manumission. There's a small ceremony that's supposed to go along with it, but ceremonies bore me. The ring means I've freed you. You're no longer a slave, Jonah ben-Aden."

Jonah blinks his eyes and stares at the ring, which becomes a blur through his tears. His hand shakes. He can hardly breathe.

"I had Laertus put out a tunic for you, and a freedman's toga. Manumission gives you the full status of a citizen of the Empire; I suppose you know that. Theoretically, legally, there are certain obligations you still owe me, for life if I wish; but we needn't follow the letter of the law. You're free to travel wherever you wish. I also had Laertus fill a small bag with coins. There should be enough to take you back to Jerusalem, if that's what you want."

Jonah feels a strange compulsion to crawl across the floor and kiss the man's feet. Fabius can read his thoughts. He looks down on him scornfully and shakes his head. "We shall never see one another again, Jonah ben-Aden. You were an amusing toy—you amused me far longer than I thought you would. Now I cast the toy aside. There will always be others. Look me in the eye, Jonah."

Jonah can breathe now. He can even control the shaking. Still, he has to struggle to lift his eyes to Fabius.

Fabius curls his upper lip. "You're a beautiful youth, Jonah

ben-Aden; I've never seen one more beautiful. Your body, your face
. . . and yet to look at you now only fills me with boredom, and
more than a little disgust. I've wrung you dry, Jonah. I look at you
and see nothing at all to tempt me. Now go. You have no business
here. You're trespassing, and if Laertus catches you he'll do what
he does with all trespassers. Men who trespass on my land never
trespass again after Laertus is through with them." Fabius turns
and leaves the room.

Jonah rises to his feet. He reaches for the tunic and pulls it
over his head. The fabric is light and airy but seems to rest like a
coat of thorns against his bruised flesh. The toga confounds him;
he has never folded one and cannot imagine how. He throws it over
his shoulder. He slips his feet into the sandals. He reaches for the
bag of coins and clutches it tightly in his fist. Limping a little, he
hurries from the room.

He finds his way to the main vestibule. The door stands open.

The sunlight in the courtyard is dazzling. The sun is high
overhead; he must have slept until midday or after. He hurries
down the road that will take him out of Fabius's domain.

He passes a vineyard heavy with grapes on the left; on his
right is a field being tended by slaves, working together in a group
at the far edge. One of them has displeased Laertus; Jonah can see
the hunchback wielding his whip against the bare back of a crouching slave. They are so far away that he sees the blow descend a
moment before he hears the crack it makes, faint but quite distinct
on the wind. They seem not to notice Jonah. He hurries on.

The walk is a long one. The way is straight, dusty, and shade-
less. The ground tilts gradually upward. At last a short steep climb
takes him to the lip of the valley and the very edge of Fabius's
estate. Two gateposts surmounted with terra-cotta eagles mark the
entrance. Jonah stops to catch his breath and for the first time turns
around. Stretching below he sees everything: the villa, the vineyards,
the cattle in the fields, the slave quarters. The place looks peaceful
and calm, the very scene a genteel Roman author might describe
to invoke the essence of Roman virtue drawn from the serenity of
the Roman countryside.

What Jonah feels he cannot put into words; he cannot even allow himself to feel it fully, all at once, or else he would drop paralyzed to his knees, unable to go on. He quickly turns his back and strides through the gates, feeling his heart beat like a hammer in his chest and clutching the bag in his hand as if it were a bird that might escape. On his finger the ring shines bright and glittering beneath the harsh Roman sun.

REGINALD JACKSON

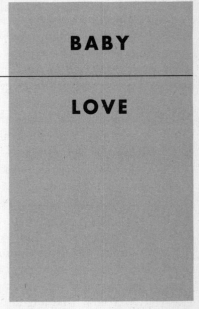

BABY

LOVE

A HAND, COLD, ROUGH, BLACK, COVERED MI-
chael's mouth the way the darkness of the night covered what was
happening to him. Michael squirmed and struggled, half screams
escaping whenever he managed to shake his head hard enough to
loosen the attacker's grip.

"Don't fight me, I'll hurt you if you fight me," said the attacker. Michael stiffened his body, determined to make it as difficult
as possible for the attacker. If he wanted to drag him into the
bedroom, he would have to drag half of the living room in there
with him, Michael decided. The attacker pushed him in the direction of the door, but Michael refused to move, locking his knees
tighter. His assailant whispered, "So, you want to play rough? I
can play rough." He shoved his knee into the back of Michael's
knees. First the left, then the right, causing Michael to lose his

balance and fall back onto the attacker. Michael could feel the strength of his size. His body was twice that of Michael's 135 pounds. Michael stood five feet, eight inches, the attacker well over six feet.

All at once the attacker scooped Michael up like a sack of potatoes and carried him, wrapping one hand around Michael's waist, pinning both of Michael's arms to his side. The attacker's other hand was around Michael's mouth. As they reached the doorway, Michael thrust out his legs against the frame of the door, refusing to go through.

"Move 'em or you drop to the floor. Move 'em!" the attacker said in a deep voice that filled the room. Michael didn't respond.

"Bitch," said the attacker. Michael pressed harder against the sides of the doorway as the attacker tried to push him through. Finally the attacker let go of Michael's waist and instead grabbed for the space between Michael's legs. He squeezed harder and harder until Michael finally let go and was carried through the doorway and flung into the air. Michael landed on the king-sized bed that occupied almost the entire bedroom, leaving room only for the brown dresser and the night table next to the only window. Michael bounced on the bed from the impact of the attacker's toss like a Raggedy Ann doll. The attacker took one hand and cleared the dresser of its contents: a jewelry box with a white ballerina that Michael had colored brown with a Magic Marker, various expensive colognes—Polo, Chanel—and a stack of self-help books.

The light from the miniblinds covering the windows cut across the room, dividing it like bars of a cage or prison cell. Michael knelt on all fours on the bed, looking for a way out. The attacker stood, skin so dark that it seemed to absorb what light was available in the room. The attacker appeared only as a black figure in the darkness.

"I'm tired of your shit. Be still and it'll go quick," said the attacker, breathing heavily from the struggling at the doorway.

"Fuck you!" Michael yelled back.

"No. Fuck you. I'm gonna fuck you. Believe it," said the attacker, regaining his breath and removing his leather jacket to reveal a bare, barrel chest that gleamed like a black pearl, it was so drenched in sweat.

Michael's heart pounded so hard that he thought it would come clean out of his chest. He moved from one side of the bed to the other, looking for something to grab, to throw, to fight with; there was nothing. The attacker moved closer to the bed; Michael could sense that he was smiling; Michael was a trapped animal.

"You motherfucker," Michael yelled.

"No, I'm a papafucker," whispered back the attacker as he pounced on the bed and Michael, wrestling Michael until he had him pinned face down. With one hand he pushed Michael's face into the black-and-white down comforter now half on the floor. Michael began to scream, "Help!" as loudly as he could. The veins on the side of his forehead bulged and his arms flailed behind him like the untied shoestrings on the big floppy sneakers worn by the tough guys who play basketball at the corner park. The attacker grabbed at Michael's behind and eased down Michael's red bicycle shorts and black underwear.

"No!" Michael pleaded. "No!"

"Shut up! Damn, look at that ass, that sweet, tight little ass." The attacker slapped Michael hard on the left cheek of his behind. Michael jumped. The attacker hit him again and again, first on the left cheek, then the right. Michael squirmed uncontrollably and screamed into the comforter. The attacker stopped slapping Michael's behind and began massaging each cheek with his hand, as if it were dough or clay he was working on, trying to get it just right. Michael continued to squirm slowly, his behind stinging from the attacker's slaps and the cold breezes blowing through the open window.

The attacker slowly lowered his head to Michael's left cheek and stroked it with his tongue, moving his tongue along both sides, then down the middle until it found Michael's hole. The tongue slowly traced the outside of the hole, moving more and more slowly. Michael's body movements came to a full stop and his body went limp. The attacker's tongue continued to outline Michael's hole, occasionally fluttering wildly at its center. With each flutter, Michael's legs would tighten and his back would arch like that of a cat preparing to fight.

Suddenly the attacker lowered himself onto Michael's back. His hot breath covering Michael's neck, his enormous body totally covering Michael's thin frame, he whispered, "You want it?"

"Yes," Michael said.

"Say it," the attacker said.

"Yes!" Michael was breathing harder.

"Say it!" commanded the attacker, slapping Michael's behind again for emphasis.

"I want it," Michael yelled out.

"All of it?" the attacker whispered.

"Yes," Michael said.

"All of it?" the attacker said more slowly, stressing each word.

"All of it!"

"Grab it and tell me you want it," the attacker said, as he leaned back on his heels.

Michael reached between the attacker's legs and unzipped his black jeans. The attacker's dick popped out like a clown's can of snakes. Michael popped a red condom in his mouth and then slipped it on the huge cock, quickly, as it jumped and spasmed in his mouth. Then Michael lay back on the bed. The attacker began pressing his cock against Michael's ass, rubbing it up and down between the crack. A wet spot formed under Michael as a river of sweat drained from his now throbbing asshole.

"Please," Michael whispered, clutching his head between his two hands.

"What?"

"Please!" Michael forced out in an uncontrolled, breathy voice as his body began to tremble with want and need and desire and expectation.

"Give it to me," Michael begged.

The attacker laughed and slapped Michael's behind again. "You really need it bad, don't you?" he whispered with a devilish grin on his face.

"Bad," Michael said, shaking his head up and down in his hands.

"When I put it in, you better not scream. You hear me? No sounds," the attacker said as he threw Michael's legs wide apart.

"Nothing. Not a sound," Michael said, bracing himself on the bed, his hands grabbing the sides of the mattress. The attacker took his finger and thrust it deep into Michael's ass, wiggling it side to side.

"Nice and tight," said the attacker, as if it were a warning or challenge.

Suddenly the room filled with a scream. "Ugh!" Michael called out as the attacker shoved his dick into Michael's ass quickly, forcefully, and without warning.

"I said no sounds!" yelled the attacker as he pumped in slowly, one hand squeezing Michael's left cheek.

"Sorry," Michael replied, trying to muffle another scream bubbling at the top of his throat. Michael bit down on the comforter until he could taste the feathers inside it. The attacker quickened his pace, pumping faster and harder, faster and harder, deeper and faster, harder and deeper, deeper, deeper still until Michael's whole body trembled uncontrollably and sounds forced themselves out of Michael's mouth. Michael was far beyond control, beyond reality, beyond time and space, in a place where pleasure and pain were the one and only sensation.

Just when Michael thought he had had enough, the attacker pulled out quickly and with one hand flipped Michael over on his back.

"I want you to see me fuck you," the attacker said as he put Michael's legs on his shoulders and thrust in again. Michael bit down on his bottom lip so hard he tore into the skin, as his head hit the headboard. Michael scrambled for the sides of the mattress to brace himself, but it was too late. He reared up and wrapped his arms around the attacker's neck.

One thrust, then another, and another. Michael was screaming out loud, filling the room with the raw, naked sounds of a good fuck. Suddenly, "Ugh!" exploded from Michael's mouth as he exploded all over the attacker; come like shooting stars flew from Michael's cock to the attacker's neck and chest. "Shit . . . shit . . . shit," fell from the attacker's mouth as his own body began to rock and spasm and shake. He thrust in one last time with all his might and planted himself deep within Michael as Michael's spine shivered and Michael screamed, "Jesus!"

All was still and quiet. The attacker lowered himself slowly onto Michael's body, clasping the wet warmth of his flesh as he whispered, "You okay, baby?"

Michael paused to catch his breath, then replied with a twenty-syllable "Fabulous!" Alan nestled into his lover's chest and quickly fell into a well-earned sleep. Michael softly began singing the Supremes hit, "Baby Love," Alan's favorite song. Michael mimicked the stage choreography with his left hand while his right hand held his man ever, ever so tight.

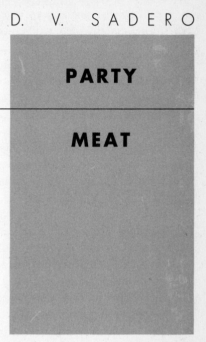

D. V. SADERO

PARTY

MEAT

I SHOVED THE GUY AGAINST THE JUKEBOX, forced him down against the glass and metal and acid-bright lights, and sank my cock into him. Angelo's rape, just before mine, could have ruined my fun, but the hole contracted fiercely around my cock, went rigid with pain and fright. I was in fucker's heaven. My two buddies stood watching. And only an hour or so before, around midnight, I was sure I hadn't a chance in the world to score.

Around twelve o'clock I'd wakened with a stiff, hot dick. Outside it was pouring and howling, one of those sudden storms that sweep over Southern California once or twice a year. "Well, shit on it," I said to myself. Just today I'd gotten back to San Pedro after four long months on a gigantic oil tanker, and I had it all planned: tune up the Harley, check out the action around Pedro, Wilming-

293

ton, Long Beach, the whole harbor area, and get my wad off as much and as wild as I could.

A little afternoon snore that had gone on too long, and now the storm, and that was the end of my hot plans. Too horny to get back to sleep, but at least there was the bar downstairs. Wouldn't even have to get wet, just down a flight and in the back door. Almost my living room anyway, Dewey's Place was.

I slipped on my jeans, cool and tight on my thighs and buns. Pushing my meat to the left, I buttoned up, then zipped my legs firmly into my black chaps. My worn black vest settled smooth and familiar across the contours of my back. No use for a shirt: I've got a good body, twenty-eight years of age, and not to brag, but hard work makes me muscular and hard living keeps me lean—and I like to show it, what the hell.

Everything looked the same downstairs in the bar, which made me feel good. Not that it was anything special—just a barroom with plenty of space and a big jukebox. Dewey's Place had been a waterfront hangout for years, and it stayed tough when it turned gay, so no need for decor. Dewey knew what his clientele wanted, being ex-Navy himself, and a warm, kind of fatherly guy in his forties, raised in rural Georgia. If he was crossed, though, his red face and lanky, wiry body turned hard and dangerous in a second. There he sat, on the usual stool at the bar, way up in the front of the room.

"Hey, it's Big Red!"

That was Angelo roaring at me, from his seat next to Dewey. Not very tall but beefy as they come; his arms, chest, and shoulders stretched his XL black T-shirt to the limit. Angelo had a swarthy, dumb-handsome face with steely-dark five o'clock shadow along the jaws, and a lot of black, very curly hair that he combed with his fingers. I'd worked a couple of ships with him and we buddied for bike cruising pretty often.

As I went toward my friends Dewey and Angelo, Devereux came over from the jukebox, out of the shadows. Even if I didn't get laid tonight, I'd have a good time drinking with my three closest buddies.

I smiled to see that even on a night as shitty as this, Devereux, "Dev the Dude," was dressed as sharp as ever. Handsome as a movie star, body lanky and wide shouldered and super-trim, he looked great in white jeans and perfectly fitting leathers. When he'd first started coming around Dewey's Place I'd checked him off as just another costume tripper. But one night, when a mess of straight bikers came in to "punch us out some queers," Dev was in the middle of it. We decked three or four of the guys and ran the others out.

Dev had enjoyed every moment of the brawl; he was not only tough but also the most expert sadist I've ever seen in action: he could do more to a body with thumb and forefinger than most guys can manage with a whole darkroom.

After Dewey and Angelo and Dev and I finished slapping and hugging and sat back down at the bar, I picked up on the bartender. Hard to believe my eyes: early twenties, blond hair in a short military cut, good looks that were maybe a touch pretty, and a solid but slightly thin build. Easy to check out his body, because he wore only a leather harness, chaps, and a black leather jock. His harness was so new it creaked when he turned around to get me a beer, and that's when I was surprised at the sight of his little white ass.

Now a bare behind is no shock to me, even one as beautiful as this; I've had as good or better. But, I mean, Dewey's bartenders were usually young and hot, but generally tougher than this kid and always his punks. They changed often enough, but while a punk worked for and put out for Dewey, he was nobody else's, so he'd never be allowed to parade around with his butt hanging out.

So the bartender, Lon was his name, made me feel a little uneasy, but my friends and I were piling up the laughs and the bullshit and the beers, so I didn't think much about it until a little later, when Angelo and I were in the toilet, giving the urinal a double spray. "Dewey's fuckin' that guy?" I asked.

"Nah. Lon can't be punked, don't hit on guys, either. Been here about a month, started mouthin' off all the time lately, last week or two." Angelo shook the drops off his thick cock and let the long, heavy foreskin droop back down over the big, dark head. "An' he's been teasin' a lot, ya know? Shit. You can picture that kind workin' downtown in one of them lightly leather joints, sure. But here? And Dewey won't listen to a word."

Back at the bar, as we joined Dev, I noticed somebody was missing. "Where's Dewey?" I asked.

"Went upstairs." And with that Dev went over to the jukebox to play some music.

Angelo leaned forward on the bar and said, "Hey, Lon, how come you show ass, huh, if you don't want a cock up it?"

"Good for business."

"That your business? I thought you was a bartender."

"You wish I peddled it," Lon answered.

What a snot, I thought, as I joined Dev over at the jukebox. The Dude caught the look on my face, I guess, because he said, in his always quiet voice, "Not to be repeated, but Dewey dropped a bundle on the stock-car races, and I think he needs business to pick up a little."

"Oh, shit," I said quietly, wondering if my one and only bar was going to soften up, "go Hollywood."

We rejoined Angelo as he was saying to Lon, "Hey, what about a little buddy-fuck?" Joking, but it was clear that my friend couldn't take his eyes off those buns.

"Aw, that's bullshit," Lon answered. "Fuck or be fucked, 's the way it is."

"Or hold on tight to your cherry, hah?'"

"Eat your heart out," was the bartender's answer.

A Hank Williams song was playing, but next to me Angelo's big body stiffened so fast that I heard his shirt stretch. On the other side Dev watched, his cool blue eyes alert, like a cat's when it has just spotted something moving.

Now Angelo, his face darkening, spoke in a low, whispery growl: "There's only three kinds of people that tease cock, ya know—cunts, queens, and punks."

Lon stopped washing glasses, came and put his elbows on the bar, and leaned square into Angelo's face. "Who are you to call me names, you with your buddy-fucking. Shit, that's just an excuse to get a lot of dick up your greaseball ass. If anyone's the queen around here, it's—"

With one hand Angelo grabbed the bartender by his shiny harness and in one swift move jerked him over the bar. Dev and I sprang to our feet. We watched him shoot a fist to Lon's jaw. Lon's head snapped back hard, but the punch must have been pulled a little, because the kid remained standing. Wobbly, Lon jerked himself free of Angelo's grip, then came at him, cursing and swinging. Angelo grabbed one flailing arm and gave the kid a spin that sent him crashing against Devereux.

The Dude locked one hand on the harness and flurried a mess of forehand-backhand blows across his smart mouth. "Satisfaction" by the Stones began to blast from the jukebox. Dev shoved the staggering bartender in my direction. I tapped one fast little stunner into his hard, flat gut.

When Lon recovered his breath a little the three of us bounced him off the walls, the furniture, and one another as bar stools, ash trays, and bottles crashed all around the place.

We eased off after a while. Barely able to stand, panting, sweaty, bruised, and scared, Lon waited at bay in the middle of the room with the three of us around him in a circle. Dev was the first to pull his cock out of his white pants.

It was as ugly as I'd remembered it, very dark meat for such a fair-skinned guy, shaft all knotty with veins, head bare of foreskin, high-flanged and shiny purple, and coming to a fat, hard point.

The kid turned away in fear, to see that Angelo had his meat out, too—not as long as Dev's or mine, but long enough and fatter than both of ours put together.

Wide-eyed, Lon looked from Angelo's crotch to mine—where my prick's stiff inches glowed a bright rosy color, which is how I got the nickname Big Red.

"Look, guys," the bartender said, "I don't take it. I never take it. I can't. You're too big." We moved closer, backing Lon into a corner. "Listen," he said, voice high and dry now, "I'll suck cock, I'll even eat ass, I'll drink piss, but please, don't make me take—"

"Shut up, punk!" Dev ordered, voice pure steel.

We closed in and grabbed the kid. With one hand Dev ripped the leather jock off, exposing a pale, half-hard cock and a pair of young-fuzzed, high-riding scared balls the size of hen's eggs. Devereux grabbed the fat pair and milked them downward until they lay squeezed together inside his fist. He curled one long finger down the taut, shiny scrotal skin, and Angelo and I let go of our captive.

No problem of escape: Lon was in what Dev called his high-control hold. I'd seen him make guys do all kinds of things, even pass out.

"Spread!" Devereux barked, eyes blazing directly into Lon's agonized, terrified young face. Gasping with the surge of pain that the Dude sent through him, the kid stood wide at once. Dev motioned with his head to Angelo.

Moving behind the kid, stroking that incredibly thick, uncut meat of his, Angelo took Lon in a bear hug. "Greaseball, hah?" He stuffed his dry cock, the size of a tall beer can, steadily into the crack of the bartender's hard little ass.

Lon began to scream. And kept screaming, even when Angelo motioned Dev away and crushed the kid downward, fucking him flat to the dirty floor.

The Dude stepped behind the bar and turned up the volume control on the jukebox. The bartender's shrieks, as Angelo brutally jammed his dick in and jerked it back, harder and faster, were lost in competition with "Sympathy for the Devil" and with the storm blowing outside.

In a while, after a grunting ejaculation, Angelo got up and went into the toilet. The kid managed to rise to his feet. As he tried to get to the door, I shoved him against the bright-lit, blaring jukebox. His body quivered in my grip and stiffened when I thrust my blazing red cock up him in one shove. I kept pushing for deeper, taking all I could get as hard as I could for as long as I could hold out. Which, after months at sea, was not long.

It felt as if my prick had exploded inside him. I stepped back panting and dripping sweat.

The kid slithered to the floor in front of the jukebox. He was

sobbing and trembling. Devereux straddled him, jerked his hips
upward, and forced his big, ugly cock up Lon's ass. "Respectable"
was playing. Whatever the Dude was doing with his hands on the
kid's chest, it made Lon scream and, fucked and beat as he was, fight
to escape. He crawled around the floor like a madman, desperate to
get away from Dev, who dog-fucked him with a harsh rhythm and
never missed a beat.

Eventually he left the bartender groaning in a heap in a back
corner, leathers scuffed, smeared with sweat, come, and dirt, harness
half torn off.

The bar and ourselves cleaned up, we returned to our usual
stools and drank some more beer. I guess my buddies and I were
all thinking the same thing, that Dewey was not going to like this.
It looked to me like the end of a fine friendship and eighty-six for
the greatest bar around.

Dewey came in by the back door; Lon was the first thing he
saw. He picked the kid up and laid the half-conscious body face
down on the bar just south of where the three of us sat.

Dewey looked at us from behind the bar. "You guys fuck
'im?" he asked, voice hard and quiet.

"He asked for it!" Angelo shouted. "Goes around insultin'
everyone, then he can't back up his own bullshit. I mean, man, he
begged us, really begged us, not to fuck his ass. Shit, he's not even
a punk . . . He's nothin' but party meat."

Devereux and I agreed.

Silence. Just the storm outside. Then Dewey smiled, a weird
grin. "Well, y'all, see, this kid came and said he'd work free, but
in return, after a month or so, he wanted to get the guys to turn
on him."

Angelo looked the most surprised of the three of us. "Wha-
at?"

Dewey went on: "If you kicked the shit outta him and fucked
him cross-eyed, it was just what he wanted. The kid's a rape freak.
I went for it because I needed to cut my overhead, and I thought
it'd be some fun for my friends . . . So yer right, Angelo. He damn
well is party meat, just something to have a good time with."

"Shit if we haven't been suckered," Angelo said. "Well, this is one time I enjoyed every fuckin' minute of it."

Lon moved slightly as he groaned. His left leg slipped from the counter and slowly dangled downward, coming to rest on a couple of bar stools. Now his beautiful little butt lay wide open. A whitish liquid oozed from the hole, which was bright red and thickly blistered, and slowly drooled down onto his big, fuzzy balls. They bulged out on the bar counter, torture-swollen, beneath the crack of his ass and between his hard young thighs that were tightly bound in black leather chaps.

As I drank with my buddies, Dewey began to apply a towel full of ice to Lon's black eye and swelling jaw, in his tough-fatherly way.

GAVIN GEOFFREY
D I L L A R D

RACE

"I WANT TO KNOW WHAT YOU KNOW," I SAID, "and I want you to teach me."

He smiled from one little ear to another, his topaz-blue eyes looking diligently within me.

"Yes. I would like that," he responded.

He was the regional chairperson of the National Leather Association, a group that I had had no previous interest in whatsoever. *Now* I was interested. . . .

As soon as the two of us could schedule an encounter we did.

I drove out to the Valley, to a small house on a rather wholesome middle-class street, parked my car in the drive, and was let into the front room through a steel guard-door.

No sooner was the door latched behind us than we were at each other's mouths, faces, necks; our clothes fell to the floor and

301

we tossed into a waiting sofa, locked in each other's clutches as though the walls were about to tumble down upon us.

They did; I couldn't get enough of this man's sex, his power, his radiant aura; *this* was a master—a *master of sexuality*.

His face wasn't essentially handsome—in the way that many are—but it was beautiful. His physique wasn't flawless (at least above the waist), but to me it was perfect. Whatever it was, this was the most sexually powerful man I had experienced since my second husband, Vince.

Yet unlike Vince, Race had the understanding of his sexuality to accompany the physical passion.

We exploded. Race confessed to me his obsession with bearded and long-haired men (rare among his peculiar subspecies), that I was his erotic ideal. But more, he knew that I was a man of awareness, that I would challenge him, and that I could reward him with my own ability to learn. He had my books; he said he had admired my words and my beauty for years.

His legs were strong as they wrapped about me; his arms could salve any emotional bruise. His genitals were without compromise, just slightly larger than mine, his dick hard at a moment's breath. And his *butt* . . . !

I would have that butt. And I told him so.

"You can have it, baby," he said, "if you can earn it . . ."

I was tied by my wrists to an overhead rod that ran the length of his ex-garage "playroom." My ankles were bound at either end of a thick wooden dowel. I was naked in a flittering candlelight and the sonorous drone of Jean-Michel Jarré created a solemn surreality.

The Master removed his own clothes, slowly for me to enjoy, kissing me before each article fell to the floor, until he stood there naked, exquisite in every detail. He didn't blindfold me, but ordered my eyes shut.

Then he began.

The first and most constant sensation was that of his lips against mine, that almost-familial warm kiss that fed me like a bottle.

"Just remember," he said, "all that I will ever do to you is make love to you. I am here to fulfill *your* fantasies. I will never let pain come to you unless it is the pain that I want you to feel. You are beautiful and I love you. Now I am going to make love to you."

He began with a vibrating prong that he moved about my limbs, genitals, and sphincter. The sensation was pure pleasure, but this was too easy and I experienced fear of what must surely follow.

"Relax," he kept saying, "let go, go with it, give it to me, give me your pain, your love." It was as though he were reiterating the words of Big Mama, once my guru, from times before when she pressed me into her bosom in the effort to bring me to enlightenment.

I submitted, and the pleasure seared through me in waves that caused me to tug at my bonds so that I had to hold them with my hands to prevent the ropes from tearing my wrists.

Then the pleasure was over. *That* pleasure. His kiss returned. "Keep your eyes closed," he ordered. I did.

I heard the pop and whirr of an electrical device being turned on.

"Open your eyes. Look," he said.

I saw him touching a tiny glass dome to his chest, which created a burst of blue flames that sparked into the salt-and-pepper fur, then went silent. When he pulled it away again the sparks shot back out and it seemed as though his chest sizzled.

I knew what would happen next, that he was simply showing his novitiate helot that the machine was not lethal, that it was merely a toy, a tool of his heart.

He reached out to me and the blue light popped against my flesh until he had made contact. It hurt. It hurt as he dragged the rod back and forth above my skin, my abdomen, touching my nipples, the head of my cock, my scrotum.

Then I understood: *I was supposed to react!*

And I did. Starting with a whimper, as he encouraged me, "Come on, baby, let me have it."

He stepped against me and I broke down, pressing my face

into his shoulder. *Daddy, save me, protect me from this pain. Protect me from all pain!* And I sobbed as I saw the doctor pull me from my hideaway and spank me for no reason, cut my dick, cut the umbilicus. The years of spanking and drunken abuse. And the love that I always maintained for that man, that father who meant more to me than any god in any heaven. And that was *Race. Now. Him. God!* This man whom I wanted to make happy more than I even desired to be happy myself. Even if that meant extreme pain to my own person. *I was his.*

Again I felt his salivating kiss on my tear-wet face. He was licking the salt from his subdued quarry, drying me with his daddy breath. I could taste the acrid aromas from his sweating nakedness, and feel the pressure of his rigid column, excited by my tears and my release.

"This will only be on you for five minutes," he said while inserting a cold leather knob into my mouth, fastening it at the nape under my hair.

"I am going to give you fifty of these," he spoke as he held up a black whip of many thongs.

The saliva ran uncontrollably in my mouth and it seemed that I had little ability to swallow; I aimed my face toward the ceiling in an effort to allow gravity to pull the spit down my throat as I contracted it to keep from choking.

"One." He struck me very gently. "Two," a bit harder. "Three. Four. Five. . . ."

It was easy at first. A game. But I knew the lashes would grow in intensity. That's the way Race works, gradually, steadily, building in trust, in power. As my flesh became raw. . . .

I didn't cry. The tears would have drowned me, with that damned thing in my mouth. I was relieved when he had reached his "Fifty," but even more relieved when he finally removed the leather nipple. He took a cheekful of water from a plastic bottle and fed it into my mouth. He was Daddy. He was Mommy. God feeding me. Saving me. Nourishing this mewling with his fluvial grace. *Then* I wept.

He untied my hands and I wept more while he held me.

"Let me have it," he kept saying, "give it to Daddy."

I realized that I was disappointed that he had untied me. . . .

We chatted while he was unlashing my feet. He pulled me down on top of him on the floor and we rested like that, forgetting the pain, our demanding dicks—the complete erasure of all that was outside of this room—just *being*.

He corrected a popular myth that I, like so many others, have always maintained about the S&M community, that, in fact, it was nothing but a bunch of callused and tired old queens who needed a barrage of tools and equipment to register any physical sensations whatsoever through their jaded old hides.

Race explained that, in fact, the experienced "bottom" (or *masochist*) relates to pain much more acutely than does the average person, and that, as he or she becomes more centered in his or her "craft," the pain becomes such that the brush of a feather—under the proper circumstances—is experienced like the gash of a razor. And yet imagine the people who swing on ropes by hooks placed through their tits and their flesh; they, he insisted, hypersensate to degrees of absolute cosmic bliss!

By contrast, the trained "top" is one who is equally sensitized to the care and needs of the person for whom he is "giving" the pain/pleasure/sensation, with rules of care, conduct, and etiquette so strict that one infraction can have her or him banished from the professional leather circuit forever.

"It is the master, in fact," he whispered as though revealing the forbidden arcane truth, "who is the ultimate slave. It is the master's duty to serve his slave."

I felt my vesicle muscles contract and my gut ignite with the revelation.

He then ordered my eyes closed again.

"This is what I consider the most important form of bondage," he said, pulling my legs and my arms out straight by my sides. No restraints.

"Don't move. Keep your eyes closed. I'll be right back."

He was gone for only a moment before he told me to open my eyes again; I saw him place a lighted candle upon my chest. The illumination on his face that should have made him look strange and monster-like in fact made him all the more lovely. I knew what would follow.

He held the candle above me and let fall one drop of wax. I winced.

He dropped another on another part of me. And continued until the hot wax was raining like a storm all over me, burning my balls, my ram, everywhere but my face.

I detached from my body, as is my habit when I am in pain, and he reprimanded me. "Stay with me!" he commanded.

I came back. I felt the pain. I started screaming and he sank down on top of me, glued to my body by the torrid paraffin; he made love to me, with his words, with his breath, with his heart.

And afterward, when he had peeled me off and showered me clean, he pulled me down on top of him again and allowed me to possess him inside. But it was as though he were a different person altogether, as though I were a different person as well. Oh, it was splendid, being inside him, watching that big and beautiful man give himself to me as would a delicate girl; but those were two different people, different Race, another Gavin, somehow less multi-dimensional, like shadow puppets that we were watching cast upon his bedroom wall. Beautiful, in all its complexity, alive with the smells, the sounds, and all the warmth of this kingdom; but we were just two men then, enjoying love, allowing our sex to be satisfied. The Being that had stirred my soul with his games, his words, and his devices was infinitely richer. That was my Guru. That was my Self. Race, the Avatar. The Divine. The Ultimate Lover.

Race Bannon, my urban shaman.

PART EIGHT

WOMEN

AND GAY

PORNOGRAPHY

Jim Merrett first wrote about his encounters with women who create gay pornography in *The Advocate*. He seemed stunned by the idea that his homosexual masturbation might be brought to a head by members of the opposite gender.

His investigation of what happens when women write gay porn is another analysis of porn itself; he's asking over and over again what it is that turns him, a gay man, on? What kinds of intrusions by someone else's fantasies can he let into his consciousness without losing his appreciation for the material?

One of the writers who most impresses him is V. K. McCarty, a woman who is also known as Mam'selle Victoire, her stage name for her life in the sex world of New York, as well as Victor King, her pseudonym as a gay male pornographer.

McCarty has owned up to her gay erotica in her interviews

with Merrett, and I've included "Knife Litanies," a story Merrett especially appreciated, in the collection as a fine example of gay-themed erotic writing. It is a fantasy for many a woman to become a gay man; it certainly was a decade ago, before AIDS, when it appeared that gay men might have all the privilege of endless sex without the slightest repercussions for their actions. Why wouldn't someone want to be a homosexual male if the reward were endless sexual gratification without any accountability? McCarty went further than most in her sexual life; often she was the only woman allowed into such male sex clubs as the Mineshaft, and she took it even another step, by recording the very sexual existence of gay men in her stories.

The queen of gay male erotica is, of course, Anne Rice, writing as A. N. Roquelaure. For Rice, pornography is, she says, "not a place where one lives. It's a place where one visits." Her goal in her three Roquelaure novels has been to create a place where the visit can be maximally safe and enjoyable, but also one where the distracting realities of our lives don't intrude on what is sexually possible.

Rice took the ancient fairy tale of Sleeping Beauty and transformed it. When the prince finds Beauty in her trance and kisses her, she doesn't end up married to him and living happily ever after. Instead she is taken off to become a sex slave in his palace in a far-off land.

In this exotic place there is little evidence of gender or other forces of societal power at play. The princes and princesses are used by the women and the men interchangeably. Even a royal prince such as Tristan can be handed over to common street boys on a master's whim, and there is no recourse. The whole point of Rice's erotic fiction is that there is no recourse from submitting to sexual pleasure, certainly a theme that many gay men—readers and writers—have identified as important to them.

JIM MERRETT

DO YOU KNOW

WHO YOU'RE

JACKING OFF TO?

A LOOK AT THE WOMEN WHO PEN GAY MALE PORN

NOT LONG AGO, I ATTENDED A PORN-WRITING workshop appropriately titled "Let's Fuck with Words" and learned, to my surprise, that the workshop leader was a woman. I had always assumed that the overwhelming majority of practicing porn writers were men. But that was nothing compared to the second surprise of the day. The workshop leader, a writer named Carol Queen, primed the group's porn-writing pumps by describing a story she had published about a gay boy and his male English teacher. The story was loaded with gay sex and Queen had published it, unapologetically, in a gay magazine. She was then at work on another story with horny gay male characters, which she also had high hopes of publishing. Queen's stories sounded promising, but what really excited was a possibility that had never occurred to me before: were there really women out there fashioning porn stories meant to be consumed exclusively by gay men? And could it even be that, in my many years of reading gay porn, I had actually jacked off without knowing it to a story written by a woman? Because I never like to leave a titillating stone unturned, I decided to do some research. It took a week of digging—making phone calls and consulting friends and editors and other porn fans—but soon I uncovered a small nest of women writers willing to come out from behind their pseudonyms and send me samples of their gay porn.

And that's why on a hot summer night not long ago, I found myself alone in my bedroom around midnight, stripped to my Calvins, preparing to jerk off to a gay porn story written by a woman.

"Big Brother's Buddy" was published by a woman in a well-known porno magazine.

I'm an open-minded queer. I don't discriminate against other transgenderists, so why should I object if a woman writer wants to pretend to be a man for pornographic effect? Besides, if straight men can activate lesbian clits with fictional lesbian scenes, might it not be possible for women pornographers to raise hard-ons on gay men?

On the other hand, I'm no pushover, and in porn, nobody gets points for trying. Success in porn is counted in hard-ons and shooting cum, an area in which women just don't have firsthand knowledge. I'm aware of the argument that was so eloquently stated in an Emily Dickinson poem about her never having seen a moor and yet still possessing the imagination to write about one. But, with all due apologies to the dear old dyke of Amherst, no amount of imagination can substitute for possessing a working cock and balls.

You can't just *imagine* what it's like to feel your dick stiffening against denim, then popping through your fly and into a wet mouth. The mind's eye alone can't conjure up how it really feels to slam-dunk your aching cock into some cute punk's greased butthole and then squirt pepper-hot cum all over his naked chest. My queer's intuition told me that this time my hard-on wouldn't even get out of the gate, much less shoot across the finish line. Which is to say that I was prepared to be cheated out of an easy bedtime boner by the simple fact that the author of "Big Brother's Buddy" was suffering from the extreme physical challenge of being born with a pussy.

With all these thoughts swirling, I turned on the student lamp next to my bed and settled into a mess of pillows. (For a good porn turn-on, these are essential to me: a comfortable place to recline; my lover away for the evening, ensuring absolute privacy; a little clothes fetishism; and a tendency to believe that what I am about to read might have happened, somewhere, at some time. This last ingredient, I suspected, would be the debilitating handicap of "Big Brother's Buddy.") One hand on my thigh and the other on "Big Brother's Buddy," I began to read.

As the story opens, a young man named Dillon is recalling a boyhood crush he developed on his older brother's friend, Donnie. Donnie is "a golden blond with wild and curly hair, and a body like a ballplayer's—narrow at the waist and then tapering up to a V-shaped torso to his big shoulders."

Maybe it was the wild and curly blond hair, or the V-shaped torso, or the synergistic effect of both, but I immediately found myself enjoying "Big Brother's Buddy." At the very least, the author had somehow tuned into such details of men's bodies as are eroticized by male admirers.

But admiring a writer's technique is nowhere near getting the piece of lead with wings to fly.

I plowed on. We quickly learn that though still a virgin, Dillon is hungry for a glimpse of Donnie in the nude. His wish is fulfilled one day when he discovers Donnie doing laps at the local swimming hole: "I watched the powerful muscles of his shoulders and back ripple as he swam a perfect crawl," Dillon observes (again, keenly homoerotic, this image of a young man's muscular back cutting through water).

Dillon decides to hide behind a rock and spy on Donnie. "It was then that I saw his bathing suit lying among the rocks. I stared at it and then at him, my eyes widening." And then Donnie finishes his laps and leaves the lake.

He was walking up out of the water, his lower body still hidden. I felt my cock begin to stir. It's not that I never saw my friends at school naked. But only in the shower and locker room. This was different. And it was Donnie. He stood before me. His long, dark blond hair was slicked back on his head. Light glinted off his sea green eyes. His chest and leg hair was tugged down by the weight of the water. And his huge cock hung proudly between his legs.

I don't know about you, but, despite my reservations, this heady combination of Tom-and-Huck innocence and secret lust was suddenly and unmistakably setting my loins ablaze. I quickly forgot the author's true gender. I didn't have a hard-on at this point, but the next passage, where Donnie walks to the shore of the lake and massages suntan lotion into his chest, started inching me closer to the promised gland:

I thought for a moment he was going to put suntan lotion on his cock, too, but he had something else in mind. I stifled a gasp as he began kneading it, lubricating its length with his hand. . . . His whole body was glistening in the sunlight like a Greek god's. I could feel the strain of my dick as it stiffened in my shorts and I hastily unzipped them. I was not surprised to find my own hard-on stretched to its full length.

I, on the other hand, *was* surprised—to find my own tool taking a stretch. There was something magical about this writer's grasp of the intrinsic horniness of golden youth and innocence. The image of a "Greek god" rubbing cream up and down his elongating prick, as seen through an eighteen-year-old boy's eyes, is about as potent as this kind of end-of-innocence porn gets. By the time Dillon finally got Donnie into the same bed with him, I was ready to rethink my whole position on the issue of women writing gay porn. I was especially touched by the way the writer had handled the end of Dillon's virginity:

> Then something began to push against my ass ring and I realized with a start that it wasn't his finger. It was his huge cock. My asshole was tight but he reached down his hand and fondled my balls.
>
> In my ear he whispered, "You're so tight, don't you want me?"
>
> "Yes," I moaned, my body shuddering as I struggled to get up on my knees so that he could take me doggy-style.
>
> "Then show me," he said, inserting a finger into my ass.
>
> "Yes," I moaned again, rocking my ass back and forth against his finger. I felt him push it in and then add another finger.
>
> I grabbed for his cock to shove it inside me but he pulled it away.
>
> "Not so fast," he said. "I have a few questions to ask you."
>
> "What? Anything," I gasped, wiggling my butt around his fingers.
>
> "You saw me at the lake that day, didn't you?" he asked, cupping my balls with his free hand.
>
> "No," I lied.
>
> Then, as he started to stroke my cock while still working my ass with his fingers, I admitted the truth. "Yes," I moaned. "I saw you."
>
> "What did you want, Dillon? Tell me."
>
> "You," I groaned. "I wanted you!"
>
> "How, how did you want me?"
>
> "I wanted to fuck you," I panted. "I wanted to fuck your ass!"
>
> "Like this?" he hissed.
>
> I gasped as he forced the head of his cock past my

burning ass ring. I buried my face in the pillow for a moment, then lifted my head.

"Yes," I groaned, feeling the pain and the cold chills run along my spine.

The whole notion of a fresh little cherry butt being penetrated for the first time imbues this passage with vital heat. That final line, where the pain and cold chills run along Dillon's spine, suggests a valid meeting point for gay men's and women's sexual experience. Both straight women and gay "bottoms" can know the exquisite pain of getting fucked for the first time. The pain/pleasure of anal receptive intercourse is what binds us at first to this most submissive of sexual pleasures, and we go back again and again, though, eventually, the pain becomes a memory and we take it up the ass with complete relish unadulterated by ache. The sweet memory of getting busted becomes delicious nostalgia for gay men, and perhaps also for women.

With visions of Donnie's nude baseball player's body wrapped around mine, his big cock plunging into my virgin ass, I splattered my chest, wiped myself clean with the Calvins, and fell into a deep sleep.

The next morning I awoke convinced that "Big Brother's Buddy's" effect on my Johnson had been a fluke. The writer had just stumbled on erotic gold—youthful lust, voyeurism, dream fulfillment, rape fantasies. "Innocent schoolboy teases muscular jock and gets fucked in his virgin butt as his reward." This is hot porn simplified; what reasonably talented writer could miss reaping a hard-on harvest using that formula?

But what about the world of real men? How well would a woman handle adult male sexuality? Though boys and girls may share many of the same feelings while still virgins, I was sure the end of empathy lay where the paths of gay and straight sexuality diverge. With her own memories of virginity, a woman might have the key to slipping inside a male virgin's head. But there's a great divide between the sex life of a woman and a gay man. How could a woman penetrate the inscrutable brow of the modern adult gay male, a complex being capable of reaching heights of romance and ecstasy unknown to heterosexuals?

For a possible reply to this challenge, I selected "Heart of the Matter"—a gay porn story by J. L. Brewer, who has some forty published wanking tales to her credit—and retired to a hot bubble bath. (Like Leopold Bloom in *Ulysses,* I just love whacking off "naked, in a womb of warmth, oiled by scented melting soap, softly laved. . . .") I figured that this steamy sanctum sanctorum would act as a kind of literary affirmative action, allowing me to give my undivided attention to "Heart of the Matter," eliminating distractions that might disturb the still waters of my libido. And even if "Heart of the Matter" didn't raise the periscope, I could softly lave my dick into shape while fantasizing about Donnie's buck-naked swim in "Big Buddy's Brother."

Drying the bathwater from my hand with a towel next to the tub, I picked up "Heart of the Matter," settled back against the cool porcelain, and began to read. Brewer's main character is Jesse, a young stud whose heart belongs to a bedridden sugar daddy who doesn't mind Jesse's occasional one-night stands. The only description of Jesse we get is from Sugar Daddy: "You're young, alive, and so enchantingly beautiful . . . ," which allows the reader to identify easily with Jesse, whereas hair and eye color, stature, and other vital statistics might exclude readers lacking these characteristics from identifying. Score one for J. L. Brewer.

Leaving home, Jesse heads to a local gay bar, where he briefly cruises a young blond before settling on an immediate prior fuck-buddy named Kurt:

> I slipped into the smoky room, saw Kurt bent over the table and ogled his alluring buns. My cock immediately began to throb with interest as he skillfully banked the eight ball and watched it glide into the corner pocket. Dimples creased his cheeks as he collected some money from the defeated player.

But Kurt is pissed at Jesse over an earlier sexcapade, when Jesse left in the wee hours of the morning while Kurt was sleeping. Says Jesse:

> I lowered my gaze. Knowing that he had every right in the world to be angry with me ... I shivered as he walked toward me. Kurt was a real stallion, but he didn't even seem aware of the fact. His body was hard and well-developed, the muscles accented by a short sleeveless shirt. I felt the heat creep steadily up the nape of my neck as he stood before me.
>
> "You lied to me," Kurt says, placing the cue stick between Jesse's legs and running the shaft along his nuts.
> "I know, I'm sorry," Jesse says, meeting Kurt's eyes.
> "You're never going to leave him, are you?"
> Jesse looks away.
> "Why don't we go to my place and fuck," Kurt whispers in Jesse's ear, before nuzzling his neck.

In several well-chosen images—the smoky poolroom, Kurt as a "stallion" in a "short sleeveless shirt," Brewer taps into the Colt model/James Dean school of bad-boy muscle hunks. That Kurt is oblivious to his own beauty makes him all the more appealing in a butch sort of way. The pool cue phallic symbol (Vincent Van Gogh uses a pool cue and two balls as an image of sexual tension in his painting *Night Café*, and the quick come-on juice up the action pretty quickly.

But Brewer has even more on the ball. In *The Homosexual Matrix,* gay sexpert C. A. Tripp argues that a certain amount of "resistance" binds both gay and straight couples together. "This resistance may be in the form of the partner's hesitance ... or any other impediment to easy access. ... Zest begins here, not twenty minutes later with what may or may not 'feel good.' "

In "Heart of the Matter," Kurt's pride won't allow him to jump into bed with Jesse, so he plays hard to get. In turn, in order not to alienate Kurt, Jesse has to conceal his aggressive animal lust, which breaks out in a shiver, and take the submissive role by apologizing. Only then does Kurt pounce. Zest indeed begins here, and Brewer's story is better for including this sexual mechanism common to both men and women. (This is no fluke; in another of her stories, Brewer plays one character's fear of being abandoned against another's fear of commitment.)

With this psychological underpinning—the resistance that plays out in both gay and straight relationships—I now believed that this story might have happened sometime, someplace, and, in recognition of this, my prick was starting to raise its soapy head out of the watery womb of warmth.

In the next scene, Jesse and Kurt embrace. "Our crotches rubbed together and I knew by the hardness of his cock that he was just as hot as I was." They take a wild ride on Kurt's Harley, "with the wind in my face, and a star-filled sky overhead. I closed my eyes to savor the sensation."

Inside Kurt's place, the main event begins.

> His massive, uncut cock slapped against my thigh. "Fuck me, Kurt," I begged, when we finally came up for air. "Fuck me raw."
>
> He back-stepped me to the bed, pushed me down and fell upon me. "You like it rough, baby? You like the way my meat tears into your tight ass?"

Jesse gets handcuffed, rolled over onto his belly, smacked on the ass with a leather strap. Kurt rolls him over and sits on his chest, wagging his big prick in front of Jesse's nose.

> I flicked my tongue across the head of it, tasted the tiny drop of cum that clung to the head and silently begged him for more.
>
> "You want to be fucked? Well, I'm just the man to do it," Kurt said, pausing to lube up his tool before ramming it in.
>
> "Do you like it?" Kurt cried, embedding his boner

to the hilt, pulling back to the head, then driving it in again.

"Yes," Jesse screamed, as Kurt pounded in and out of him. Kurt pulled out and shot his load down Jesse's throat.

"Fuck, Kurt, you almost killed me," Jesse stammered.

At this point, my dong was poking through the suds like a whale taking a breath. As Kurt and Jesse had their second boff of the evening, with Jesse plugging Kurt's greedy hole—"I slapped his enticing buns. I rammed it in once, twice, three times"—I was sending gorpy cumspouts into the oily bathwater.

Vanquished twice by gay porn written by women, I rose from the bath, changed into my softest pajamas, and hunkered down for some deep thought.

How had I, a savvy consumer of gay porn, been so utterly taken in by these presumptuous hussies? Was there something going on behind the scenes that I wasn't aware of?

I remembered a recent article I'd read by Simon LeVay, the research scientist, about the much-ballyhooed structural differences between gay and straight male brains: "Psychologists have accumulated an impressive body of evidence that some mental processes in gay men (verbal ability for example) are more typical of straight women than of straight men."

Was my response to womynporn being programmed by some peculiarity of my gay brain? Maybe, but so what? Even if a woman can get inside my head, she can't get inside my skin. Not unless she can put on a cock and balls for the occasion.

But then I thought, hey, isn't that what the queer movement is all about—a license to gender-fuck?

I suddenly recalled a scene in the teen flick *Heathers,* when a girl cheerleader tells a rival, "Suck my dick." I've always loved that raunchy line coming out of those lipsticked lips. It's as unexpected as it is sexy. Maybe the idea of a woman co-opting our penis power and fucking up the butt with it is sexy in and of itself.

My theory sounded even better a few days later when I talked to V. K. McCarty, a very womanly editor at *Penthouse Variations* who straps on a fictional phallus to become Victor King, author of gay S&M stories in such magazines as *Drummer* and *Mach*.

Said McCarty: "The heart of it all is imagining the feeling of my dick pressing in for the first time. It's like no other sensation in sex. It's predatory and magical and totally satisfying."

A half hour later, as I squatted in front of my fax machine, McCarty's "Knife Litanies" came peeling into my lap.

"Knife Litanies" is so viscerally real that you'd think McCarty is the queer Jekyll and Hyde, liberated woman by day, sex-addicted leatherman by night. The narrator of "Knife Litanies" seems real enough to be standing in the room with you, hissing orders:

> What was it about that kid that drove me so nuts?
> I could skin myself just remembering the smell of him.
> I remember one time I woke up forgetting I'd let him
> spend the night and I was stuck up his ass. He was so
> tight he was grabbing me wrong and I actually thought
> about pissing in him but I was getting longer by the
> minute and I couldn't. The velvety back of his neck was
> in my mouth and it was such a sweet moment really but,
> poor kid, I smacked his ass silly till he mushed up inside
> some and slid easier on my plank.

It wasn't easy maintaining myself in a half-squat on the floor, the fax paper limply draped over my knees, my dick inching up into the stiff fabric of my blue jeans, threatening to send me splaying, but I was lost in V. K.'s underworld:

> He could reach the most transcendent enlightenment
> sliding his guts on my fist. In retrospect I regret the
> times I'd plow him hard and wide first so he'd be swollen
> tight and struggling and to think how I cherished the
> grainy vein-pumping feeling of his ass almost too sore to
> take my knuckles.

I had to stop: my knees were cramping up.

But in the time it took V. K. to fax me, I had proof enough that a woman can indeed get inside a gay man's skin. The first line establishes her cock-bearing authority—what gay man wouldn't be entranced by "the smell of him"—and each following sentence presses another heady sense-memory button: "stuck up his ass . . . pissing in him . . . velvety back of his neck." Chill upon chill.

McCarty pays closer attention to the sights and sounds of the penis than many a gay male writer. She traces every vein, every fold of flesh, every inch of us. In her diction you can hear the whoosh-whoosh of a prick sliding in and out of a wet hole. A sound, perhaps, that only someone with a pussy can hear accurately. The squinchy in-out is even louder in another McCarty tale, "The Basic Training."

> One night under an almost full moon, after a particularly grueling session in my favorite part of the Ramble in Central Park, I strapped his hands together over his head and bound them overhead to a branch. And sucked him off. Patches of moonlight flashed gently on his sighing face. I let his cock swell slowly in a limp, wet mouth, sliding almost imperceptibly back and forth at random, feeling each heartbeat fill the mucous opening. Then, wetting space for my hand with each stroke, I penetrated my mouth with him, kneading the swelling flesh in with rolling fingers. Finally, with his glossy skin stretched taut over the iron shaft, veins arching out, I grabbed his hips and jammed my throat onto the flaming rod. It roughly skimmed the roof of my mouth, trembled a moment at the impasse, and suddenly broke down into the inner depth.

Because McCarty writes with such authority, the issue of her gender becomes moot. McCarty's narrative voice is so commanding, her erotic imagery so compelling, her language so poetic—I immediately became her captive. Her gritty, veiny, spit-drenched fiction proves she's a coxwoman par excellence.

Another woman with a mighty big dick—and imagination to match—is Pat Califia, a former editor of *Advocate Men* whose column of sex advice is read by both gay men and lesbians. Though Califia is known as one of our foremost lesbian writers, her own sexual adventures have provided fodder for the hot gay male sex she sprinkles through her stories. ("I have tied gay men up, beaten and fucked them," she told me. "I have direct experience here.") That evening I fortified myself with some wine and settled in with Pat's *Doc and Fluff,* a full-length novel chronicling the apocalyptic adventures of polymorphously perverse biker gangs. *Doc and Fluff* contains one of the nastiest gay sex scenes I've ever read.

As the action begins, a bunch of male bikers are holed up inside a barn, abandoned by their "bitches." One of their number, Anderson, wants like hell to fuck another, Prez.

"When Prez opened his eyes, the man was standing in front of him, his hips at eye level. The denim was faded below and to one side of Anderson's fly, where the fat head of his uncut dick had worn it down."

Then Anderson climbs into the hayloft. Knowing Prez will soon follow, he heats up his bone-handled boot knife, puts a can of Crisco next to his sleeping bag, and then pulls his stiff dick out and begins to play with it.

When Prez appears at the trapdoor a few minutes later, Anderson "slaps Prez's face with his hard dick."

Then Anderson hauls Prez through the trapdoor by his ears and pulls his jacket down over his shoulders.

> And with the hot knife, he slashed apart the T-shirt underneath it, leaving deep, bloody cuts and angry red burns underneath the ribbons of knit white cotton.
>
> Prez didn't scream, but his face was contorted like a gargoyle's. Then Anderson grabbed one of Prez's nipples between the knife and his thumb, and bore down. "Suck

it," he said, pushing his hips into Prez's face. "Suck my cock or by God I'll cut this thing off."

Anderson sucks hard on Prez's bleeding nipples. He yanks Prez's balls high with his fist, threatening to cut them off, then touches "the tip of the glowing knife to Prez's cockhead." Prez screams. Anderson runs the hot knife all the way up the underside of Prez's rigid shaft.

It gets even nastier. Anderson uses the Crisco to fist-fuck Prez, then fucks his own fist still jammed up inside Prez's asshole. There's blood all over the place by the time they're finished.

Throughout this passage, Califia turns the classic rape defense—"she asked for it by the way she acted"—back against men. The more Prez protests and flails and screams, the more slashing Anderson's sex assault becomes. Anderson knows that despite the protests, Prez really wants to be debased and fucked half to death. (When Anderson falls asleep, Prez sucks both his cock and balls into his mouth, drinking his piss while he jacks off. Anderson wakes and kicks him away, groaning, "*You* are a *pervert*.")

Califia suggests that the classic rape defense is projected onto women *by* men, that it is the men who really want it so bad they are secretly complicit in male-male rape. As I lay on my raft of pillows, I tried to resist being ravished by Califia's violent sexuality, skipping over the bloodier passages. But each time I found myself going back to the parts I'd skipped because I *wanted* to. I too am a *pervert*; I wanted to be violated by Califia's prose.

I relished Califia's gigantism, these titans exploding with titanic passion. At one point, Anderson cums "like a flamethrower . . . as if a grenade had gone off in the small of his back." Her language plays on the excesses of gay porn—does anybody in gay porn ever have anything less than an eight-inch dick? She's the female Tom of Finland; her giantly endowed, completely uninhibited men seem improbable, but if they do exist somewhere . . . wow!

I found fresh heat in Califia's plain language; she rejects overheated synonyms in favor of such perfectly serviceable Anglo-Saxonisms as "dick," "cock," and "ass." (Does anybody really holler, "Oh ram your throbbing tower of manmeat into my super-heated love orifice!") Califia's dialogue is ripped from life: "Fuck that ass!" Perhaps it is expressly because Califia is a woman that she can avoid the strained metaphors that drag down a lot of gay porn; pioneers don't have to worry about who's covered the territory before.

And Califia balances her more outlandish descriptions of sexual gymnastics with details drawn from more down-to-earth eroticism. Anderson crouching next to Prez, surreptitiously sniffing his crotch; Prez noticing the faded spot on Anderson's jeans. These are things that I, as a gay guy, can relate to, and that helped me to stick with the narrative when it became anatomically improbable.

Is there something in Califia's porn that betrays her womanhood? Besides all that flowing blood, it takes a woman to think up a last line like this one: "Before he slept, it seemed to Prez that he heard Fluff somewhere behind him in the darkness, and she was laughing."

Can we really let women writers get away with this kind of transgression? Can they bring female characters into the action without trashing the hard-on? My queer's intuition told me no again. I was glad Califia had saved her laughing woman for the last line. Knowing that a woman was spying on me would have deflated every one of the porn hard-ons recounted here thus far.

And yet, Carol Queen, a bisexual sex worker from San Francisco, has the nerve to have a teenage girl narrate the sex in her story "The Golden Boy." As I prepared for bed on a cool summer night, I was ready for "The Golden Boy" to fail. I even hoped it would. Summer was ending; it was time to get back to work; enough jerking off. If I kept it up I'd become a raving porn addict, grow hair on my palms, go nuts. I showered, brushed my teeth, put on a new pair of pajamas, and slipped between crisp white sheets. I felt good and clean and full of purpose. Here was a piece of womynporn that wouldn't make me spoil my bedclothes.

"When I met Jon he was just past chubby," she begins, "melted down into a lithe boy who was starting to show signs of man. He was a young man the way a colt is part gangly animal."

My pajamas were safe so far.

Immediately we are introduced to Mr. White, a drama teacher with wire-rimmed glasses and "bright, lavishly lashed eyes and a mustache that curled." The narrator has a crush on Mr. White, but she soon realizes that as much as she wants him, Mr. White has his eyes on Jon, and Jon is just as interested in Mr. White.

One night, both students are invited to spend the evening at Mr. White's home. The girl soon finds herself watching from an armchair as Mr. White seduces Jon into a nude massage:

> Then Mr. White began sweeping strokes down Jon's body and I realized I didn't have to pretend not to be there, nor to see: my presence had not prevented their touching. . . . The man was exploring him, every inch of skin oiled now and gleaming in the light, every muscle traced and kneaded, every curve of his body voluptuously stroked. Every time he stroked up Jon's thighs and over the muscles of his ass, Mr. White brought his hands closer together, testing the boy's response as he came nearer the cleft of his asscheeks.

The narrator finds her own cunt getting wet as the massage heats up:

> Jon squirmed in an encouraging way each time the hands neared, raising his ass for more pressure. Mr. White responded by stroking harder, pulling the cheeks apart each time.

The narrator finally cums for a full five minutes as the teacher-student relationship ends in a mighty orgasm:

> John had begun to murmur: "I want it, I want it . . ." rhythmically, entranced. He was twisting his torso, trying to reach Mr. White's cock with his mouth, trying to suck him in return. Mr. White finally knelt over him

on the table, obliging him, and Jon went for his cock with the hunger of an overripe virgin. He held the man by the waist and tried to bring him down closer, tried to get more of his cock, and Mr. White swallowed all of Jon's cock and, with a moan, began thrusting into Jon's mouth. Jon took it, moaning too. His oiled body still gleamed in the lamplight, golden, and he fucked up into his teacher's throat.

I had been coming for five minutes by the time they finally came, Jon shooting with a last hard thrust and what would have been a yell if his mouth hadn't been so full, and Mr. White with a long groan, in immediate response. The boy took the man's cum like he'd sucked cock before, but I don't think he ever had.

So much for my no-whack-off pledge. This time my prick was striking through the fly of my pj's, and I took the liberty of baptizing the crisp sheets. Against what I would have considered great odds, even seeing gay action through the eyes of a teenage girl can give me a boner. Maybe I'm just oversexed.

Or maybe this honest narrator represents a fresh new approach to gay porn. No sexual bragging here, just an innocent girl telling what she saw the night her English teacher and her best friend sixty-nined.

If this sounds subversive, it's probably meant to be. Queen is one of America's leading bisexuals, and her porn pushes the envelope of what's acceptable—both to straight and gay readers. Queen once told me that adopting a gay male persona allows women to enjoy the sexual freedom they perceive men as having. And that's the secret of women writing gay porn. In this conservative climate, women are still being asked to chain themselves to dull, submissive lives. Witness Hillary Clinton's censure for *not* wanting to stay home and bake cookies. It's liberating to think that women can be sexual outlaws, that McCarty, Califia, and Queen can preserve their essential femininity while parading around as big-dicked, promiscuous faggots.

As barriers fall between gay men and women and the queer movement progresses, I believe we'll hear more from the women who write gay porn. (The next march on Washington is for lesbian, gay, and *bisexual* rights!) Perhaps a recognized body of queer literature will emerge with stories like "Knife Litanies" and "The Golden Boy" at its core curriculum. Meanwhile, next time you retire to the bathroom with your usual stroking material, think about it: those steamy buttholes and spewing orgasms just might have been conceived by a woman.

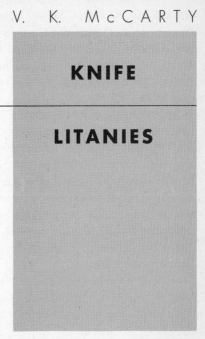

V. K. McCARTY

KNIFE

LITANIES

SUNSET KNIFES THROUGH THE WOODEN SLATS OF
our bar by the water for half an hour some days, especially now,
and the memory of that kid materializes in front of me so intensely
I can smell him. That wonderful, alive, dirty-puppy-dog smell in
his flannel.

What was it about him that drove me so nuts? I could skin
myself just remembering the smell of him. I found him in that
dark secret intimacy, the center of my universe some nights catting
around looking for trouble. The heads pass by along our side rim
of the Piers. You can audition the feel of their mouths, and tits,
trying to figure who'll put out. I bet I go through half a pack some
nights, staring at the black waves, waiting for the right head to
pass by.

But this kid was a jewel: silky hair that disappeared in my

fingers and dreamy cheeks I wanted to crush to know. His shoulders were cool and waxy with sweat and he smelled like some fine raw chicken in my hands. He felt impossibly young but, damn if his nipples weren't swollen with God-knows-what experience.

Usually I plug straight in, but he was so crushable in my hands, it was hard to let go of his face, and I kissed and tongued him through my fingers, feeling my cock press down into the cool part of my leg.

His smart-ass mouth kissing back made me crazy and I wanted him to shut up, just hang in my hands, and I gripped him hard until he did. With his mouth screwed shut in my fist, I jammed my tongue between his lips and prayed, with such jaded tits, that he have an ass as tight as I was making his mouth.

He snaked up his hands between us, I shook him to stop him, and he did the most amazing thing. He stood quietly with his face under my fingers and put his hands behind his back.

I was hooked. I thought, if this kid has a tight ass, I'm gonna have to marry him.

Of course he didn't. But he sure did make a mouthful of thermal underwear feel like oven-warmed heaven. Stuck his tongue right inside the bottom two buttons just like a pro.

I was so astonished by the initial feel of him, I jerked that boy off the line, and ducked him into the light of the garbage fires in the center of the transept so I could see him. In the phantom strobe lights of the flames, I had positively Tom of Finland flashes about him, but when he lit my cigarette, he looked more individual in the Bic light, and I could see his mustache was darker than his hair.

We stood for several minutes, saying nothing in the great space. I find the very moment I'm hooking up, the most unfathomable desire for solitude, something I never feel alone, even here other nights.

Then, as I took in a long drag, he was standing so his ass was in my free hand. I pushed at it, feeling him up, letting the spongy cush of his rump razz my balls, just meditating on it like that, until I was game for action. Then, gathering impulse, I shoved his tight butt ahead of me down the whole length of the pier.

The Hudson yawned up at us through patches in the broken flooring; the vaulted ceiling overhead creaked from men prowling on the metal roof. Silhouetted figures posing in the entryways beckoned to us but I wanted him out on the far end where it fans out into a concrete-and-brick beach. I hoped I was intimidating him down to his toes, but as I maneuvered him into place, I realized he was posing for two of the guys who were watching—and the sleaziest smile spread across his face in the dim light.

Just as I was considering throwing him around some to get his undivided attention, he melted down my leg and practically unbuttoned me with his teeth. I wasn't half hard and I didn't want him fishing for it, so I bagged up my balls in my fist and let my sleazy smirking jewel of a boy swab them down while I mused on the sight of him.

It was too dark to see that we were dwarfed by the Keith Haring and Tava cartoons on the corrugated wall behind us, but I wondered whether he hadn't been here like this before anyway. He'd certainly done the cocksucking line out on the side ledge.

Speaking of which, I realized my shaft was solidifying nicely under my hand. No wonder, persuasive little minx, he was leaning on it. I pulled my meat over my balls, unfurled it so to speak, and let it thud on the kid's face.

This was going to be fun, giving him the ride of his life, trying to swing on it.

He came off my balls with a sucking noise and I fed him my cockhead, back and forth across his lips, into him, and then all the way down on it in one shove.

Well, this was some tongue—like a squirmy little animal in there. It made the pleasure so sudden and intense, it was almost like a charley horse. And he acted as if he was gagging from the size of me, which was hard to believe, but it sure made me feel great in front of the little crowd that had congregated around us.

Eventually I let him keep his hands on it and he backed off

a little and drew my foreskin way down, pursing it up on the end. He played his lips all sloppy around the puckered tip, and then pressed his tongue inside, holding his hand tight.

In and out he prodded his tongue, holding my curtain in his fist down on my glans; and I suddenly realized what he was doing. He was imitating exactly what I'd done before to his mouth.

I went nuts. Just thinking of it, as he fucked the puckered end of my foreskin, was excruciating, he was so good. I couldn't help myself, I grabbed his head. Even loving all of this so much, I couldn't help just fucking right through it all, but that boy was with me every stroke of the way. He let me saw in and out of his creamy face a while and then lapped under my foreskin again, pulling it over his widened, cupped-out tongue in jerk-off strokes with his hand.

I grabbed it, too, and slammed into him, feeling the incredible thickness of my jacking strokes with his flat tongue stuck along in there. It was wild, galloping for my load with the flap stretched on his tongue like that.

As the kaleidoscopic end of it came, I pulled off and shot straightway into his mouth, ramming home, planting the first volley deep in him.

I tell you, having that kid in hand could sure make me feel all-powerful, but weathering those blow jobs of his always made me a little older.

After that first night, I thought I'd settle in with him and retire from the world. I began to think maybe he was my reward for teaching a generation of young men to suck cock and make coffee. But he had his drawbacks.

Even while I trusted I was soundly ravishing him from one end to the other, savoring him like fine cognac or almost-too-young Brie, he often ended up controlling our play in a way that mystified me. I honestly think I never do anything twice, but no matter what combination of leverage and distress I put him under, somehow he always seemed to dance right through it. And so nimbly choreographed my come-shots, every time he turned up at my door.

And his apocryphal explanations of what he'd done that day!

Every day was mythologically adventurous for him. Almost getting a job. Almost getting arrested. Almost getting tied up and kept by a man he said did big oil paintings for sheiks.

Lots of sheiks in his stories. I've never seen one or met one, certainly not in our circle. But to hear him tell it, he was being sold to sheiks in back rooms I'd been in the weekend before. Crazy boy banter.

One time I was trying to watch the news, and he was on his knees in front of me babbling away with my cock soft in his mouth, about two hot guys pissing between buildings the other night who ended up passing his mouth back and forth. And, sure enough, one of them was a bodyguard to a Philadelphia jeweler who sold to sheiks.

Of course I must say, those little stories of his always got much simpler real fast when I was pulling out my belt, but I could never tell if they were getting more truthful. And of course—it wasn't the dubious jeweler to sheiks who bothered me but the two dudes who might have actually made the acquaintance of his hot, squeegee mouth.

And yet, here I sit, missing him, trying to remember what I was chasing with this beer.

He's been in here, too. In fact, he started doing something in here I'd actually fantasized about. It was something else I got to see him do as if he'd read my mind.

I think he knew I didn't want him in my bar, but he burst in late one afternoon and started eagerly yammering out some wild tale, and then suddenly realized maybe this wasn't such a good idea.

Almost immediately he was squat down on the floor with his arms wrapped snug around my thigh. Just waiting there. I stared down at him, amazed he'd do something I'd been meaning to make some boy do. Smart kid.

It became a safe place for him, koala-bear–stuck on me like that. Sometimes he'd stay like that for hours, it seemed like.

During Pride that spring, he came up to me out on Hudson when I was talking with friends. We'd gotten separated by the parade crowd but there he was, snug-in-waiting on my left thigh almost before I realized it was him. Felt good wearing him warm on me like that.

Makes me stupid lovesick, but sometimes I do wish I'd been kinder. I remember one time I woke up forgetting I'd let him spend the night, and I was stuck in his ass. He was so tight he was grabbing me wrong, and I actually thought about pissing in him, but I was getting longer by the minute and I couldn't. The velvety back of his neck was in my mouth and it was such a sweet moment really but, poor kid, I smacked ass silly until he mushed up inside some and slid easier on my dick.

Whether it was his belted bottom dancing on my cock as I planked him, or his pretty mouth doing its Lolita majick, his memory burns and sparkles in my head during these sunset cocktails.

I always dreamed of making a man of him and it seems like I was always halfway angry with him, but even when I was just planning to tan his hide the next time he came back, he still kept me hard.

He could reach the most transcendent enlightenment sliding his guts on my fist. In retrospect I regret the times I'd plow him hard and wide first so he'd be swollen tight and struggling. And to think how I cherished the grainy vein-pumping feeling of his ass almost too sore to take my knuckles. Makes me a little melancholy behind my Scotch.

Something about knowing I'd been in there good made me want to sport his ass out in the Village and I even got the old chaps out, knowing perfectly well they didn't fit anymore. That kid could do that to me, get me doing pull-ups in the showers, oiling my leathers, you know what I mean.

Just about killed me then, it did, the time I heard a good buddy of mine really losing it, gasping and groaning away in the john behind the table where I was playing pool. When I went in to piss, there he was with his foreskin all stretched down over my kid's tongue. My friend was arched up, hissing at the ceiling, and my boy was knifing my heart out, doing what he's prone to do so well.

I don't know what I could have expected, but I didn't answer the door for quite a while after that.

I do keep dreaming about it all lately, and I know I've been bragging on that kid a lot, haven't I, but you know what it is? After thinking they'd never really do it, demolition equipment came in and took out the Piers. It makes me think a lot about those days.

Now more Hudson River light cuts across under the West Side Highway. And just at sunset, that hazy orange radiance is stronger lately, and I sure do see that pretty boy beaming up at me, like he was here so close I could smell him.

ANNE RICE
WRITING AS A.N. ROQUELAURE

TRISTAN IN THE

HOUSE OF NICOLAS,

THE QUEEN'S

CHRONICLER

IN A NEAR DAZE, I THOUGHT OF BEAUTY'S WORDS, even as the auctioneer called for the bids, my eyes half closed, the screaming crowd a swirling current around me. Why should we obey? If we were bad, if we had been sentenced to this penitential place, why must we comply with anything?

Her questions echoed through the cries and jeers, the great inarticulate din that was the crowd's true voice, purely brutal, endlessly renewing its own vigor. I clung to the silver memory of her exquisite little oval face, eyes flashing with irrepressible independence, as all the while I was poked, slapped, turned round, examined.

Maybe I took refuge in the strange inner dialogue, because it was too excruciating to bear the blazing actuality of the auction. I was on the block, just as they had threatened I would be. And the bids were rising from everywhere.

It seemed I saw everything and nothing, and in a dim moment of excruciating remorse, I pitied the foolish slave whom I had been, dreaming in the castle gardens of disobedience and the village.

"Sold to Nicolas, the Queen's Chronicler."

Then I was being roughly shuffled down the steps, and the man who had bought me stood before me. He seemed a silent flame in the midst of the press, the rough hands slapping at my erect cock, pinching me, tugging at locks of my hair. Wrapped in a perfect stillness all his own, he lifted my chin, and our eyes met, and with an exquisite shock, I thought, yes, this is my Master!

Exquisite.

If not the man himself, robust enough for all his slender height, then the manner of it.

Beauty's question thudded in my ears. I think I closed my eyes for a moment.

I was being pushed and shoved through the crowd, told by a hundred taskmasters to march, to lift my knees, lift my chin, to keep that cock erect, while the auctioneer's loud bark called the next slave behind me to the platform. The roaring din enveloped me.

I had only glimpsed my Master, but in the glimpse all the details of his being were fixed perfectly. Taller than I by only an inch, he had a square but lean face and a wealth of white hair curling thickly well above his shoulders. He was much too young for the white hair, almost boyish despite his great height and the pure ice of his gaze, his blue eyes full of darkness at the very centers. He seemed much too finely dressed for the village, but there were others like him on the balconies over the square, watching from high-backed chairs set in the open windows. Well-to-do shopkeepers and their wives, surely, but they called him Nicolas, the Queen's Chronicler.

He had long hands, beautiful hands that had almost languidly gestured for me to follow him.

At last I reached the end of the square, felt the last rough slaps and pinches. I found myself marching with low panting breaths in an empty street walled on either side with little taverns and stalls

and bolted doorways. Everyone was at the auction, I saw with relief.
And it was quiet here.

Nothing but the sound of my feet on the stones and the crisp
click of my Master's boots behind me. He was very close. So close
I almost felt him brush against my buttocks. And then with a
shock I felt the wallop of a stout strap and his voice very low near
my ear: "Pick up those knees, and hold your head high and back."
At once I straightened, alarmed that I had let myself lose any
measure of dignity. My cock stiffened, despite the fatigue in my
calves. I pictured him again, so puzzling, that smooth young face,
and the shining white hair, and the finely stitched velvet tunic.

The streets twisted, narrowed, grew a little darker as the high-
peaked roofs jutted overhead, and I flushed to see a young man and
woman coming toward us, all crisp in clean starched clothes, their
eyes dusting me carefully. I could hear my labored breath echoing
up the walls. An old man on a stool at a doorway glanced up.

The belt walloped me again just as the couple drew alongside
and I heard the man laugh to himself and murmur, "Beautiful,
strong slave, sir."

But why did I try to march fast, to keep my head up? Why
was I caught again in the same anxiety? Beauty had looked so
rebellious when she asked her questions. I thought of her hot sex
clamping so boldly to my cock. That, and the sound of my Master's
voice again urging me on, maddened me.

"Stop," he said suddenly and jerked my arm around so I faced
him. Again I saw those large shadowy blue eyes with the black
centers, and the fine long mouth without a single line of mockery
or hardness. Several shadowy shapes appeared ahead of us, and I felt
a dreadful sinking feeling as I saw them pause to watch us.

"You have never been taught to march, have you?" he said,
and he forced my chin so high I groaned and had to exert all my
will not to struggle just a little. I didn't dare to answer. "Well,
you will learn to march for me," he said and forced me down on
my knees in the street before him. He took my face in both hands,
though he still held the belt in his right, and tilted it up.

I felt powerless and full of shame gazing up at him. I could

hear the sound of young men nearby murmuring and laughing to
themselves. He forced me forward until I felt the bulge of his cock
in his breeches, and my mouth opened and I pressed my kisses to
it fervently. It came alive under my lips. And I felt my own hips
move, though I tried to still them. I was trembling all over. His
cock pulsed like a beating heart against the silk. The three observers
were drawing closer.

Why do we obey? Is it not easier to obey? The questions tormented me.

"Now, up, and move fast when I tell you. And lift those
knees," he said, and I turned and rose, the belt cracking against
my thighs. The three young men moved aside as I started off, but
I could feel their attention; common youths they were, in coarse
clothing. The belt caught me with fast thudding wallops. A disobedient Prince cast down lower than the village louts, one to be
enjoyed as well as punished.

I was drenched in heat and confusion, yet I put all my strength
into doing as I was told, the strap licking my calves and the backs
of my knees, before it lashed hard against the undercurve of my
buttocks.

What had I said to Beauty, that I had not come to the village
to resist? But what was my meaning? It *was* easier to obey. I knew
already the anguish that I had displeased and might be corrected
again in front of these common boys; I might hear that iron voice
again and this time in anger.

What would have soothed me, a kind word of approval? I had
had so many from Lord Stefan, my Master at the castle, and yet I
had deliberately provoked him, disobeyed him. In the early hours
of the morning, I had risen and boldly walked out of Lord Stefan's
chamber, breaking and running to the far reaches of the garden,
where the pages saw me. I'd led them a merry chase through the
thick trees and shrubbery. And when I was caught, I fought and
kicked, until, gagged and bound, I was put before the Queen and
a grieving and disappointed Stefan.

I had deliberately cast myself down. Yet in the midst of this
terrifying place with its brutal, jeering throngs, I was struggling

to stay ahead of the strap for another Master. My hair was in my eyes. My eyes swam with tears that had not yet started to flow. The twisting lane with its endless shingles and glistening windows dimmed in front of me.

"Stop," my Master said, and gratefully I obeyed, feeling his fingers curled around my arm with a strange tenderness. There was the sound behind me of several pairs of feet and a little eruption of masculine laughter. So the miserable youths had followed!

I heard my Master say, "Why do you watch with such interest?" He was talking to them. "Don't you want to see the auction?"

"O, there's plenty more to see, sir," said one of the young men. "We were just admiring that one, sir, the legs and the cock on that one."

"Are you buying today?" asked the Master.

"We haven't the money to buy, sir."

"We'll have to wait for the tents," said a second voice.

"Well, come here," my Master said. To my horror, he went on, "You may have a look at him before I take him inside; he is a beauty." I was petrified as he turned me around and made me face the trio. I was glad to keep my eyes down, to see nothing but their dull yellow rawhide boots and worn gray breeches. They gathered close.

"You may touch him if you like," said the Master, and lifting my face again, he said to me, "Reach up and hold tight to the iron bracket on the wall above you."

I felt the bracket jutting out from the wall before I actually saw it, and it was just high enough that I had to stand on tiptoe to grasp it, with some four feet of space behind me.

The Master stood back and folded his arms, the belt gleaming as it hung at his side, and I saw the hands of the young men closing in, feeling the inevitable squeeze to my flaming buttocks before the hands lifted my balls and pressed them lightly. The loose flesh came alive with sensation, tingling, quivering. I squirmed, almost unable to stand still, and smarted at the immediate laughter. One of the young men spanked my cock so that it bobbed sharply. "Look at that thing, hard as a stone!" he said and spanked it again this way and that as another man weighed the balls, juggling them slightly.

I struggled to swallow the huge lump in my throat and stop shaking. I felt drained of all reason. In the castle there had been those lavish rooms devoted exclusively to pleasure, slaves decorated as exquisitely as sculptures. Of course I'd been handled. I'd been handled in the camp months before by the soldiers who brought me to the castle. But this was a common cobblestoned street like the streets of a hundred towns I had known, and I was not the Prince riding through on my handsome mount, but a helpless naked slave examined by three youths right before shops and lodging places.

The little group shifted back and forth, one of the men pushing at my buttocks and asking if he might see my anus.

"Of course," said the Master.

I felt all the strength go out of me. At once my buttocks were pried apart as they had been on the auction block and I felt a hard thumb pushed in me. I tried to stifle a grunting cry and almost let go of the bracket.

"Give him the belt if you like," said the Master, and I saw it held out in his hand just before I was twisted to the side, and then it struck at my buttocks viciously. Two of the youths still toyed with my cock and balls, tugging at the hair and skin of my scrotum and cradling it roughly. But I was shaken by each stripe of pain across my backside. I couldn't help but moan aloud again, as the stinging strap came harder from the youth than it had from my Master, and when the prying fingers touched the tip of my cock, I strained back, desperately trying to control it. What would it mean if I were to come in the hands of these loutish youths? I couldn't bear the thought of it. And yet my cock was deep red and iron-hard from its torment.

"How's that for a whipping?" said the one behind me, reaching around and jerking my chin toward him. "As good as your Master?"

"That's enough sport," said the Master. He stepped forward, taking the leather strap, and received their grateful thanks with a polite nod as I stood trembling.

It had only begun. What was to follow? And what had happened to Beauty?

Others were passing in the street. It seemed I heard a faint distant roar as from a crowd. There was a thin unmistakable blast of a trumpet. My Master was studying me, but I looked down feeling the passion in spasms in my cock, my buttocks tightening and relaxing involuntarily.

My Master's hand rose to my face. He ran his fingers down my cheek and lifted several locks of my hair. I could see the dusty sunlight striking the big brass buckle of his belt and the ring on his left hand with which he held the stout strap beside me. The touch of his fingers was silky and I felt my cock rising with a shameful, uncontrollable jerking motion.

"Into the house, on your hands and knees," he said softly.

PART NINE

POST-AIDS,

PAST

ROMANTIC?

If there is anything that must be transgressive about writing, it's writing about gay sex in the age of AIDS. The connection between a deadly disease and outlaw sex is too tight for comfort. It's nearly impossible to write about sex, it sometimes seems today, without adding to it retribution, though the expression of sex was meant to be an escape from judgment through action.

One of the most vital publications in the country dealing with these issues is *Diseased Pariah News,* an underground 'zine from San Francisco that's published by people who have AIDS for other people who have AIDS. There are none of the crystals or chimes of the New Age in this magazine. "Get Fat, Don't Die" is one of their rallying cries.

Scott O'Hara, a major figure in the gay sexual world, wrote a series of vignettes that were published in the 'zine. "How I Got

AIDS or, Memories of a Working Boy" is a powerful example of how a gay writer can take any material and reconceptualize it. The vignettes, as O'Hara explains in his introduction, all involved real-life activities that he experienced as a gay man and as a porn star, each of them possibly the act that brought about his disease. It's transfixing to read the material; it presents to us much more of a clash of enticing fantasy and impossible results than we would like to experience.

"Sucked In" is another head-on example of transformative writing. Here is a new voice from San Francisco, Will Leber, examining one of the most difficult questions of all: how can we gay men be attracted to the very things we despise? The Marine fantasies that begin this volume should ask those questions, but they are more likely to retreat into a state of innocence where, really, the bad guys are just good kids. Leber won't take that way out. Here he presents an AIDS activist who is confronted with the contradictions of his desire.

"Wall" by another new voice, Patrick Carr from New York, describes an encounter by the narrator with a man who holds his fantasy, but then withdraws it, producing a raw urban rage that won't be quieted by a romantic veneer. The wall between desire and reality is too thick for the narrator to stand.

Michael Lowenthal from New Hampshire is still another new voice. Lowenthal uses every wile of the pornographer to turn around reality. Lowenthal is quite young; he was only twenty-three when he wrote this piece. He is one of the generation of gay men who came out after AIDS became an identified epidemic and after safe sex became a necessity of gay erotic life. How could a new generation of gay writers re-create that reality into something that was not only safe, but erotically exciting? Lowenthal's answer in "Better Safe" is a fine ending to a book that, while it contains all the contradictions that might come out in gay pornography, also aims to highlight its essentially romantic and transformative purpose.

SCOTT O'HARA

HOW I GOT

AIDS, OR,

MEMOIRS OF A

WORKING BOY

THE GIMMICK HERE IS THAT EACH INSTALLMENT IN the continuing saga will describe, in as much detail as I can stomach, one of the times I might have gotten AIDS. I would write about how you, too, can get AIDS, but presumably everyone reading this is the Right Sort of People and already has it. Whether or not I ever get to the right episode (and who knows? not me) is fairly irrelevant, as long as I keep readers and editors entertained.

EPISODE ONE: HAWAII

My beach-bum phase. Actually, since I never learned to surf, this may be just a wee bit presumptuous. But I *was* living just two blocks from the beach, and working as a janitor at a club just off the beach. Well, all right, the baths. And you don't have much in the way of physical needs in Hawaii—I could've (and did, from time to time) slept on the beach and lived on the cum I slurped at Diamond Head. So maybe "beach bum" isn't too far off the mark.

I was staying well exercised, bicycling and swimming, so surfing didn't seem essential. Waikiki is a two-mile strip between Honolulu and Diamond Head, and I frequented both places, mostly by bike. So it rains every now and then—who worries? In five minutes, you're dry.

So I was not feeling too unattractive. In shape, tanned, just twenty-one. Perhaps I was a trifle overconfident. Fucking arrogant is more like it. Then Joey showed up. Isn't that how it always is? The snake wriggles into Paradise and instantly gives you a hard-on. Well, maybe you don't get hard-ons for snakes, but I do. He was visiting from the Mainland, S.F. in fact—with his lover, who'd never been to the Islands before. Before we get into the jokes about giving him a proper lei that make every current or former resident wince, I must protest that I've always been the honorable type: I wouldn't think of deliberately setting out to seduce anyone's lover. Unless it was quite clear in advance that he wanted to be seduced. Both lovers at once, though—that's another matter entirely. It's one of my favorite positions. So I went at it, with gusto. Playing tour guide, that is. That's the way residents generally go about seducing tourists—as if seduction were necessary. Though, truth to tell, Joey knew the island quite as well as I did. Went bodysurfing with them for a whole day at Makapuu, and watched their bodies turn an alarming shade of red. No seduction *that* evening. And the next day they had friends to visit on the North Shore. And the day after that—oh, something came up, I forget what. It was the day before departure when I finally got them down to the tubs for an evening of debauchery.

For proper orientation and political correctness, let me date this episode. Pre-"HIV Disease"; pre-"AIDS"; even pre-"GRIDS." It was still just a "gay cancer" then. And the baths were still a pleasure dome, not a political arena.

What happened that night? I suspect you know as well as I do, and if you don't, I'd like to know how *you* acquired this quaint little virus. Besides, this also dates to the middle of a drug-induced haze that lasted for a year or two, and to be certain of the details I'd need to consult with Joey or his lover, and neither one is available. But we must've had a ball-busting good time, because I looked them up on my next two visits to The City. I guarantee that if one of us was previously infected, the other two had the perfect opportunity to acquire it.

So we were lying there, pretty thoroughly exhausted, in the movie room—that's another thing that's changed: you could make it in the movie room without being yelled at, then—and Joey turned to me. No, not exactly, he stayed himself; but he rolled on his side, and in an admiring tone of voice, said, "You could make a career of that."

So I did.

HOW I GOT AIDS #2—BONNY DOON

You all know how difficult it can be to guess what the weather's like on the other side of Twin Peaks. Now imagine how hard it is to guess the weather sixty miles down the coast. Can't be done. Best you can do is wait for September, drive down there every morning, early, and wait for the fog to burn off. If it doesn't, you go home and come back tomorrow. At least, that's what you do if you're filming porno there, because gooseflesh is not very attractive on film. Hard-ons tend to wilt under heavy fog. And besides, part of the illusion we try to convey via celluloid and videotape—especially in a video called *California Blue*—is that California is eternally sunny. And on my very first foray into the demimonde of Hollywood, I *would* run into a director who insisted on natural, outdoor settings. Yes, the results were spectacular, worthy of a *National Geographic* special; but the trauma! the expense! the loss of sleep!

Anyone want to guess how many trips we made down the

coast? Each time getting up before dawn, douching and doing makeup, skipping breakfast and driving sixty miles—and like as not, sitting around shivering for three hours before heading home. There are few things in this world as depressing as sitting on the beach in the fog, waiting for it to burn off. Not that we did this every day; we'd all have rebelled. But the whole process took about a month—the longest I've ever spent on one set. It shows, too: the hair length (and, in my case, the hair *color*) changes from scene to scene. Of course, we assume our viewers' minds (?) are occupied with other things, and are far too busy to notice such details.

And just a word or two, for those of you who still have romantic notions about sex on the beach: you haven't *lived* until you've been fucked using lube with sand in it. Even jerking off becomes a seriously masochistic act. You know that look of ecstasy on my face as I finally reach my climax? Try using a belt-sander on your balls, and I bet you could re-create it.

Eventually, of course, the weather cooperated, and we got all the scenes filmed. The most memorable one (for me) was being, um, "disciplined" by a "farmer" and a "cop" and a cucumber. Farmer and cop changed back into street clothes after we finished shooting, but the cucumber stayed in character—I'd been sent out to the produce market that morning, before leaving, to pick it out, along with some ears of corn. (Only in the Mission do produce markets open at those ungodly hours.) I named him Dennis—I've never liked to fuck anonymously—and took him home with me afterward. And Dennis is the only one of the three who, I'm reasonably certain, *couldn't* have given me AIDS. Perhaps this wasn't quite what my mother had in mind when she told me that veggies were good for me, but it might have had something to do with Ms. Browning's elegant phrase "vegetable love."

On a cautionary note, I would recommend that those of you who are of such a persuasion should *avoid* zucchini—or scrub them very well first. Those little hairs that grow on them don't seem offensive to skin, but can be quite abrasive to more delicate parts. Zucchini, I think, are strictly for oral satisfaction. (And if anyone has a good, high-caloric recipe, you should definitely send it in to Biffy Mae immediately. I have a gardenful and I need inspiration.)

Anyhow, I played it safe (on at least one level): I fixed a cucumber salad that evening. Dennis died happy.

HOW I GOT AIDS #3—TENDERLOIN

The Tenderloin, to most people, indicates decay and decrepitude. To those who live and work there, though, it's just a neighborhood—one that calls for a little more nighttime caution than most, perhaps. I lived there once; I worked there for several years; and many of my friends lived there also. These memories may be physically anchored in the Tenderloin, but my mental associations are anything but seedy. Some of my fondest memories, in fact.

For instance, there was Bob. First guy I met who actually lived there. He was a law student at Hastings, and we carried on a protracted fuck-buddy relationship—a misleading description, since he was rabidly opposed to fucking. He'd been fucked twice in his life, he said, and hated it both times—once when he first came out, in the seventies, and once, more recently, by a man who was soon to become his ex-lover. His sex life revolved around cocksucking; unsurprisingly, his oral technique was superb. My cock is no beginner's toy, but he was undaunted—and furthermore, he taught me something about obsession. Without his tutoring, I might not be where I am today. I wish he were still around to share the results with.

Memories of Bob take me back to the first time I saw him. Class, how many of you remember the balcony at the Strand, back when Thursdays were gay porn days? Raise your hands, please. I didn't show up *every* week, but often enough that there were some familiar faces. He was the only guy I ever went home with, though—and he insisted on waiting for the end of the movie. Always had this irrational respect for movies—maybe because he'd been in one. *El Paso Wrecking Corp.,* I think. And, come to think of it, if I'd had a role like that one, I might have a little more respect for the medium. Unfortunately, far too many of my videos were what might be called Tenderloin roles. Dogs. Poor judgment on my part.

The nadir of my career came with a video called—no, I don't suppose I should name it—on the other hand, I don't want any of you renting it—*Hung & Horny,* in which not only does the boy on the box cover have a dildo shoved in his pants to give him a basket, but the cumshots were mostly faked with milk. *Cold* milk, straight from the refrigerator. All over my chest and stomach. Three different times, for camera angles. Trust me, fans, not even notoriety is worth this sort of abuse.

To end on a happier note—oh, carry me back to old Savages, yes, that's where I belong . . . Maybe you can't go home again, but I found a good substitute in Savages. I wrestled there, jerked off on stage, won a contest, and met a lot of long-term friends in the back rooms. Even in a place like that—I'll concede it was a dump— there is a certain, um, team spirit, and I played around a lot with my fellow performers. Sarge, who pierced my tits after a performance; Francesco, whom I sucked off in the "dressing room" (a closet-sized lean-to next to the stage) while I was waiting to go on; John, who later played cop to my punk, on screen; and David, the shy one who drew me like a magnet. (My titrings were steel.) I must truly have been "innocent" still, whatever my past; because when David smiled at me, and agreed to accompany me to dinner one evening, I remember feeling—and acting—like a petted puppy. Puzzled, he asked, "Hasn't anyone ever been nice to you before?" And oh, of course people had been; hundreds, if not thousands. "Not someone I respect," was my reply, and I still can't say how truthful it might have been; but there's a large part of me that wants to be that innocent again.

Did I promise you a happy ending? Matter of opinion, I suppose—but I think this is one.

HOW I GOT AIDS #4—LITLAND

Some of you have noticed that in three episodes, I have yet to get nitty and gritty about sex. Yes, Virginia, there is a reason. I'm fairly good at rendering situations and contexts, lead-ins and conflicts, well enough to give the average reader a hard-on; this is the very stuff of erotica. What trips me up is the transcription of the moans and groans of the sex act. So I generally fall back on the "omniscient reader" technique: flatter the reader, tell him he already knows what's happening, "so why should I bore you with details?" Read *Lady Chatterley's Lover,* you'll find the same evasion. Besides, the hard-on quotient of graphic terms derives from their rarity, their taboo—repetition dulls both them and the reader. Now, I admit that the reason I euphemize is not because I aim to create great erotica; I'm just plain uncomfortable with dirty talk. On-screen, you'll hear me grunt and groan, squeal like a stuck pig whenever I get stuck, and generally make more noise than two bull elephants in heat—but I use no words. I become utterly inarticulate. In those rare cases when I *do* speak, as for instance in the mind-boggling "Wussy" scene, you can be sure that the director had a precise script, from which he would not budge. Scripts can make a video great, but only if the actors are equal to the drama. I never felt quite up to it.

The advantage of my Neanderthal approach to sex is that you *can* tell I'm enjoying myself. I can't say as much for some of my coworkers. I don't blame them (mostly I blame the directors)—but if I had been as uncomfortable as some of these guys seem to be, I'd've quit on the first day. Haven't you noticed? The ones who do all the moaning and dirty talk—but keep their eyes closed and heads thrown back so they can't see their partners? Who act like they're digging ditches, not fucking? Call me old-fashioned: I like guys to be *turned on* to each other.

The worst offenders, of course, are the *real* straight boys. I understand the motivation: it's called Money. (Straight porn pays even less than gay—for the men.) But nothing's more boring (to me) than watching a guy have sex without lust. Without love, sure; but without lust, why bother? I'd rather watch him mow the lawn.

And the funny thing is, it's usually in those "rape" scenes that the top has the most trouble with his hard-on. It annoys me to hear an aggressor *tell* his victim what he's going to do to him, repeatedly—while his dick looks like boiled spaghetti. And it puzzles me that, if two guys *do* hit it off and start sucking up a storm, the director inevitably breaks it up: "Okay, boys—time to fuck." Why? Why can't the director let go and let the performers create the scene? All he needs to say, to any competent sex star, is "I don't care what you do, just so you *have a good time.*"

Unfortunately, the Gage Brothers aren't making videos anymore.

The longest oral scene I know, offhand, is in a video called *Wild Oats.* For twenty minutes they go at it like anacondas trying to swallow each other—and you hardly notice it's so long (the *scene,* you filthy pervert), because they are two of the most turned-on guys you've ever had the privilege of viewing. Cocks like rocks. I doubt that the cameraman stopped shooting once. The scene *cries* to be capped right there with a cumshot; but nosirree, fucking is required. So they change position, as directed, and it takes fifteen minutes to get a half-hard insertion. I don't expect our pornographers to be Eisensteins; but wasting a shot like that is simply criminal.

Is this just sour grapes? Am I bitching and moaning because I made too many turkeys? Partly. Yes, it's painful watching myself do all the things I've just described. And again, I marvel that the scenes in which I got fucked are some of the hottest ones I ever did. My career might've been very different—and longer? or cut shorter?—if I hadn't been pigeonholed as a top.

Mostly, though, I'd like to get one simple message across to directors: as a member of the audience, I prefer videos that *aid* my imagination, rather than trying to replace it.

HOW I GOT AIDS #5—APRIL

April, I understand, is not a geographic location unless you happen to live in Amsterdam. It seems to be an emotional state for me, though, and that's close enough. My equivalent of *"Au revoir"* is "See you in April"—loosely translated as I Sure As Hell Hope To See You Again, and Real Soon—which does, admittedly, confuse people when I use it in midsummer. Nevertheless, it implies to me a perfectly torrid climate.

In one particular year, April included two videos, on subsequent weekends (yes, most of your favorite videos were shot in the course of one long, hectic weekend—don't ask how). And somehow, I managed to fall in love each weekend.

In the first one, that was all to the good: we were scheduled to perform together, and I think I can be justifiably proud of the fireworks that resulted. The second time around, I wasn't so lucky. The director was insistent that Michael and I be on opposite sides of the set all weekend. A more frustrating experience I can't imagine—but come to think of it, that could be what was wanted. That company seems to specialize in videos of eternally frustrated youths screwing each other just to take the edge off horniness ... God forbid any of their characters might fall in love. So perhaps a scene with me and Michael would have wound up on the cutting room floor anyhow. No matter: I got his phone number.

It was almost a month before I made it down to L.A.—like most good San Franciscans, I habitually avoided it, but lovelust makes a person behave oddly. I was to discover later (almost two years later) that Michael was in the throes of Great Romance himself at the time, but that didn't stop us from burning up the sheets. Few things *could* stop him. It stands out as one of the best weekends in my recorded history. "And yet ..."

I was quite accustomed to condoms by that time—even if we weren't yet using them in videos, in private life I did. Almost always. I still can't explain (or excuse) it; for some reason, even mentioning condoms to Michael was impossible. Talking about any aspect of sex has never been easy for me (writing is only a little bit easier), so I usually rely on actions. With several years of hind-sight, I think this is an error: if I can't bring myself to talk about it, I shouldn't be doing it. But the result, at the time, was that for the duration of our affair (which continued sporadically for two years), Michael was the *only* person in my private life with whom I was having seriously unsafe sex. Doubtful that it made any differ-ence to either of us, health-wise; but if there is responsibility to be taken for spreading it around, I can't exactly duck.

But this is not supposed to be True Confessions time. I want to tell you about the Good Times, which were numerous. Most memorable: April of the following year, when we met, half by chance, half by desperation (my half) in San Diego. Neither of us had a place to go for sex; we rode around on his motorcycle, and ended up in Balboa Park. He parked, and led me down a ravine to a spot next to a freeway, but screened from it by trees . . . and he pulled out his dick and dared me to suck it. It seemed to be a reasonably well-protected spot, and I've always had a passion for outdoor sex—what could be more natural?—so I had no hesitation. When I came up for air, sometime after he'd cum, the first thing I saw, atop the ridge, was the silhouette of a mounted policeman. So much for *my* imminent orgasm. Either he didn't see us, or just wasn't interested; but he certainly added to the Drama of the scene.

Come to think of it, *that* scene is the one between Michael and me that should have been captured on video for eternity. Except, of course, that then he would've had to pull out to cum.

HOW I GOT AIDS #6—GRANTS PASS

This episode doesn't fit in very well, since I left Grants Pass in '79 and haven't been back for more than two days running since. And it's questionable whether even today there is a documented case within fifty miles. Among other things, it's the seat of Josephine County, which you may remember from the news awhile back as the locale of an "AIDS-Free Zone" initiative. Made the cockles of my heart go all warm and fluttery to think that I was born there. If I still lived there, I'd hesitate before becoming "documented."

Anyhow, back to the question at hand: how would I have gotten the bug in good ol' G.P.? Short of time-traveling, which is what my visits back there always remind me of anyway, but in the other direction.

Answer: I wouldn't have. Except perhaps in the most general of terms. I spent a good deal of time there learning how to do the things that later backfired on me; and I contracted a serious case of Living there, which could be said to have led directly to AIDS. That is to say, I spent the years '75–'79 learning that Life Is A Banquet, and making a pig of myself.

My first opportunity (or at least, the first one that I had guts enough to grab) came along in the person of a friend of a friend of my sister's, who was on a bicycle tour around the country and stopped in for a weekend. I was eager to show him around; even then, I had a weakness for well-developed calves, and he had an eighty-mile-a-day habit. Yum. I'd also been "warned" in advance that he was gay. Wedding bells. For twenty-four hours I dogged his footsteps, making myself as obviously available as I knew how— then broke down and asked him if something was wrong, didn't he like my looks? Why hadn't he made a pass at me? I think I scared the poor fellow out of his wits (bear in mind, I was only fifteen!), but he eventually cooperated . . . and then skeedaddled for the California border bright'n'early the next morning.

After that it became a little easier.

Five years had gone by before I realized what was *really* wrong with this picture. I mean, I'd been jerking off over the Sears catalog and Parr of Arizona for five years before I finally met this guy; I'd read (and cried and jerked off over) *The Front Runner* and *The Fancy Dancer* (just about all the gay fiction available at the time and place); and yet, if they'd caught him, he'd *still* be behind bars. I have a friend who is locked up right now for a very similar "crime." Do I understand? No.

So, like I say, I've been back for the occasional visit with my folks. Twice I've even shown up with boyfriend in tow. They always treat him real formal and nice, but there's a certain tension in the air. So I don't stay too long. Some polite conversation; we have lunch; we leave. I can usually keep my claws retracted. How difficult is it? Well, I strongly suspect that they voted *for* that AIDS-Free Zone. Nevertheless, they're making progress: they still won't talk about AIDS with me, but my father recently sent me a clipping about a "doctor" who uses high-frequency waves to vibrate the dear little virus to death. I hated to break the news to him, but the fact is, I've already *been* to a disco, and it didn't work. (I don't wish to devalue experimental treatments; it's just that my father has a habit of picking up on the oddest of the odd. Like father, like son?) And I send him clippings about the experimental aircraft association, which meets in Oshkosh, Wisconsin, near where I live. Somehow, I think just that one concession—letting him know that we *do* share some interests—has allowed him a whole new perspective on AIDS. Me, too.

And if that initiative came up again today, you know? I think they'd vote against it.

HOW I GOT AIDS #7—BUENA VISTA

Just for variety—this is how I definitely did *not* get AIDS.

I met Bob Chesley at the Los Angeles premier of *Jerker,* and was instantly in awe of him. Anyone who can come up with that sort of intense fantasy, who can keep an audience hard in their pants for ninety minutes without even showing dick, has a mind to be reckoned with. My talents impressed him, too, so we hit it off pretty well. I saw him often after that, socially: at his place, or mine (two blocks apart), or in the Haight—actually, we showed up at many of the same sorts of functions. I was still performing at the Campus then, so my evenings were chaotic, but I managed to take in my bite of culture.

One afternoon, he'd invited me over to his apartment—anyone who was ever there remembers it vividly: the bird's-eye view of the best parts of Buena Vista Park—to take some photos. In tights, naturally: his *primo* fetish. We had a great time; and the photos, when I saw them, were eye-poppers. I'd owned tights for years, but never realized what I looked like in them, or the possibilities inherent in them. Hot-diggity! But after we were finished shooting, while relaxing over coffee, we got into the depths of his fascination with the image—particularly, with cartoon characters. Now, I grew up without television; it can only be a matter of speculation for me what it's like for a gayboy of six or seven to watch tights-clad superheroes jumping around the TV screen. (I do recall, vividly, seeing a Silver Surfer comic book, when I was about ten; it excited me, yes, but I was greatly disappointed that he seemed to be neutered.) Bob described it all too clearly for me, though. Again, he had the knack of creating a fantasy from scratch and inserting it into your libido fully formed. By the time he got out his custom-made Superman costume to show me, I was all worked up. I asked him, with a strange sort of hunger, if I could borrow it for a few days. He agreed; I rushed home with it, promptly put it on, began posing in front of the mirror and figuring out how to jerk off in and out of it . . . and I got the sudden urge to call him and tell him how good it felt.

Now, phone sex is not my thing. Emphatically. Phones make me nervous; talking about sex in graphic terms embarrasses me. With Bob, though, anything was possible: he was the man who *defined* phone sex for the stage. We had a brief, mind-blowing trip; both of us came; and I told him to be at the Campus next evening for the ten o'clock show.

Yeah, I did it. Started out as Clark Kent, to a tape of the Superman theme, followed by cries of distress—at which point C. K. looked around, found a "phone booth," and tore off his suit and tie—and the rest is pretty predictable. The audience ate it up: they always liked watching acts that could be rationalized as Art, rather than Just Jack-off Shows. And I found it unexpectedly sexy, jerking off while still wearing the tights. The management demurred, though. Not vigorously, I had carte blanche around there; but they thought that performers should strip down *all* the way. Always. Okay, it wasn't worth making a fuss over, and I'd had my fun. I

still think it was one of the best shows I ever did. It impressed
Bob, too, I guess: two months later, he presented me with the script
of his latest play, in which—*voilà*!—was the character of Skip ("as
in 'Skip to the good parts,'" he explained to me), doing a show
very like mine. The play is called *Come Again,* and of course no
respectable theater will touch it.

Okay, no unsafe sex in this episode. No Hollywood backstage
wheelin'n'dealin'. Just some brilliant soft-core photos; a dirty phone
call; a jack-off show in tights; and a fucking literary event (unpro-
duceable). Some of my fondest memories. Thanks, Robert.

HOW I GOT AIDS #8—SILVERLAKE

. . . but of course, I have strayed significantly from my subject. The
(alleged) connection among all these disparate tales, remember, is
"How I Got AIDS." Do I seem to have forgotten that? With the
secondary goal being the memory of an exhortation from a certain
editor to "keep it spicy. We wanna know what *really* goes on on a
movie set." So—I'll give you the spiciest of the lot: *Oversize Load.*
Now, this one's sorta tricky to talk candidly about, since I believe
most of the principals are still alive, and therefore offendable. But
at least three of them aren't: one technician, who, alas, I didn't get
to know as well as I would've liked, and two performers, with
whom I did have sex (though not onscreen), are dead. The others?
Well, as I say, I assume they're in good health. Mention of any
person in these pages should not be taken as an indication of said
person's health, etc. These caveats taken care of . . .

Rumors of the casting couch aside, there is only one time in
my career when I was called upon to bed the producer/director
before (or, for that matter, after) being cast. And I can hardly
complain, since he was someone I would've swooned for in a New
York minute under *any* circumstances. I was more than eager—
whether or not he would've cast me if I hadn't been so eager is, in
my opinion, a moot point. And the sex was good: well orchestrated,
as befits any experienced director, inventive and memorable. I was

quite royally screwed—which left me eagerly awaiting the weekend of the shooting. Maybe that was his intent: to leave his performers panting for more, keep them ever ready. It worked. I came back, all right; and all weekend, while I was being thrown at partner after partner, I kept wondering, "All right, guy, when do I get *you* again?" It worked, as I say: my passion was sufficiently deflected (certainly not sublimated) into those other encounters. Viewing that video, I still shake my head in amazement—and get a roaring hard-on. In episode one, I get fucked—and it's a graphic example of just how noisily incoherent I become when totally aroused—and do a little slobbering on my own dick. It was one of the most "natural" scenes I've ever been in—i.e., there was very little stop'n'fluff time. Both of us were seriously into it. Not in love; just randy. I never saw him again.

Scene number two was a little more labored. To begin with, it was a standing fuck, which is never the most comfortable of positions—and, hell, I'm seldom an inspired fucker. It would be libelous to claim that my partner wasn't a turn-on—we would have spontaneously ignited, under more propitious circumstances. And we came up with a perfectly adequate scene, too—the edited version is damn hot—it just wasn't the stuff of which legends should be made.

Which brings us to scene three, and the ultimate, crowning frustration of the weekend. I've got this fetish, you know? For dark, hairy, uncut, Latino-looking men. Why is it that I'm always paired with blonds? Poor planning on someone's part. So now, we're doing a three-way in the shower room, with me and two numbers from Italy or the south of France or Brazil or someplace—and I'm supposed to stand there at the washbasin jerking off while these guys fuck—and I can only watch, in the mirror. Major case of blue balls, here. And you know—I think it shows, on film. The fact that I'm *dying* to get in on this sex—but for some reason or other, don't dare to. Tension. Conflict. Suspense. Is this director a genius, or what? Yeah. So was de Sade.

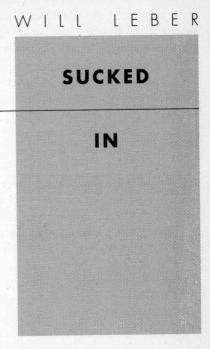

WILL   LEBER

SUCKED

IN

February 25, 1992
WE ARE OUTSIDE THE ST. FRANCIS HOTEL ON A
blue San Francisco day. There are at least three thousand of us,
though I am certain that the press reports of the demonstration will
reduce us to "an unruly contingent of several hundred." I'm in the
back of the group joining in the chants: *"We're here, we're queer, and
this is your last year! 150,000 dead from AIDS—where was George
Bush! Fight AIDS, not people with AIDS! AIDS won't wait—more
funding now!"*

Inside the St. Francis, at least a thousand of them are hobnob-
bing, shaking hands, and toasting President George Bush at his
$1,000-a-plate campaign banquet. I add it all up; it's a million-
dollar lunch. I remember watching the TV news report of Bush's
visit to Japan a couple of weeks ago. I witnessed the President

unexpectedly slumping in his chair at the state dinner. His bile overflowed from his frozen mouth. I wonder if he felt any pain, if he remembers how it feels to be sick and out of control? I am overwhelmed by the wish that they—all of those backslapping, banqueting bastards—would throw up en masse, turn a violent purple, choking on their own vomit.

They are *in* and we are *out*. I am thinking that they—Reagan and Bush—have been *in* for most of my adult life. I am thinking that their reactionary, rightist agenda is winning. I wonder if it could be merely coincidence that the AIDS virus suddenly struck us when Reagan first came to power. I wonder why the virus prefers *us* to *them*. I suspect that AIDS was born of a conspiracy, that it is a diabolical plot to decimate unwanted populations: drug addicts, faggots, and niggers. Didn't the invading U.S. cavalry pass out blankets to the Injuns, blankets infected with invisible smallpox?

I remember arguing with my friends on the way to the demo. They rebuffed my conspiracy theory. But I countered, "Don't you think if more of them started dying, they'd find the cure?" With that they had to agree.

As I see it, they just can't stand that we have sex with each other. God forbid that we enjoy sex, lust for sex, hunt for sex. They think that fags deserve to get AIDS for doing all those bad, bad sex things. We don't fit into their tidy little notion of traditional family values.

I am scanning the crowd. We are almost uniformly dressed in black. I survey a shouting sea of angry faces. Many of us wear black motorcycle jackets, the backs plastered with peeling, political bumper stickers: QUEER, ACT-UP, SILENCE = DEATH, LICK BUSH, ALL PEOPLE WITH AIDS ARE INNOCENT. I feel like the whole demonstration is inside me, a riot in my head.

I'm gazing to my right along the side of the crowd. I feel the impulse to smash something. I try to take my mind off the rally for a minute, keep myself from rushing up front to the police line, keep out of trouble. I've been doing this for six years and I'm tired of our pathetic protesting, of die-ins and actions. I'm sick and tired of struggle and consensus and caring. I want to lash out, break some glass, shatter their crystalline complacency.

I try to distract myself. I observe a middle-aged tourist couple, man and wife. The man snaps some shots of drag queens and leathermen with his Instamatic. They scurry along, satisfied they've captured something to prove to all their cronies back in Bum-fuck that they've been to San Francisco. A couple of dykes sit on their bikes parked along the sidewalk. They wave fists and toot their horns.

Beyond them, I spot a young man dressed in a suit. He stands out among us up on a bench, a dark, angular profile against the sun. I move toward him and circle around to face him. His muscular shoulders jut up above the throng. His blond hair is crew-cut and his tanned skin glistens in the sun. His complexion is buffed like a prize apple. I instantly think about doing those bad, bad sex things. I think about cock.

He wears dark, aviator-style sunglasses with mirrored lenses. He looks in my direction, but I can't tell if he can see me.

Shouts and the high-pitched trill of whistles snap me back to the rally. I stand up on my tiptoes, but waving placards and arms block my view of the action. I glance toward the man alone on top of the bench and decide to jump up there. From the higher vantage point I can see the police up front in riot gear, helmets on, shields over their faces, gloved hands holding black batons. The more militant protesters are kicking on the metal barricades, taunting the authorities. The man shifts his weight behind me; the slatted wood of the bench seat flexes under my feet. I can feel his heat. One of the barricades overturns and a phalanx of police troopers swarms forward. I twist around to catch what's happening on the edge of the melee. My arm brushes his elbow and sends a jolt of sexual adrenaline down to my dick. The cops drag screaming queers away into a paddywagon. I feel an urge to rush to the front, but my attraction to the man beside me helps to hold me back. Keep out of trouble, I tell myself.

The police resecure the line and the crowd resumes a chant. My attention turns back to the man. I follow the pressed seam of his pants up to his crotch. He forces one hip out and the pendulous head of his penis swings loosely inside the expensive fabric of his suit. The pants drape with a casual swagger down to a distinctive cuff atop his highly polished cordovan wing tips. His left hand adjusts his balls. The cuff of his white shirt, rigid with starch, extends perfectly just beyond the sleeve of his navy-blue jacket. I see a thick, glimmering gold band on his second finger. I remember the three reasons why my friend Ron, the traveling salesman, says he prefers married men: "One, they don't kiss. Two, they don't tell. And, three, they don't want to get married."

The wind gently waves through his wide silk tie. I follow the flying fabric up to the knot at his throat. I want to bite him there, run my tongue up the long, taut sinews of his sweaty neck.

Then I notice a black line running worm-like up from his collar. Something black is stuck in his ear. We are face to face as he raises a little black, antennaed box to his full-lipped mouth. It takes a second for the realization to hit me . . . Shit! He's Secret Service!

I reflexively jump down. I stop a few yards away and lean against a light pole. He stares, dead ahead, straight at me. What am I doing? Why do I lust for men like him? How could I want him? He's the enemy! But how couldn't I? He's the man in the underwear ads of my youth, the tennis coach, the Marine sergeant in a porno centerfold.

"We're here! We're queer! And this is your last YEAR!" The rhythmic cry of the crowd breaks over me. He's still eyeing me. I'm swept by a guilty wave of panic. Why don't I get turned on by my buddies—lanky men with broccoli-boy haircuts, buzzed around the sides with a bushy mane on top; the pierced dudes with diamond-studded nostrils and so many hoops hanging from their ears that they tinkle when you fuck? A video runs through my head: *A highway patrolman on a motorcycle pulls over a kid in a speeding convertible along a deserted stretch of mountain road. Surfer boy behind the wheel frantically tries to button up his holey denim shorts. Surfer has been beating his meat, driving like a maniac, a free spirit with the wind blowing through his hair.*

Get real! I scold myself. This is life, not video! A man wearing a suit and sunglasses and holding a walkie-talkie? He's definitely Secret Service—SS—one of the President's men! He's a pig!

I glare at him—one of *them*! I focus my anger on him, like the sun's rays through a magnifying glass, into a pure beam of hatred that could burn a hole right through him. But he is not fazed. *Shiny, knee-high boots kick roadside gravel. Cop leans two hands on the driver's door. He stares down—his eyes pools of silver, hidden behind sunglasses—at seated, shirtless boy. The top button of kid's shorts is still undone, exposing his hard cock.*

The man nods his head slightly as he seems to study me up and down. I'm wearing a black leather jacket, and a white T-shirt. Is he reading my T-shirt? Silk-screened on the front is a photo of two bare-chested, shave-headed, tattooed guys nibbling one another's nipples. The message of the moment shouts out in fluorescent, three-inch-high lettering: SAFE SEX IS HOT SEX, and in smaller capitals, USE A CONDOM EVERYTIME.

I gaze into his shining shades and feel my heat reflected back at me. A ball of fire hits my chest like angina. My nipples pulse to a tugging erection beneath the intertwined boys pictured on my shirt. *Patrolman orders kid, "Get out of the car. Down on your hands and knees!" Fast-forward to cop-meat pounding into surfer's gaping mouth, fucking him down his throat. Boy squats with arms wrapped around black motorcycle boots. His cock spills out the side of ripped shorts, erection rubs against boots, rosy dickhead oozes precum running in streams down shiny leather.* Mesmerized by his power, I curse quietly, "You Nazi son-of-a-bitch." My scrotum contracts to protect my balls and my cock rises to the challenge. I can't help it! "You Aryan, blond, indifferent, chiseled-bodied Adonis. I want to crawl at your feet."

I center him in my sights, lock my eyes onto him. I want you. I want you. I refuse to break my trance as the rally marches off and we are left behind. I hear the echoes of the protest, slogans amplified through handheld bullhorns: *"Every seven minutes someone dies of AIDS! Had enough?"*

The man jumps to the ground, level with me. He wets his lips, still staring me down. A leer crosses his face. It's an expression

I've seen before, full of hunger. I automatically grin back and join in the escalating cruise.

He starts to move away and I pursue him through the leaflet-strewn street. He glances back at me as I pace behind him across Union Square. Sheets of white, pink, and lavender paper swirl at my feet, nip at my heels. He stops for a moment to wait for me, then turns down an alley.

When I round the corner he is suddenly walking toward me. I panic momentarily, fearing that I have fallen into a trap. He barks something into the little walkie-talkie and folds down the antenna. He comes straight at me and stops, broad-shouldered, in front of me. I see myself as a miniature reflection in his mirrored lenses.

"So," he says, "you've been watching me all afternoon. Do you want something from me?"

"I think you know what I want," I return. Already there is an agreement between us about what is said or, more importantly, not said.

"Let's go have a drink." He motions me toward his car. It is a white Cadillac, a rental car. He unlocks the door. I slide in and he slams it shut behind me. I'm enveloped in the hush of a blood-red interior. Everything I touch is blood-red, the seat, the roof, the dash, the door, the ashtray.

He jumps in behind the wheel, reaches across the wide expanse of bloody leather, and grabs a handful of my knee. I let out a sigh. So this is what it's going to be: a front-seat quickie. My foot kicks involuntarily as he runs a squeezing hand up my thigh. I stroke his hard-muscled forearm and lean into his fist, forcing my crotch against his knuckles.

I bend over into his lap. I want it. But I want it over. I mouth his mound through the slippery gabardine. I feel his penis firmly shifting beneath my chin. I fumble at his belt buckle, eyes closed, like a blind man feeling my way. "Not here." He wrests his arm back from me. "Not yet." He pulls me up by my hair.

As he starts the engine and we pull out from the curb with a lurch of acceleration, I feel my stomach contract and vomit rise, which I force back down. He drives up the hill into the courtyard of a big hotel and a fleet-footed valet runs up to the Caddy like a stableboy to fetch his master's stallion. He drops the keys and a folded bill to the bowing boy.

In the elevator going up, he pulls me to him, hard against the starched white shirt. He smells like crisp new money. He gropes me, weighs my crotch, fondles my ass. He gooses me and I lean into him.

He slips me into his room like a morning newspaper and spreads me out on the bed, arms and legs wide. I read the political button on his lapel: PRESIDENT BUSH '92: FAMILY VALUES. I am somehow certain he is the father of two fair-haired, sun-freckled children, one boy and one girl. I recall what my friend Ron always says: "Daddies know what to do with it. Daddies are proven!" It's one more taboo. It heightens my arousal.

He starts to take off his sunglasses and I say, "No, leave them on."

He pops his bulging biceps out of his jacket. He tosses the coat over a chair.

As he turns back toward me, I see it—the pistol. The little gun is tucked into a tight shoulder harness, just below the rise of his left tit. The handle waits there to be grabbed. I flush with anticipation; I want to feel that power in the palm of my hand. I remember all my favorite cop shows as a child. I remember Michael Douglas in *The Streets of San Francisco.*

He unlocks the minibar, asks, "What do you want?"

"You know what I want." I sit up on the bed and unzip my jacket, feeling like a cheap whore in a fleabag motel.

He pours me a whiskey straight up. I down the double shot in a gulp. It burns down my throat. He unknots his tie and drops it in a puddle of silk sliding down beside my leg. He takes hold of my hand, rubs it against his stiffening phallus. He finishes his whiskey and pours another. I wiggle out of my leather jacket and push it off the bed. It hits the floor with the weight of a dead body. A few plastic packets of condoms spill out from the pocket onto the carpet.

He is reading my T-shirt, SAFE SEX IS HOT SEX. He yanks it

out of my jeans and peels it up over my head. He takes hold of my arms in his crushing hands and flattens heavy on top of my bare chest. His breath is sharp with liquor. He pants down my neck. The gun presses between us, rough, raw against my tit. His wet tongue strokes up my throat, hungrily parts my lips. The saliva-slicked tip slithers through my gritted teeth. I feel an urge to bite it off. I think that I shouldn't let him in so deep, his whiskey-wet tongue tickling my tonsils.

He knots my T-shirt around my wrists, unbuttons my jeans, pushes them down to the boots on my feet. He stretches up off the mattress. He drops his pants, kicks them off with his shoes. He towers above me in bleached white boxer shorts. The pink head of his huge prick peeks through the pee slit. He climbs out of the underwear back onto the bed. I lie back, feeling bound, and wish he'd gag me with his blond-haired cock.

He rips open his shirt, starts to slip the holster over his head. I say, "No, leave it on."

The open shirt frames the lean V-shape of his tan torso in white. A sparse fur swirls from the center of his chest out over the humps of his pecs. The shirt spreads wide just beyond his copper-colored nipples, which shine like lucky pennies. The holster hugs his side intimately.

He bites my nipples and I can feel the sharp stubble of his late-day beard piercing my skin like a thousand hypodermic needles. I feel his penis, the master of the universe, prying open my thighs. My erect cock rests against the leather-holstered gun. I think that yes, he must be Secret Service, and I peer into his mirrored eyes and ask, "Are you SS?"

He doesn't answer. He slaps the side of my butt—whap-whap, whap-whap—and I yelp little pleas of more, more, more. He chokes my dark dong in his golden grip just below the brown scar of my circumcision. He rises up on his knees and the swaying head of his prick slices the air, touching the tip of my penis. The shafts cross like swords.

He slides up my body; sweat slickens our contact. He holds my hands up above my head, positions his cock between my eyes.

I feel a damp trail of precum cool on my face as he tickles his prick down my nose. My nostrils flare with the smell of it. He coats my lips with his gloss. I try to pull my arms out of his vise-grip. I bend my elbows, but he pulls down my wrists, tightening the binding by twisting another loop of my T-shirt around his left hand.

"Suck it," he demands as he batters his blunt, heavy cockhead across my jaws. I open wide and wordlessly swallow the eight inches back against the tender membranes of my throat, so deep I choke. I can't breathe around it. He holds it in me until I stark to kick, struggle for air, then pulls out. I gasp and pant for breath, yet crave for the feeling of it plunging down my windpipe.

He presses the slippery head back in again and again. The stabbing rod violates the inner cavity of my throat. The pulsing pressure on the back of my tongue provokes my gag response. I convulse around the swollen head of his cock.

Don't let him cum! My gagging triggers a survival instinct and I twist and kick violently against his ribs with my knees. I clamp down with my teeth—just enough to get his attention—on the hairy base of his cock. A jolt of fright locks up his body. He slowly pulls out as I maintain the constant sharp pressure of my incisors.

"Not yet," I smile at him, renewing a trust. I work my hands free from his lock. I move up onto my elbows. I hold my T-shirt in one hand and its slogan runs through my head. I think about rolling on rubbers, protected sex insulated by layers of latex. I fling the T-shirt from the bed. I know that there is nothing safe about this sex. Already, we have broken some barrier, trespassed into forbidden territory. I want *him* to feel that sense of helplessness, the perverse thrill of danger at the end of a shooting prick.

I reach up to pinch his nipples, little teasing tugs. "Pull 'em, twist 'em," he pleads. I pull on his left tit so hard that I lose my grip and my hand jams into the gun holster. I caress it from inside the flap of his shirt. "The gun," I say, "take it out, I want to feel it. I want you to hold it to my head."

He pulls the pistol out with his right hand, rests the cold, hard steel shaft alongside my cheek. Goose bumps shiver through my extremities and my cock leaps. I beg him, "Let me hold it."

He presses the pistol into my palm and I immediately take control. I order him, "Get down on your hands and knees." He obeys like a good dog, sliding down to the floor. He needs to feel what it's like.

I spread open his fuzzy, angel-hair–covered butt. His anus is red-hot like sunburned skin. I poke it with the gun, twisting the handle as I ply his sphincter. I drive it at him and he crawls forward, bumping head first into the chair. His jacket hangs limply, collar down, off the back. I read the upside-down button, FAMILY VALUES. How could you? How couldn't I? He's one of *them*!

"Lie down," I command, the gun still pointed up his ass. He collapses flat. I stretch out beside him. The scattered condoms crumple on the carpet beneath us. He turns to face me. I bring the gun up and rest it between his massive pectoral muscles, nuzzle it up under his chin. He needs to taste this.

I aim the barrel right between his eyes, press the cold, round end of it against him. I tilt back the handle so only the sharp, bottom edge contacts his skin. I trace down his nose, pause beneath his nostrils so he can inhale the full smoky horror of his fear. The edge travels over the hill of his top lip, then settles against his pouty, lower lip. I force it down, revealing the moist, gaping vulnerability of his now open mouth. "Go ahead, suck it," I tease.

I revel in holding the upper hand. But he bucks with a surprising force that flings me onto my back. He rolls on top of me, straddles my chest, pins me down by my wrists. I wrench and writhe beneath him. But he outweighs me and seems so much stronger that he's almost omnipotent.

He rips the pistol from me. I have lost the prize. I go slack and he frees my arms. He hoists me up by my boots, slips his square, crew-cut head between my legs, catches his shoulders under the jeans which bind my feet. He leans into me and without resistance folds my knees back against my chest.

He stares down on me, digs into his mouth with his left hand, carries the dripping stream of spit to my ass, wipes the slime onto my hole. I tense my buttocks when he presses his middle fuck-finger into my ass. He forces it in past the knuckle, then pulls partway out and marries me to his second finger. The cool metal of his wedding band pistons my rectum. I moan when the intruders withdraw.

With a sudden, merciless stab he buries his stake inside of me. I scream out, "Fuck me, fuck me, fuck me. Fuck me Daddy, fuck me sir. Fuck me mister, master, sir!" I claw at his dimpled asscheeks, pull him harder into me. I squeeze down his flexing arms. Then my hands grasp the gun and I guide him to shove it into my mouth. I pucker around the cold steel stub, tongue the slightly oily shaft.

He pounds against me like a pack of mugging teenagers pummeling me with bats. I sweat like a fever, lost in a spinning vacuum. I want it. But I want it over. His cock tortures me like an electric cattle prod stuck over and over against an uncooperative prisoner: Confess, confess, confess! My body leaps, out of control, each time he sticks me.

He drives into me, searching, struggling, straining for his orgasm. He jerks me in his fist, timing his thrusts with the strokes on my cock as if it were an extension of his own.

He lets loose of the gun and I hold it in my mouth. We work in sync toward orgasm, toward climax, toward relieving the friction between pleasure and pain in shot after shot of white-hot release. I look up into the mirrored pools covering his eyes as I slide the pistol from my swollen lips. I offer it like a lollipop for him to lick. He sticks out his tongue and I lay the barrel against its warm embrace. He sucks it, then I suck it. Him, then me, him, me.

I suck in hard. I suck in hard my stomach, my chest, my ass, my throat, my mouth, my lips. I suck him in, suck it all in, suck with all my might. I suck his cum like deadly pellets into my gas chamber. I suck the shaft of the gun, probe the opening of the barrel, caress and lick and suck the thing as my fingers find the trigger—and I watch in his sunglasses for the flying bullets.

PATRICK CARR

WALL

MAYBE I'VE GONE CRAZY, STAYING INDOORS SO much. Work and home, work and home, work and home. Perhaps a larger apartment, although I can't now imagine my moving. I just need to get more rest: I stay up so late, I get no sleep. I try to occupy myself, find something to do around here. I need to be productive again. But I spend my hours listening. Listening for sounds in the hall, footsteps up the stairs and going to that apartment.

I am listening for a knock at my door.

He used to sit outside all the time then, on the step in front of the building. And he wore what seemed to be the same clothes every day, although they were plain to the point of being generic: jeans and a white T. Black boots. His hair was dark and straight and long and his eyes were black and his skin a stubborn sallow, never tanning in the sun. He listened to a radio, turned down low, and seemed immovable. I became accustomed to veering around him as I came and went.

He paid little attention to me when I'd leave the building, but upon my return I could see him cock his head toward me, just slightly and without his eyes. Sometimes, if my hands were full, I'd need to take a minute at the door and would use my fumbling for the key as an opportunity to get a closer look at his face. But he never looked up at me.

Except once.

It was on a Friday this past June, in the early evening when he sat with his hair shining an almost-blue in the leftover sunlight. I took the one step up to the door, put my key to the lock, and glanced quickly at him from the corner of my eye almost reflexively. And I stopped, looking him full in the face for the first time. A surprise, perhaps, but no great event in itself. Except for the fact that he was extraordinarily handsome, one might even say beautiful. Very grave beauty; a look of brutal royalty.

We stood for what must have been upward of a minute, silent and studying, before I introduced myself. He shook my hand, seeming generally underwhelmed. But I was more than impressed. I heard my breathing get a little harder and got that feeling in my middle: that one where gut and cock overthrow authority and run the show alone. Want him? I wanted him so badly, you'd think I'd been chasing him for months.

He remained mute, finally tilting his head toward one shoulder and arching a brow impossibly high. *"Well?"* it asked.

"I'm going . . . to . . . be getting inside . . . my apartment . . . I guess, now," I fluffed stupidly. I didn't want to leave, but didn't know how to stay.

"Yeah," he said. "Me too. It's gettin' kinda chilly."

Which told me I'd made some headway: it was eighty-something degrees that night.

■　●　■

He walked behind me through the dirty hallway until we reached the stairs at the back of our little tenement. He lived, as something would have it, on the second floor, at the opposite end of the hall from me. He had been living there for six months, though I had only noticed him when he took to sitting out front in the warm weather.

"Yeah. I see you all the time," he said.

I confessed to being surprised at never seeing him elsewhere, never hearing him come or go, what with the paper-thin walls in this place.

"But I see you," he said again. "And hear you. I always knew you were here."

I entered the apartment after him. Just for a drink, we said. And I was thirsty, really.

Seeing him from behind, I noticed for the first time how broad his shoulders were, and how much broader they looked with stray flying wisps of hair reaching out to touch the top of each arm. His shirt wasn't skin-tight, but displayed hard, sharp shoulder blades moving under it, moving almost too much. And through his shirt I caught a shadow of something—darkness, like animal markings.

We walked down a short hall toward the main room of the apartment. There he stopped suddenly, so suddenly I almost walked into him. He wheeled around and we were face to face, and so close that a loose piece of his hair reached out and rested itchily on my chin. I left it alone.

"Kitchen's in there," he said, with a little nod to his left.

His mouth was an inch from mine. His breath was cold.

We lounged around awhile, drinking beer and staying quiet. He sat in his one chair, with me on the floor after deciding to avoid the rumpled bed in the corner. For the time being, I thought.

I felt as though we'd been there for hours, although I knew that couldn't be. It was just the silence, and the chill of the over—air-conditioned room. And the way he rocked back and forth in that chair, letting it tilt back toward the wall, then forward, back and forward. With four fingers in each pocket, and thumbs resting out over his crotch.

The silence was becoming too much, and the initial sexual rush was starting to fade fast. I figured it was time things moved one way or another.

"So what do you do?" I tried.

"Nothing."

"Uh-huh." Great, I thought. Deliberately vague and dead silent. I figured he'd had second thoughts about having me here. Which underscored my own second thoughts, so I decided to leave. I stood to start my goodbye.

"Don't go," he said suddenly. He jerked his gaze up to me. "I'm not talking much, I know. But I want you to stay." When he finished he left his mouth open slightly, enough so that I could catch his tongue as it pressed against his lower teeth and ran along their sharp edge.

He'd stopped rocking and leaned forward, resting his elbows on his knees. He never turned his eyes from mine. He never blinked.

This is it, I thought, and allowed myself a little smirking smile. That feeling was coming back, a little at a time. I took the couple of steps to him. And ran the back of my hand down his cheek.

His eyes widened, his head rolled, and he took my fingers in his mouth.

I could feel his mouth grow warm around them. So I moved them in deeper. And out and in again so that his mouth got slicker and softer. I smiled more at that and the fact that I was getting hard as a rock doing it. I wanted to fuck his mouth so badly I clenched my teeth.

I ran my other hand over his chest, feeling it smooth and hard if not really built up. I found a nipple with a forefinger, and brought my thumb to roll and pinch it. He breathed harder at that, so I took the other hand, wet with spit, to the other. His nipples were tough and hard now, so I put some real pressure on them, and pulled him up to standing.

He was breathing hard warm breath quickly. "I make music," he said.

What? I just stared at him. Was he high or what? The mood started its way out the window, so I tugged on his tits a couple of times to bring him back to speed.

"I record in the basement," he said, "where my equipment is."

I got it. And laughed a low laugh that made him crack the only smile I'd ever see on him.

Downstairs things were a mess, the epitome of filthy, cluttered basements; furniture and paper, old clothes in piles halfway to decay. I swore I'd heard something scuttle, and so was relieved to pass through a wide metal door into the "studio."

It looked neurotically clean, and larger than any of the apartments I'd seen before moving in. A long rectangle mazed overhead with the building's pipes. One door, no windows, and a bare bulb with enough wattage to make me squint. As to "equipment"—the room seemed home to every piece of machinery that ever created, transmitted, or amplified a sound. I knew what very little of it was.

Chief among the equipment, and the only things I easily recognized, were four speakers: huge black boxes in each corner of the room. Tall as the man was, he looked only average standing next to them. An impressive setup, I admitted, mostly to myself.

"Yes." His back was to me, and he was fiddling with something I couldn't see. Something in his hair. Then from the speaker next to me: "I like it."

He turned to face me, and I saw the mouthpiece of a small headset poking toward his mouth from one side. He crossed the room to some other doodad, reaching up to whack the lightbulb into swinging as he passed. Shadows grew and shrank; they took a step to one side, to the other.

He was turning knobs, and his voice boomed from the boxes: "For the next sixty minutes we will be conducting a test of the emergency broadcasting system. This is only a test." And he wheeled around suddenly, grabbed the lightbulb in midswing, and dashed it against the wall, into darkness.

■ ● ■

My eyes struggled to adjust to the darkness, but the room was too black. I thought I'd eventually focus on something, but I didn't have time. The room was suddenly all sound—loud rumblings and screechings. They swirled and throbbed; they were deafening.

Above all I heard him, a low little sound from his throat, before words. "Ready?" His voice shook my gut. "Clothes."

I tried to say something, to ask him to turn the noise down, to get some light. I could feel my mouth move, but heard something slight and far away. I held a hand in front of my mouth to make sure I was actually using breath.

"Now." And I could feel him in front of me as he said it, and then his hands ripped open the buttons of my jeans. Another quick hand tore open my shirt, tugged on it until it fell away.

I sucked in a quick breath. He traced things on my chest with the backs of his fingers, with their cool nails. "Pretty boy." If my eyes had adjusted to the dark, they still saw nothing. All I knew of him was his fingers. All I knew of myself was the dots and lines he touched onto me. The assaulting noise made me deaf to everything but the rumble of his voice. Whatever I was when I'd come in here had become almost inaudible.

I could feel my cock grow harder in my underwear, bobbing up as my jeans slid down around my knees, my body rocking on its own. The strange here-and-there lightness of his fingers traveled my body, skirted round back, stopped on my backside for a second, and wandered on. I didn't hear a moan, but I felt its roughness in my throat. Ready, I thought. Make me something.

His hands clapped down on the sides of my skull, and he tipped my head back. He pressed his mouth to mine, sharply, and his tongue pushed in. It searched my mouth—my tongue, my teeth, deep reaching back to my throat. I sucked it in, closed my lips around it as it fucked in and out of me. Then it was gone, and our open mouths bounced on each other. He slipped his hands down my face, held my mouth open, and spit deep into me. And again.

My body was slipping, but I braced myself to keep near him. He smeared his spit on my face, reached deep into me, pushing his fingers down deep into me. "Hole." Far away I was saying yes, yes, mumbling far away with him in my mouth.

He wiped his hands on my chest and belly. He plunged one into my underwear, grabbing my cock roughly and drawing out more of the sticky precum I'd started soaking myself with. "So bad. So, so bad." He yanked brutally at my balls, and I buckled.

"Ah, a wiggler. You are incorrigible really. Hands up." I raised my hands into the air, where they brushed against a water pipe right overhead. "Stay." I stood still, and felt him behind me. He wrapped my wrists in something, something soft. Tied my wrists to the pipe.

I started struggling, panicking some. This was too much: I couldn't move, I couldn't hear, I couldn't see. "You're really troublesome." He bound my ankles together. I can't remember . . . if I heard . . . myself, telling him to stop. The noise in the room was an almost music now, a chord held until maddening. I threw all my focus onto his voice; it was the only piece of reality I had.

He reached around front and was at my cock again. "So excitable. Hard as steel, huh?" I was. I fell still and he pushed it down, let it spring up to slap my belly. "You like that, baby boy?"

I did. I let my head fall back and listened to him through the insanity of the noise.

"I thought I knew what you wanted. How you wanted. Was my thinking right?"

I nodded.

"Yes." He spit in his hand and rubbed it roughly over the head of my dick. "And I think you know how to give me what I want." He worked up and down the shaft. "Don't you?"

Yes yes yes yes.

"Don't you?"

Yes oh yes yes.

"Come on, you fuck. *Answer me!*" He slapped his hand on my balls and I could feel my groaning. And my hips as they bucked. "Enthusiasm, boy. I expect the right energy." He pulled his dick out and ran it through the crack of my ass.

I pushed back for it, almost convulsively. "Yes! Yes yes. How we want it." He swatted it back and forth on me and laughed. He pressed himself against my back, humping his cock on me.

His hands moved, and I felt him take the belt from his jeans. "You want, but lack the—what?—proper fervor in the asking." He drew off me. With a matter-of-fact sarcasm he continued. "I just don't think we've reached the proper pitch yet."

The blow tore through me like a jagged blade. My shoulder, my back stung from right to left. And caught fire. The belt hit again, the broad of my back: the sting; the burn; a surge, a fist from my guts to my head. It rolled on my shoulders, drunk.

"Yeah." He let the belt go on my ass, again, over and over. Hundred times. My hands clawed at the pipe overhead, I felt my shorts soaking. I thought I pissed myself, but I was too hard for that. I was rutting wildly, moving my dick against the cotton of my underwear, I was so close, and over and over he brought the leather down on me hotly could feel it come up in me my balls pull up toward me.

He brought the belt around my neck tightly, and his breath was in my ear "piggy piggy piggy little pig hole" and he pulled my shorts down. My dick stood out free. "Little boys shouldn't rub themselves that way." He grabbed my balls and yanked them down. "Unless they're told to." He ran a hand, like barbed wire, down my back. And up. And up my arms to my wrists. In a move they were free, and I fell hard to my knees.

"Behind you." An instinct I didn't recognize brought my hands to the small of my back, where they were rebound. He pushed my face to the floor, and shoved a wet finger in my ass. I inched back toward it. "Greedy boy," the room screamed. "But perhaps we've come to a proper appreciation—"

Yesyes. I could feel his dick rubbing against my hole and I rocked toward it please please fuck

"Yes?"

mememe fuck me fuck fuck fuck over and over I said it I screamed fuck yes please yes

"Yes?"

banging my head on the floor and his dick oozing and rubbing

against my asscheeks stinging and hot the pressure on my hole yes
scream fuck fuck sirsirsir

"I think—"

I could feel whimpering and shaking his hands on my head
around my face rubbing my head my hair smoothing petting grabbing my shoulder hand over my head over my face in my mouth
drooling on his hand in my mouth pull my head back in me in
me in me in me

"—yes." And pushed and in, in me all at once deep up inside
me all all at once full up inside me

"Fuckhole."

all that yes, I was only that all hole pulling him in all hole
pushing back around him all a filled place each inch sucking him
down deep pulled back by his hands onto him all hole he used all
his pleasure

"Attaboy, work for me."

tighten now on him all of me tighten on him pull

"Work hard, boy."

back on him his voice raspy grab him hole

"Yeah."

deeper deeper harder pound

"—good—"

pulls me up into me fucking hard

"—boy—"

clawing pulling biting thrusting pushing deep scream

"Fuck—"

hold him hold him hold

"—fuck."

come come yes

"—shit."

Hold. Hold. Release. Tighten. Release. Again.

I was aching, I ached and rocked while he held me for a
minute. His hard breathing filled the room, my ears. Got slower.
Quieter. Faded away. He stood up, and stepped in front of me.
Knocked my mouth open with a gentle fist. Spit for me.

"Dog."

Yes. Anything. Everything. I rubbed my head against his thigh. Felt his hand through my hair. I inched forward on my knees to his leg and he raised his toe into my crotch. I started rutting against rubbing my stillhard dick fucking against it. Like an alley mutt.

"Listen."

And the room filled with whimpering, whimpers along with each buck of my hips. Me whimpering and rubbing humping please sir

"Well, there's something to be said—"

his hand by my face licking it licking his hand

"—for having no shame. Though at the moment I can't think of what it is."

please please haven't I

"Up."

done well?

"*Up.*" He pulled me to my feet, let my wrists and ankles free. Opened the door; pushed me toward it.

"Tune in tomorrow, kids." He shoved me through the door, slammed it shut.

I stood for I don't know how long. It was quiet there, and bright; my ears rang and I had to keep eyes shut for a while.

I stayed there, more horny than before. I'd come so close I hurt from the buildup, the not-release.

I waited for him to come out.

He never did. I went upstairs and cleaned myself up. I washed the spit and cum off me—their slick wet covering a hard grit. I wanted desperately now to come myself. But couldn't. I sat down near the door, and listened for him on the stairs.

I sit and listen for him, every morning. Every evening.

During the first month, I paced a lot. I ate lots of take-out, drank gallons of coffee, stayed awake and wired, wondering when he'd come home.

By the second month, pizza or beans and rice from Luisa's

made up my diet. She had them ready and waiting, so I'd grab and run. Wait for him on the stairs, sometimes. In my apartment.

The third month brought drunkenness on the weekends, the pathetic pollution of drinking alone. Watching television turned down low, helping myself to sleep and a little relief.

The fourth month is just about over now. It has been the worst. It has been the month when I started my drumming on the walls, on the floor—there seem to be no neighbors to complain. Four days ago I came in my sleep.

For the first time in all these months. In my fucking sleep. All I knew of it was the stain in the morning.

The next night I drummed on my walls again. I walked through the apartment, pounding things, tore through the closets and the kitchen drawers. Took a hammer and sank its claw into the fucking wall.

MICHAEL LOWENTHAL

BETTER

SAFE

SAFE SEX IS THE BEST THING THAT'S EVER HAP-
pened to me. It has turned my secret fetish into the moral high
ground, made my lifelong fantasies suddenly PC.

You see, I am a condom queen. A certified latex addict. These
days people are always talking about this or that dysfunction being
the last closet, the final taboo. You get three people together on
Oprah and suddenly you've got a new oppressed minority. I don't
want to stake a claim to any special status. I'm as tired as the next
guy of hearing about equal rights for vampires, or inclusive language
for lesbians with facial hair, or whatever the latest "last" taboos are,
but I can certainly sympathize. I know all about closets within
closets.

I came out with a bang. 1974. New York City. I was twenty-
one years old. My hair was long, my shorts were short, and I was

ready for action. I knew there were faggots into just about every-thing—enemas, titclamps, piss-drinking, and more—so I was sure I would find a community of condom fetishists without much problem.

Naive baby fag that I was, I plunged head first (pun intended) into the scene. I would go down to the Village in my cutoff jeans and fringe vest, swivel my hips a little bit, and I'd have a man in my apartment in no time. But as soon as I would bring up the idea of using a rubber, the other guy would pull away, horrified, and look at me as if I'd just suggested we not fuck on the first date or something equally unimaginable.

"That shit's for the heteros," I heard more than a few times. "What kind of self-hating faggot are you?"

It seems that condoms—like marriage, courtship, and sex with people whose last names you knew—were a hindrance to be borne by the puritanical straight oppressors, something that we freedom-loving, unrepressed queers could do without, thank you very much.

This rapid string of rejections came as a rude and painful shock. I had assumed that of all people, other gays would accept me for who I am. My condom fetish is an essential part of me, just as natural as my being gay. In denying my preference, they were denying my very being. In fact, my obsession with rubbers began even before I was conscious of being attracted to boys.

I was twelve. My parents had just divorced, and my dad had moved into a genuine bachelor pad a few miles from our house, where I spent weekends even though he was hardly ever there. One Saturday morning when he was gone as usual, I stalked into his room and started poking through his stuff. His room was a mess, which I guess isn't a big surprise considering this was the first time in his life he'd had to clean up after himself.

I waded through a heap of dirty socks and underwear on the floor, past an avalanche of mail between the night table and the bed, making my way to the dresser against the far wall. I'm not exactly sure why I was drawn to it. I just had a hunch I'd find something: a stash of M&Ms maybe, or my father's emergency cash. What I found, of course, was better than anything I'd imagined.

I knew about condoms in a vague, naughty kind of way. (It's not like we had sex ed back when I was in junior high.) I think I'd seen a dispenser in a truck-stop bathroom once on a family vacation. And I'd heard that my best friend Tommy's big brother had been dumped by Barbara Mason because he refused to use one.

But here, in the top drawer of my father's dresser, under the boxer shorts and his little-used jockstrap, was the real McCoy. The box itself was a thrill: a soft green color with a blurry romantic picture on the front, and on the back full directions for use, complete with a diagram. I just held the box for a little while, turning it in my sweaty hands.

After a minute or so I worked up my courage and opened it. I took out a small foil packet and squished the contents from one side to the other. It felt almost fluid inside and a tingle shimmered through my stomach as I imagined all the moist places this was meant to go. Finally I tore open the packet and squeezed the condom halfway out. It was definitely wet, but in a different way than I had imagined, slippery but also kind of tacky. Rolled up at the edges, the rubber was a dull muddy yellow, the color of a fading summer tan. But in the center, where there was a little nipple poking up toward the ceiling, the rubber was clear as cellophane.

I held the condom up to my nose and smelled it: musty and fresh at the same time. A little bitter, but not in a bad way. The smell was intensely familiar, but it took me a minute to place it. Then a rush of memory flooded over me: my mother, towering above the tiny four-year-old me at the kitchen sink after dinner. Her yellow dishgloves teasing me, tweaking my nose, the latex squeaky-smooth and smelling clean like just-folded laundry. Then ducking to get away from her hands, pretending to be shy, nudging up against the back of her heavy wool skirt, to the soft chalky skin at the back of her knees.

I let my pants fall to the floor and without even bothering to step out of them I grabbed my stiff dick. The rubber rolled on as if it were meant to be there all along, a missing body part that now finally made me complete. As I pushed the tight circle of rubber all the way to the base of my dick, I felt the blood being forced to the tip. I couldn't believe how much bigger the rubber made my erection. The veins swelled like thick purple vines wrapping around a post. It was like looking at my dick through a magnifying glass.

I ran my finger lightly over the smooth surface of rubber. My own touch was electrifying, sending shock waves of pleasure up and down my spine. Somehow the tightness of the latex made my finger seem like ten fingers, its gentle heat the burn of a blazing fire. I grabbed my dick just below the tip and made a fist. I didn't even have to pump it up and down the way I normally did. I just held it there, enjoying the sensation of having every square inch of my dick squeezed in its tight rubber wrapping. With the other hand I took hold of the clear nipple at the top of the condom. I pulled it as far out as I could without tearing the rubber and then let go. It snapped back against my piss hole with a cold sting. The pain made me wince, but I noticed that my dick swelled even larger. I stretched the nipple again and let it whip back, then again, and again. The pain was like an ice-cold needle being stuck down the middle of my cock, but at the same time my balls were tingling with pleasure. The rubber was tight all over me, the acid smell of the latex filling my nostrils like a drug. I snapped the rubber nipple one more time and the muscles in my groin gave way. I fell to my knees, shooting a solid stream of sperm into the latex capsule, watching the clear nipple swell with my milky whiteness.

After that first time, I was hooked. I went back to my father's bedroom the next weekend, and the next, and the next. . . .

Pretty soon I was spending all my allowance on rubbers. I found a drugstore on the other side of town where the clerk didn't give me a hard time. I experimented with different kinds: ribbed, lubricated, foreign brands. Sometimes I would wear a rubber all day in school, hiding my hard-on under extra-baggy pants.

It wasn't long before my fetish became a genuine addiction. I had to jack off at least once a day into a rubber, usually more like two or three times. I couldn't get off unless I was wearing one.

■ ● ■

You can see why it was so painful when I finally came out about
my fetish, only to be ridiculed by all my potential partners. But I
won't bore you with my tales of misery. We can just fast-forward
for a decade or so after my disappointing debut. I was your better
basic, run-of-the-mill Manhattan queen. I went out dancing,
marched in the pride parade, changed my wardrobe with each fashion wave. Your standard-issue faggot . . . except for the small issue
of sex.

I still had sex every now and then, but it was hardly worth
the effort. I was as turned off by the men as they were turned off
by condoms, and the act itself caused me as much tension as it
relieved. After so many rejections I stopped letting myself even
bring up the subject of rubbers. It was like being in the closet all
over again.

Imagine my surprise ten years later when everybody started
talking about safe sex. Suddenly the same self-righteous queens who
had shut me out in the seventies were telling me with equal conviction that using rubbers was my duty to the community.

In the next few years I was surrounded by condoms. Drugstores
put them out in the aisles with all the other merchandise, and right
up front, too, not tucked away with the feminine hygiene products
and hemorrhoid medication. Rubbers were on posters, in magazines,
on the sides of public buses.

I'll never forget the day I came home from work, turned on
the news, and there's the Surgeon General of the United States
urging everybody, gay and straight alike, to indulge in my long-
hidden fetish. I could have kissed that sweet old Republican!

Don't get the impression that my sex life changed overnight,
because it didn't. In fact, as condoms became more and more socially
acceptable, I had less and less sex. As elated as I was by the change
in attitudes, I couldn't quite get up the courage to go out and take
advantage of it. When your entire life has been based on denial,
the prospect of satisfaction can be somewhat overwhelming. On top
of that, with so many friends starting to die of AIDS, it would
have felt wrong to gain so much pleasure from the very circumstance
that was killing them.

■　●　■

I'm not sure what finally turned me around. Part of it, as the eighties ran into the nineties and we'd been living with the plague for almost a decade, was watching my infected friends reclaim their sexuality. What I saw them learning, and learned with them, was that with so many forces out there to destroy us, we should get everything we can out of life while we have the chance. If that sounds kind of *carpe diem* hokey, so be it. When you've seen twenty-six-year-old men on their deathbeds, talking about all the things they wish they'd had time to do, it's all too real.

But the bottom line was, I was *horny*. I'd had almost no sex for a couple of years, and I had still *never* had the kind of sex I wanted. Now that sex with condoms was happening all around me, it was simply too much to bear.

I get giddy just thinking about what happened next. I'd like to be able to tell you it was spontaneous—maybe then I'd seem less like the vulture that I am. But the truth of the matter is I meditated on my plan for weeks. After almost two months of plotting, the perfect opportunity arose and I knew I couldn't pass it up. It was then that I executed the first of what by now are many similar conquests.

It was January 1991, the country in a yellow-ribboned hysteria. With almost half a million American troops standing poised in the Persian Gulf, an equal number of citizens gathered at the Mall in Washington, D.C., to protest the imminent war. Some had traveled ten hours or more—from Michigan, Florida, and Maine—to stand up for justice and truth.

And why was I there, pushing my way briskly through the crowd? Why had I taken the Metroliner down from New York on a weekend when I should have been at home catching up on correspondence? Because I knew ACT UP was going to have a large contingent in the march, and what better place to meet a young, horny, safe-sex fanatic? (I had considered going to a regular ACT UP demo in Manhattan—and eventually I would—but for this first time, this experiment, I needed the safety of being in a city where I was totally unknown.)

The Mall was jam-packed with people. There didn't seem to be any order to the way groups were lining up, but the ACT UP contingent was not very hard to find. I simply followed the chant: *Suck my dick. Lick my labia. U.S. out of Saudi Arabia.*

I hovered around the edges of the group for a few minutes, trying to blend in. I had worn my oldest pair of jeans, the ones with holes in both knees, and a plain white T-shirt under the big leather jacket my friend Steve had lent me. I had carefully affixed stickers to the arms and back of the jacket: MONEY FOR AIDS, NOT FOR OIL;; SODOMITES FOR SADDAM.

Nobody gave me the hairy eyeball, so I figured the uniform was pretty authentic. I kept a low profile and scanned the crowd, searching for the perfect victim. There were probably a score of safe-sex radicals to choose from within fifty yards of me, but one stood out above the rest. He was tall and extremely thin, a male Olive Oyl. He was dressed about the same as I was, except on the shoulders of his leather jacket, in place of studs, he had glued strips of condom packets: blue, green, and red. The jacket was unzipped to reveal a SAFE SEX IS HOT SEX T-shirt that pictured two naked men tangled in a wild fuck.

As he walked closer to me I saw that his face was smooth and sharply hewn, tapering to a solid, slightly cleft chin. Even more appealing was his shining strawberry-blond hair: crew-cut, but still somehow endearingly disheveled. His sideburns were sculpted precisely, creeping down below his ears and then jutting inward like two furry maps of Italy.

He wove through the crowd with graceful ease, as if he could sense all the gaps. "Die-ins are at Twelfth Street, Fourteenth, and in front of the White House," he chanted to everybody he passed. "Die-ins at Twelfth, Fourteenth, and the White House."

He must have shouted the same line two dozen times, yet each time he repeated it with wonderful conviction. If he took all his assignments seriously, I knew he must follow the rule book on safe sex down to the letter of the law. This was definitely my man.

"Die-ins at Twelfth . . ." he started the mantra again.

"Fourteenth, and the White House," I deadpanned before he could finish.

He looked startled, and then embarrassed. "I guess everybody's pretty much heard, huh?"

"I think that's a safe bet."

He looked down sheepishly and fiddled with the zipper on his jacket. It occurred to me that underneath all the radical crusader paraphernalia, he was just a kid, probably no older than twenty.

"You think it's okay to stop, then?" he asked.

So he was the type who needed orders. This would be even easier than I'd expected. "Listen," I said. "You did a great job. Maybe now you should take a new assignment."

"Sure. What needs to be done?" He was *so* eager-beaver it was frightening.

"You don't have to if you don't want to. But I'm from out of town, and I don't know a single person here. I could really use some company for the march. You know, like a local escort."

"Oh, well, I'm from here," he said. "I mean, I guess I could do that. Sure."

I extended my hand. "I really appreciate it. My name's Jerry."

"Arlo," he said. "Good to meet you." As he held out his hand to take mine I noticed for the first time that it was sheathed in a latex glove.

When the march moved out into the street we walked together through the seas of people, trying not to get separated. Arlo lived up to his activist image right away, shouting all the ACT UP slogans with the conviction of a Baptist preacher. When one chant died down he was always the first to start another.

After a few blocks we passed a small group of counterprotesters, mostly prudish-looking women whose husbands were serving in the Gulf. Arlo said we had to stop and slipped the backpack off his shoulder. I had no idea what he was doing as he reached inside and then flung his hand grandly in the protesters' direction. To the women's absolute horror, dozens of miniature packets of lubricant showered down on them, glimmering in the winter sun like so many giant snowflakes.

"Safe sex is for Republicans, too!" Arlo shouted. "Spread love, not AIDS."

Arlo's activist adrenaline was really pumping. I began to imagine the kind of sex we could have. I knew it would be extreme, like everything about this kid.

When we all "died" in the middle of Pennsylvania Avenue Arlo took the metaphor seriously. He gave up all control of his muscles and collapsed to the ground, 150 pounds of dead weight. I know because he died right on top of me. It was such a wonderful feeling to have him pressing on me, covering me with his skinny length. One of his gloved hands fell across my face, and I just couldn't help myself. I took his pinkie into my mouth and sucked it like a calf at the teat, letting the bitter dryness of the latex spread over my tongue.

When the rally was over, I asked Arlo what he was doing next.

"Well, they're making posters over at Mark's house to publicize the big action next week. I thought I'd go over and maybe help."

Even after my finger-sucking routine, he didn't get it. This generation has no appreciation for the art of seduction, I thought.

"Arlo," I said firmly. "I've really enjoyed being with you today."

"Me too, Jerry. I had a really good time."

"Good, I'm glad." I was going to have to make it even clearer. "I'm kind of pooped, so I'm going back to my hotel. I was hoping you might want to come with me."

Arlo flinched and looked quickly into my eyes, as if he wasn't sure he'd heard me correctly.

"Oh," was all he said. *Now* he got it.

■ ● ■

We didn't say anything on the way up to the room. I watched Arlo in the mirrored walls of the elevator. He seemed nervous in a way he hadn't been before, rubbing his sideburns obsessively and scuffing the carpet with his shoes. The radical activist's bravado had disappeared.

We stepped off at the twelfth floor and followed the maze of hallways to the room. Our leather jackets creaked awkwardly with each stride, punctuating the silence between us. I was beginning to wonder if I should go through with this after all. Maybe I should level with Arlo about my motives. But we were already at the room, and I figured if he hadn't freaked out by now, he wanted this as much as I did. He'd had ample opportunity to run away.

As I was fumbling to slide the credit-card–like key into its slot, Arlo touched me gently on the shoulder. "Um, Jerry? Can we be clear about something before anything happens?"

"Sure," I said, leaving the key in the lock.

Arlo looked into my eyes with a devastatingly serious expression. "I'm safe," he said plainly. "Totally. I mean, that's the only way I'll do it."

I'm safe. Totally. The words raised the hair on the back of my neck. I wanted to ravish Arlo right there in the hallway, to shove my throbbing hard-on into his earnest face. But I suppressed my desire and tried to match his serious demeanor. After a sufficient pause I leaned forward and pecked him drily on the cheek.

"I wouldn't feel comfortable any other way," I said. "That's what I like about you younger guys. You've got that commitment."

A wide smile bloomed on Arlo's face and the swagger returned to his air. We rushed into the room and he immediately tossed his backpack onto the giant bed. Neither of us said anything, but with some kind of telepathy we moved so we were facing each other, about five feet apart. The rules were clear for this stage: no touching, just looking.

First we both stripped off our leather jackets. Then Arlo pulled his T-shirt over his head and I saw that his long torso was smooth except for a small patch of reddish hair just above his solar plexus.

His nipples were hard, small burgundy cylinders rising out of his otherwise flat chest. I yanked off my own shirt quickly, wanting to keep up with the kid without missing any of the show. I'm proud of my muscular chest, but Arlo hardly seemed to notice me. He was concentrating intently on the removal of his own clothes. He slipped off his shoes and socks, and I did the same. I wanted to let him think that he was calling the shots.

Then Arlo moved his hand to his belt and paused, staring directly into my eyes. This was clearly the centerpiece of the ritual. Taking in a big gulp of air and holding it, as if even breathing would destroy the sanctity of the moment, he undid his button-flies and in one smooth motion stepped out of the jeans and his Jockeys at the same time.

At first I was so overwhelmed it was all I could do just to look at his legs. They were long and lean, not a millimeter of fat. His skin was pale, with just the slightest wisps of curly hair. He looked almost frail, in need of protection. It was more than I could have hoped for.

Finally, I steadied myself and raised my eyes to his crotch. His circumcised dick was just like his legs, long and thin. In fact, it was about the thinnest cock I'd ever seen, hardly bigger around than my thumb. It hung limp in the wide space between his legs, its squarish knob well below the sac of his balls. But then as I watched, it twitched to the side and then lurched upward in small bursts, filling with blood until it stood straight up to his belly button. It must have been eight inches long, and still hardly as thick as a hot dog!

I took a step back and admired the bare fullness of him. He was completely naked now, all except for the latex gloves that he'd been wearing since the moment I laid eyes on him. Something told me he didn't take those off.

Now it was my turn. I unhooked my belt and lowered the zipper slowly, trying to look in control. I pulled off the jeans deliberately, one leg at a time, folded them, and placed them on the dresser. Then the excitement of the moment got to me and I couldn't keep up the charade any longer. I yanked off my underwear,

ripping it in the process. My bulging cock protruded like a light-
ning rod in front of me, as long as Arlo's but more than twice as
thick.

We stood there for a few moments, ogling each other. Neither
of us had said a word since we'd entered the room. Nor had we
touched. This was so different from the frenzied groping and exaggerated "I'm-gonna-fuck-your-tight-ass" talk that I had experienced
as sex in the seventies. With Arlo, everything was calm and controlled. He was all concentration, like a surgeon about to enter O.R.
The restraint was driving me wild.

Just when I had decided I'd have to make the next move, Arlo
reached over to the bed and got his backpack. He unzipped the
main compartment and an army's worth of safe-sex paraphernalia
spilled out. He tossed me a pair of surgical gloves identical to the
ones on his hands.

"Boy, you're serious," I said. I knew the rationale, but I was
hoping I could get Arlo to explain it out loud.

As if he could read my mind, he said, "Most people have small
cuts in their cuticles, all around their fingers. Even putting a condom on somebody else could be dangerous if you're not protected.
What if some precum leaks?"

I began to swoon just from hearing Arlo talk that way. I
stretched the translucent latex over my fingers and let it snap tightly
on my wrist: the sound of a palm slapping flat on a bare ass. Then
the other hand. Smack. I realized as I wiggled my fingers in their
tight new covering that our roles had reversed. Despite his youth,
Arlo was the experienced one here.

Arlo grabbed a rubber from the pile and ripped open the foil
packet. "I have to put this on myself now," he said. "It's kind of
tricky with—" and he looked down at his thin cock. When he
stretched the condom over his length I saw what he meant. The
rubber hung too loosely on his thin prick, clinging only in a few
places. In all my fantasies about rubbers, I'd never even thought of
this.

Then it got even better. Arlo reached again into the backpack
and pulled out a small, blue rubber band. He looped the band

carefully around the head of his dick. He twisted it once and then looped it over again. Then again. And once more before rolling the band down to the base. He winced a little as he pushed it along, but I could tell from the way he sucked in his breath that there was pleasure mixed in with the pain. It was tight all right, so tight that the veins in his dick pumped to almost double their previous size. My own dick bulged, too, as I watched the display.

"There," he said casually. "I'm all set."

My heart was racing. My hands and arms felt like jelly. I was too buzzed to think straight, let alone maneuver a rubber onto my own cock. I picked up one of the foil packets from the pile and handed it to Arlo. "You look like an expert. Why don't you dress me in my armor?"

He *was* an expert. He tore open the package and pulled out the rubber, holding it up like a prize. Kneeling before my crotch, he grabbed the base of my shaft firmly with one gloved hand. The touch of the latex sent a wave of warmth through my tight stomach. My knees weakened and I almost fell back onto the bed. With the other hand Arlo positioned the rolled-up rubber on the tip of my cock, and suddenly his mouth was on me, sliding down, tight and warm and wet, although I knew I must be imagining the wet because he was covering me with the rubber, stretching it over my length with his teeth, miraculously getting it on me without ever having touched my bare skin with his mouth or tongue.

Now I did fall onto the bed. I took Arlo with me, tackling him and kissing his chest, gnawing at the tiny island of hair just above his sternum. His skin was as tight and smooth as the rubbers we were wearing. Slowly, I worked my way up to his neck. I licked around his Adam's apple and pretended to take a bite. Then I put the whole bulge into my mouth and sucked on it the way you would someone's ball-sac. Arlo loved it. He ran his gloved hands frantically through my hair, creating waves of static that lit my scalp on fire.

I moved back down the center of Arlo's chest, leaving a trail of hickies that bloomed on his skin like a polka-dotted necktie. I lingered over his belly button, rimming it gently and then plunging its depth with my tongue. At the same time I reached up and squeezed his rock-hard nipples between my rubber-covered fingers. Arlo shivered at the touch and squirmed under me, whimpering unintelligible phrases.

Finally I made my way down to the prize. In its clear wrapper, Arlo's cock glowed in the bright hotel-room light. It lay elegantly on his pale belly, like an exquisite centerpiece on a banquet tray. I lowered my mouth and took a tentative taste of his encased shaft. He was wearing a mint condom! The fresh tingle of the mint and the bittersweetness of the latex mingled on my tongue, and I sloshed my own saliva around in my mouth like a sip of fine wine. I took another lick, longer this time, up the full length of his prick. It jerked in response, lifting a full inch off his body. Then I lost any hint of self-restraint. I began lapping at the shaft wildly like a dog at a bone, nudging it all over Arlo's belly. I rubbed my lips against the velvet-smooth rubber, reveling in the touch of latex against skin. This was better than any of my fantasies.

I climbed back up Arlo's body and brought my face level with his. As we started to kiss he reached down between our bodies and circled my cock with his fingers. He pumped a few times, forcing more blood into the already swollen head. I thought my cock would burst right out of the rubber. Arlo jerked me again and the friction of latex against latex produced a loud squeak that was pleasure-pain in my ears.

I was already close to coming, so I took Arlo's hand and guided it away from my crotch. He seemed to get the message, moving his hand up gingerly along my chest. But when he got to my shoulder he grabbed suddenly and rolled over, pinning me to the bed. There was a shocking strength in those thin arms of his. I took the maneuver as a sign that he was ready to fuck. I started to ask him if he wanted to, but as soon as I spoke he covered my mouth and nose with his hand, not letting me finish the sentence. When I tried to breathe in all I got was the latex smell of his glove. I was immediately drunk with it, the aphrodisiac scent of my years of fantasy, of all the men I'd dreamed of having. I wanted to tell him how good it was but Arlo held his hand there, squeezing tightly, and the lack of breath was like a dagger in my lungs. I squirmed, trying to get out from under his grip, but I was losing energy fast, my empty throat burning. I was sick with dizziness, about to black out, when suddenly he released his hand and as I drank in a mammoth intoxicating gulp of air my cock opened with a rapid-fire of cum. I groaned loudly as I shot out more and more, thick gobs of sperm that filled the tip of the rubber and then oozed down, surrounding me with my own warmth.

Arlo saw that I had come and grabbed his own cock. He circled the base of his shaft with one hand, holding the tight rubber band. With the other he jerked himself wildly, so fast that his hand was a pink blur before my eyes. It only took a few seconds. Arlo shuddered a few times and let out a sharp grunt. I saw the tip of his rubber swell with fluid and then he collapsed on top of me and panted into my ear.

We lay there together for a few minutes, letting our hearts and lungs slow down to normal pace. I breathed in deeply, enjoying the bittersweet tang of another man's sex sweat. I felt as if a whole new world had opened up for me, as if this had been my very first time. And in a way it had.

When Arlo was dressed we kissed unromantically for a few seconds and then I showed him to the door. He seemed so nonplussed by the whole situation, and I couldn't help wondering if somebody like Arlo took it for granted that this was what sex was, or if he had any idea what things were like before AIDS. Just as he was about to step outside, I asked him if he'd ever had unprotected sex.

"God, don't I ever wish," he laughed. "But it's just not worth the risk."

"Do you think it will always be this way?" I asked.

Arlo nodded emphatically. "Even if they come up with a cure, it's not like AIDS is going to go away. Yup. Safe sex is here to stay."

My whole body felt buoyant, as if a heavy weight had lifted.

Arlo stepped into the hallway, but after a few paces he turned and looked at me strangely, as though he were seeing through a wide expanse of distance and time.

"It must have been a blast in the old days, huh? When you didn't have to do everything through a layer of latex."

"Oh, I don't know," I said as he disappeared down the hall. "Every age has its good points and its bad."

CONTRIBUTORS

RANDY BOYD is a native of Indianapolis now living in Southern California. A 1985 graduate of UCLA, he has published fiction in the anthology *Certain Voices* and *BLACKfire* magazine. His essays and nonfiction work have been featured in *Au Courant,* the *Washington Blade,* and *Frontiers* magazine. He is the author of the forthcoming novel *Bridge Across the Ocean.*

MICHAEL BRONSKI is the author of *Culture Clash: The Making of Gay Sensibility.* He is a columnist for *Z Magazine, First Hand,* and *The Guide.* His articles on books, film, culture, politics, and sexuality have appeared in *Gay Community News, The Village Voice, The Boston Globe, Fag Rag, Radical America, American Book Review,* and *The Advocate,* as well as numerous anthologies including *Hometowns: Gay Men Write About Where They Belong, Personal Dispatches: Writers Confront*

AIDS, Leatherfolk, A Member of the Family: Gay Men Write About Their Families, and *Gay Spirit.* He has been involved in gay liberation for more than twenty years and lives in Cambridge with his lover, the poet Walta Borawski.

PATRICK CARR was born and raised in New Jersey and received his degree in theater from Rutgers University. He lives in New York, where he works in publishing and is a member of ACT UP.

GARY COLLINS is only one pseudonym of the author of scores of pioneering gay porn paperbacks that began appearing in the late 1960s, including the recently reissued futuristic fantasy *All-Stud* (written under the name Clay Caldwell.) While not cranking out classic tales of lust among frat boys, hayseeds, truckers, and military men, "Collins" (also known as Lance Lester, Thumper Johnson, and Lance LaFong) made a living writing dialogue for Disney comics. Now retired, he divides his time between running a small farm in Southern California, volunteering at his local public library, and producing new stories under the Caldwell pen name.

WILLIAM COZAD is a graduate of San Francisco State University and lives in that city with his boyfriend. He is a regular contributor to *Inches, Stallion, Playguy, Honcho, Hot/Shots,* and *Beau.* Many of his gay erotic novels and stories were published under the pen name Wes Cranston.

JOHN DIBELKA is a contributing editor to *Bear* magazine, for which he writes an opinion column, "Bare Pause." His short fiction has appeared under the pen name Jay Shaffer in most major gay men's magazines since 1985. He has published two collections of his Jay Shaffer stories, *Full Service* and *Wet Dreams.* He lives in San Diego.

GAVIN GEOFFREY DILLARD is an artist and poet currently living in Yosemite, California. His autobiography *In the Flesh: My Life As Art,* is forthcoming from Dutton.

LARRY DUPLECHAN is the author of four critically acclaimed novels: *Eight Days a Week, Blackbird, Tangled Up in Blue,* and *Captain Swing.* Duplechan's work has appeared in *LA Style, The New York Native,* and *Black American Literature Forum* and in the anthologies *Black Men/White Men, Relationships: A Collection of Gay Male Coming Out, Hometowns: Gay Men Write About Where They Belong, A Member of the Family: Gay Men Write About Their Families,* and *Calling the Wind: Twentieth Century African-American Short Stories.* A native of Los Angeles, Duplechan lives there with his life-partner of seventeen years.

LARS EIGHNER is the author of two collections of erotic fiction, *Bayou Boy* and *B.O.M.C.,* and a volume of memoirs, *Travels with Lizbeth.* His autobiographical essays have appeared in *The Threepenny Review, Harper's,* and *Utne Reader;* his essay on "Dumpster Diving" was selected for the 1992 edition of *The Pushcart Prize* anthology. He lives in Austin, Texas.

ANDREW HOLLERAN is the author of the novels *Dancer from the Dance* and *Nights in Aruba,* and a book of essays, *Ground Zero.*

F. VALENTINE HOOVEN, III has been published extensively in the alternative press, for which he also does illustrations and creates crossword puzzles. He is the author of *Tom of Finland,* a biography of the gay erotic artist.

REGINALD JACKSON is the founder and director of the Rainbow Stage Company in New York City. He lives in New Jersey with his lover, Greg.

JAMOO is the associate editor of *Interrace* magazine, a publication for people of mixed races. He has contributed to many gay male periodicals including *BLACKfire, BLK, SLC, Black and Gay,* and *Advocate MEN.* Jamoo (who is Black, Cherokee, Spanish, and white) is known for his erotic writings about mixed-race gay men.

DAVE KINNICK was raised in Berkeley and moved to Hollywood in

1982 to attend UCLA. He began a career in erotic journalism while managing the campus gay newspaper, *TenPercent*. Close friends were occasionally alarmed by his rampant and notorious interest in gay pornography, and in 1988 an editor friend suggested he try his hand at writing about it. He has been the monthly video review columnist for *Advocate MEN* magazine ever since, and he chronicles the small world of pornography and its denizens for *The Advocate, Manshots,* and *Adam Gay Video.* He also contributes to numerous 'zines including *Sin Bros.* and *Steam,* and co-founded a sex party organization named Mondo Penis.

WILL LEBER highly values his family: his boyhood boyfriend (and lover of eighteen years) and their demanding miniature dachshund. They live on a hilltop in San Francisco.

MICHAEL LOWENTHAL was born a month and a half before Stonewall, and still didn't manage to come out for eighteen years. He tried to make up for the delay when he graduated in 1990 as the first openly gay valedictorian of Dartmouth College. His writing has appeared in *The James White Review, Lambda Book Report, Gay Community News, OutWeek,* and *Berkeley Fiction Review.* With Carrie Wofford he co-edited *From Now On,* a multicultural anthology of fiction and poetry by young gay men, lesbians, and bisexuals. He lives in New Hampshire with his lover, Koko.

V. K. McCARTY was born in Boston and made a theater career in New York City. For the past fourteen years she has been the editor of *Variations* magazine and was recently called in to take over *Forum.* Under her pseudonyms Victor King and Mam'selle Victoire she has started *Stroke* magazine, written for *Penthouse, Mach,* and *DungeonMaster,* and enjoyed the attentions of promising young men.

JIM MERRETT resides in New York with Cesar, his work- and love-partner of six years. He is a contributing writer at *The Advocate* and publishes feature and news articles regularly in *QW, The Guide,* and *Frontiers* magazines. He has also published in *The New York Times.*

His gay-themed poetry has appeared in *The James White Review, Bay Windows, First Hand, SPSM&H* (a publication of *Amelia*) and *Ellipsis . . .* , and his short fiction has also appeared in *R.F.D.* and *Ellipsis. . . .* He has been sexually active since age eight.

SCOTT O'HARA (formerly known as "The Biggest Dick in San Francisco") performed in video porn from 1983 to 1988. Since retiring, he has lived in Cazenovia, Wisconsin, writing and gardening. His articles, fiction, poems, and photography have appeared in *Advocate MEN, Drummer, James White Review, RFD, Diseased Pariah News, Inches, Thing,* and other magazines. He edits *Steam,* a quarterly review of bathhouses and sex clubs.

ROBERT PATRICK wrote the play *Untold Decades: Seven Gay Comedies,* and a novel, *Temple Slave.* He welcomes correspondence at 2848 Wathen, Atwater, California 95301.

JOHN PRESTON has written or edited more than forty books, including such erotic landmarks as *Mr. Benson* and *I Once Had a Master and Other Tales of Erotic Love.* He lives in Portland, Maine.

ANNE RICE was born in New Orleans, where she now lives with her husband, the poet Stan Rice, and their son, Christopher.

JOHN W. ROWBERRY has been involved in gay erotica and publishing for over two decades as a writer, editor, and critic. He has worked for a number of periodicals, including *The Advocate.* He was the editor of *Drummer* during its golden age. He currently edits *Stallion* and *Inches* magazines. He has a published short story collection, *Lewd Contact.*

LEIGH RUTLEDGE was born in Chicago and raised in northern California, and now makes his home in Colorado. He is the author of *The Gay Book of Lists, Unnatural Quotations, The Gay Fireside Companion,* and *The Gay Decades.* He is also the author of *The Left-Hander's Guide to Life* and a humor book, *Excuses, Excuses.* He lives with his lover of fifteen years; they share their home with thirty-one housecats and four dogs.

D.V. SADERO is a former lifeguard and newspaper reporter. He began writing erotica twenty years ago, writing six or seven paperbacks in quick succession when he needed some fast money to pay for an operation. Then he happily retired. About ten years ago, in a line of work (private investigation) that involved a good deal of waiting around and hanging out, he was able to indulge his erotic imaginings, some of which he put on the office computer. From there, it was only a step to mailing them to magazines. Twenty of his stories are collected under the title *In the Alley.*

STEVEN SAYLOR is the creator of the ancient Roman sleuth Gordianus the Finder, hero of the novels *Roman Blood* and *Arms of Nemesis.* Under the pen name Aaron Travis, he has published his erotic fiction which includes the novel *Slaves of the Empire* and a number of short-story collections. He divides his time between homes in Berkeley, California, and Amethyst, Texas.

NORMAN SHAPIRO had been a closet pornographer for some thirty-five years before starting Euphemisms Publishing Company. His purpose was to come out with his artwork and find an audience who might appreciate it for what it is. He also wanted to offer his art at an affordable price. So he rented a good copier machine. This was in 1983, two years before his retirement from teaching art in the public schools. His artist's books and mail art have since found their way into the hands of private collectors, museums, and college libraries. You can ask to see his books at the New York Public Library or at the Kinsey Institute at Indiana University. Printed Matter in New York City has been carrying his titles from time to time since the mid-1980s.

DAN VEEN is a native of San Francisco. At sixteen, he wrote and sold his first erotica, inspired by his experiences as a whore and an escort. His fiction has appeared under various pseudonyms in numerous publications. He has degrees in sociology and German literature. He currently resides in New Orleans and Mexico.

CHRISTOPHER WITTKE was the features editor of *Gay Community News* from 1990 to 1992. His essays have appeared in *Hometowns: Gay Men Write About Where They Belong, A Member of the Family: Gay Men Write About Their Families*, and *Art Issues* magazine. He is a contributing editor and media analyst for *BEAR* magazine. His work has also appeared in *Z, Guys*, and *In Touch* magazines.

"Absolutism" first appeared in *Advocate MEN,* August 1991. Copyright John Preston 1991.

"Baby Love" copyright Reginald Jackson 1993.

"Better Safe" copyright Michael Lowenthal 1993.

"Bush League" first appeared in *Advocate MEN*, May 1991. Copyright F. Valentine Hooven, III 1991.

"Do You Know Who You're Jacking Off To? A Look at the Women Who Pen Gay Male Porn." An early version of this essay was published in *The Advocate,* issue 603, May 19, 1992. Copyright Jim Merrett 1992.

"Fatherless" copyright Leigh Rutledge 1992.

"Herzschmerz" originally appeared in *Christopher Street* magazine, Issue 184. Copyright Andrew Holleran 1992.

"How I Got AIDS, or, Memoirs of a Working Boy" first appeared in *Diseased Pariah News*. Copyright Scott O'Hara 1991.

"How Sweet (and Sticky) It Was" copyright Michael Bronski 1993.

"If New Orleans Were Paris" first appeared in *Daddy* magazine. Copyright Jamoo 1991.

"Just Do It." Parts of this essay appeared in different forms in *Gay Community News* True Safe Sex Stories series and were published anonymously in Boyd McDonald's anthology *Lewd: True Homosexual Experiences.* Copyright Christopher Wittke 1993.

"The King and His Virgin Boy" first appeared in *BLACKfire* magazine, issue number 3. Copyright Randy Boyd 1993.

"Kit" copyright Robert Patrick 1993.

"Knife Litanies" copyright V. K. McCarty 1993.

"Party Meat" first appeared in *Honcho,* August 1980. Copyright D. V. Sadero 1980.

"The Pawnbroker" first appeared in *Inches*, September 1991. Copyright William Cozad 1991.

"Race" is from *In the Flesh: My Life as Art* copyright Gavin Geoffrey Dillard 1993. Used by permission of the publisher, Dutton, an imprint of Dutton Signet, a division of Penguin Books USA Inc.

"Scenario for a Porn Flick" copyright Norman Shapiro 1993.

"The Sergeant" is taken from *The Sergeant* by Gary Collins, New York: 101 Enterprises, 1968. Copyright Gary Collins, 1993.

"Shooters" first appeared in *Advocate MEN*. Copyright J. S. Dibelka 1989.

"Slave" first appeared in *Mach,* number 20 and number 21. Copyright Steven Saylor 1990.

"Slaveboy Weekend" originally appeared in *The Advocate*. Copyright Dave Kinnick 1992.

"The Stories of V" copyright Dan Veen 1993.

"Sucked In" copyright Will Leber 1993.

"Tau Delt" by Lars Eighner was originally published in *Freshmen,* February 1992. Copyright Lars Eighner 1992.

"Travelers' Tales" are taken from *Lewd Conduct* by John W. Rowberry, New York: BadBoy Books, 1993. Copyright John W. Rowberry 1993.

"Tristan in the House of Nicolas, the Queen's Chronicler" is from *Beauty's Punishment* by A. N. Roquelaure. Copyright 1984 A. N. Roquelaure. Used by permission of the publisher, Dutton, an imprint of Dutton Signet, a division of Penguin Books USA Inc.

"Video X-Press" copyright Larry Duplechan 1993.

"Wall" copyright Patrick Carr 1993.